DOCTORS AND DOCTORS' WIVES

DOCTORS AND DOCTORS' WIVES

A NOVEL BY

FRANCIS ROE

NAL BOOKS

NEW AMERICAN LIBRARY

A DIVISION OF PENGUIN BOOKS USA INC., NEW YORK
PUBLISHED IN CANADA BY
PENGUIN BOOKS CANADA LIMITED, MARKHAM, ONTARIO

Copyright © 1989 by Francis Roe

All rights reserved. For information address New American Library.

NAL BOOKS TRADEMARK REG. U.S. PAT. OFF. AND FOREIGN COUNTRIES
REGISTERED TRADEMARK—MARCA REGISTRADA
HECHO EN CRAWFORDSVILLE, INDIANA, U.S.A.

SIGNET, SIGNET CLASSIC, MENTOR, ONYX, PLUME, MERIDIAN and NAL BOOKS are published by New American Library, a division of Penguin Books USA Inc., 1633 Broadway, New York, New York 10019

Library of Congress Cataloging-in-Publication Data

Roe, Francis J. C.
    Doctors and doctors' wives / by Francis Roe.
        p.   cm.
    ISBN 0-453-00706-6
    I. Title.
PS3568.034896D6   1990
813'.54—dc20   89-36907
                                                         CIP

Designed by Leonard Telesca

First Printing, January, 1990

1 2 3 4 5 6 7 8 9

PRINTED IN THE UNITED STATES OF AMERICA

*This book is for Frederick Paul Roe
and Dominique Eve Roe.*

PROLOGUE

Willie Stringer had just started rounds with his team when the call came over the paging system: "Code Blue, Harkmore Pavilion, Room 2104, Dr. Stringer, Room 2104 . . ."

"Go on without me," he told his chief resident, and by the time the call had been repeated, Willie was on his way, hurrying down the corridor toward the elevators, trying to keep his stethoscope, flashlight, and the rest of his paraphernalia from leaping out of the pockets of his white coat. As soon as he'd turned the corner, Willie broke into a run.

A hard knot formed in his stomach. Room 2104 . . . The elevators were at the end of the corridor, and as usual there was a crowd waiting. Willie glanced up at the indicator. Nothing even close. The emergency stairs . . . In a moment he was clattering down the steps, his slapping footsteps echoing around the bare concrete cylinder. Four or five floors above, he heard a metal door crash, then a fast tumbling of feet as someone started to run down the stairs behind him. That would be the anesthesia resident answering the same call. By the time Willie reached the bottom, his knees felt like jelly and he could only take the steps one at a time. He must be getting old. It was easier in the tunnel, although he had to watch out for the low pipes and cables hanging from the low, curved ceiling. Willie half jogged, half ran, head low, sticking to the centerline. The tunnel joined the main hospital building to the Harkmore Pavilion, passing under the visitors' parking area.

First, establish an airway . . . In his head, Willie went through the familiar routine of resuscitation. His penlight fell out of his pocket and it took him a few seconds to pick it up. Maybe

he should have just left it there. The anesthesia resident was
far behind, walking. He was too far back for Willie to hear
him panting, but he must be. He'd run down five more flights
than Willie.

It was unusual for an attending surgeon to go to a code, but
this was a special case . . . he might need to put in one or more
intravenous lines . . . Room 2104 . . . Oh, sweet Jesus Christ,
what could possibly have gone wrong?

The wait in the lobby for the Harkmore elevator was inter-
minable, but Willie knew better than to try running up to the
twenty-first floor. 2104 . . . He checked his notebook; maybe
they'd made a mistake, given the wrong room number, or
maybe they'd moved the boy . . . but he knew it was him. He'd
seen him less than an hour before, and everything had been
all right then. Edward Hopkins, his best friend's son, the
twelve-year-old kid the nurses had all fallen in love with . . .
They'd operated on him yesterday. What on earth could have
gone wrong? His stomach tight with anxiety, Willie got into
the elevator, opened the small steel door by the console with
the special key, and pressed the override button. The other
passengers looked at him but didn't say anything. They moved
away from him, giving him room. Willie looked at his watch
just before the doors opened at the twenty-first floor and a
wave of frustration swept over him. Eleven minutes had passed
from the time they had called the code; surely, for chrissake,
there had to be a better system.

He ran past the nurses' desk. The secretary looked over and
pointed down the hall. "Room 2104, Dr. Stringer," she called
after him. Twenty-one oh-four, was what she said, with a soft,
cultured voice. She must be from England, or somewhere . . .
Room 2104 was at the far end of the corridor.

There was the usual crowd outside the door, and the medical
resident was just going in with his intern. Willie recognized a
couple of physiotherapists and an X-ray tech, and with a
sudden constriction of his throat he saw a man in a business
suit peering into the room. Greg . . . Didn't all those people
have anything better to do? Willie felt his adrenaline rising as
he approached the door. A nurse stood with a defibrillator cart
right in the doorway. He nodded quickly at Greg, pushed the
defibrillator aside with more than necessary force, went in and
closed the door.

Inside it was like bedlam. The room was full of nurses and doctors talking, shouting over each other. A student nurse was holding the patient's hand and sobbing as if her heart would break. Edward was sitting up, propped by pillows, and at first Willie didn't recognize him because of the blood. It was a dark, maroon color, and it was all over his face, especially around his mouth. The boy's big, terrified brown eyes shone wide and luminous from behind it, a few chalk-white patches of skin showing around them. There was blood all over the sheets, the floor, even some on the wall next to the bed.

"You, get out!" the medical resident was shouting at the student nurse. "Get the hell out of here!" He turned. "Do we have an IV running? Let's get this show on the road!" Sol Leibowitz was a second-year resident. He glanced up in surprise when Willie came in but didn't stop giving orders. "Get six units of whole blood up here, and get them to cross-match another six!" he shouted at nobody in particular. Bob Wesley, Willie's junior resident, came in, breathless. Willie quickly assessed the situation. Edward had had a major hemorrhage, that was obvious, but he was conscious. There was no immediate need for airways, defibrillators, and especially no need for this kind of self-indulgent shouting. He pushed his way through to Sol. "Take it easy, Sol," he said. "The IV's running, it's an eighteen-gauge, and Bob here'll put in another. We've got blood for him from yesterday."

He smiled at Edward, who was too terrified to smile back, but Willie could feel that the boy was glad to see him in this welter of shouting, unknown faces. He took his hand. It was big for a twelve-year-old's, but cold as ice. Arvid Donoghue, the anesthetist, came in, glanced at the patient, and looked questioningly at Willie, who nodded reassuringly. He wasn't going to need Arvid—not now, anyway. "Do we have a blood pressure?" he asked. He pitched his voice with emphatic and deliberate calm, as much for Edward's benefit as for the sake of the others.

"Eighty over forty, Dr. Stringer," replied the staff nurse. She sounded relieved. "It's up from sixty over nothing."

"Take it and record it every five minutes," said Willie, and turned back to the boy.

"We need to put in another IV, Edward. Can you stand being stuck one more time?" Edward nodded, just barely moving his head. He seemed too frightened to move any more than that, in case he started to vomit blood again. "Let's get your head down first." Willie supported him while one of the nurses removed the pillows and gently let him lie back. There was no blood where the pillows had been.

"He looks pretty stable right now," Bob murmured, more for Dr. Stringer than for anybody else. Poor old Willie looked as pale as if he'd been the one who'd had a hemorrhage. Bob wiped Edward's inner arm and slipped the needle into the vein. Edward didn't move.

"I think we can take care of it from here," said Willie to Sol. "Thanks a lot for coming."

Sol looked rather strangely at Willie. He didn't like having the initiative taken from him. "Where's he bleeding from? Do they all do that after surgery?"

"No, they usually don't." He stared bleakly at Sol; he wasn't used to this kind of implied insubordination, especially from some insignificant junior.

"Pressure's up, Dr. Stringer. One hundred ten over eighty."

Edward lay completely still while Bob poked around with the needle; it was more difficult to get it into a vein because they'd shrunk from blood loss. Then a thin trickle of blood came out of the back of the needle. A nurse handed him the plastic tubing; fluid was running out of the end.

"Ringer's lactate?" asked Willie, looking up at the bottle, and the nurse nodded. "Turn it wide open . . . good." He straightened up and smiled reassuringly at Edward. "Would you like to wash your mouth out? That stuff doesn't taste too great, does it?" He nodded to Barbara, the staff nurse, who came up with a glass of water and a plastic kidney-shaped dish for him to spit into.

The boy moved his eyes to Willie and managed the barest of smiles, but it was enough to bring tears of relief to the nurses in the room. The thought of something terrible happening to their Edward was unbearable, although they were all used to terrible things happening every day.

"Okay, now could somebody tell me what's been going on here?" Willie sought the head nurse with his eyes.

"He was fine until"—the head nurse consulted the records she had on the clipboard—"until 11:22, when he rang the bell.

I couldn't hear what he was saying, so I came to the room and he was vomiting. . . ." She looked at Edward as if for confirmation. Barbara was gently washing around his mouth with a washcloth and talking quietly to him. "There was so much blood, I called a code. I'm sorry if—"

"Look, we're wasting time here," said Sol. "Shouldn't you take him back to the OR and fix whatever got screwed up yesterday?"

"Nothing got screwed up, Dr. Leibowitz," said Willie. He'd talk to Neil Harmon, his boss, and in no time at all Sol would be out in the cold world looking for a job. Nobody talked to Dr. Wilbrahim Stringer like that. "And don't feel you need to stay. As I said, I think we can take care of things from here on in."

Sol gave a little shrug, hesitated, but didn't leave. Somebody came in with half a dozen blood bags, and Barbara, the staff nurse, started the precautionary routine of checking each one against Edward's hospital number.

"Don't bother with that right now," Willie snapped. "Hang a couple up and check them as you go along."

He looked down and forced himself to smile at Edward, who was looking pale but human again now that the blood had been cleaned off his face.

"Well, young fella, are you feeling better? That was quite a ruckus you started up!" Edward's color was already starting to return as the blood ran fast into his veins, and the fear was leaving his face.

"Sorry about that," he murmured, and one of the young nurses laughed loudly but stopped suddenly when the head nurse looked at her. Willie rubbed his nose and gazed at Edward, trying to figure out what had caused this unusual postoperative complication.

"Did you sneeze or anything?" he asked, thinking that the strain might have pulled a suture off a blood vessel. He lifted Edward's pajama top to make sure the incision was all right.

"No, I was just looking at a magazine." His voice sounded shaky but was quite audible, and he glanced at the bloodstained periodical at the end of the bed. "Maybe I was reading too fast or something." Edward's confidence was coming back, and he essayed a smile. The atmosphere in the room relaxed almost palpably; even Sol grinned, then pulled the stethoscope off his neck and stuck it in his pocket with a flourish. The nurse in charge of the defibrillator looked at Willie questioningly and he nodded. She turned the machine off and put the paddles back in their holders. The X-ray technician muttered something and slipped quietly out; it was obvious he wasn't going to be needed now.

Willie checked over the situation. Both intravenous lines were running, and Edward's blood pressure was almost back to normal. The cardiac monitor showed a steady, normal rhythm, a little fast but otherwise satisfactory.

"Let's get some clean sheets in here and tidy the place up a bit," he said.

Now the tension was off, he could feel the tightness leave his throat, and his voice sounded confident, relaxed. One of the student nurses went quickly to the closet and stood on tiptoe to reach the linen. Willie picked up Edward's wrist to check the strength of the pulse, and smiled at him reassuringly. He was about to say something but checked himself when he saw a peculiar look come over Edward's face, which seemed to stretch and grow thinner. The boy pushed himself up on one elbow and stared at Willie with eyes that seemed to get bigger by the second, full of growing panic. He tried to speak, and his mouth opened but no sound came out. A moment later a weird gurgling noise came from the back of his throat.

"On his side! Turn him!" Willie put his hands under Edward's shoulders and heaved. He hadn't noticed before how thin he was. The shoulder bones . . . The dark blood came out of his mouth in a rush and poured out so fast and thick, the boy couldn't draw breath without choking. He turned his eyes back to stare at Willie, then coughed and bubbled; it was a torrent that no intravenous infusion could ever keep up with. Edward's eyes, still fixed on Willie as his only hope, started to go glassy.

"Give me the laryngoscope! And an endotracheal tube!" Willie's hands were shaking badly as he reached for the instrument. He turned Edward's head and put his left hand under his chin to stabilize him while he slid the blade of the scope along the back of Edward's tongue.

"Suction!" he yelled. "Get me the suction!" He heard the sound of the pump starting up, and a stiff plastic tube was pushed over his shoulder into the boy's mouth. For a second it looked as if it couldn't keep up with the blood gushing out so relentlessly, but finally the pool lessened and Willie was able to see the epiglottis. "Tube!" Into his hand went the transparent tube with a floppy, collapsed balloon around it. He slid it down and by the grace of God got it into the trachea. He blew into the end and could feel Edward's chest move. "Inflate the balloon now," he said, his voice quieter, and Barbara the staff nurse pushed the little syringe full of air into the balloon, although her hands were trembling so much, she almost dropped it. Now the blood couldn't pour down his trachea and into his lungs, and the kid would be able to breathe. But the blood kept on coming, and Willie sensed a kind of floppiness to Edward's neck as he lowered his head back onto the sheet.

When he looked up, Sol was shining a light in Edward's eyes. "He's dilated, both sides, and unreactive," he said loudly, as if to imply that this wouldn't have happened if he'd been in charge. "Pressure's down to zero," said the nurse. She had tears in her eyes. The horror of it seemed to strike Willie only now.

"We can't let this kid die!" he said desperately. He grabbed Edward's limp wrist, hoping to feel a pulse. His eyes went to the monitor hanging from the wall by the bed.

Sol followed his gaze. "Dying heart pattern," he said. "He's gone."

Edward lay very still; his chest didn't move. The blood had stopped gushing out and was beginning to coagulate around his mouth and on the sheet. The eyes were still turned toward Willie, but now they were glazed and fixed. With a sudden fury of impotence, Willie got up and smashed his fist against the wall. The room was suddenly silent, in awful contrast to the frenzied activity of only a few moments before. The only sound was from Barbara, biting on her knuckles and trying to stifle her sobs. The head nurse, tight-lipped, steadfastly looked the other way.

The silence deepened, and Willie suddenly realized they were all waiting. Waiting for him to pronounce the boy dead. Sol ostentatiously headed for the door, looking around for a second to survey the bloody wreckage.

Stringer went up to the head of the bed and gazed at Edward's face for a second. "You'd better get him cleaned up," he said curtly to the nurses. "His father's waiting outside, and he'll want to come in and see him."

PART ONE

CHAPTER
ONE

1955

Greg Hopkins looked around the courtyard, but he didn't see anyone he knew. Suddenly it started to rain, a noisy summer rain with fat drops that plopped and splashed around his feet. He ran for the steps leading down to the Anatomy Department; at the bottom, the big door was still closed. The rain was now pouring down; the other students were already there, huddled damply around the closed, blue-painted door. To one side, separate from the throng, Greg saw a large multicolored umbrella held up by a tall, confident-looking young man wearing a new English-style raincoat. For a second Greg hesitated, then a cold trickle down his neck made his mind up for him. He came and stood under the umbrella, and the young man obligingly moved it over. He was a couple of inches taller than Greg, but it seemed more; there was an aura about him of freshly laundered clothes and expensive after-shave, and his thick dark hair was carefully styled.

Greg glanced up at the huge canopy of the umbrella and grinned. "It looks like something your chauffeur should be holding."

"Yes, he usually does."

Greg blinked, then shot a quick glance at his companion. The young man grinned, a wide, confident, attractive smile. His voice was clear, well-educated. The women must go for this guy like sharks in a feeding frenzy, thought Greg.

"But where is that low-class fucker when I need him? On vacation in Hawaii."

There was a pause while Greg took this in. He'd never met anybody who had a chauffeur, and he couldn't tell if the other was joking. He decided to let it pass. "My name's Greg Hopkins," he said finally.

The elegant young man stuck out his hand. "Stringer," he said, quickly taking in Greg's stocky build, dark hair, and rather brooding, square features. He also noted the shabby coat and cheap black shoes. "Most people call me Willie."

He didn't add that only his mother called him by his full given name, which was Wilbrahim, pronounced "Wilbram." But as she so rarely spoke to him, that hardly counted.

Two minutes later, on the stroke of ten, the blue door opened from the inside, and a short, white-haired man with a fresh complexion and a spotless white coat said, "Come in, boys and girls, come in, don't just stand out there in the rain!"

They made a knot around the door, pushing past him one by one. The rain was still pelting down, and everybody got in as fast as possible. One of the repeat students muttered to Greg, "That's Professor Lockhart. He wouldn't open that door one second early if it was raining white-hot meteorites out here, the old bugger!"

They trailed down a long, white-tiled corridor to the lockers. The repeaters had already taken the ones nearest the door, and Greg and Willie took adjoining ones. They put on the mandatory white coats and headed for the main dissecting room.

The entire first-year medical class was packed just inside the door, about a hundred of them, clutching their new instrument boxes and dissection manuals. Three rows of steel dissecting tables stretched the length of the room, each bearing a new corpse, visible only in sinister outline, mummified in preservative-soaked wrappings. At the far end, an overhead lamp was on and two people were busily working on something at one of the tables.

The place stank of formalin, and Greg felt his eyes burning from the chemical. One of the white-coated assistants was shouting out names.

"Bradford?"

Somebody in the crowd muttered an answer.

"Bradford, you're at table five. Davidoff . . ." He looked up. "Davidoff, if you're not here, please say so!" There was a faint titter of respectful laughter. As their names were called, the students left the group and wandered around checking the numbers of the tables.

Greg soon found the body he'd been assigned to; there was only one other student at the table, the one who'd said something about meteorites while they were waiting to get in. He was a cheerful-looking fellow with chubby cheeks and a twinkling look about him. His name was Martin Penrose. They surveyed the grisly thing on the table in front of them, and Martin said with the voice of experience that he hoped it wasn't a fat one. The fat ones were the worst, particularly if the air-conditioning broke down, as it had last session.

They were about to start unwrapping the body when the young man who'd been holding the umbrella came up and put his instrument box on the table.

"I'm joining you, if you don't mind," he said airily. "My table had four people, and this one has only two."

"It's because this body had the plague," said Martin, eyeing the newcomer with some suspicion. "They wanted to limit the exposure."

"Go ahead and unwrap it, my man," said Willie, taking a copy of the *Times* out of his leather briefcase. "Don't let me interrupt your studies."

Martin hesitated, wondering if he should take offense, but he just shrugged and grinned. Greg put on his rubber gloves and Martin did likewise. Each started to unwrap an arm, the first part they were going to dissect.

"There's somebody like that in every class," Martin said in a loud voice, looking at Willie, who was now immersed in the financial section. "Thinks he's a big shot."

Under the outer layers of coarse bandaging there was a thick covering of some kind of gauze tubing, and Greg went off to find some heavy scissors to cut it. Willie had put away his *Times* and was now leafing through his dissection manual.

"What are you going to do when you finish medical school?" he asked when Greg returned with a huge pair of angled scissors attached to a long chain. "I mean, what specialty?"

"I'm not sure," replied Greg, surprised. "Probably general practice, I would think. I like the idea of dealing with patients, getting to know them. . . ."

"Excellent. How about you?" he asked Martin.

"How about me what?" asked Martin.

"I was inquiring about your future plans, after you qualify. That's assuming that you finish, of course."

Martin took his time answering, and watched while Greg inserted the flattened end of the scissors between the gauze and the skin of the corpse.

"I'm going to do psychiatry," he said finally. "I've always been interested in the motivation of megalomaniacs. Tell me," he said, fixing his eyes on Willie and putting on an expression of intense but spurious interest, "what made *you* decide to become a doctor?"

Willie ignored the question. "Psychiatry, huh? Excellent. I'm going to be a surgeon, so it's obviously more important for me to study the intimate workings of the human body. Therefore I shall take one of the arms, and the two of you will share the other." He held up his hand as Martin was about to protest. "You shall have the right arm. It's always better than the left, as the muscles and bony structures are better defined and will need less dissection. No, don't thank me, it's only fair."

Greg grinned and chopped away with the scissors, but the material was thick and difficult to cut.

"Hold the arm for me, Martin."

Martin steadied the arm, holding it with both hands while Greg worked on the coverings. Willie had returned to his *Times* and was paying no attention to what they were doing. Slowly a brown, leathery hand started to appear as the gauze parted. The fingers were old and clawed, the fingernails long. Greg prodded gingerly at one of the fingers. It felt like a piece of wood.

"God, this is a really old one," said Martin. He had done the course before and was in a better position to compare. "Everybody gives their bod a name; I think we should call this one Methuselah."

Willie leaned over to examine the arm, which was now fully exposed up to the shoulder. He picked up the hand and tried to move the fingers but they were completely stiff. "This is— or rather, was—a woman," he pronounced.

Greg looked up and down the arm. "How can you tell?"

"First, the bone structure," said Willie. "For the size of the body, the hands are small. The skin on the palms is smooth, without calluses . . . usually the males who finish up here have had a lifetime of manual work. But of course the real tip-off is the nails."

Martin and Greg looked at the nails. They were tobacco-brown, looked as if they had been poorly cared for, but otherwise didn't seem to have any obviously unusual characteristics.

"Okay, Sherlock," said Martin, "I think you're full of shit, but go ahead, tell us."

"Wait a minute," said Greg, who was examining the nails minutely. "There are some ridges here across them, near the root."

"On females, the nails tend to be narrow, whereas on men they're often wider than they are long, especially on the thumb," said Willie, ignoring Greg. "Also, these ones here are rounded from side to side . . . look at your own for comparison; ours are much flatter."

Greg and Martin looked at each other, then they both peeled off a glove to examine their own fingernails. "Look," said Willie, pointing at Martin's hand, "if you ignore the faint rim of dirt under the fingernails, you can see precisely what I mean."

Greg laughed and handed Willie the big scissors. "Why don't you cut away the dressings and see if the other side's any different," he said.

Willie started to chop at the bandaging. Greg watched him, not satisfied with his explanation. "I think those ridges across the nails must mean something," he said. "There aren't any like that on mine, or on yours or Martin's."

"Transverse ridges are signs that the person suffered a recent major illness," said Willie, hacking at the gauze. "In fact," he said, looking across at them with a sudden grin, "I guess for this lady it was a fatal one."

He went back to his task. The gauze was impregnated with some kind of gum, and he was having problems cutting it. The edges of the scissors were slipping on the material.

They laughed, still not quite sure how to take him. Did Willie Stringer really know what he was talking about, or was he just putting them on?

"How do you happen to know all that stuff?" asked Greg, watching the stubborn expression on Willie's face as he struggled with the arm coverings. *He's like me,* he thought, *he doesn't give up.* It had taken both Martin's and his combined efforts to cut the coverings off the arm on their side.

"My father's a pathologist," replied Willie. "I've seen him do autopsies." Suddenly he sounded more human to Greg, who could imagine Willie watching his father work, asking questions all the time.

Finally Willie had the coverings off, and massaged his fingers where the scissors had made an angry red pressure mark.

"I think that Ayeh would be a more suitable name for her, don't you think?"

"What's Ayeh?" asked Greg, who was busy with the arm on his side, making a cut along the skin of the forearm from the wrist to the elbow.

Willie gave them a cool look with his gray-blue eyes. "That's the name of Methuselah's wife."

He came around the table to see what Greg was doing, and they were trying to tell the difference between the veins and the arteries when Professor Lockhart came bustling up to their table.

"Well, boys, are you all finding your way around? Let's see now . . ." He picked up a pair of tweezers and Greg's scissors and snipped away at the tissues, skillfully separating and exposing the different structures. He had bright pink hands, and Greg couldn't help looking at his fingernails. They were flat and wide.

"Look, boys, this is a vein, the median cephalic." He picked up a gray, stringy, flat structure. "Feel it, roll it between your fingers. Can you feel how thin the walls are?" Greg tried but couldn't really tell much. Willie nodded, appreciating the texture.

"Now, here . . ." Lockhart spread some tendons over the wrist with the scissors and slipped a small hook between them, emerging with what looked like a piece of thick gray string. "That's an artery. The walls are thicker, there's more body to it."

"So to speak," said Willie.

Lockhart smiled cherubically at him. "Right, more body." He tugged on the hook. "Can any of you tell me the name of this artery?"

"The radial artery," said Martin promptly. It was all beginning to come back.

Lockhart looked at him, and his smile faded a little. "Weren't you in the last group?"

"Yes, sir," said Martin. "Martin Penrose, sir."

"Yes, well, better luck this time." His smile reappeared. "And what are your colleagues' names?"

Willie told him.

"Stringer . . . Is your father the distinguished pathologist, by any chance?"

"He's the only pathologist we know with that name," said Willie, for once sounding genuinely modest.

"Good, well, I hope you have as fine a career as he has had." Lockhart looked quizzically at Willie, and they thought he was going to say something else, but he went on to the next table.

Willie went back to his arm, carefully peeling back the stiff, mummified skin to uncover the underlying tissues. Watching him, both Greg and Martin could see that he was totally enthralled with what he was doing. There was a kind of intensity about him when he worked that almost made the two of them talk to each other in whispers. Not willing to be overawed by a fellow student, they reacted by chatting and laughing a little more loudly than they otherwise would have. Willie paid not the slightest attention to them for at least two hours, then he looked up at the clock.

"Lunchtime, gentlemen," he said.

They carefully rewrapped the arms, soaked the thick gauze in formalin solution from a gallon can kept under the table, and went over to the sinks to wash their hands. That morning, everybody scrubbed under their fingernails and lathered with the coarse red soap up past their elbows with particular care.

"Every damn thing here tastes of formalin," complained Willie, seated in the cafeteria twenty minutes later. He pushed away the uneaten half of his hamburger.

"You'd better get used to it," said Martin. "Until we finish this course, everything you eat, drink, lick, or suck is going to taste of the stuff."

"I hope you're not being crude," said Willie,

Greg put his knuckles up to his nose and sniffed. "You're right," he said. "And I washed and washed . . ."

"You sound like Lady Macbeth," said Willie, crushing his paper napkin and dropping it onto his plate. He struck a pose. " 'Will all great Neptune's ocean wash this blood clean from my hand? No, this my hand will rather the multitudinous seas incarnadine . . .' "

"I never knew what that meant," said Martin, looking at Willie with a kind of amusement. He wasn't feeling hungry, either. Only Greg went on eating, and that was because he knew that this might also be his supper. His student loan barely covered necessities, and even secondhand, the books and instruments had strained his budget.

" 'Making the green one red,' " went on Willie. "Actually, Lady MacB was referring to medical students who puke after eating disgusting cafeteria food. First they're green with nausea, then they—"

"Shut up, Willie, for God's sake," said Greg equably, munching on the piece of lettuce which had formed a bed for his hamburger. "I'm having enough trouble getting this down without your comments."

"You know, there's only one thing that's really missing down here," remarked Willie, after they were back at work trying to identify the flexor muscles and tendons of the forearm.

Greg and Martin looked up, waiting to hear what new gem of information Willie was about to produce. But he wouldn't say until one of them asked.

They looked at each other and grinned. "Okay, what is it?" asked Greg. "What is it we're missing?"

"Nurses," said Willie, and went back to his work.

CHAPTER
TWO

"He has the information, all right," said Willie reflectively. "The problem is, he doesn't have anywhere to put it."

"That's not very kind," replied Greg, lifting the lid on his plastic coffee container. "He certainly works hard enough; you have to give him that. In fact, he works harder than you seem to."

"There are two kinds of people who succeed in medicine . . ." started Willie.

"Yeah, I know," said Greg, a trace of acid in his voice. "The brilliant ones like you, and the ones like me who work hard and have a good memory."

"Basically, that's right," replied Willie modestly. "And unfortunately our friend Martin doesn't belong to either group."

"Don't you think we should do something to help him?" asked Greg. "After all, he's at our table, and he's our friend."

Willie put a cigarette into a long silver holder with engraved scrolls and designs on it. He lit it and looked at the glowing end thoughtfully, while Greg waited, his feeling of friendship and camaraderie tinged, as always, with a kind of irritated envy.

"Yes," said Willie slowly, adjusting the velvet collar on his jacket, which seemed to be rubbing uncomfortably against his neck. "I really must stop buying clothes in New York." He sat up suddenly, and his eyes lit up. "We must tutor him," he said. "That way we'll review the material ourselves. At the same time he can have the benefit of our superior intellects."

Greg looked at him to see if he was joking, but Willie was quite serious.

"You're so conceited, you take my breath away," said Greg, laughing in spite of himself.

"Not at all," replied Willie loftily. "Conceit is pride in *imaginary* attributes. Anyway, let's start tomorrow, okay?"

"Okay," said Greg resignedly. "Tomorrow evening in the library, right?" That would mean giving up a session in the blood bank, which would have provided some much-needed cash, but what the hell.

Not that Greg was so confident of passing the exams himself. He had memorized everything, but the examiners didn't always stick to the same kind of question. With a shudder, Greg remembered his last oral exam, where the visiting professor had given him a tiny dried bone and asked first if it was human, then what sex it was!

"Okay, Martin, let's go over the cranial nerves again." Greg kept his voice low, almost a whisper; for a place that insisted on silence, the medical library, with its wooden floors, metal bookcases, and reverberating ceiling, could not have been more ineffectively designed.

Martin took a deep breath, and Greg could see him raking through the shallow waters of his memory. "Number one is the olfactory, runs along to the front of the skull and emerges through the cribriform plate into the nose, innervates the nasal mucosa, responsible for the sense of smell . . ."

"Good. Number two?"

"Optic, one from each eye, collects branches from the retina, passes back along the base of the brain to the visual cortex—"

"Hey, wait a minute. What about the optic chiasma and the optic tracts?"

"Right. Sorry. The optic nerves meet inside the skull at the optic chiasma and interchange fibers so that half from each side go along each optic tract."

"Right. Which are the fibers that interchange, medial or lateral?"

Martin hesitated. His mind had a terrible tendency to go completely blank during this kind of question-and-answer session, even when it was being conducted by one of his friends.

"Lateral." Sheer guesswork, but he tried to look as if he were quite sure about it.

"Wrong. The lateral ones stay on the same side and the medial ones cross over. Look, here's the diagram."

Martin shook his head in despair. "I look at it, remember it, and when you ask me the next time, it's just a blur in my mind, and the damn nerves swim from one side to the other."

"Hey, listen," said Greg, his eyes lighting up with amusement. "I heard this new mnemonic for the cranial nerves—"

"I know it already," interrupted Martin. "On Old Olympus' Towering Top—"

"Not that one; nobody can remember how it goes on from there. Okay, listen to this. Oh, Oh, Oh, To Touch And Feel A Girl's Vagina, AH!"

Martin grinned and repeated it, getting it right the second time. "I certainly won't forget that one," he said, counting the words on his fingers, "but it's not long enough for the twelve cranial nerves, is it?"

"Sure it is. The AH at the end is for the Accessory and the Hypoglossal. Now, let's go over some normal lab values, real quick." Martin's eyes turned up, trying to visualize the printed list he'd been memorizing while he ate his lunchtime hot dog. His fists tightened with effort. "Right," he said, "sock it to me."

"Number of white cells in a cubic milliliter of blood."

"Five to ten thousand, increases with infection and leukemia, goes down with radiation, overwhelming infections."

Greg remembered the lecturer demonstrating how small a cubic milliliter was; it was the size of a tiny drop hanging off the tip of a needle.

"Good. How many red cells per cubic milliliter?"

Martin hesitated and his eyes wavered. "Five million?"

"Right. Terrific!"

"Where's Willie?" asked Martin, looking around. "He hasn't been in the library for ages."

Greg looked at the clock. That goddamn Willie! It was far too late for him to be coming in now. It had been his idea to give Martin the tutorials, but he hadn't shown up since he first mentioned it, and that was a week ago.

"You're standing on my foot!"

"Smiley, can you see my name there?" Panic in the voice.

"Willie Stringer failed!" That brought a general titter from the crowd around the bulletin board. They all knew better. The exam results were posted at eleven in the morning on two bulletin boards about ten feet apart, and about a hundred people, not including girlfriends, boyfriends, dogs, and an occasional anxious parent, milled around the glass-fronted lists in moods that ranged from complacency to terror. Only the names of those who had passed were on the lists, and some students who'd reached the front were going through the list again and again, in case their name had been misplaced or was somehow misspelled and out of alphabetical order.

Greg was as anxious as any of them.

Margie Chapman, a pretty girl who'd worked two tables down from them, was walking away in tears, head down, fists clenched, repeating, "Fuck, fuck, oh, fuck!"

Ralphie Gobel was happily hugging his parents. He looked just like his father, same squat body, same gray, jowly face.

Willie had not bothered to show up. When Greg got near enough to read the typed names, he deliberately looked first for Martin's. Penrose, Penrose . . . Mitchell was there, and Pabst, and Quigley, but no Penrose. Greg's heart leapt when he saw his own name, and then, at the top of the honors list, Willie Stringer's name. Good old Willie, Willie the Great . . .

It was Martin's second failure, so he was not invited to return for another try. Willie and Greg took him out to get drunk the evening the results came out. In a way, it was an intimation of academic mortality to all of them, and it sobered both Greg and Willie to see a proportion of their classmates disappear into the wilderness.

Even at this early stage in Willie's career, people knew about him, pointed him out. The taller one, they said, the good-looking one with all the black hair, walking beside that other guy . . . Some of the junior faculty looked on him as just a precocious, immature brat; medical school, they said with a knowing smile, will eventually take care of him, one way or the other. The more senior staff tended to look at Willie with interest and curiosity. That's a boy who'll go far, they said.

Greg periodically got annoyed at his own relative anonymity; he grew angry at being constantly in Willie's shadow, but finally decided it was better to be there than nowhere at all.

The watering hole usually favored by the trio was a bar near the university campus, but Martin wanted to get as far as possible from the institution that had rejected him, short of going over to New Jersey.

They went to Arthur's, uptown, on Amsterdam Avenue, a place frequented by the students from Columbia-Presbyterian Hospital. It was a long, tunnel-like establishment with a low ceiling and a heavy-looking bar of dark wood with a brass foot rail. There were Tiffany-type stained-glass lamp shades and a big mirror behind the bar with the Guinness logo across it. Greg noticed the swirls in the corners where the mirror had been carelessly wiped. The beer taps had old-fashioned, rounded, imitation ivory handles.

It took a little while to get used to the gloom inside; the place was almost deserted, and they sat halfway up the bar, with Martin in the middle, the guest of honor. All three of them felt uncomfortable, and Greg's sense of failure and loss was almost as strong as Martin's. To Martin it was as though Greg and Willie had already left him; he felt as if he'd been abandoned in a small boat at sea, the mother ship steaming off into the future without him.

"So what are you going to do now?" asked Willie abruptly after their drinks had been put on the shiny bar in front of them. Greg and Martin had beer, but Willie had ordered some foreign concoction called a Pimm's.

Martin didn't answer immediately, as if he felt it was too early in the proceedings to be asked that kind of question. Maybe later, when they'd gotten tanked up a bit, he might raise the subject himself.

He took a long swig, then wiped the foam off his top lip with his sleeve. "I don't know. Maybe I'll go into law, to defend you guys against malpractice suits." Greg laughed, a bit too loudly, but Willie just kept on looking at him with that intense, questioning gaze.

"Come on, Martin. Really, what are you going to do?"

Martin slammed down his glass on the bar, and some of it slopped over the edge. The bartender, washing glasses a little farther down, looked up but didn't say anything.

"Willie, I don't fucking know *what* I'm going to do. Does that answer your question?"

Willie stared at him in astonishment, and Greg took a big, embarrassed swig from his glass. Sometimes Willie just didn't see the raw places on people, the painful abrasions on their self-esteem.

"Well, Martin, that's all right," Willie replied quietly, "there's no need to be like that. It's just that I had an idea, and if you were already fixed up, there was no point mentioning it."

"Let's talk about something else," said Greg with a diplomatic yawn. "I don't know about you guys, but I just want to get bombed and forget exams and everything else that ever happened in my entire life, good or bad."

"If *you* get drunk, Greg," said Martin, good-humored again, "the rest of us'll be dead first. You're like Rasputin the way you can hold your booze."

Greg was worried about Martin. He knew that he didn't come from a wealthy family, and the local scholarship he had had from his hometown would end abruptly now that he'd failed the exams.

Several beers later, Willie went off rather unsteadily to the men's room, and Greg took the opportunity to hand Martin five rolled-up ten-dollar bills. Martin pushed his hand away.

"Thanks, Greg, but I don't need it. I'll be okay."

Greg stuffed the bills inside Martin's jacket. "It's just a loan," he said. "And for chrissake, don't make a fuss or we'll get thrown out." As the money left his hands, Greg had a momentary pang. To him, it was a lot of money.

Martin mumbled an embarrassed thanks, and just had time to put the money safely in a pocket, when Willie reappeared, pulling something out of his parka. It was a small but expensive-looking package wrapped in gold foil.

He handed it with a flourish to Martin, who examined it carefully, then held it up to his ear before slowly opening it. Nestling inside the silk-lined box was a gold Cross pen-and-pencil set.

Martin looked from the set to Willie's face and back. The muscles around his mouth twitched, and for an awful moment Greg thought he was going to burst into tears.

"Now that's really thoughtful," he said. "Really thoughtful, indeed."

"Actually, that's only half of it," said Willie, offhanded as usual. He pointed at the set. "They're just for taking down your orders." There was a silence. Greg and Martin looked at Willie expectantly.

"Okay, Willie, what's the rest of it?" asked Greg resignedly. Everything had to be done Willie's way.

"Well, actually, the rest is up to Greg's father," said Willie. Greg's mouth fell open. "*What* did you say?"

"I called him a couple of weeks ago." He turned to Martin. "Mr. Hopkins is in pharmaceutical sales, did you know? Anyway, he said they have a job in his company for a trainee, with good prospects, and in a few years you could be making more than either of us."

Greg put his head down between his hands and laughed incredulously. Fucking Willie!

"He said they were looking for people with some medical exposure, and that's what you've just had." Willie was in his element, at the center, organizing the rest of the world. He took a piece of paper out of his pocket and squinted at it in the dim light. "You have an appointment to see him in his office next week," he said, passing the paper over. "He'll tell you all about it then."

Willie sat back and called for another round of drinks. Suddenly Martin grabbed him by the collar and shook him, his eyes slitted. "You said you called him two weeks ago. We hadn't even taken the exams then!"

"Foresight, my boy, just foresight!" Willie gently disengaged Martin's hand. He didn't like people touching him; well, not men, anyway.

Martin slowly backed off, not knowing whether to knock Willie's interfering block off. Then he laughed. "Willie," he said, "I've never in my life met anybody like you."

Right, thought Greg, *and I've never met anybody who manages to get all the credit for something but leaves all the work to someone else.*

Martin fell very quiet and left soon afterward, but Willie and Greg stayed on for a final drink.

"Well, Greg," said Willie, raising his glass, "it's just you and me now."

CHAPTER

THREE

1958

"Oh, God!"

"What?"

"This bookcase! I don't believe it! You must have made it yourself!"

"Right. Greg and I—"

"For heaven's sake, don't you ever do *anything* on your own? Always Greg this, Greg that . . ."

"Mother, I haven't even spoken to you for six months. How could it always be anything?"

"Actually, that's rather a nice desk," his mother said with a sudden change of tone. Now it was Mrs. Andromache Stringer, ex-actress, Smith graduate, socialite, three-pack-a-day nicotine addict, furniture expert. She walked across the Kashan rug to the old English mahogany desk placed against the far wall of the living room and pulled on one of the brass handles. "Where'd you get it?"

"Down in the Village."

She turned on her high heels and scowled at him. Her makeup was so thick, she could have been going onstage, and the curved lines of her eyebrows gave her a glassy, surprised look. "Don't you start that sulk routine with me, young man. When I ask you a question, I expect the courtesy of a proper answer."

Willie opened his mouth, but she was already examining the two-gray-hills rug on the back of the sofa, the one he'd bought in Santa Fe. A cigarette was stuck in her mouth like a ther-

mometer. She flung the hair out of her eyes in a well-
remembered theatrical gesture, for which Willie had gotten
smacked hard at the age of four for innocently imitating. Mrs.
Stringer dropped ash on the rug and went into the bathroom.

Oh, shit! thought Willie. She's going to check the medicine
cabinet. Sure enough, a few moments later Mrs. Stringer came
out, bearing a can of hair spray, a bottle of nail varnish, and,
oh, God, a small blue-and-white cardboard box of tampons, all
clutched in one scarlet-nailed hand.

She dropped them at his feet. "You didn't tell me about your
sex-change operation," she drawled, taking a fresh cigarette
out and lighting it. Her hand, Willie noticed, was trembling.

"I need a drink," she announced, sitting down on the sofa.
"That was the last straw."

Willie went into the kitchen where his gray Persian cat,
Fortescue, was hiding under the table. It had taken Fortescue
three seconds to understand more about Mrs. Andromache
Stringer than Willie had in all his twenty-four years.

"Vodka, please," she called out. "Don't bother with the ice."

"Well?" she said after half emptying the tumbler.

"Well, what?"

"Are you getting yourself tested regularly?"

"We have final exams," said Willie, deliberately obtuse. From
his childhood he had always feared his mother's dreadful rages,
but now he didn't give a damn.

"I mean for the filthy diseases all your sluts and whores
expose you to," she said, addressing an audience of thousands,
her eyes fixed belligerently on him. She got up and started to
shout, but still enunciating every word with thespian clarity.
"You're just like your father, whoring around, fucking anything
that moves—"

Willie stood up. "Get out," he said quietly.

She stopped in her tracks. "*What did you say?* How dare you
talk to me—"

Willie reached for her arm and she slapped him hard across
the face. He grabbed her elbow tight and pushed her toward
the door. She was heavier than she looked, with a doughy,
corseted feel about her.

"I'll have your father stop your allowance!" she shouted,
forgetting that it came from his grandfather's trust. She turned

her head toward him and her face sagged, for the first time afraid at his expression.

"You never . . ." she started, and began to weep. Willie pulled the door open. She stood there, suddenly old, pathetic, with tears rolling down her cheeks and leaving tracks in her makeup. At that moment, Willie could have killed her.

"Don't ever come back here," he said. He put his hand on the small of her back, giving her a push, slamming the door behind her.

He could feel his pulse racing as he went back to the kitchen. Fortescue started to purr and wind himself around his feet as if to congratulate Willie on his courage.

"Okay, Big F," said Willie, after washing the tumbler and picking the ash off the rug, "I have to get some work done here."

He pulled a book from the top shelf of the sagging brick-and-plank bookcase, sat down, and put his feet up on the sofa. He thumbed through the fifteen-hundred-page Davis textbook of surgery, then hefted it in his hand. It weighed at least twice as much as a human brain; there had to be some kind of significance to that fact. Fortescue snuggled down in his lap.

Willie's six-week surgical rotation started the next day; this was *his* subject, and he was determined to shine like no other student before him. He turned the pages; he'd read the textbook many times before, and he knew most of the stuff already, but now he couldn't concentrate. "Like your father," she'd said. No way had his father fooled around. She really had it all wrong. He remembered a dinner party at the house when he had been about four or five. They were all dressed up, going to the opera or something, and his nanny had brought him down to be introduced to the guests. His mother was surprised to see him and for a few moments didn't seem able to remember his name. Everybody thought it was terribly funny; she spilled some wine out of her glass, and everybody was laughing, laughing. . . .

Willie's group was supposed to report to the Department of Surgery office at eight, and Willie was there on the dot, panting with anticipation, in company with three other students, two women and one man. Greg's assignment was to Medical Outpatients, ten floors below; he'd finished his surgical rotation three months earlier and had hated every moment of it.

"They treat you like shit," he'd told Willie indignantly on his last day. "They make you run errands, fetch X rays, hold retractors in the OR. That's the worst; you stand there for hours and hours, you can't see anything, and they don't explain what they're doing." Greg's tales of woe did nothing to dim Willie's enthusiasm. He knew he was going to spend the rest of his life being a surgeon; and the sooner he got started, the better.

They waited for twenty-five minutes outside the frosted glass door. Finally, just as they had decided to go down to the cafeteria for a quick coffee, a figure in a white coat with the sleeves rolled up over OR greens came around the corner toward them, pulled a set of keys out of his pocket, selected one, and unlocked the door. He said nothing and didn't look at them until the door was open.

"Okay, inside," he said in a flat, uninterested voice, and they all trooped in obediently, like schoolchildren.

"My name's Janus Frankel," he said, sitting on the corner of the desk, glancing around at them with clever, aggressive eyes. His tone suggested that they should already be aware of who he was. Willie had heard of him from Greg; he looked as if he was in his mid-thirties and was rather smaller than average, with delicate, mobile hands. Under the rolled-up sleeves, the muscles moved very visibly in his thin forearms. He had a pale, intense, triangular face, the white skin shining over his cheekbones.

"I'm assistant professor in this department, and it's my unhappy lot to be in charge of student teaching." The girl next to Willie gave a little laugh, thinking he was trying to be funny. He froze her with a stare.

"Let me have your names, please."

His voice was formal, distant. When Willie gave his name, Frankel looked up, stared at him for a moment, and then went on. Willie, uncomfortable without knowing why, tried to feel a proper admiration for this man, who'd not only finished medical school but also had completed a long surgical residency, passed his surgical boards, and gotten himself this prestigious post in a university department of surgery. He must be quite a guy, although he didn't look that impressive. Frankel glanced down at the list he'd just written.

"The first two, Harding and Miss Stone, will join Dr. Gold-smith's team. Dr. Goldsmith is our senior resident. Miss Serafin and you, Stringer, will be assigned to me."

Edie Serafin and Willie exchanged a quick glance, which Frankel caught. He glared coldly at them.

"I want you to be quite clear about what will be expected of you all," he said. "Ward rounds start at six-thirty every day. That gives us time to see all the patients on the service before we start operating at seven-thirty."

Both Harding and Edie Serafin were taking notes, and Frankel looked at Willie as if he should be writing all this down too.

"You will be responsible for all X rays and charts coming with the patients into the operating room, then if the team leader needs you, you'll assist during the operations."

Frankel's humorless eyes swept over the group. This is not a man who enjoys teaching, thought Willie, but that's all right. He's probably a damn good surgeon and researcher.

". . . complete medical histories and examinations on all new patients, and discuss your findings with the junior resident." Frankel's voice droned on; each Monday there were full Surgical Department rounds at ten, and all students had to be there, come hell or high water. Surgical pathology rounds followed that, in the Path Department. The list of meetings, duties, and responsibilities was long, but Dr. Frankel assured them that they would pick the routine up very quickly. If they weren't able to do that, he suggested, maybe they should consider another profession.

Edie Serafin and Willie followed Dr. Frankel to the operating room.

"The case we're doing next is a hernia," he told them. "Do you remember the anatomy of the inguinal region?"

"I think so," replied Edie nervously. She knew she didn't remember enough to withstand a quizzing.

"Yes," said Willie confidently.

"We'll see," said Frankel, smiling. Both Edie and Willie noticed how thin his lips were.

Edie went into the nurses' changing room, as there were no

facilities for women doctors, and Willie followed Janus into the doctors' lounge, which led into their changing room. He pointed out the students' lockers and the piles of clean green shirts and pants.

"They come in three sizes," he informed Willie. "You find out what size you have after you've put it on."

Willie spent most of the morning in the operating room, but it wasn't quite as he'd hoped. Frankel taught, but only out of a sense of duty. His method was to ask questions until the students ran out of answers, then zero in on the question that had stumped them. It was an exhausting experience.

When he talked to Willie, he called him Stringer. Edie he called "You." He didn't hide his opinion that women should have a full and complete freedom of choice in their medical careers as long as they chose nursing or became laboratory assistants. He told Willie to scrub up so he could hold the retractors; Edie was told to look over his shoulder and not touch anything. "It's all sterile," he snapped, looking at her as if he expected that she was too.

"All right, Stringer, what's this structure I'm holding up here?" Dr. Frankel had a curved clamp under a cord of whitish tissue, about the thickness of a pencil.

"The spermatic cord?" hazarded Willie.

"You, what do you think it is?"

Edie said nothing, shaking her head slightly. She wouldn't demean herself by simply agreeing with Willie.

Frankel kept going. "This group of veins here, what's that?" Willie had no idea, and neither did Edie.

"It's called the pampiniform plexus. Didn't you people learn anatomy a year or two ago, or is that no longer on the curriculum?" Frankel was happier now that he'd found something they didn't know about. "You, how do you think the pampiniform plexus got its name?"

"It was named after Professor Pampini of the University of Genoa," said Edie promptly, and Willie grinned at her over his mask. She wasn't anybody's fool.

"I don't expect that kind of levity in the operating room," said Frankel severely. Willie noticed that he kept on operating throughout the conversation. "The term *pampiniform* relates to the Latin word meaning a bunch of grapes, and the early surgeons noted a resemblance to this structure." Willie stared at the pampiniform plexus. The knot of veins looked less like a bunch of grapes than a sack of potatoes, but that, he figured, must be part of the mystique of surgery.

When the time came to close the incision, Frankel suddenly asked Willie if Greg Hopkins was a friend of his. When Willie said yes, Frankel said, "I thought so. Not one of our best students . . . he couldn't care less about surgery. I certainly hope you don't plan on following in his footsteps." The way he looked at Willie showed that he expected the worst. Willie was astonished. He knew Greg hadn't been happy on the surgical service, but he knew that he was conscientious and hardworking. Maybe he'd upset Frankel in some way.

What Willie didn't know was that Frankel made up his mind about students the first day. From then on, the lucky ones were tolerated and the others could not do anything right.

After escorting the patient to the recovery room and learning how to hook him up to the monitor, Willie went to grab a bite of lunch before going up to the surgical floor to examine his new patients. Gordon Hogan, the junior resident, went with him.

"How did you enjoy working with Janus Frankel?" he asked as they came into the cafeteria. The lunch line was slowly moving forward, the unmistakable cafeteria odor of grease and hot steam wafting by them in gusts. "Pick up a tray," he went on, "we don't have to wait in line. Do they give you guys lunch vouchers? Here, have one. I can get as many as I need." He winked lasciviously, indicating the pretty girl just beyond the counter working the cash register.

"Thanks," said Willie. "Frankel? Well, I got him through the case, all right, although his anatomy was a bit shaky. Why?"

"He's an asshole, that's why. We call him Janus the Anus. He gives the house staff a real hard time. Sarcastic, loves to get people in trouble, so watch your step."

Gordon put a carton of milk, a piece of chicken, and a plastic cup of yogurt on his tray. Willie wasn't feeling hungry, so he made do with a chicken sandwich, an orange, and a glass of water. He followed Gordon to a table where the rest of the team were sitting in greens, rushing through lunch.

"This is Willie Stringer, he's working with the Anus."

They looked at him briefly, grinning a moment's sympathy. They had other things to think about. Edwin Goldsmith, the chief resident, had a stack of cards in his hand; he was going through the patients on the service, keeping tabs on everything that was going on. Willie sat watching, eating his food, quietly learning how a clinical surgical service works. Ed Goldsmith was careful, methodical, meticulous to the point of obsessiveness. Willie could see his writing on the cards; tiny, cramped, slightly backward-leaning.

Monday morning. Gordon Hogan, the junior resident, was getting ready for rounds. As usual, he was flustered with the responsibility; if anything went wrong, he had let his side down, and he also got all the blame.

"Willie, where the fuck did you put the films on Sarah What's-her-name, the pancreatic abscess?"

Willie raked quickly through a stack of about fifty large brown envelopes. Some of them were old and falling apart, and dozens of black X-ray films threatened to fall out. If that happened, it would be a total disaster.

"Here."

Gordon took them with relief, but a second later he shouted, "Where's the report? It's not in here!" Willie looked quickly through the stack again, then ran down to the Radiology Department for a copy. He enjoyed the rushing around but saw why it had bothered Greg so much. On the Internal Medicine service, there were people hired to do that kind of clerical work, the medical residents having simply refused to do it anymore. The surgeons, more driven and more compulsive, needed to be in direct control of every detail and continued to scurry around, week after week, spending hours that could have been better utilized taking care of their patients.

At ten A.M. everyone gathered in the auditorium. The chairman and the attending physicians, in long white coats, occupied the front two rows of benches; the residents and interns, wearing white jackets with big round blue hospital badges at the top of the sleeves, filled the rest. The house staff slated to present cases sat nervously near the front, hugging envelopes of X rays. The students, nurses, and residents from other services sat wherever they could find a seat. Willie, next to Gordon Hogan, who had more or less adopted him, saw Janus Frankel sitting with the chairman, talking animatedly. Gordon followed his gaze.

"Sycophantic prick that he is," he whispered. "Look at him, always trying to smarm his way in with the boss."

There were several cases to be presented. First was a patient suffering from acute pancreatitis who had been admitted to the medical floor as a heart attack. This was followed by the case of a physician who had had a malignant melanoma excised from his back twenty years before, had had no problems until he had a simple hernia operation six months ago, and was now dying of disseminated melanoma in his liver and brain.

"Is his present tumor-cell type the same as the one removed twenty years ago?" asked the chairman.

"We believe so," replied Ed Goldsmith, the chief resident. "It was done at Mount Sinai."

"Don't you have the slides?" chipped in Janus Frankel. "Surely our own pathologists should make the comparison."

"I called the Pathology Department there, and they got the report out for me." Ed sounded tired, deliberately patient. "The slides are in storage, and they said it would take a week or so to get them out."

"Isn't there a messenger service?" snapped Frankel, with a side glance at the chairman. "Or couldn't you have sent one of your students across town to get them?" His tone was hectoring, disdainful.

"You see now why he's called the Anus, huh?" Gordon whispered as Frankel continued the attack on his chief resident.

"Do you consider that you're taking proper care of this patient, one of our professional colleagues, when you don't even know it's the same cancer he had back then?"

"Your point is well taken, Dr. Frankel," said the chairman, obviously anxious to move on. "I'm sure that information will be available next week." He looked pointedly at the chief resident. "Now let's get on with the next case."

Janus sat back with a self-satisfied smile. If you once let the residents get away with this kind of thing, he thought, the entire standards of the institution began to crumble, and he was not about to let that happen, even if some of the others in authority didn't feel the same sense of responsibility.

"This is case number 88-033297," said Ed, "and Dr. Hogan will present it."

Gordon stepped behind the small podium. "This was the case of a previously healthy eight-year-old male who presented at the emergency room at seven P.M. with a twelve-hour history of abdominal pain."

Willie tried to remember if he'd seen this one; so far it didn't ring a bell.

"The pain started around the umbilicus, was steady in character, and passed to the right lower quadrant after about three hours." Gordon took a deep breath. So far so good, but he could see Frankel watching him with his beady eyes. "He vomited twice, and his mother brought him to the emergency room. There, he was found to have severe tenderness with rebound in the right lower quadrant, maximal over McBurney's Point."

The chairman looked over the rows of students. "Can any of you tell me where McBurney's Point is?"

A female voice, which Willie thought he recognized as Edie's, replied from near the back of the auditorium, "Two thirds of the way out between the umbilicus and the right anterior superior iliac spine."

"Correct. Low on the right side of the belly." There was a faint titter from the audience. They can get you coming or going, Willie thought. If Edie had said that, the chairman would have laid into her without mercy.

"Some tenderness on the right side on rectal examination, white-cell count was 7,000 with a normal differential, hemoglobin 14.2. The clinical findings and the slightly raised white-cell count strongly suggested acute appendicitis."

"Well?" asked the chairman.

"We took him to the operating room. His appendix was normal, but he had enlarged mesenteric glands. We took the appendix out."

"Your final diagnosis?"

"Mesenteric adenitis, sir."

"A difficult problem," said the chairman after a pause. He addressed the auditorium. "Mesenteric adenitis is a benign, self-limiting disease that causes similar symptoms to appendicitis; and only too frequently results in the patient being operated on unnecessarily."

"Couldn't they have waited?" asked Dr. Frankel. "The child would have improved by morning."

"We felt we shouldn't take the risk of the appendix rupturing," said Ed Goldsmith, taking the heat off Gordon. "There is much less risk in removing a normal appendix."

"Didn't we have a similar case a few weeks back?" Frankel went on, getting into his stride. "Are you people opening up everybody who comes to the hospital with abdominal pain?"

"Now wait a minute, Janus," said one of the other attendings from farther along the bench. "Most hospitals run something like a fifteen to twenty percent error rate on diagnosing acute appendicitis." The chairman turned in his seat to see who was talking, but Frankel stared straight ahead. He did not appreciate being criticized in front of the entire staff and the students. The attending continued, "If every diagnosis they made was correct, and they never operated on suspicion, they'd be missing cases of perforated appendicitis, possibly with fatal results." He paused for a moment. "I entirely agree with the way the residents managed this case."

"I'm sure our overall error rate in this institution is well below fifteen or twenty percent," said Frankel, tight-lipped, "but I'm sure it'll be in that range soon, with the kind of residents we seem to be getting these days!"

"Does anybody know what the error rate actually is in this hospital?" asked the chairman mildly. There was a silence. Nobody seemed to know.

"Well, I will find that out and report the results this time next week," said Frankel, furious that his attack on the residents had been deflected by the other attendings. "In my opinion, diagnostic errors of this sort are inexcusable."

Gordon came back to his seat, looking a little short of breath. "That bastard . . ." he said softly. "Now you see what sort of a person he is. Just be careful working with him."

At the end of the meeting the chairman and the attendings filed out, and the others followed. When Willie got to the door, Frankel was waiting for him. To Willie's surprise, he sounded calm and friendly.

"I'd like you to get that data for me, Stringer," he said, ignoring Gordon. "About the appendectomies. You should be able to get it all from Medical Records; it shouldn't be too much of a big deal."

"What exactly will you need, sir?" inquired Willie, feeling honored to be asked. Frankel made a movement of impatience.

"Total number of appendectomies, the percentage with actual appendicitis, the pathological findings, other diagnoses, and so on. I'll need it first thing next Monday morning, okay?"

He hurried off to catch up with the chairman. Gordon looked resigned. "Typical. You do the work; he presents it and gets the credit. Anyway, it'll be good practice for you."

The rest of the week was extremely busy for Willie. He managed to get a couple of hours off on Wednesday afternoon and went downtown to Columbia's School of Music to buy tickets for a concert. Between what happened there and all the work and reading he had to do, it wasn't surprising that by Friday afternoon he'd completely forgotten about the assignment Dr. Frankel had given him.

CHAPTER
FOUR

On Wednesday, during their brief lunch break, Willie mentioned that he was taking a couple of hours off that afternoon to pick up some concert tickets. The house staff looked at him as if he'd suddenly grown horns.

"You're in Outpatients this afternoon, Willie," said Ed Goldsmith, as if that were the end of the matter.

Willie took a deep breath.

"Sorry, guys. I've been on this service four weeks now, and I've barely been out of the building. It's for the Menuhin concert, and I have to get them today."

"Isn't he the violinist guy?" asked Gordon. "I saw something about him in the papers."

"Okay," said Ed grudgingly. "Up to now, you've done a good job on this rotation. Just make sure you're back for the five-o'clock rounds or I'll have your ass on a plate."

Willie spent the rest of the brief meal in heaven. In this environment, praise was as rare as hens' teeth.

Going outside into the bright sunshine after the weeks of almost total incarceration felt like getting out of bed for the first time after a long illness. Even the touch of his clothes was unfamiliar, and the collar and tie felt constrictive after the loose-fitting OR greens.

Since his first year in medical school, Willie's taste in clothes had become more restrained, but he still liked to look snappy and well dressed. His face had taken on some maturity, and there was something about him, maybe a slight haughtiness, or the jaunty way he walked, that made people look around at him with a kind of envy, even in jaded New York City. He took the subway to the Columbia campus; he was to pick up the tickets at the front desk of the music school.

A crowd of students was coming out through the revolving doors, some carrying instrument cases, some hurrying out silent and preoccupied, intent on music only they could hear.

None of the women he saw wore makeup, except for an unusually attractive girl who jammed the revolving door with her cello case just as he came up. Through the glass Willie could see her pulling, trying to free it. She glanced at him for a second, half angry, half apologetic. Willie, annoyed at being held up, pushed on his side of the door, thinking a little extra pressure might do the trick. The door moved a few inches, and through the plate glass he heard the splintering of wood, followed by her furious scream. He'd never seen anybody's face change so fast; he backed away as she pounded furiously on the glass at him. She looked at the case, its neck angled and crushed, then put her head between her hands and started to cry. Willie felt terrible, but there was nothing he could do. And the girl was so pretty, so obviously desolate, that he felt even worse. Probably her boyfriend was waiting outside for her, a seven-foot, three-hundred-pound giant who would want to break him in two. It took almost ten minutes for the security guard to take a panel out, then rotate the door slowly around to free her, while Willie waited guiltily for her to come through.

She kept her eyes on him for the last few moments before she emerged, saving her pent-up fury.

"You pig!" she yelled at him as soon as she was out, her eyes flashing, standing with her aged cello case beside her, splinters of white wood showing against the black of the case. "Look what you did! You clumsy idiot! You broke my instrument!" The tears were standing in her eyes again, and she laid the case on the grass at the side of the door.

"Let me help you open it," said Willie, his voice very quiet, very apologetic.

"If you touch it, I'll kill you," she said, and although she was now on her knees in front of the cello, she looked as if she meant it. Willie stood uncomfortably, watching her while she unlocked the case and eased it open. The hinges creaked, and Willie held his breath. The green velvet lining was torn where the bow was clipped to the case, and the bow itself was bent.

She ignored it and pulled the cello out. To Willie's huge relief, it seemed to be undamaged. Still ignoring Willie, she started to replace the instrument gently in the case. Sighing with relief, Willie had a sudden urge to ask her to play something for him but prudently decided this wasn't quite the moment. The bow was bent, but it straightened when she unclipped it and turned the little knob at the end to tighten up the horsehair.

"You're lucky," she said, turning to Willie. "That could have been the most expensive mistake of your life."

"I'm terribly sorry," he said. "I was just trying to free the door. Here, let me get that dent out of the case for you. I'll be happy to pay to get it fixed, or get you a new one."

Willie got down on his knees and gently pressed on the case, straightening it out. Still silently furious, she replaced the bow, shut the case and locked it, and picked it up. She must be stronger than she looks, thought Willie, for she handled it like a violin.

"Please, let me take you for coffee or something," he begged. "I'll need to give you my name and address, for the case, that is, and I'm glad it wasn't damaged, I mean the actual cello—" He stopped, and she cracked a small smile through the ice when she saw his confusion. He was very good-looking. She could tell he wasn't one of her fellow students.

"That won't be necessary," she said curtly, but Willie thought he detected a minuscule softening of her attitude, and after all, her cello was intact.

"Come on," he said, pleading. "There's a place just around the corner, on Broadway."

She wouldn't let him carry her cello, and even with that burden she walked as fast as he did.

They found a table near the window, and she laid her cello carefully down against the wall.

"My name's Willie Stringer," he said, pulling her chair out. She seemed quite composed now, her expression still serious but not solemn. She had perfect, smooth skin and large gray-green eyes with a touch of eye shadow around them. She was totally beautiful, and Willie was enchanted.

"I don't know if I should give my name to a total stranger," she said rather coldly. "Especially one who shows signs of being some kind of destructive maniac."

"I gave you my name," he replied, smiling. "And if anybody was bent on destruction five minutes ago, it was you."

She looked him over, trying to place him. He didn't look like one of the people who hung around the campus trying to pick women up. Nor did he look like a businessman; maybe he was junior faculty, or at law school? He had nice hands, she noticed, like a musician's.

"My name's Liz," she said. "I'll decide later whether I'll tell you the rest of it. What I'm trying to figure out"—Willie felt her eyes go straight through his heart—"is why I'm sitting here. Maybe I should take off, before you do more damage."

Willie tried to figure out if she was being coy. Her accent was hard to place, but it was educated, with a decisive tone to it. Maybe she came from some nearby town and hadn't yet learned New York City habits. She obviously didn't have the New Yorker's inborn distrust of her fellowmen.

"You can take off screaming if you like," he said mildly, "but you'd better leave them a forwarding address for your big fiddle there."

As it turned out, Willie learned more about Liz in the next half hour than she did about him. Her anger quickly evaporated and she became lively, funny, and easy to talk to. She was a second-year student, preferred Mahler to almost any other composer, was learning about computer analysis of musical structure, and her home was in Bridgeport, Connecticut, where her father was an accountant.

He also learned that she had a lisp, barely noticeable when she was calm; that her lower eyelids came up just a fraction when she was about to ask a question; that one of her very white front teeth had a tiny chip on its outside corner; that she had an exciting and marvelous figure; and finally that there was something about the way she moved that he found irresistible.

Willie looked at his watch with a start, paid the bill, said good-bye, and headed back to the hospital. He was in a kind of dazed glow; not until he was in the subway, halfway to his destination, did he remember that he hadn't picked up the tickets to the concert.

Liz had written down her telephone number for him on a piece of paper torn out of her diary, and Willie fingered it continuously in his pocket, like a talisman. He couldn't wait to tell Greg the news; he'd found the woman in his life, he was sure of it.

He was a few minutes late for rounds, but nobody said anything. He was unusually quiet; normally he could be counted on to contribute something to the discussions, even if he wasn't always correct.

Willie was made to pay for his time off; they kept him so busy for the rest of the week that he was exhausted, didn't know if he was coming or going. When he told Greg about Liz, Greg was consumed with curiosity. Anybody who could affect Willie Stringer like that must be something really special.

Willie talked to Liz several times on the phone but simply could not get away to see her. By a stroke of sheer good fortune, though, he had the next weekend off.

"I'm going up to see her parents," Willie said. He tried to look his usual cool self, but his eyes were sparkling. He was down in the medical Outpatients Department, visiting Greg. It was Friday afternoon, and things were momentarily quiet.

"Isn't that a bit soon?" asked Greg. "Seeing her parents, I mean?"

"No. It's not an official visit, not yet, anyway. She'd promised to go home this weekend and said I could come, too, if I wanted."

"When are you going?"

"Tonight, after we finish late rounds. She's got a car, and she's picking me up at eight. I'd really like you to meet her."

When eight o'clock came, Greg was busy dealing with a child who'd come in with severe asthma, so he missed seeing Liz, anyway.

The call from Janus Frankel came about an hour later. Had Greg seen Willie Stringer? Frankel sounded furious. Not recently, answered Greg cautiously.

"Well, he was supposed to do some research for me. I just want to be sure he's done it. Tell him to call me when you see him," and he hung up.

Greg sat and pondered for a moment. He was sure Willie would have mentioned a research project, especially if he had had to do it for the Anus. He reached for the phone and paged Gordon Hogan. He might know what was going on.

The phone rang a few seconds later.

"Gordon? This is Greg Hopkins. Do you remember me? I did my surgical—"

"Yes, I remember," Gordon said, interrupting. "What do you want?" It was a major breach of protocol for a mere student to page a resident.

Greg told him about the phone call from Frankel. There was a long silence from Gordon's end.

"Oh, shit!" he said finally. "Willie was supposed to find out how many people we operated on for appendicitis, how many actually had it, and what the final diagnosis was on the others. Where the hell is he?"

Greg explained that he was gone and wouldn't be back until Monday morning.

"Well, God help him, then," said Gordon. "The Anus'll make his life hell and give him a failing grade at the end of his rotation, you can be sure of that."

Gordon hung up, having better things to do than talk to a damn medical student who wasn't even on his service.

Greg put his head between his hands. That goddamn Willie! And he didn't even know Liz's surname, so he couldn't call him, although he knew she lived up in Bridgeport.

Maybe he'd done the work and just hadn't mentioned it? But Greg knew that he hadn't. For one thing, he hadn't had time; they kept him so busy up there, he didn't have time to go to the toilet, let alone the Records Department.

The Records Department . . . Greg reached for the phone and dialed the number. After a long wait the duty clerk answered. No, nobody had done a chart search for appendectomies, not that he knew of.

"Are you going to be there for a while?" asked Greg. Then, "I'll be over in a few minutes."

Greg went to see how the asthmatic child was doing. The intravenous aminophylline had worked wonders, and the child was asleep, breathing easily. He gave the nurse the number where he could be reached.

It took a total of three hours, on and off, plus a substantial bribe, before Greg emerged with several sheets of computer printout. Actually it had been quite interesting to do, although he was seething at Willie for putting him to this additional trouble. He laughed, thinking that some time on Sunday Willie would suddenly remember and would absolutely shit himself. Then he would call in a panic, try to get it done over the phone. He was so anxious to be thought of as the best student who'd ever been on the service, and he knew what such forgetfulness would do to his hopes.

But Willie didn't call. Monday morning came, and Willie didn't appear. Frankel came in about nine and went gray when he found that neither Willie nor the data Frankel had boasted about to the chairman was anywhere to be found.

At ten Greg waited anxiously for Willie outside the auditorium, while the rounds got under way. Frankel was beside himself, thinking about faking a fainting spell—anything to get out—when the chairman called on him.

"Dr. Frankel tells me that some interesting facts have come out of the research he kindly undertook to do last week. Dr. Frankel, if you'd like to come up . . . ?"

At that moment Willie appeared outside the door.

"Where the hell have you been?" Greg hissed at him. "Frankel's in there, waiting for your appendectomy research!"

Willie's jaw dropped. "Oh, Christ!"

"Here," said Greg urgently, "it's all done. Here's the summary, read it quickly, then get in there. I put a copy on Frankel's desk, but he doesn't know it's there."

When Willie went in, a silence had fallen. Frankel was on the podium, stammering, red in the face. When he saw Willie enter, he looked as if he were going to explode.

"I'm sorry, Dr. Frankel," said Willie meekly, stepping over and handing the printout to him.

"Perhaps *you* can give us the report, Mr. Stringer?" said the chairman sarcastically.

"Dr. Frankel has all the data there," said Willie briskly, "but I can give you a brief summary if you wish."

When he finished, the chairman gave him a quick, approving nod. "There's one other thing, Mr. Stringer. Did you not know that this conference starts at ten, *precisely*?"

"I'm terribly sorry, sir, but my cat had a stroke, and I had to take care of him." There was a moment's silence, then a roar of laughter burst from the audience. They'd been able to restrain themselves, except for a few quiet, joyous giggles during the spectacle of Dr. Frankel's embarrassment, but this was too much.

"That will do, Mr. Stringer, thank you." The chairman's tone was calm, and he was doing his best to control his amusement. He'd heard all kinds of things about Stringer, and he certainly was turning out to be a character.

Later, while they were getting ready to start the afternoon operating schedule, Gordon Hogan asked him curiously, "Willie, what was that about your cat having a stroke? Were you just pulling their leg?"

"Not at all. It's an old cat, and this morning when I got up, it was making this funny noise."

The cat had been trying to walk across the living room but was falling over at every step. Finally it could only scrabble with its left paws; the right ones, both front and back, were held stiffly out, and it couldn't balance on them. All the time it was making a continuous, pitiful meow that must have awakened him. Willie, still stiff with sleep and with one hand on his pajama drawstring to keep the pants from falling, came over to look at the cat and bent down to stroke it.

"Hey, Fortescue, what's the matter?"

The meow became louder and the cat tried to bite his hand. Willie was sure it didn't recognize him. He hesitated, looking at it hard for a moment. Spastic paralysis of the right side . . . either a stroke or a brain tumor. One way or the other, not good news. If he left it like that, it could drag on half paralyzed for weeks or even months.

He thought hard, hand on his chin. He could drown it, but it would be difficult to hold it under water, and he'd almost surely get severely bitten and scratched. Maybe if he put it in the oven and turned on the gas? After considering a few alternatives, he went into the kitchen and rummaged around in the drawer where he kept his tools. There was a roll of copper wire at the back. He cut off a length, about a couple of feet, and looked around for something to use as handles. Finally he settled for two stainless-steel knives out of the cutlery drawer; he carefully wound an end of the wire several times around the middle of one knife and twisted the end back around the main part of the wire. He repeated the process with the other end and finished up with quite a serviceable-looking garrote. He made a big loop with the wire, holding the knives so his knuckles were touching, and went back into the living room. Fortescue was on the floor in front of the sofa, scrabbling, trying unsuccessfully to get up on it, and falling down each time.

"Okay, Fortescue," he said quietly in his usual voice, so as not to alarm him. The cat heard Willie and, to his surprise, started to purr. "Sorry about this, Fortescue," he said quietly, and slipped the loop over its head. He tightened it suddenly, and the cat let out a dreadful screaming noise just before its windpipe was shut off. Willie gritted his teeth and pulled, but the loop slipped, bending the cat's neck at a grotesque angle. There was a bubbling, squirting noise and a pool of semi-liquid feces appeared on his Kashan rug. "Goddamn!" he said angrily, he should have known that would happen; he'd read *The Godfather* only a few weeks before.

While he cleaned the rug with a wet cloth, the cat lay still, its dead eyes protruding. Willie picked it up by the tail and noted that it was already stiffening. He took it back to the kitchen and dropped it into a garbage bag. Poor old Fortescue, he thought. But it was still the best way.

At the end of Willie's rotation, Frankel wanted to fail him, but he was overruled by the chairman after consultation with Ed Goldsmith and the other house staff.

The final opinion of those on the service who knew him best was that Willie was very bright, arrogant, hardworking, and well informed. He had two major failings, they felt: he had a tendency to be erratic (on several occasions he had missed a diagnosis because he hadn't taken the necessary time but relied too much on his intuition); and he tended to be unfeeling and thoughtless with his patients—he should try to remember that they were human beings too.

The last day of rotation in the medical Outpatient Department was always set aside for student exams, so they could take an "informal" clinical test of their diagnostic abilities. They weren't forced to take the exam, but everybody did it as a matter of course. It appeared as an "optional" in the students' final transcript, and it gave them some idea about how they were doing in relation to their peers. The residents and staff members gave critiques, and the tests were generally thought to be a valuable experience.

Greg was given the end cubicle, next to the exit door. He pulled the curtain and went in, his heart hammering, wondering what kind of rare disease they had in store for him. A woman was lying on the stretcher, dressed only in a hospital gown. There could be no excuses for not doing a full examination; a nurse was available when the student wished to do a rectal or vaginal exam.

The lady was fat, middle-aged, with a round, sunburned, jolly face. Her name was Dominica Fernandez; she came from Puerto Rico and spoke enough English to get by.

Before Greg had time to introduce himself, she heaved up on her elbow.

"Doctor, please, do I have to lie here? I am so uncomfortable."

"Sure, of course, why don't you sit up." Greg went over and helped her. She was seriously overweight and wheezing.

"My name's Greg Hopkins, and I've come to examine you. We need to find out what's the matter."

"You're a doctor?" She beamed at him in a motherly way. "You're very nice-looking doctor. I like you!" She sat on the examining table, the top sheet across her knees, and watched him with dark, interested eyes.

Greg sat down in the green chair facing the stretcher. Although this was a test, he felt instantly comfortable with Mrs. Fernandez; she seemed a really nice, pleasant lady, obviously anxious to please. His tension decreased; he had examined enough patients by now not to worry about the mechanics of it; he already had a good bedside manner and was learning to make patients feel confident and relaxed in his presence.

"Well, Señora Fernandez." He smiled, stretching out his legs in front of him. "What's been the matter with you?"

Her face clouded. "I been *mucho* sick," she said, using what Willie called Spanglish, referring to the linguistic word-soup happily used by many Spanish-speaking immigrants in New York.

"*Dolor?*" he asked. Greg could speak this lingo as well as anybody.

"No, Doctor, no *dolor*, well, maybe *poquito* . . ." She smiled uncertainly at him. The other doctors had told her that she was going to be used for a test, and she wanted to help this nice-looking boy as much as she could. Tell him everything, they had said, don't leave out anything at all, even if you don't think it's important.

"Where was the pain?" he asked.

"Well, Doctor, it wasn't really a pain, but it started at the time my husband . . . that's Emilio, my husband, he's waiting for me outside—" She stopped and looked at him to be sure she was saying the right kinds of things. Greg smiled encouragingly. Sometimes it took a while for patients to come to the point.

"It was when he was working for his Cousin Roberto at the fruit stand. Emilio, he's really a steve something at the docks, mostly at Elizabeth, New Jersey—"

"You mean *stevedore?*"

"Right! Steeveedore!" She beamed at him. This was such a nice doctor, so interested, not like some of them.

"This Roberto is not a nice person, not like you, Doctor. He was starting to give my Emilio a hard time, like if he came just one minute late to the market where they get their fruit, he'd start hollering—"

"Right, Mrs. Fernandez." Greg interrupted gently. "You were going to tell me about a pain you had?"

"Oh, no, Doctor," she said, a surprised look coming over her face. "I didn't have no pain, just a little one, and it went away."

"Did you only have it that one time?"

Mrs. Fernandez rubbed her huge side thoughtfully. Obviously the pain hadn't made too much of an impression on her, so Greg decided to leave that line of questioning. Maybe he'd come back to it later.

"Are you taking any medicines, Mrs. Fernandez?" This was one of the first things he'd learned about clinical exams— always find out what medicines the patient is taking; often it's the best clue to the diagnosis.

Dominica threw up her pudgy hands. "Oh, Doctor! *Medicinas!* All the time I take medicines!"

Greg smiled with relief. Maybe he'd be able to find something out about Dominica's medical history, after all.

"What kind of medicines, Mrs. Fernandez? Do you remember their names?"

Dominica's brow wrinkled with effort. "I think so. One of them was Dr. DaCosta. I can't remember the other one; he was short, with no hair. His office was terrible, Doctor, not like here, but dirty, di-i-i-rty, full of dirty men, and the smell!"

"He prescribed medicine for you? Here in New York?" Greg took out his pen. "Do you remember his address?"

"One fourteen Casa della Vittoria, in San Juan," she replied triumphantly, and Greg began to sweat. He looked at the clock; he'd been there for fifteen minutes and so far all he'd gotten for sure was her husband's name. Maybe he'd be able to find out more on physical examination.

"Would you like to lie back, Mrs. Fernandez, so I can listen to your chest?"

"Sure, for you, Doctor, yes, you're such a *nice* doctor," she said, slowly sliding back onto the table. By the time she was down, with Greg's help, she was wheezing with the effort and smiling apologetically. Greg put his stethoscope on the front of her chest and listened. He could hardly hear anything; her heart was going rather rapidly, but then, he thought, so was his.

He moved the stethoscope to the side of her chest to listen to her breathing, but because of her obesity the sounds were so faint, he could say nothing about them, except that she was wheezing. And he didn't need his stethoscope for that; he could hear it from where he was standing. Greg was beginning to feel panicky; there had to be something seriously the matter with the woman or she wouldn't be here, but so far he hadn't the vaguest idea what her problem might be.

Her abdomen was vast; for a moment Greg thought that a long scar under her right ribs might give him a clue, but it turned out that she had had her gallbladder removed about twenty years before.

He had less than five minutes left; he was about to call the nurse to do a pelvic exam in a final desperate attempt to reach a diagnosis when he heard a noise behind him. He turned and saw Willie Stringer's head poking around the curtain; then the rest of him appeared and he came into the cubicle.

"You're not supposed to be here, Willie, I'm in the middle of my clinical exam."

Willie glanced at the patient for a second, then said, "Come outside for a second. I need to talk to you."

Greg threw a despairing look at the clock; he knew that

whatever he did now, he wouldn't have time to make a diagnosis.

"Okay," he said resignedly. He turned to Mrs. Fernandez. "Excuse me, Dominica, I'll just be a moment. You can sit up if you want."

Dominica was looking at Willie with disapproval, then smiled at Greg. That doctor who had just come in, she knew that kind, just from the way he looked at her. He was the kind of doctor she didn't like at all.

"What's up, Willie?" They had gone into the corridor, out of sight of the nurses' station.

"Not much. I just wanted to know if you were free for coffee."

"Willie! Goddammit!" Greg was furious. "Here I'm in the middle of an exam, I don't know what the hell's the matter with my patient and I'm going to flunk it, and you want to go for coffee!"

Willie looked at him in astonishment.

"What do you mean, you don't know what's the matter with her? She's got SLE, systemic lupus erythematosus."

Greg goggled at him. "What the hell are you talking about? She doesn't even—"

"Greg," said Willie urgently, "didn't you see the butterfly rash on her face?"

"I thought that was just sunburn."

"Well, go back and look at it. She's also in congestive heart failure; her neck veins were engorged and she could hardly breathe when she was lying down. She had a moon face, so they're probably giving her steroids in pretty big doses, which means she's probably in kidney failure or approaching that point. You need to check her blood urea nitrogen, look for casts in the urine, follow that up with a kidney biopsy . . ."

Greg didn't say anything, just turned and ran back to Mrs. Fernandez's cubicle. It took him only a few moments to confirm what Willie had told him.

While he was checking the faint rash on her face, Dominica smiled at him. The closer he got, the better-looking he was.

"That other doctor who came in," she said, "I'm sure he's very good, but I like you *mucho* better."

"Mr. Hopkins?" A voice behind him made Greg jump. It

was the senior clinical instructor. "How did you get on with Mrs. Fernandez?" he asked, smiling at the patient.

"Pretty well, I think, sir."

"Did you come to a diagnosis?"

"Yes, I think so," replied Greg confidently.

"Good. Let's go outside and discuss it." He sounded surprised.

"You give him a good mark now," said Dominica. "He's the nicest doctor I ever seen!"

Willie was still waiting when Greg finished ten minutes later, and they walked to the cafeteria together.

"How did it go?" asked Willie.

"Just fine. You saved the day, Willie. He was surprised that I'd gotten the correct diagnosis after only half an hour. I almost told him how long you'd taken—"

"And was she on steroids?"

"Fifty milligrams a day for the last eight months. When they cut down or she forgets to take it, the lupus flares up. I'd never have guessed she was so sick."

Willie nodded; obviously that was what he had expected. They turned into the main hospital corridor, Willie deep in thought. Suddenly he spoke, in a modest and unassuming tone that surprised Greg. "Before you spread the rumor that I'm the greatest diagnostician since Paracelsus, there's something else about the case that you should know." He was hesitating about something, and Greg waited, almost respectfully; his friend was beginning to carry the aura of some kind of clinical superman.

Willie didn't say anything more until they had carried their coffee containers over to one of the round, Formica-topped tables. He still seemed to be having trouble getting out whatever it was he had to say.

"I know Mrs. Fernandez well," he said finally, a broad grin slowly spreading across his face. "I had to put a catheter in her bladder when she was in about two weeks ago. Boy, does that lady hate me!"

CHAPTER

FIVE

"I swear the guy's gone gay," said Suzanne, who worked in Pediatrics. She dropped a slim wrist in a faggy gesture. "You know his friend, Greggie . . ."

"No, I don't think so," replied Jasmine, a pretty, petite Eurasian girl from the Records Department. "Honestly, you can't say he didn't try. . . ."

They giggled over their own memories, but there was a kind of wariness about both of them. After all, nobody knew yet what had caused the sudden change in Willie Stringer's attitude.

"Well, even at his best, he reminded me of a cocktail sausage," said Suzanne, smiling but watching Jasmine closely. It might quite possibly be her.

Jasmine shook her head. "Maybe you weren't doing the right thing," she purred in her silky accent. "The way I remember him, it was more like a salami." She giggled again, and Suzanne's lips tightened for a second. Then she saw that she and Jasmine were doing the same thing: both putting a brave face on a distressing situation.

Jasmine collected the paper napkins and sandwich wrappers on the tray. "If I find out who it is," she said sweetly, "you can hold her arms while I scratch her eyes out."

"It's a deal," Suzanne agreed.

Elsewhere, silent tears were shed.

Willie's work habits had changed too. Maybe he'd gotten burned out on the surgery rotation; that had been his biggest effort, because he knew he was going to be a surgeon, and the other subjects didn't matter as much to him. Anyway, he now felt he could coast for a while, and rely on his clinical intuition and good memory.

Most of the time that he wasn't at the hospital he spent with Liz, who shared an apartment near Columbia University with Ellen Petrini, who was studying hotel management. According to Liz, Ellen's father was a big-shot politician in Connecticut, and the only reason she was sharing an apartment was because he wouldn't allow her to have one on her own.

"You think *he's* bad," said Ellen, "you should see my grand-father from Palermo. Females in this family barely exist for him, and he told my father that sending me to college was not just a waste, but sinful too."

Willie spent a lot of time at their apartment—at first in order to fix the cello case, which he did using one of the new epoxy resins. He repaired the torn lining and varnished the outside so carefully that it took a detailed examination to see that it had ever been damaged. He had to work on it for a long time before he got it exactly right. Meanwhile, Liz missed school; she couldn't just trundle her cello through the streets without a case, and she wanted to spend time with Willie. She had fallen in love so hard, it made her breathless.

"Let's go for a picnic," said Liz. They were both lying on the floor in her apartment listening to an old Dizzy Gillespie record. "It's Sunday, and it's beautiful out. Let's go up to the Cloisters. We can sit on the grass in Fort Tryon Park . . . it should be cool up there, above the river."

Willie rolled over toward her. "Can we screw in the grass?"

"Sure, if you don't mind getting arrested. God, I can just imagine my father reading about it in the paper: PROMINENT FUTURE SURGEON ARRESTED FOR PARK RAPE."

Willie sat up suddenly, then came down again, all in one movement. "Rape?" he asked.

"What d'you think I'd tell them? That I had my legs up in the air of my own free will? Sorry!"

Ellen came out of the bathroom, and her eyes narrowed for a second when she saw the two of them together on the floor. "Ahem!"

"We're all going for a picnic," said Liz. "Fort Tryon Park."

"All?"

"You, me, this young fellow here, and we're going to call his friend Greg to come with us, aren't we, Willie?"

"He's been complaining that he's never met you," said Willie, smiling at Liz, "although I've told him enough about you to turn a normal person's stomach."

"And you've told me plenty about him," said Liz, rolling over on her back and then sitting up. "I feel like he's a brother already."

"All right already!" said Willie. "You're certainly picking up the lingo around here." He put his arms around her from behind and was about to slide his hands up to her breasts, but she caught his wrists. Liz was stronger than she looked.

"I don't know if I can go," said Ellen. She didn't look particularly happy at the thought of a picnic with the two lovebirds. "I should be doing the laundry and stuff."

"You don't have to do it now. You're coming." Liz slid out of Willie's grasp, went to the phone, and took it on its long extension cord to him. "Here, Willie. Call him."

Greg was free. They decided that he should come over to Liz's apartment at once and they'd all go up to the park in Willie's car.

When the doorbell rang, Ellen went to answer it; Liz and Willie exchanged a quick glance.

Willie made the introductions in his usual suave way; Greg looked at Liz with curiosity, and he was impressed. Not only was she stunning to look at, but there was something about her, the way she moved, an aura, something magic. Maybe it was the same quality that had enchanted Willie.

He barely noticed Ellen at first, although she was very attractive, too, in a quick, vivacious Mediterranean way, with flawless olive skin, long black hair, a flamboyant figure, and dark, long-lashed eyes.

It was a perfect Sunday morning; even the breeze was right, coming from the ocean and blowing the effluvium of New Jersey back where it came from. There was less traffic than usual, and Willie drove up Amsterdam at breakneck speed, then onto St. Nicholas toward the east gate of Fort Tryon Park.

"It's just being overrun," said Greg, looking out at the dirty streets full of people hanging around the open bodegas, and the little groups of two or three kids zipping through the lazy crowds on roller skates. "Look, there isn't a shop sign in English in this whole area."

"Right," said Willie. "I had an aunt who lived in the Heights before she went to Florida. On Sundays you couldn't see a soul on the street; the whole area was closed down. I like it better like this."

The picnic was a qualified success. They had brought a couple of long baguettes of French bread, a big chunk of Bel Paese from Zabar's, grapes, dark chocolate, and a jug of Gallo red, which Willie told them was the best oenological bargain in the world.

"Oenological?" asked Liz, spreading a red-and-white-checkered tablecloth on the grass. She leaned forward, and Greg's heart started to beat faster. "What's oenological?"

"He means it's a logical wine to own," said Greg, smiling, and Willie groaned.

Superficially they all seemed to have a good time, but there were invisible undercurrents that everybody felt, without quite being able to identify their source. Greg was affable but quiet; he spent some time talking and joking with Liz because he was anxious to get to know more about her. The two of them got along well, and then Willie chipped in and the conversation became general again. Greg then chatted with Ellen, but with less enthusiasm than he had with Liz. When their conversation petered out and she was talking to Willie, Ellen looked up and Greg's eyes were on her, thoughtful, observant. Ellen thought he might be getting interested in her, and turned her attention back to him for a while. "My brother Fredo's thinking of going into medicine," she told him. It would be quite convenient if Greg . . . but for some reason she wasn't able to give him her full attention; there was a restlessness about her. Greg figured his end of the conversation wasn't too interesting, because she seemed to be simultaneously listening to him and trying to keep up with what Willie and Liz were discussing.

On the whole they had a good time, though, and it was a welcome relief from the heat and bustle of the city. If one ignored the four high-rise buildings straddling the Cross Bronx Expressway, and the distant roar of the traffic making its relentless way across the George Washington Bridge, they could have been out in the country, upriver somewhere. The

Cloisters was just visible through the trees, and when they went to sit on the benches after lunch, shaded from the sun by the maples and birch trees, they could look over the clifflike banks across the Hudson to the hazy New Jersey shore. It was very relaxing.

The next few months were full of activity for Willie and Greg, who were approaching the end of their medical school training and starting to think about the approaching, looming specter of the board exams.

Greg in particular had to work hard; he didn't have the same effortless ability with which Willie soaked up information. Greg had to write it down, summarize, memorize the summaries. Willie wasn't always as reliable on the details as Greg was, but he had a brilliance about him that seemed to excuse that.

One evening they went to the bar across the street from the hospital. It was dark, grubby, and the bartender was abrupt and unfriendly; the only thing it had to recommend it was its convenience. Willie liked it for all the reasons Greg didn't.

"Have you ever seen such a place?" he said, delighted when a big flake of plaster fell off the ceiling onto their table, shattering into a splash of whitish dust. "There's only one thing that mars its pure perfection," he said, wiping his glass with his handkerchief. "They should serve inedible food here. Don't you see it, a pile of rancid sandwiches curling up there on the counter, under a fly-spotted glass dome?" He held up the glass and poured slowly from a bottle of Heineken in the other hand, like a pharmacist filling a bottle of medicine.

Greg didn't know what he was talking about.

"How's Liz?" he asked, the chair creaking alarmingly as he sat back.

"Fine. We went to a show two nights ago, *My Fair Lady*."

"How was it?" Greg drank gingerly from his glass. He had wiped it, too, but felt he'd just smeared the teeming colonies of bacteria around the surface.

"Great. Sometimes I think I should have been born in England; I'm sure I'd be much more comfortable as an aristocrat."

"Did Ellen go with you?"

Willie raised his eyebrows expressively. "Yes. As a matter of fact, the only reason we went was that her old man was able to get tickets. You know, I wish you'd come out with us sometimes."

Greg looked uncomfortable and stared into his beer.

"I'm hitting the books a lot."

"Yeah, I know. So am I. But it would be fun, and Ellen could use a little action, I know the signs. Don't you think she's a pretty hot number?"

"How come she doesn't have a guy of her own?" asked Greg, looking squarely at Willie.

"Maybe she's waiting for you to reappear," answered Willie. "I know she liked you at our picnic."

Greg shook his head. He didn't know if he should tell Willie who Ellen was really interested in.

"She's not my type. Anyway, I don't have the time to work on a real relationship. Right now an occasional roll in the hay with somebody whose name I barely know is more my speed."

"Relationships don't need that much work," protested Willie. "Get the right one and she'll cook for you *and* do your laundry. It's worth a candlelight dinner from time to time!"

Greg was surprised by his own anger.

"You certainly are a cynical bastard," he said. "Does Liz really wash your socks?"

Willie stared at him in surprise. "Cynical? *Moi?*" He sat back in his chair with a look of injured innocence. "Christ, I bought them a washer *and* a dryer, and yes, they do my socks. It's only fair."

Greg grinned. "Willie, there's nobody quite like you. Talking about girls . . . you remember Martin Penrose? Did you ever see him in action?"

"God, Martin! I'd almost forgotten about him. Have you heard from him?"

"He's apparently doing very well. He joined one of the drug companies, not my father's, one of the big ones with a head office over in New Jersey, I think."

"We should get him to come over sometime. I'd really like to hear how he's doing. Maybe we can take him out and get him drunk again, like the time he failed his exams."

A large cockroach suddenly appeared on the table, its antennae quivering. Greg, disgusted, was about to flick it off onto the floor when Willie stopped him. Willie drained his glass, and then with a quick movement clapped the inverted glass over it. It tried to run up the foamy sides of the glass but kept on slipping down. Finally it stopped in a vertical position near the rim.

Willie waved to the bartender, a scrawny, sallow-faced man in a gray waistcoat. "Same again," said Willie when he came over. The bartender picked up the inverted glass and was about to wipe the table with his cloth when the cockroach climbed onto the back of his hand. He started, dropping the glass on the floor with a crash.

"Your idea of a joke?" He growled threateningly at Willie as he stooped to pick up the shards.

"Just be thankful I'm not from the Board of Health," said Willie, without bothering to look at him.

"I was telling you about Martin in action," Greg continued. "Well, he has a technique I've never seen before or since. Didn't he ever tell you about it?" He waited while the bartender came back with two bottles and two fresh glasses, slamming them down on the table without a word.

"I went with him to this bar downtown," said Greg, "in one of the big hotels, I don't remember which. Anyway, it was very quiet, and there were just the two of us at the bar, and this woman comes in, very nicely dressed, glances at Martin, and sits down at the far end of the bar."

"You may have told me this," said Willie, grinning, "but go on, anyway."

"Martin keeps looking over at her, and finally he says to me, 'Would you excuse me?' in that kind of formal way, and he goes over to the woman. A second later there's this loud slap, and Martin comes ambling back and sits down again, totally unconcerned. You could see the marks of her fingers right across his face."

"No, you never told me this one," said Willie, smiling because he could visualize the situation perfectly. Martin would have been whistling nonchalantly under his breath.

"Anyway, I was shocked, and I didn't say anything for a minute, then I asked him, as diplomatically as I could, how he knew her." Greg shook his head in wonder at the recollection. " 'Never seen her before in my life,' he said. 'Then why did she slap you?' I asked him. I couldn't understand what was going on at all. 'I just said to her, "Excuse me, but would you like to fuck?" ' Martin said. He sounded totally unconcerned, and I couldn't believe my ears. I couldn't believe I'd heard him right, and I asked him again."

Willie was already laughing. He could imagine Greg going beet-red, glancing over at the woman in embarrassment, expecting her to call the cops.

" 'Martin,' I said to him, and I was really shocked, 'you must be completely off your rocker! What on earth possessed you to say something like that to a woman you've never seen before?' " Greg was appalled again, just thinking about it. "He said, that's how he found his women friends!" Greg gulped. "He said he gets slapped a lot, but one in every ten says yes, and he doesn't have to go through all the crap of taking them out to dinner and a show, which is always a gamble, anyway."

Willie leaned back dangerously in his chair, howling with delight. The bartender looked up from his newspaper and glowered at him from the other side of the bar.

"How come you never told me this before? That's the funniest story I ever heard! Martin Penrose! I tell you, Greg, I now have a totally new respect for that man!"

Willie was enjoying his evening with Greg. He'd been spending a lot of time with Liz and Ellen, which was great, but it was a relief to be able to enjoy a good laugh about things that Liz and Ellen might not appreciate.

They finished their last beer; as usual Willie was a little unsteady on his feet and Greg was entirely sober.

"Are you going to grand rounds tomorrow morning?" asked Greg as they were leaving.

"I guess so. When is it?"

"Ten. I'll see you then. Say hi to the girls. And you take good care of Liz, okay?" Greg put his hand on Willie's shoulder. "She's really special."

"Yeah, I know."

Greg headed back toward his dormitory. All he could think about as he walked along was Liz Phelan, the way she looked, the funny laugh she had, the way she moved her shoulders when she talked—and how totally inaccessible she was. Greg tightened his lips. Just as long as Willie was good to her . . .

CHAPTER
SIX

"**I** think we should stop at my parents' on the way up."

"For God's sake, Liz, we only have a weekend. Cape Cod's far enough away as it is."

"Come on, Willie, we have to go through Bridgeport, anyway. I can't just go past. . . . We only have to stay a few minutes."

"Well, I don't think your father likes me. Okay, okay!"

Willie was shocked to see tears in her eyes; he had difficulty understanding that anybody might *want* to see their parents.

Liz went on with the packing.

Willie, Willie, Willie . . . her whole life seemed to center around him now; she could hardly remember what life was like before she knew him. Everything she did, she did with him in her mind somewhere, whatever it was. She would hear somebody say something funny or interesting and would look around instinctively to share it with him. It was all very strange, and a contrast to her previous self-sufficiency; sometimes it made her nervous. Sometimes, if she hadn't seen Willie for a day or two, she started to get this awful gnawing feeling in her stomach, just below the breastbone, and she'd become restless. Then she couldn't concentrate, couldn't practice her cello, couldn't read, couldn't do anything. When that happened, she had to work at something very physical, like cleaning the kitchen floor or going to the park and forcing herself to run until she was so breathless it hurt. It frightened her when she realized how dependent she had become on him for her sense of well-being.

Ellen wasn't that much help, either. Maybe it was because of her different background, but recently she seemed a bit malicious; if Willie called when Liz wasn't home, often Ellen didn't remember to mention it. She was always very apologetic, but still . . .

It must have been difficult for Ellen, especially at first. After all, the two of them had been sharing the apartment for several months before Willie showed up, and they were good friends, really close, with the same kinds of problems, the same kind of things to talk about. Since Willie had appeared on the scene, Liz's time had been totally taken up with him. Willie came first; there was no question about that. It must have hurt Ellen's feelings. She probably felt that Liz had rejected her, so it was natural for Ellen to be more distant, grumpy from time to time, and even on occasion really quite bitchy; a side of her Liz had not seen before.

Not that she wasn't nice when Willie was around; at least Liz could be thankful for that. But for all these reasons, a kind of distance, a discomfort, had grown up between them, and Liz was glad to be taking off with Willie and getting away from Ellen.

The Cape! What a great idea that was. The week before, they had been browsing around in Brentano's, and Willie had picked up a big book near the door with wonderful color pictures of sturdy lighthouses painted dazzling white against the cloudless blue sky, with sparkling sand stretching out as far as you could see, and no one in sight. They decided to go there the very next weekend. Liz felt a sudden warmth throughout her body as she thought about making love on the sand at night, with only the quiet lapping of the waves, the high bright stars, and the two of them, wrapped together under the silent night sky.

Willie had an old gray-green Chevrolet with scratches down each door and missing the door trim on the driver's side. He said there was no point in having a good car in New York, and that other drivers took one look at his beat-up Chevy and steered clear.

They thought about taking a tent and sleeping on the beach somewhere, but Liz had heard that the weather forecast wasn't terrific, so they decided to stay in motels. She didn't like not being able to shower or wash her hair, either, but she didn't

have to bring in that extra argument. Willie liked the idea of
the big double beds in the motel, so the tent concept was forgotten.

They were like joyous kids going off on vacation, packing
blankets, a frying pan, and a boxful of emergency sardines
and chocolates and cookies. Liz forgot the suntan lotion and
had to run back in after Willie had started the motor, and in
the bathroom she found the toiletries and makeup kit she'd
put specially on one side so as not to forget them.

It was almost three o'clock on Friday afternoon by the time
they finally got going, and the day was hot and full of promise.
They wound the windows down because the air conditioner
was broken, and sang songs at the top of their voices as they
drove along, smiling and waving at the tight-lipped New York
drivers who snarled back at them, hating the thought that
anybody might be enjoying themselves.

They drove up the FDR Drive with the river on their right,
passing a Circle Line boat chugging up the East River, full of
sightseers. The traffic was still heavy when they rattled across
the Willis Avenue Bridge, then up the Major Deegan to the
Cross Bronx Expressway. By the time they reached the New
England Thruway, they were hoarse from singing and from
the highway fumes. Liz yawned, leaned back against the
doorpost, and closed her eyes. She felt his right hand sliding
up under her dress and turned toward him with a smile,
already half asleep. He swerved and nearly broadsided a small
panel truck driving in the next lane on his left. Liz woke with
a jolt, just in time to see the bearded driver flash a furious
single-digit message to Willie, who waved back, open-handed,
shouting, "Yeah, one of these is for you too!" Liz went back to
sleep.

They went through Greenwich, past Stamford, where the
first new building in years was going up near the highway, a
strange-looking edifice that seemed to be built entirely of glass.
Willie woke up Liz to look at it, and they decided that it was
time for a cup of coffee, so they stopped at a roadside coffee
shop, parked the car, and walked over to the restaurant, their
arms around each other's waists. They felt free, free of the
constraints and noise of the city, free from the dirty air. Here
the air was cool and crisp, and they both felt a wonderful sense

of adventure, of being with the person they most wanted to be with in the whole world. They were both as happy as they had ever been in their lives.

When the first Bridgeport sign came up, Willie slowed and turned off at the ramp. Five minutes later they pulled up outside her parents' old Victorian-style house.

"You see, Willie, it's hardly out of our way." Liz sounded apologetic.

Mike Phelan was putting down some cement on the short path to the front door. He was a heavy, square-set man, red in the face from exertion. He wore a whitish porkpie hat with sweat stains around the band. He straightened up, pushed the hat back with his wrist, and grinned at Willie while Liz came around and kissed him on the cheek.

"It runs in the family," he said, indicating the crusted shovel and cement-loaded wheelbarrow. "My father built his own house too."

"You remember Willie," said Liz.

"Sure. I won't shake . . ." The drying cement covered his hands with gray smears rimmed with powdery white. "Here's your mother."

Mary Phelan had a big smile on her round face as she came out and stepped carefully clear of the patch of wet cement. She held her hands out to Liz and smiled welcomingly at Willie. A noise, something between a grunt and a bubbling snort, escaped her lips. Luckily Liz had told him that she had been deaf and dumb from birth, but it still surprised him. She looked entirely normal. Willie said it explained Liz's musical talent because she was making up for her mother's deficiency.

They stopped long enough for a cup of coffee and a chat. Somehow Liz understood the sounds her mother made, and her mother lip-read. Occasionally they supplemented words with sign language. Willie felt left out, and soon he was restless and eager to get going. Mike hadn't come in, so they said good-bye to him on their way out.

It started to rain about an hour later, as they were crossing the bridge over the Thames at New London, and by the time they got to Mystic, it was more than the wipers could handle. Willie had to slow until the blurry black shapes in front of him turned back into cars.

"Why don't we stop at Newport, Willie? At this rate we'll be driving all night before we get to the Cape."

"Take a look at the map," he said, leaning forward, straining to see in front of him. "I think Newport's quite a way off the beaten track."

The light had faded when the rain started, and after another half hour it had become dark enough to switch the car lights on. The main beam reflected dazzlingly on the teeming bright raindrops, and Willie pushed the foot switch to dip the lights. The rain was coming down so hard, it gave them the impression that they were alone in the world. Suddenly the car in front of him started to weave, and for a moment Willie thought it was his own car doing things, but before he had a chance to think any more, the car in front fishtailed, slammed into the central barrier, bounced off it, slid sideways to the left and turned over. To both Willie and Liz it all seemed to happen in terrible slow motion, except when their own car shot past and narrowly missed the capsizing vehicle.

Shocked, Willie slowed down as soon as he safely could, then went into reverse. Two cars went past him, both in the outside lane with their headlights on; maybe they hadn't even noticed the accident. The rain was so heavy, he couldn't see anything through the back window, so he stuck his head out and slowly backed up along the hard shoulder, every few seconds using his sleeve to wipe the water out of his eyes. He backed for about twenty yards without spotting the car and was beginning to think that maybe he had hallucinated the whole thing when he saw some small flames flickering a few yards farther behind him. He stopped and the two of them jumped out and ran to the overturned car. One of the front wheels was still slowly spinning. The fire was in the engine, and the rain hissed as it landed on the hot metal. Willie looked through the window, but all he could see was a heap of clothing lying on the ceiling. As he watched, a trickle of blood started to ooze along what had been the top of the window, and it dripped out and ran back along the roof of the car. Liz ran around the car; all the windows were closed. Meanwhile Willie tried to open the doors; they were jammed tight. There was no movement inside. Willie banged on the door, and the heap of clothing moved so that they could just see the grayish blob of a child's face, with blood coming from a gash on her forehead. She moved closer to the window; her face was white, shocked. She looked about ten years old. Her lips moved, but of course they could hear nothing.

"We have to get her out!" said Willie, sweating with frustration. The flames seemed to be increasing, and he could feel the heat even through the rain. He thought for a second, then ran back to his car and opened the trunk, rummaging around until he found the jack. He pulled it out, tearing a piece of skin off his thumb as he did so, ran back, and started to smash at the window. At first the toughened glass just cracked, then he broke through. As he pounded away at the rest of the window he became aware of voices, somebody at his side, and then of a runnel of flame licking along the underside of the car from the engine and back toward the gas tank.

There were lights, flares going on in the roadway behind as he reached into the darkness of the car, feeling for the girl. Somebody was pulling at his coat. "Get back! She's going to go up any second!" He shook the hand off. If it went up, he went with it. He could hear Liz's voice behind him, and as his hand reached desperately around, he felt an arm, a shoulder. He caught it and pulled, but he couldn't get the right leverage because of the back of the seat. Then something gave and the girl's body, suddenly light, slithered along the inverted ceiling, and then her head was there and two thick arms joined his and they pulled the child through, gashing her thigh on the broken window.

Willie could feel the heat on his face and then on the back of his neck as he ran, stumbling, with her in his arms along the slippery wet grass. He felt rather than saw other people running with him, panting, and the smell of panic was like ammonia in his nostrils. They were about fifteen yards away when the car exploded and lit up everything in front of him in one bright orange moment, and then the blast hit them and he was sprawled flat on his face in the cold wet grass. It seemed like dozens of hands came to pull the child out from under him, and then they helped him up. He pushed the arms away from him, and then Liz was there, and he didn't mind her arms, not one bit, and everybody was quiet now and standing around watching the flames, the light flickering on their faces, except for two people in yellow slickers uselessly spraying the flames with small fire extinguishers.

Willie sat down on the wet grass and shivered until his teeth rattled audibly, while Liz, who had run back to set out the road flares, now took the little girl from the men as if by some primeval female right, bundled her up in somebody's coat, and held her tight to keep her warm. The child was expressionless, big-eyed, but aside from the cut on her forehead, she appeared to be unhurt. She was limp, nonreactive, and listless in Liz's arms, and Liz kept her head turned away from the blaze. A white ambulance with a red stripe and all its lights flashing howled up into the area, lit by half a dozen vehicle headlights. They found Willie sitting shivering on the grass and wanted him to go to the hospital, too, but he refused. He was all right, it was just some mud on his clothes.

He didn't want to see the little girl, find out her name or who she was or anything about her. He grabbed Liz as the ambulance doors closed; he wanted to get out before the State Police came with their flat-brimmed mountie hats and cold hard eyes. They went back to their car and Liz got in the driver's seat. They sat quietly for a minute before he insisted on driving off. The flames were still licking around the burned-out wreck, and Liz shivered, thinking of the bodies still inside. The little girl's parents? Uncle and aunt taking her for a weekend? Brothers? Sisters?

They stopped at a motel about twenty miles farther along, and Willie spent a long time in the shower. There were some things even Willie couldn't just wash away. They opened the two tins of sardines they'd packed, ate them, and then went straight to bed. They slept tight in each other's arms until early the next morning, when Willie woke and made love to her with a ferocity that was almost frightening.

Willie's jacket had blood on it, and the sleeve was all cut. When he picked it up off the chair where he'd dropped it, a shower of small fragments of glass fell onto the floor.

After breakfast they decided to go on to Newport, only about an hour's drive away. It was still raining, the unending, relentless rain of a nor'easter. Willie refused to get a newspaper, although Liz wanted to see if there was anything about the accident. There might be names, something to fill in the gaps. . . .

"Are you sure we shouldn't just go back to New York?" she asked. "It might be like this all weekend."

Willie was stubborn, and the pain in his thumb where he'd hurt himself with the jack did not improve his humor. The storm worsened, and the traffic went at a crawl, particularly on the narrow roads and the bridges leading to Newport. From the high Narragansett Bridge, through the swirling rain, they could intermittently see gray ships below them, wallowing in the heavy swell, struggling up the bay to get away from the storm. They found a motel and were both soaked to the skin by the time they'd gotten out of the car and gone up the steps to their room on the top level.

Willie was coldly uncommunicative by now, although Liz, who had never seen this side of him before, tried to jolly him out of it. He paced up and down the room like a caged tiger, looking through the rain at the shiny, deserted motel parking lot.

"Why don't we get in the car and take a ride around?" asked Liz. "Maybe we can see the ocean."

"Later," he said. "Take your clothes off."

And that was how they spent their weekend; mostly in bed, coming up for food and an occasional ride around the soaked and rain-glittery town, deserted except for a few hardy tourists striding down the main street with bravado, leaning courageously into the wind in their streaming, brand-new slickers. The cliff walk was closed by a police barrier; it was unsafe in this weather, they said. The Breakers was closed for repairs; the massive structure was surrounded by scaffolding. In a rare moment of lightness, Willie said it reminded him of an orthopedic patient in multiple traction.

And Liz loved him all the more; the desperation of his lovemaking, the grim silences, the subterranean rages made him more three-dimensional, more real to her, although the flashes of his passion sometimes disturbed her.

They left Newport after lunch on Sunday, and both the weather and Willie's mood lightened at about the same time.

"I think maybe I'm going through withdrawal," he said, which was as near to being apologetic as he ever got. "I need the chemicals in the air that comes over from New Jersey. . . ."

Without mentioning it, they both looked for the place on I-95 where the accident had occurred, but they couldn't remember the exact location. They saw nothing, and both had the weird feeling that maybe it hadn't really happened.

Liz felt that by now it was safe to talk about it.

"You were a real hero, you know, Willie," she said quietly. "If it hadn't been for you, that kid . . ." She shook her head and left the sentence unfinished.

He felt her eyes on his face, trying to look inside him, and didn't answer. In fact, from that moment on he never spoke about the accident, although he had dreams about it for a long time afterward. He could never remember the exact content of the dreams, but he knew what they were, because nothing else gave him that panicky, choking feeling that made him suddenly sit up in the middle of the night, soaked in sweat.

After they got back to New York, Willie immersed himself in his studies, and in a way it was a relief to Liz not to see him quite so often. She caught up with all the things she hadn't been doing, she got her cello out and played for hours on end. She was working on Elgar's Cello Concerto, and she could feel her daily improvement. Her relationship with Ellen improved too. It was like a plateau, a settling in her life. She was now secure in her feelings about Willie; she'd seen the worst of him, his dark moods, his erotic nature, and it all cemented her love, which she knew was reciprocated. She had never played her cello so well, and her teacher said that there was a new maturity about her interpretation, and that if she would only work hard at it, she could be good. Really good.

A few weeks later she went to spend a weekend with her parents. She went alone, partly because Willie was preparing for his boards, but also because her father indicated, none too subtly, that Willie would not be welcome, at least not by him. Liz was hurt and couldn't understand it. They had barely spoken to each other. Maybe her father was beginning to see Willie as a threat; Liz had never been so involved with a man before, and her father must have seen how much in love she was. Her mother, on the other hand, was a devoted fan of Willie's and was quite openly waiting for Liz to announce that she and Willie were going to get married.

On Saturday, Liz woke late; she felt overtired and dizzy for a little while after she got up and didn't feel like any breakfast, but her mother made her drink some coffee and eat a piece of toast with marmalade. Later they went shopping in downtown Bridgeport, and Liz found a tiny ivory chess set in an antique shop. Her heart jumped; it was just the right thing for Willie, he would love it. She had it gift-wrapped and bore it back home in triumph. Her father snorted when she told him about it. But she enjoyed her weekend, in spite of her father's unexplained disapproval of Willie.

She felt a sense of lightness, almost of floating on air, as she got on the train on Sunday just after noon to go back to New York. She had planned to take the five o'clock train, but she was already missing Willie and couldn't wait for him to see her present. He appreciated quality, and he would understand the love that went with it. The train sped back through the Connecticut countryside, and she hummed the cello part of her concerto. An old lady across the aisle smiled at her and after a while leaned over to her and whispered, "You must be in love!" Liz smiled back, feeling warm and happy that it showed.

She decided to splurge and took a taxi to Willie's apartment; it would have taken too long to go by subway. She ran up the stairs, the package in her hand, getting more excited by the minute, pulling the key to his apartment out of her purse. She opened the door and ran in. He wasn't in the living room, so she went into the bedroom. There he was, in bed, looking at her with a surprised expression. And Ellen was in the bed beside him.

PART TWO

CHAPTER
SEVEN

1988

Greg Hopkins closed the door of his office and walked around to the small parking area behind it. He left the lights on inside because it was Wednesday, the day the cleaning lady came: Greg didn't want a lawsuit because Millie had fallen over something in the dark. His office had been a private home before he converted it when he first came to town. It was conveniently close to the hospital.

The sticker on the windshield of his Pontiac was a month out of date; Liz usually remembered that kind of thing. He'd have to remind her. He looked at his watch. He was an hour late for dinner, as usual. He wheeled out into the street, making a left turn at the light, onto Main Street. It wasn't a bad place, this little town, but nothing much happened here. When you wanted some excitement, New York City was a couple of hours' drive away.

Greg was wearier than usual, and the tiredness seeped into his bones as he drove home. The well-lit shops and streetlights sparked and flicked by. *There's so much in my daily life I don't even notice,* he thought. *If somebody asked me what I had for dinner yesterday, when I last had an intelligent conversation, or even whether the radio was on, for the life of me I couldn't say. My life slides past and I don't notice it because it doesn't demand my attention.* Greg focused for a moment on the car radio; yes, it was on. Some kind of raucous music. He turned it down till it was just loud enough to touch some bare and lonely spot in his mind, but not so loud that he had to listen. *Maybe I'll die before I can stop and smell the flowers.*

His father had been the same, but as a salesman for a drug company his concerns didn't seem to Greg so weighty. His mother used to get furious when his father came home and spent his time writing reports, and then couldn't sleep for worrying about some account that wasn't going well. Would she have minded less if he'd been worrying about a little girl with typhoid? Being a doctor is a great excuse, Greg reminded himself, and if you want, you can use it to get away with just about anything. People really conspire to make you feel heroic. "Totally devoted, that Dr. Hopkins. Thinks only about his patients, we're so lucky."

As if other people didn't take their work seriously and worry just as hard.

"And Mrs. Hopkins—what a woman! Talk about dedication. Runs the house like clockwork. The doctor never has to worry about putting up screens or mowing the lawn, or the kids— she takes care of everything. So he can concentrate on us, us, *us!* What other doctor do you know who makes house calls anymore?"

Greg turned into Haven Road, where the sidewalk was lined by a bridal guard of thick-trunked chestnut trees, their branches joined in the darkness high overhead. The headlights tunneled below the canopy of bright new leaves, touched on a white-painted fence, then lit up a couple of ornamental lampposts outside the Macklins' house. His own home, number 18, was next, a big yellow-and-white Colonial set back from the road. The driveway was marked by a mailbox with a cast-iron horse and buggy on the top. Greg turned left between two old stone pillars, and a low branch scraped the top of the car. He pulled up with a quiet scrunch of gravel behind Liz's station wagon and sat still for a moment, leaving the motor running. Had he remembered to order electrolytes for Mrs. Wellbourne? Her potassium had been quietly going up for a couple of days and she might be edging into kidney failure. He'd call the hospital and check, although the nurses would probably take care of it.

There were lights on upstairs, and in the living room. The rest of the house was dark.

He switched off the motor and let himself in through the

back door, almost falling over Douglas's bicycle. He found the light switch, picked the bike up, and leaned it against the wall. Edward's bicycle was parked next to Patsy's old Raleigh, now gathering dust against the far wall. He touched the handlebars for a moment, remembering her first rather wobbling foray into Haven Road on her eleventh birthday. The bike had been so shiny new then, and a little too big for her—seven years ago! Time was beginning to pass too quickly for comfort.

He opened the door to the kitchen and walked in. Only the light over the stove was on. He heard Liz's footsteps coming from the living room.

"Greg? Dinner's in the oven. I didn't want to keep the children waiting." She appeared through the door, her slim figure outlined by the light behind her. "There's a couple of messages for you, but they can wait. Here, let me get it. You'll burn your fingers."

"I can do it, thanks. Looks good, what is it?"

"Boeuf bourguignon," she said, putting the white porcelain dish on the counter between his knife and fork. "It's really good, even the children liked it. Not that you could tell the difference, my poor tired man; it could be a can of microwaved cat food and you'd say, 'Liz, that was lovely, I'm sorry I'm late again, but tomorrow's going to be easier. I should be done by six.' "

"Are the children in bed?"

"No, it's only just after eight." Liz sat sideways on the stool next to him. "I really believe you think they're about seven years old. For your information, Douglas is fourteen, Edward is twelve, and Elspeth was ten three weeks ago. They're all upstairs doing their homework."

"You forgot to tell me how old Patsy is. Or doesn't she matter anymore, now that she's left the nest?" Greg smiled at Liz and reached over to stroke her cheek for a second.

"Well, I didn't think I'd need to remind you about her. You really miss her, don't you?" Liz sat on the stool next to him and watched him eat.

"Ech!" said Greg, moving his hands in a poor imitation of Yiddish unconcern. "Louella said somebody called from the school about Edward. I was doing a pelvic and they didn't leave a message."

"I've told them not to call your office. They wanted permission for him to run in the state championships, so I said sure, okay."

"Great! Good for him! When are they? I mean, the state championships?"

"In a couple of months. Why don't you ask him? He's just thrilled about it."

"Great. Yes, I will ask him. This is lovely. What did you call it? Boeuf . . . ?"

"Bourguignon. Would you like some salad?"

The phone rang, unnaturally loud in the quiet, semidark kitchen. Liz picked it up, listened for a moment, and gave it to him.

"Surprise, surprise. It's the hospital. Something about Mrs. Wellbourne."

Greg held the phone for a moment while he swallowed the last mouthful of mashed potatoes, then put it to his ear.

"No, actually, I just finished. . . . Yes, thanks. I was going to call you. . . . You'd better run a rhythm strip on her. . . . No, on second thought, do a full ECG, and get a potassium level *stat*. And put in an IV. I'll be there in fifteen minutes."

Greg got off the counter stool and stretched. "I'll go up and say hello to the kids first," he said.

Liz picked the dishes up and put them in the dishwasher. *Another candlelit, romantic evening with my husband the doctor.* The dishwasher rumbled. It had a comforting, kitcheny sound.

Greg went through the butler's pantry to the front hallway and listened at the foot of the stairs for a moment before going up. Douglas's thumping music made the banisters buzz. Apparently he couldn't do his homework without it. When Greg opened his door, a wall of sound hit him like an avalanche, and Douglas looked up, grinning. He was lying on his bed with a book in front of him, his face spattered with acne. It didn't seem to bother him. He opened his mouth and said something, but Greg couldn't hear him, so he fought his way through the noise to the stereo and turned a few knobs until the volume dropped suddenly, but a row of lights kept on flicking up and down in time with the beat.

"Oof! That's better. I didn't hear what you said."

"I just said hi, Dad."

They looked at each other silently for a moment, and Greg

felt the usual twinge of discomfort. It was really ridiculous not to know what to say to one's own firstborn son. He sought the healer's refuge. "I'll get you some stuff for your face from the office."

"Don't bother. I got some cream from the drugstore."

"What's it called? Some of those proprietary creams aren't so hot."

"I don't know, but the guys say it works great. Can I have my music back on? It's Dire Straits."

"What?"

"Yeah, right." Douglas grinned again, got off the bed, and turned the sound up. Then he flopped back on the bed and picked up his book. The volume lessened abruptly as Greg closed the door behind him. The entire three-minute visit made him feel as if he'd been narrowly missed by a truck.

Edward and Elspeth had their rooms at the other end of the hallway, with a bathroom between them. Greg poked his head into Edward's room. He was writing at his table by the window, the pen in his left hand, arm curled around the notebook. A red bulb in his reading lamp cast an eerie glow around the room. He had his back to the door. Greg watched him for a few moments in silence. Although ideally he would have preferred to feel the same way about all his children, for some reason Edward was the one he communicated with most easily, the one in whom he saw an improved version of himself. Maybe when *he* grew up he wouldn't get sucked into whatever he did for a living to the point where his other interests died on the vine.

"Edward?" The boy turned around. He moves just like his mother, Greg thought as he went into the room.

"Hi, Dad. Did you just come in? Mommy tell you about the state championships?" He got up and sat on the bed, looking up at his father. His face looked strange in the red light, and his normally brown hair and eyes shone jet-black.

Greg put a hand on his son's head and ruffled his hair affectionately. "That light makes you look like a zombie," he said. "Why red?" He sat down on the bed next to his son.

"Experimenting," replied Edward. "Timmy has a strobe light. Have you ever tried to read with one? He got a headache that lasted a whole day."

"What's this about the state championships? I didn't know you were so good." He realized that if he weren't so busy, he could see Edward on the track most afternoons.

"They're putting me in for the two-hundred-meter. My time isn't good enough for the hundred, but Coach Lenahan's putting Timmy up for that. Do you think you could come? They're going to be in Hartford."

Greg hesitated for a fraction of a second, but Edward saw it and grinned. "You don't have to, but it would be great if you could."

"I'll certainly try. When are they?"

"June. I've got the dates here somewhere." Edward got up and rummaged in his desk.

The bathroom door opened and Elspeth came through. She looked at Edward. "Fourteenth and fifteenth, Saturday and Sunday," she said.

Edward straightened up and looked around at her. "And how do you happen to know that, Twerpette?"

Elspeth looked at him seriously. "Somebody has to keep your schedule straight, and you obviously can't. Daddy, can I go with him?"

"I'm really proud of you, Edward, and I hope we'll all be able to go," said Greg, getting up. "Now I'm afraid I have to go back to the hospital." He grinned at Edward's expression. "I know," he said with an apologetic tone to his voice that both children recognized well. "What can I tell you?"

Two minutes later he was backing down the driveway, his head craned around. *Darn that branch,* he thought, *I'll have to tell Liz . . . Or, of course,* said a quiet voice, *you could make time to cut it down yourself.*

The parking lot in front of the hospital entrance had only a sprinkling of cars, and somebody was getting into a big white BMW that Greg didn't recognize. It had New York plates.

The emergency room was quiet when he walked through on his way to the new wing. Mrs. Harris was at the desk talking to Derek, the new male nurse, finding out about him. They both looked up and smiled. Mrs. Harris stood up in her old-fashioned way, although her arthritis and her weight must have made it difficult.

"Here's the ECG, Dr. Hopkins. They just finished doing it.

The lab hasn't called yet with the potassium. Janet had to come in to do it." She handed Greg a small roll of gray paper with a rubber band around it. He flipped it off and spread the long strip down the counter.

"How's she doing?"

"She was having some chest pain, and she's, well, agitated. She just had a visitor and maybe that disturbed her."

Greg stared at the tracing. There was no question; the peaked T-wave of excessive potassium showed on every lead. He rolled the tracing up and replaced the elastic.

"She's quite hyperkalemic, and we're going to have to move right along. Does she have an IV?"

"Yes," said Derek. "I just finished putting it in myself." He spoke with just the trace of a lisp. "Five percent dextrose in water, if that's all right?"

"Good. We're going to need some Kayexalate enemas." The little computer terminal beeped and Greg came around to look. A short stream of figures rolled onto the screen.

"Sodium 147, Chloride 102, Potassium 6.8. Wow, that's quite a jump. Let's you and me go and see her." He looked at Mrs. Harris when he spoke, indicating that Derek could stay at the desk.

The two of them went down the quiet corridor toward Room 12, at the far end. "I think it would be a good idea to bring her up nearer the desk," he said. "With her potassium so high, she's at risk for cardiac arrest."

Mrs. Wellbourne wasn't looking well at all; she was lying back against her three pillows and her lips had a bluish tinge. She smiled at Greg when he came in, but it obviously took an effort. He smiled back but didn't say anything; he felt her pulse—it was rapid and thready. He thought for a minute, looking hard at her. "Get me an ampule of fifty percent dextrose and fifty units of aqueous insulin," he said to Mrs. Harris.

She hesitated. "Her blood sugar's not that bad, Dr. Hopkins," she said very softly so the patient wouldn't hear. Her eyes sought his. "You're thinking of Mr. Devereaux in fourteen."

Greg grinned at her. "The insulin's to lower her potassium, Mrs. Harris. It combines with dextrose to take potassium out of the circulation. We use it only when we're in a *real hurry,*

Mrs. Harris." She picked up on that fast and disappeared to get the medications.

"How're you feeling, Gladys?" he asked the woman in the bed.

"I've been better, Dr. Hopkins, I must say," she answered. "I can feel my heart beating like a drum."

"It's because your potassium's high," he told her. "We'll get it down with some medications, and I'm going to order some special enemas for you."

Gladys groaned. "And I thought you were my friend," she said. "I'll get my own back at the Annual Fair. I'll put ptomaine in your sandwiches." Gladys Wellbourne was chairperson of the hospital's board, and an important lady around town.

Mrs. Harris came back with a big glass ampule of dextrose and a vial of insulin, and in a few moments the medications were running into her veins. Greg sat down in the wicker chair facing her and stretched out his legs. Janet, the lab technician, knocked at the door and timidly came in to draw some more blood.

The medications worked fast, and within a few minutes Gladys was feeling better, but because of their potency, Greg decided to stick around for a little while longer.

"How's Nelson?" he asked, to make conversation. Her husband, a banker, had had a hip replacement in New York three months before.

"He's doing all right. They said he'd need the other one done in a year or so, and he's not looking forward to that. By the way, I had a visit from an old friend of yours this evening— maybe you bumped into him on the way out?"

"I didn't see a soul. Tonight the place is quiet as . . . well, it's really quiet."

"Willie Stringer. He said he was in medical school with you. He married Ellen, my niece."

"My God, Willie Stringer! How's he doing?"

"Great, he tells us. Park Avenue practice, very busy. He said to say hello."

Fifteen minutes later Greg left her room and headed down the silent corridors toward the emergency-room entrance. Gladys was out of danger, although she would have to be watched carefully. Willie Stringer, thought Greg, how about that! An unexpected blizzard of mixed memories blew around him as he started down the main stairway. He'd been Willie the Great, or more usually Willie 'n' Liz, because the two of them had been so inseparable. But all that was a long time ago, and Greg had never felt a twinge of jealousy since then. Well, maybe a twinge. Odd that Willie hadn't stopped by to say hello. Greg went through the double doors out to the parking lot. Also odd that he hadn't told the nurses that Gladys was in trouble, because he must have noticed. Maybe he's too busy, had to get back to town. Or maybe he just doesn't like her.

On the way home, Greg decided they should have Willie and Ellen over for dinner sometime. He remembered Ellen well; she'd been Liz's sultry roommate, from an Italian family, very social, lots of money. Although he'd been to the wedding as Willie's best man, he'd never really known what had happened between Willie and Liz. After she'd taken off so suddenly to Edinburgh, Willie had run around like a lunatic trying to find her. Greg felt pretty sure that he'd done something bad to her, and she'd decided she'd had enough. Willie and Ellen were married after about a year. Once, a couple of years later when Liz had come back but before she and Greg were married, he'd brought the subject up, but he'd dropped it as soon as he saw the expression on her face.

Surely now, after all those years, whatever wounds remained were healed? He knew that he and Liz were happy together. And the more he thought about it, the more excited Greg got at the prospect of seeing Willie Stringer. Their friendship had been one of the great things in his early life, and, damn it, there was no reason on God's earth to lose it permanently.

CHAPTER
EIGHT

Greg knew that surgeons usually spend their mornings in the operating room, so he waited until two in the afternoon before calling Willie Stringer's office in New York. He found the number in his well-thumbed directory of medical specialists and got Louella to make the call. Meanwhile he went into the tiny lab to spin down a sample of urine; there was no point wasting time.

"Dr. Greg," Louella called after a couple of minutes, her hand over the mouthpiece. "You're through to New York." She said it importantly, as if a call to the big city were something really special. "Do you want to take it in the office?"

Greg came back on the double, took the phone from her hand, smiling in anticipation, but the smile faded when he found himself talking to Willie's secretary. Louella was watching him.

"She wouldn't put him on until you were on the line," she whispered apologetically. "You know what they're like down there, those big shots."

"Willie!" said Greg, sounding like a schoolboy. "How the hell are you?" He glanced at Louella, and motioned her to switch off the centrifuge. It was one of the old models that didn't have a timer.

"Right! I didn't know Gladys Wellbourne was Ellen's aunt. Isn't that something! Yes, she's doing fine. Listen, I know you're busy, but why don't you and Ellen come over for dinner next week, say Friday, so you won't be operating the next day?"

There was a brief silence while Willie got over his shock. He'd deliberately avoided going to see Greg when he went up

there; too many hurts, too much emotion remained. Liz . . .
God, Liz . . . He could still feel the unrelenting knot that had
formed in his stomach when he found she had gone, the panic
when he couldn't find her . . . calling her parents . . . Her
father had cursed at him and threatened all kinds of reprisals
if Willie didn't leave her alone. He'd called again the next day,
desperate, and a neighbor had answered the phone. After a
pause she'd quietly let him know that Liz had gone abroad to
stay with an aunt and never wanted to hear from him ever
again.

"Great, sure," Willie answered after a pause. "As long as
Ellen doesn't have anything planned. Tell me about yourself.
What's been happening?"

"I wouldn't know where to start, it's been so long. Listen, we
can go over all that when you come up."

Willie remembered the excited phone call after Greg had
met Liz by accident in New York. That had been the last time
he'd heard from Greg: Willie had gone to do his residency in
California about that time, and Ellen had gone with him. He
hadn't tried to get in touch when he came back; it would all
have been too difficult, with Ellen and Liz. Willie had heard
Greg and Liz had gotten married, but he hadn't been invited
to the wedding. He didn't know how much Liz had told Greg,
but he assumed Greg knew the whole story. And now, here he
was asking them to dinner after all this time. He wondered if
Liz knew about the invitation.

"Terrific. I can't wait to see you . . . and Liz." He paused in
case Greg said something to help clarify the situation with Liz,
but he didn't. "I have a board meeting, so it won't be until
around eight, if that's okay?" He paused. "Greg," he asked
cautiously, "are you sure that's going to be all right with Liz?"

"Of course," replied Greg enthusiastically. "She'll be delighted. It's such a pity we all lost touch. I can't wait to see you
both." Greg hung up, smiling; Willie the Great had sounded
the same as ever.

Sitting at his rosewood desk in Manhattan, Willie Stringer
put the receiver down slowly. For God's sake, he thought, Liz
had never told Greg! She hadn't told him anything at all! Well,
it was all a long time ago, and time heals everything. He hoped
that Liz had forgiven him. If not, he thought, Greg will be

calling back soon, trying to think of an excuse to cancel the invitation.

He got up and went to the window, becoming dimly aware of the muted roar of the Park Avenue traffic. Below, the lines of cars stretched and contracted as the lights changed from green to red and back again, but Willie didn't see them. He was in Connecticut on a bright summer's day, riding a borrowed Kawasaki in the leafy, winding roads around Greenwich, with Liz riding pillion, hugging him, her arms around his waist.

The intercom buzzed, and his secretary's voice asked if he was ready to see his next patient.

"Right," he said, pulling himself the fifty miles back to his office. "Let me see the chart first."

"It's the top folder on your desk, Dr. Stringer," said the voice, and he grinned. Vera was so efficient, he'd started making a game of trying to catch her in a mistake.

The top chart was neatly labeled with the patient's name. He turned it sideways to read it: Mrs. William R. Sheely. When they put the husband's name like that, it usually meant somebody important. Inside was the patient's history, written in Vera's neat script. He'd taught her how to take a history a few months ago, and it had been a good move. It relieved him of asking all those routine questions and figuring out all the garbled answers, and it saved a lot of time.

Principal complaint, abdominal pain. Well, that could be just about anything. He glanced at Mrs. Sheely's age: forty-five. Weight: 195 pounds. Height: five-feet-two. Gallbladder for sure, he thought, and skimmed through the rest of the chart, pausing at "Social History." Mrs. William R. Sheely lived on East Forty-fourth Street, and her husband owned a big surgical-supply company. That might be useful sometime.

"She's ready for you in Booth three," said the invisible Vera, and Willie headed for the door. Everything would be ready in Booth 3, down to the latex gloves and hematest strips.

Willie took off his pin-striped jacket and hung it in the closet, taking out one of the freshly laundered white coats. There was a small ink mark at the bottom of the breast pocket; he frowned and dropped it on the floor. The next one passed his inspection and he checked the fit in the mirror on the back of the door. Not bad. He smoothed the lapels and adjusted his tie, a dark blue Hermès silk, his Christmas present from Ellen the previous year. He had sixteen of them at home, one for every Christmas they'd been married; wide ones, narrow ones, stripes, polka dots. . . .

He spent a few more moments close to the mirror, checking his appearance; his mane of graying hair needed cutting, he noticed, but he looked good otherwise. He turned sideways, put his fingers on both cheekbones, and pushed the skin up, bringing the corners of his mouth up and smoothing out the facial lines. He didn't need a lift yet, although a lot of men were having it done these days. Maybe he'd ask Del Armitage, just casually. The last patient of Del's he'd seen wandering around the corridors with those telltale black eyes was a man surely not yet out of his forties.

Mrs. William R. Sheely was lying on the examining table, dressed only in a short white paper gown. She smiled nervously and pushed back her blond curls when he introduced himself, her fat, Caribbean-tanned face creasing under the makeup. When Willie first started in practice, he used to talk to his new patients first in the office before examining them, but he now found it took up too much time. This way was much more efficient, although some of them felt at a disadvantage, dressed only in a paper gown and seeing him for the first time, but that was all right, too, because in their embarrassment they usually talked less.

Vera stood on the other side of the table, slender and elegant, smiling when he came in. She stood there waiting for him, so demure-looking in her tailored white uniform with its high, severe neckline.

"Well, Mrs. Sheely, what seems to be the problem?" He smiled at her, knowing the power of his look. Nowadays he did it automatically, using the smallest effective pulse of directed energy.

"Well, my husband says it must be my gallbladder, but I told him it couldn't be, because—"

"Mrs. Sheely," said Willie quietly, "just tell me what symptoms you've been having." He didn't care for overweight people, especially women. Operating on them was always difficult— you couldn't get good access, and the internal tissues were infiltrated with yellow fat.

"I get this pain," she was saying, "under my ribs here." And she pointed to her right side.

"Any relationship to meals?"

She hesitated. "Well, maybe. I'd have to think about that."

Everything's in relation to *your* meals, he thought, opening her gown and poking at her abdomen. When they were that fat, there wasn't much chance of ever feeling anything except another roll of grease. Anyway, there wasn't much doubt. Fair, fat, and forty, they used to say in medical school, these are the people who get gallbladder disease. By and large, they were right. There wasn't any point wasting any more time with this one. He checked her breasts, noting the sweat rash underneath both of them.

"Well," he said, stepping back from the table, "it certainly looks as if it's your gall—" He happened to glance at Vera, who was making urgent signs at him with her eyes. He hesitated. "Excuse me," he said to Mrs. Sheely. "Vera, would you step outside for a moment?"

When the door closed behind them, he snapped, "What the hell's the matter with you, making faces like that?"

"I'm sorry, but you were just about to tell her that she needed to have her gallbladder taken out, but she had it out eight years ago, in Miami. It's all written down in the history."

Willie opened his mouth in surprise, and at the same moment Mrs. DuBois, one of the secretaries, came through.

"It's the hospital, Dr. Stringer. The resident's on the line. Dr. Wesley, I think he said."

"Okay, I'll take it in a second. Vera, make an appointment for Mrs. Sheely to have an upper GI series; she's probably got an ulcer or something."

He followed Mrs. DuBois into the big waiting room. It had cost him a fortune to have it decorated, but it really looked good now, with its thick ivory carpet, glass-and-steel furniture, and Miró lithographs. A few patients were sitting in the comfortable leather-covered armchairs, and a couple of them looked up and smiled. A large man in a business suit glanced at him from behind his paper. That had to be William R. Sheely.

Mrs. DuBois held the phone out.

"Yes, who's this?" Willie did not like to be interrupted during office hours; that's why he had a house staff, to take care of problems at the hospital.

"Bob Wesley here. Sorry to bother you, Dr. Stringer, but we had an emergency admission, and you're on call."

Bob Wesley was the junior resident on his team. Willie didn't care for him too much; he didn't seem to be able to take the kind of responsibility Willie expected of him.

"Right. What is it?" said Willie, an edge to his voice. Mr. Sheely had lowered his paper and was watching him; the moment Willie put the phone down, he would be on his feet, asking about his wife. Willie turned his back to him.

"It's a black kid, name of Elmo Harris, gunshot wound in the right upper abdomen, about an hour ago. The police got the gun; it's a .22. His pressure was down when he came in, so we gave him a quick liter of fluid by IV and he's stable now, blood pressure 124 over 68, pulse around 100."

Willie looked around his waiting room; it was filling up and he was already behind schedule.

"You say he's stable? Has Walter seen him?"

Bob Wesley put a finger in his other ear to block out the sounds of the emergency room and half turned to look at another stretcher coming in through the double doors.

"Walter's in the OR, Dr. Stringer, doing an aneurysm. Yes, we got a late start." Bob could just hear Mrs. Demajian, the supervisor, calling him from the trauma booth to check the new arrival. "I'm sorry, Dr. Stringer, I couldn't hear you, there's a lot of noise down here."

"You'll have to wait until I've finished office hours," repeated Willie in an irritated voice. "Why don't you admit him, get some X rays, and I'll see him as soon as I come in, should be around"—he looked up at the Garrard wall clock above him—"six, maybe a bit before."

There was a pause at the other end, which Willie took as a silent criticism but was in fact caused by Bob putting his hand over the mouthpiece and shouting back at Mrs. Demajian that he was coming. "And if you keep on calling me here at the office, it'll be later!" Willie was really annoyed now, and he slammed the phone down and hurried back to the examining-room area before Mr. Sheely had time to catch him.

* * *

The only available booth when they brought Elmo into the emergency room was at the end of the corridor, the one farthest from the desk. It used to be part of the pharmacy but had been taken over as part of the ER expansion program. Suddenly, from having five or six people around him asking questions, drawing blood, and examining his belly, there was nobody. Even the two policemen who'd come in the ambulance had gone. Dixie, the girl who'd come in with him, was sitting beside him as if nothing had happened, reading a magazine. The nurse who'd put a dressing over the little hole in his belly was a big-boned girl with a pasty face and blond hair straggling in wisps from under her cap. The name tag pinned to her chest read ASTER HICKS, R.N. Elmo had checked her out, purely out of habit. A lot of his friends went for blondes, but Elmo preferred a girl with shiny dark skin and lips that he could really feel when he kissed them. He turned his head and looked at Dixie, then sat up on one elbow.

"D'you have a cigarette?"

The magazine she was reading was called *Black Beauty*. He'd seen it before, full of crap supposed to raise black girls' consciousness or something, like how a girl should do her hair for a quiet candlelit dinner. Candlelit dinner, for chrissake! In a fifth-floor walk-up on 127th Street? For a slice of Ed's Take-home Pizza? This Dixie . . . he'd picked her up earlier that day and didn't know too much about her, only that somebody had gotten real mad at him for being with her. Elmo had the feeling that this wasn't the first time she'd come into the hospital like this; she was calm and seemed to know what to do. Elmo lay back, suddenly feeling very weak.

Dixie didn't even look up but started to rake around in the grubby old bag she carried. Eventually she found a crumpled pack and opened it.

"I've just got Slims," she said, then gave a muffled, hoarse scream. Elmo had fallen back on the stretcher; there were beads of sweat all over his face, as if he'd been out in the rain. His breathing had changed too. It was deeper and his nostrils were flaring every time he breathed in. He was quite conscious and knew that something bad was happening.

Dixie grabbed the call cord and pushed the button hard. A little red light lit up on the console behind him.

"Come into room . . . I don't know, the room where Elmo Harris is, something's happened." Her voice was a croak. There was no sound from the speaker on the wall. Nobody answered the call, and no footsteps came running down the hall toward them.

"Where the fuck are they?" muttered Elmo through his teeth. He was sweating hard, and the drops were running down the side of his forehead.

"I know how to get them honkies down here," said Dixie. She was a tiny slip of a thing, with skinny legs and a small triangular face. Only her lips and hair and a few dark freckles around her eyes showed that she was black. "You hold tight, honey, 'cause you're gonna hear a noise like you never heard in all your life!" And sure enough, little Dixie went to the doorway and let out a continuous ear-piercing shriek that must have raised the neck hairs on patients two floors away and would have done credit to a banshee being put into a garbage disposal feetfirst. It worked; within moments the big nurse, Aster Hicks, came running down the corridor, closely followed by Bob Wesley.

Bob didn't take long; he could recognize the signs of an internal hemorrhage as well as the next person.

"He's bleeding inside. We'll have to take him up to the operating room," he told Dixie after turning the IV up to maximum. He was following the time-honored practice of talking to relatives rather than the person most affected by such a decision. A thought struck him, and he checked Elmo's arm for needle marks. There were none, but you couldn't ever be sure. "Have either of you had an AIDS test recently?"

"Yeah, me," growled Elmo, "when I sold some blood a couple of weeks ago." The whites of his eyes were showing above the iris.

"Well?" Bob was in a hurry and didn't have time to sit there and chitchat.

"Negative," said Elmo. "Anyway, I don't go in for guys or dope." Dixie nodded vigorously, and Elmo glowered at her. What the fuck did she know?

"Get the OR to send somebody for this guy," Bob told Aster, then he hesitated. By the time the transportation people had gotten themselves organized, Elmo could be in deep trouble.

"No. Let's take him up ourselves," he said. "That way, at least he won't get lost." A week before, a new transportation aide had taken the wrong elevator and left his elderly patient at the back of the laundry storage area.

"We can't do that!" said Aster, opening her eyes with indignation. "We're nurses, not aides. And, anyway, it's against the regulations."

"Oh, for chrissake!" said Bob, going to the door and opening it wide. "Call the OR and tell them we're coming," he snapped. "And get the blood bank to send up six units of whole blood directly to the OR. Or is that the secretary's job?"

She glowered at him and went back to the desk.

With Dixie's help, Bob maneuvered the stretcher along the corridor to the elevators. As they passed the desk he heard the nursing supervisor being called over the paging system and saw Aster staring coldly at him over the desk. Oh, well, he'd been reported before. What was one more time?

But the adrenaline was starting to pump again, like a whip to a tired horse, and a kind of fear gripped him. Who was going to help him with this case? He didn't have much experience, and an internal hemorrhage like this one could be a major surgical challenge. A wave of anger came over him at the thought of Willie Stringer. That bastard! Why didn't he come in when he was needed? It was always the same: he always had something else to do. Once, Walter English, his chief resident, had been doing a difficult thyroid and had called Willie to help him. Willie appeared at the door of the operating room, holding a mask in front of his face. "Everything okay, Walter?" asked Willie. "Don't hesitate to call if you need me, just get Marine Operator 85; I'll be out on the Sound!" Then he'd disappeared, all in the space of a couple of seconds.

And right now Walter was still in the middle of an aneurysm, so he couldn't help. With a kind of scared thrill, Bob realized he would be on his own. Elmo Harris's young life would be in his hands.

There were two nurses already in the elevator, and they helped him get the stretcher in. There was just room for Dixie, who stood silently alongside, looking at Elmo's sweating face and wishing she'd never met the stupid bastard.

CHAPTER
NINE

Willie Stringer switched off his dictating machine and sat back in his leather chair. All afternoon Greg and Liz had been hovering at the back of his mind, but now there would be no more interruptions and he could reflect on that astonishing call from Greg Hopkins. It must be eighteen years . . . he calculated it out on his fingers.

What was Ellen going to say?

The phone rang; it was the OR supervisor. Dr. Wesley had taken that patient to the operating room and would he please come in because it was turning out to be more of a problem than they'd expected.

"If he's having a problem," he said, "you'd better find somebody who's right there to help him. The fastest I could get in would be thirty minutes. Who's up in the suite right now?"

"Walter English," said the supervisor, "but he's tied up with his team doing an aneurysm. Wait a minute, Dr. Frankel's light just went on. Do you want to talk to him?"

"What am I going to say to him? Tell him to go help Bob Wesley, if he can spare the time off from his committees!"

He hung up, well aware of the hostility at the other end. It was really a pain in the ass to be on call so much for the residents. The good ones rarely called him because they had learned not to get into problems they couldn't get themselves out of. That Bob Wesley, he wasn't at all sure about him. When Willie had been doing his training in San Francisco, he could count on the fingers of one hand the number of times he'd had to ask for help, maybe even a hand with a couple of digital amputations.

That had been quite a time in San Francisco; the two first years were the rockiest in their marriage. Then things had improved, not for any particular reason, except maybe that Ellen had gotten used to being far from home and was making the best of San Francisco. After watching a few Jacques Cousteau movies, she became fascinated by the underwater scenes, and they both learned to scuba dive.

Willie picked the printout of his monthly accounts off his desk and put it in his briefcase to take home. His thoughts went back to Catalina Island. God, that had been so marvelous, like another world, down among the reefs and wrecks, a world of silence, where the predator was king. They had decided to do some magazine stories; Ellen did the research and the writing, and he learned to take underwater photos. They'd even had one accepted by *Outdoor Life* and been paid for it. The arrival of the check was celebrated by a seafood dinner at Anthony's, a new place near Fisherman's Wharf, and that shared success had somehow cemented their marriage.

Willie went down in the elevator to the underground garage, still in the grip of his memories. It had been four years' hard labor at San Francisco General, and then the struggle to get back to New York. Luckily he'd done some research work and published a few papers, so he'd been able to get back into his old teaching hospital, although he was pretty sure that Janus Frankel, who by now had become quite a big wheel at the hospital, had tried to block his appointment.

The traffic wasn't bad, and when he got home to his apartment, the doorman told him Ellen had just come in. A sudden burst of worry hit him as he thought about her. Ellen was just coming out of their bedroom when he came in, and she smiled when she saw him.

"How did it go?" he asked.

"Okay, I guess." She came over and gave him a kiss on the cheek. He noticed again how much weight she'd lost; he could feel the bones of her hips through her dress.

Willie put his briefcase down on the hall table. When they moved in here, Ellen's father had had the whole place decorated for them. It was all very beautiful, expensive and in the best of taste, but even after three years Willie still felt that he was living in some kind of luxurious hotel.

"What did he say?"

"He wants some more tests. He said the ultrasound was technically unsatisfactory and I need to have a CAT scan. What *is* that?"

Willie felt his face tighten with concern. Although he couldn't admit it, even to himself, he knew that Ellen had something seriously the matter with her. Why was Carrera taking so long to find out what it was?

"It's a special kind of X ray," he said, trying to make it sound like nothing. "It's like seeing slices of your body."

Ellen shivered. "Does it hurt?"

"Of course not. It's just like any other X ray, except you lie down and they slide you into a kind of tube."

"He said he was going to call you."

"At home?" Willie was startled. It must be worse than he'd thought.

"No, of course not. At the office, tomorrow." She put her hands on his shoulders and looked at him, a small frown on her face. Her eyes were still beautiful, and seemed bigger now. "Why can't *you* take care of me, Willie? You're better and more clever than any of them."

"You know I can't, sweetheart." Willie suddenly felt tired, angry, and impotent all at once. "For one thing, I'm not a gynecologist, and anyway, it's unethical to treat members of one's own family."

"Could we eat out tonight? I just don't feel up to cooking anything."

"Sure. No, on second thought, I have a better idea. Why don't we get that woman, the one who did the catering for the Hardings' party? She does individual gourmet dinners and she'll deliver it." Willie was excited at the thought of doing something nice for Ellen, and he reached for the phone.

At that very moment it rang, and Willie picked it up.

"Hi, Phil," he said so that Ellen would know that it was Carrera. A knot formed suddenly in his stomach. Ellen had said he would call tomorrow.

"Yes, I suppose she has been. . . . Right, that certainly sounds like a good idea. Sure. . . . Yes, I'll do that. . . . Listen, Phil, I appreciate you taking the time. . . . Yes, you're right, I'd do the same for you."

Willie put the phone down slowly, not sure whether to feel happy or not.

"He says he thinks you're depressed," he said to Ellen. "He says we should take some time off, go to the Caribbean or somewhere. Sounds like a good idea to me."

Ellen's eyes lit up, and Willie suddenly felt happier. Maybe that's all it was, after all.

"I have an even better idea," he said. "Why don't we take the Concorde to London, do some shopping at Harrods, take in a few shows, *Phantom of the Opera,* a ballet, take the boat up the Thames to Kew Gardens. . . . What do you say?" He held his arms out and pulled her close to him. "And I have another surprise for you," he said, gently nuzzling into the side of her neck. "Guess who called today?"

Liz Hopkins usually woke about half an hour before Greg, and she treasured that time beside him, lying so snug and warm with the comforting sound of his breathing next to her. In some ways this was the best and most important time of her day, before the demands started to pour in on her like lead confetti.

Thirty minutes . . . that was how long she had to gather herself, reestablish contact with the rest of the world, realize that the sun was shining, that birds still sang. In addition, this was the time she planned out the rest of her day. There was never any time later; once out of bed, it was straight into the tunnel.

Decisions. Problems. Who has first rights to the bathroom (whoever gets there first), where are the shirts (usually in the shirt drawer), whose turn is it today to lose one sneaker (never both), and all the sorting and settling of end-of-the-world problems with clothes, unfinished homework, cereals (Mom, he's finished the *last* Cocoa Puff and he *knows* I don't like Rice Krispies), the school bus arriving and nobody's ready, going out in her robe to apologize to the driver, returning late library books, and laundry, shopping, paying bills, making dinner . . . Sometimes she emerged from the tunnel for a quick breath of air before the boys came home from school but usually not. She loved it, all of it.

Most of the time.

Sometimes, not very often, she felt she was coming close to the breaking point, but always something had happened to take the strain off her, a few days' vacation or an improvement in their financial situation. Liz wondered what it would be like, how she would react if things got to a point where she couldn't stand it anymore. Would she go like Mrs. Arthur, her sixth-grade teacher, who had suddenly started to scream in class for no obvious reason and hadn't stopped even when they were taking her away in an ambulance? Or like their ex-neighbor, poor Gwen Durocher, the Canadian opera singer, who'd been investigated during the McCarthy Era and was never able to get another engagement? Gwen had come to a town meeting, and just when they were about to start, she'd come up to the podium and sung three magnificent arias from *La Bohème*, then gone back home to her house and never emerged until she was carried out in a box ten years later.

Liz's own music helped her a lot in times of stress. She didn't play enough to keep up to her old level, but when she did, it was with all her old passion and commitment. When they heard her playing, usually upstairs in her sewing room, the children knew better than to interrupt. Liz had been married to Greg for two years before she forced herself to open the cello case, which still bore the fine surgical scars of Willie's repairwork. Time had passed, and now she was able to play without the bitter reminders of earlier days, the days of her innocence, the days of her youth.

In her life Liz had had two huge jolts, which had left a small, hidden part of her perpetually trembling. The first was when her mother told her the truth about her father, when she was sixteen. Liz had always thought he was a businessman who traveled a lot and seemed to have been away for most of her childhood. In fact, her present position as a doctor's wife sometimes made her smile: her father had been a "doctor" for a while in Minnesota, then in Oregon when it got too hot in Minneapolis. Other times he had been a banker, a salesman, a cardsharp . . . Liz could still make her children's eyes pop with the card tricks he had taught her between unavoidable absences at Uncle Sam's expense. Of course he'd "retired" several years ago and now led a life of blameless crustiness in Bridgeport, in the house financed by one of his earlier and more successful scams.

The second jolt, of course, had been Willie Stringer.

Today was Saturday, she remembered suddenly. No school. Elspeth appeared at the bedroom door in her little white nightie, rubbing her eyes. Without a word she climbed into the bed next to her father, who grunted and moved over a little to make room. He lay there for a few minutes with his arm across her before sitting up suddenly.

"How come they didn't call about Mrs. Wellbourne?" He looked at Liz.

She shrugged her shoulders and sighed. "It means she must be all right, don't you think?" The new day had begun.

Greg tried to clamber out of bed over Elspeth, who went stiff as a poker and pretended to be asleep, although she couldn't help letting out a tiny giggle. He picked her up in his arms, climbed carefully out of bed, and put her back beside Liz, but Elspeth had her arms around his neck and wouldn't let go. Greg started to tickle her ribs; she squealed and wriggled but hung on. "I'm never going to let you go, Daddy!" she said.

"That's enough, Elspeth," said Liz sternly. Greg was so soft with them . . . but he'd get them all excited about something or other, then he'd go off and she'd be left with a wild, unruly mob of children on her hands.

Liberated, Greg sat on the edge of the bed, picked up the bedside phone, and pressed the button that automatically dialed the hospital. The conversation was brief.

"She seems to be okay," he told Liz, putting the phone down. "They did her potassium at six and it was normal." Like many doctors' wives, Liz had developed a kind of intuitive knowledge of medicine over the years from listening to Greg. She was now used to being stopped in the street by his patients to be told about their various ailments in the most intimate detail. At first, when Greg had just opened his office, she'd gotten alarmed and embarrassed and told them to make an appointment to see the doctor, but now she listened and didn't hesitate to tell them quite authoritatively what to do about their children's colds (aspirin, plenty of fluids) or their arthritis (same treatment). After all, she took care of any medical problems with the children: Douglas's German measles, Elspeth's strep

throat, and whatever it had been that made Edward so tired
for a week last year. Liz used to joke that she had an honorary
medical degree from Bucharest, like her father.

"Go see if Edward wants to come with us to do rounds," said
Greg, picking Elspeth up gently and standing her on the floor
beside him. Taking the children with him to see his patients at
the hospital had been a Saturday routine for years; the patients,
particularly the older ones, enjoyed it, and it was a good
occasional reminder to the children that lots of people were
less fortunate than they were.

There was no point inviting Douglas; when he was younger,
it had bored him, and now he slept until noon and growled
unpleasantly if anybody disturbed him. They had given up
waking him because he would just wander around the house
in an angry daze, looking for a quiet corner to lie down and
go back to sleep.

Elspeth went off to rouse Edward, and they could hear her
poking and prodding him into consciousness.

She came back with an air of long-suffering tolerance. "He
said yes, but he wants to sleep for five more minutes. That's
all those boys ever want to do, is sleep."

Liz climbed out of bed, caught sight of her disheveled hair
in the mirror, and shuddered. Greg, watching her, thought
how little change the years had made; she was as slim as a
bride, with a firm, elegant figure virtually unchanged by bearing
four children. If Elspeth hadn't been there, he'd have pulled
Liz back into bed with him.

In the bathroom, face up to the mirror, Liz saw a different
picture. There was no mistaking the little crow's-feet around
her eyes, the slight loss of texture to the skin around her cheeks
and mouth. She stood back; the overall picture certainly
improved with distance. And with her hair brushed and her
face on, she was as attractive as anybody she was likely to meet
on the street.

Edward appeared in the bathroom door, his pajamas sagging.
God, that kid was getting tall—no wonder he could run so fast,
with those long legs.

"Go on, Edward!" she said. "If you're going to the hospital
with your father, you'd better get yourself dressed and brush
your teeth."

How many times had she said that in the last ten years?—get dressed, brush your teeth. Why was it that one reminder was never enough?

"I don't have any socks, Mom."

"Have you looked in the drawer?" Silence. Edward, like Douglas, seemed to be able to stay half asleep almost indefinitely. His eyes strayed to the window. A jay had just landed on the wheelbarrow that had been left out on the lawn, and its tail was flicking extravagantly up and down. Its mate landed in a flash of blue on the fence a moment later, but the two didn't seem to pay any attention to each other, as if their presence in the same garden were simply accidental. For different reasons, both Liz and Edward enjoyed watching them.

"Did you see their wings? What a color!" said Edward, gazing at the birds, his eyes shining. He was quite awake now; he had a quiet, almost hesitant way of speaking that made people listen, even when he wasn't saying anything very important.

"Look at the way they love each other," Liz said without thinking. She envied their mutual freedom.

"How can you tell?" asked Edward curiously. The jay on the wheelbarrow flew to a branch on one of the Japanese cherry trees. The other was on the wing instantly, and landed on the adjacent cherry tree, its tail going up and down like a pump handle. It seemed to know in advance where the first one was going.

"There are plenty of socks in your drawer," Liz said briskly. "Get going."

There were always arguments about who would sit in the front seat, so when he had two or more children in the car, Greg made them all sit in the back. Now Edward and Elspeth were trying to get in the back simultaneously. Edward was stronger and got in first.

"That's enough of the rough stuff, you two," said Greg, almost mechanically. The number of times he must have said that! The branch scraped over the roof as he backed out into the street.

"Edward, I wish you wouldn't push your sister like that. Remember, she's smaller than you."

I'll cut that branch as soon as we get home, he thought. *I hope it didn't scratch the paint.*

He parked outside the emergency room and they went in, one on each side of him. Elspeth clutched his hand firmly, and a moment later, a little to Greg's surprise, Edward grabbed his other hand. Elspeth skipped. Edward said, "If you knew how *silly* you look, skipping like that."

Elspeth stuck her tongue out at him when she thought her father wasn't looking.

"Come on, Mouse, behave," Greg told her, giving her hand a shake. He was thinking about the four patients he had in the hospital: Mrs. Albright with her kidney infection; John Worblett, the unstable diabetic; Dave Gilligan, the retarded boy with epilepsy; and of course Mrs. Wellbourne.

"Why do you call her Mouse?" asked Edward in his quiet voice. He was sometimes less thoughtful, more of a child than he sounded. "Because I would call her *rat!*" And he swung around Greg to aim a swipe at her.

"Would you like to spend the morning waiting for us in the car?" asked Greg threateningly. He couldn't appear too stern, because old Dr. Anderson was coming down the hall, smiling at them.

Beth Goodfriend was on duty that morning, a quick, friendly, capable girl with straggly blond hair under her cap and a big, efficient-looking bosom under her blue-and-white uniform. The children loved her.

"Hi, Edward, hi, Elspeth! Taking your daddy on rounds with you this morning?" This joke always got a smile from both of them. In fact, they'd have felt vaguely anxious if Beth had greeted them any other way. Beth pulled four charts out of the rack. "Where would you like to start, children? How about with Dave Gilligan?" They both nodded, smiling, and Beth looked at Greg for confirmation. He might not want them to see an epileptic child. Elspeth took hold of Greg's hand again.

Dave's room was close to the nurses' station because he sometimes howled during the night and the nurse had to be able to get to him quickly. Dave was twelve, the same as Edward, but had a mental age of about three. His epileptic fits had started a year after he was born but were partially controlled with medication. Recently they'd been getting more frequent and more severe. They went into his room, Beth first, followed by Greg, with Elspeth hanging on tight to him. Edward came last, his eyes seeking out the boy in the bed. He was lying back, staring at the ceiling and grinning, but not the kind of grin Edward would get from his friend Timmy—it didn't last as long, he decided, and his mouth was doing something else. That's where the difference was. When Timmy grinned at him, even if it was just for a second, it was the shape of his mouth that gave an instant clue about what he was up to.

Dave's mother was sitting on the bed. She'd just finished feeding him and was screwing the top back on a little jar. She was older-looking than Edward's own mother, with a thicker body. Her legs were wide, and her stockings wrinkled below her knee down to the shoes. Edward noticed the whitish cracks on the side of the dark shoes, near where the tops met the sole. She must have been out in really heavy rain with them. The lady had a kind, worried sort of expression, and she stood up when they all came in. It was nice, the way people looked at his father, as if they knew he could help them, whatever the matter was.

"Hi, Mrs. Gilligan. How's Dave this morning?" Dave's eyes were rolling around the room, but he wasn't watching anything. Suddenly his hand swung up and he hit his mother hard in the chest. Edward could see that it hurt her, but she only took his hand and put it gently away from her. She moved down the bed a little, to be out of his range. Edward imagined what his own mother's response would have been if he'd hit her like that. She would have smacked him one, hard enough to make his teeth rattle. Not that he'd ever hit her. He'd kill anybody who did that. But this lady looked at her son without anger.

"He hasn't had a fit since six this morning, Dr. Hopkins, and he's just had his breakfast." Dave started to swing his arm up and down, up and down, as if he were conducting a band. She looked at him and smiled. *I bet she doesn't have time to think about anything except him,* thought Edward. *I wonder if he has any brothers and sisters.*

Suddenly Dave stopped swinging his arm, and his face twisted. At first Edward thought it was just another strange expression, but then he started to howl, a frightening sound that made Edward's hair stand on end. Elspeth edged behind her father. Before anybody else could move, Greg quickly picked up what looked like a stick wrapped up in a bandage off the bedside table and stuck it between Dave's teeth. The howling stopped abruptly, and the boy's whole body went rigid, his back arching up in the bed. Fascinated and horrified, Edward watched as Dave's lips became puffy and blue. He seemed to have stopped breathing. Greg held the stick in position, and for one dreadful second Edward thought it was choking him. Beth grabbed Dave's knees when his whole body started to shake. The shaking seemed to last forever, then he drew a breath with a rattling, hissing noise. The shaking got less and finally stopped. Greg took the stick out of Dave's mouth, and then there was an awful smell. He'd dirtied the bed. Beth took a facecloth from the sink, and while his mother turned him on one side, she cleaned up the mess. Within a couple of minutes they'd rolled up the dirty sheet, put on a fresh one, and changed his pajama bottoms.

Mrs. Gilligan looked at Greg apologetically. "I'm sorry he did that in front of your children, Doctor."

Greg took a deep breath. "He's getting sixty milligrams of phenobarb in the evening, isn't he?"

"Yes, and it seems to be working." She was watching Dave, who seemed to be asleep now, breathing steadily with a little snort out of the side of his mouth from time to time. With her finger she gently pushed his tongue back into his mouth.

"When he was just on forty milligrams, he was having them every couple of hours, and he bit his tongue two days ago, nothing very bad, but it gave me a scare." She looked uncertainly at him, as if he might blame her. Greg hesitated; there was nothing more he could do beyond monitoring the effects of the medication. The child had been thoroughly worked over, with a brain scan and all the other tests. That was the tough part, when he couldn't help anymore, because the tragedy went on. Dave had destroyed the Gilligan family; he was the youngest of three sons, and the person his mother cared most for in the world. His father simply hadn't been able to cope with the problems associated with a retarded epileptic son and had left for parts unknown, calling home from time to time and occasionally sending money.

"Would you feel comfortable taking him home later today?" asked Greg. "His seizures are less bad now, don't you think?"

"Yes, thank you, Doctor," she said, smiling with relief. "I'd like to take him home. My sister's taking care of the others, but she has to go to work too."

"Bring him to the office on Wednesday," said Greg. "We'll

check the phenobarbital level in his blood then. Call me if you have any problems. You have my phone number?"

"Yes, I do, Doctor. But I won't call unless I have to."

Elspeth hadn't taken her eyes off Dave. He seemed all right now, but why had he done that? And why had her daddy put a stick in his mouth? Storing the questions for later, she followed the others out. The lady gave her a real nice smile as she was leaving the room, but she looked so sad.

By the time they had seen Mrs. Albright, Mr. Worblett, and Mrs. Wellbourne, it was almost eleven o'clock.

"Who would like to go to McDonald's for lunch?" Greg asked them as they all walked toward the car.

"Even Douglas'll get up for that," replied Elspeth, but she was still thinking about Dave and how awful he looked with that stick in his mouth.

When they got home, the children stayed outside; the yard was warm and the promise of spring was in the air. All the children knew was that winter was finally over, and they liked it. Liz was hanging up a large saw on a rack in the butler's pantry.

"Oh, there was a branch hanging down over the driveway, no big deal," she said in answer to his unspoken question. "Everything all right at the hospital? Did the children behave?"

"Sure. We'll tell you all about it at lunch. We thought we'd go to McDonald's, if that's okay with you."

"Fine. Douglas should be getting up now, I've already called him four times."

Greg was about to go upstairs when a thought struck him.

"Does Edward hold your hand when you're crossing the road?" he asked.

"He used to, but not anymore. Nowadays he tells *me* when it's safe to cross." Liz smiled. "Why?"

"Nothing. It's just that he held my hand crossing over to the emergency room, that's all."

Liz thought for a moment. "I'm not surprised. He doesn't see enough of you; it's his way of maintaining contact." She looked seriously at him. "Spend a little more time with him, Greg. At this age he needs to have a father around, when he's about to become a man. It must be a frightening time for a boy."

Greg nodded and went upstairs. She was right. The telephone rang, and Liz knew that once again she'd be taking the children to McDonald's without him.

CHAPTER
TEN

When Bob Wesley pushed Elmo Harris's stretcher out of the elevator, he was feeling panicky and out of his depth. Although the IVs were running well, Elmo was looking gray under his black skin, his blood pressure was low, he had a rapid pulse, and he was still sweating profusely. Bob knew that these were the hallmarks of hemorrhagic shock, meaning that he'd lost around two pints of blood or more from his circulation. As there was virtually no blood coming out of the bullet hole, it was clear that the bleeding was internal. Bob checked his pulse a couple of times on the way up; it was running fast but not out of control. Dixie, Elmo's girlfriend, helped him maneuver the stretcher through the double doors into the operating room. Her face had remained completely expressionless throughout; stress, thought Bob. She probably thinks her boyfriend's going to die.

At the desk, Bob explained the situation to Toni Berklund, the operating room supervisor. She checked the utilization board.

"You can use Room eight," she said. "They just canceled a craniotomy. Who's going to help you?"

"Whoever's around," replied Bob. "Can you get a tech to take over from this young lady here?"

"Sure. Maybe she'd like a job here; we're always short-staffed." Toni smiled at her, but Dixie just stared back, thinking, *Don't patronize me, you white slut, just get this guy off my hands!* Toni was already on the intercom, summoning a tech from the break room.

"Has he been premedicated?" asked Toni.

"No, we didn't have time."

"Good," she said, producing a printed form. "That means he can sign the release." She turned to Elmo. "Sign this, please. It says that your doctor has fully explained the proposed surgery and has gone over the risks involved."

"Yeah." Elmo grunted. "Whatever." He took the pen Toni held out to him and laboriously signed his name at the bottom. He had no idea what he was signing; he just wanted to get whatever they were going to do over and done with.

"Thanks for your help," Bob said to Dixie. "This is going to take a while, so why don't you go get yourself a cup of coffee."

Without a backward look at Elmo, Dixie took off. She'd done what she had to do, and if Elmo ever saw her again, it wouldn't be in the hospital. He was now on his own, and anyway, the whole place gave her the creeps.

"I can get you a medical student," said Toni. "Who's your attending?"

"Dr. Stringer," said Bob, taking his white coat off and turning toward the changing room. "He's at his office. Tell him we couldn't wait and that the guy's hemorrhaging internally. He knows about him. I called ten, fifteen minutes ago."

"Isn't he on his way?"

"I doubt it. He has an office full of patients, he said."

Toni looked at him and nodded. She knew what the score was with Willie Stringer. "Marianne Glover is free," she said. "She's the best tech we have. I'll send her in."

Bob smiled gratefully and went in to change into his scrubs while the anesthesia resident came up and helped wheel Elmo off to the operating room.

Bob's hands were clammy. Where was the guy bleeding from? What sort of incision should he use? Was six units going to be enough blood? Should he tell the staff to wear double gloves to protect themselves from AIDS? He knew Elmo had said he tested out negative, but people lied all the time.

A young man in greens came through the door, hesitated, and came over to Bob.

"Hi, I'm Andy Fisher," he said, coming over. "Toni told me I'm going to be helping you."

"Good." A medical student was better than nothing. "Let me tell you about the patient." Bob described what had happened to Elmo; talking about it helped him to sort out his own thoughts on the matter.

"What do you think's going on?" asked Andy.

"Well, he's bleeding, we know that. The bullet hole's over on the right, and the X ray shows the slug up against the lower ribs. Do you remember where the spleen lies?"

"On the right, inside the ninth, tenth, and eleventh ribs," replied Andy promptly. *At least he knows his anatomy,* thought Bob. *Maybe he'll be of some use to me, after all.*

Bob changed while they talked, and put his wallet and his watch in the pocket of his greens. Nobody ever left valuables in the changing room, not even in the padlocked lockers. He put a pair of paper booties over his shoes, and a paper helmet that covered the head and ears and tied behind his neck. Together they stepped into the main corridor of the suite.

"Room eight," said Bob. "I hope they've got him asleep by now."

Elmo was indeed asleep, strapped to the table in the usual cruciform position. The anesthesiology resident had already intubated him. Bob looked at the black rubber diaphragm on the anesthesia machine, going up and down inside its transparent plastic jar. Elmo's chest moved up and down in time with it.

"Ready when you are," said the resident cheerfully. Bob had worked with her before; her name was Anne something, he couldn't remember her last name, but he did remember she was good.

Bob and Andy went to the scrub sinks while the circulating nurse pulled the top sheet off Elmo.

"You want him shaved?" she called out.

Bob nodded.

"Where's your incision going to be?" she called again.

Bob hesitated. "Midline, I guess." He couldn't go far wrong with a midline incision. If there wasn't enough room, he could always extend it.

Toni came up behind him.

"I called Dr. Stringer's office, but he was with a patient, so I left a message with his nurse."

"Toni," said Bob, beginning to feel shaky, "is there anybody around who can assist? This is going to be a big case, and . . ."

"As far as I know, everybody's working," she said. "Let me check. Maybe one of the attendings can come out."

Bob's heart sank. He'd helped with cases like this in the past but didn't feel competent to handle one on his own. On the other hand, if he waited, Elmo would bleed to death.

Bob looked up at the clock. They'd been scrubbing for the statutory length of time. He took a deep breath and marched into the operating room with his hands up in front of him. Marianne, a sturdy, middle-aged OR tech, gave him a sterile towel to dry his hands and smiled encouragingly. The inflexible operating room routine calmed him like an oft-repeated prayer; Marianne held out a gown, and he slipped into it, then put his hands into the latex gloves, pulling the cuffs over the long sleeves. Andy did the same after him. Elmo's black body was gleaming with the brown antiseptic betadine solution, and Bob quickly put the drapes on, leaving a central space to operate in. So far, so good.

An aide came in with four bags of blood.

"Run a couple in real fast, Anne," said Bob. "He's lost at least two units already."

Andy positioned himself on the other side of the table and anchored the suction tubing and the wires for the electric coagulator. The scrub tech adjusted the light. She knew the surgeon usually did that, but she correctly reckoned that right now poor Bob Wesley needed all the help he could get.

"Okay to start?" Bob looked over at Anne. He hoped he didn't sound as scared as he felt.

"Okay," said Anne. "His pressure's down a bit, so I'm keeping him light. If he moves, I can paralyze him, but I'd rather not."

The scrub tech was looking at Bob, holding the knife out, the handle toward him.

"Here we go!" said Bob, and made a cut from the notch below the breastbone to just above Elmo's belly button. The incision wasn't too straight, and it wasn't very deep. How deep should he go? Bob felt his hand start to shake, but with an effort of will he controlled it. It really was different doing it himself. Andy mopped up the blood with a big gauze sponge, and Bob used the coagulator to seal up the little blood vessels. Cautiously he took the knife and cut down to the next layer. Luckily Elmo was thin, and the white, fibrous layer in the midline between the abdominal muscles showed up clearly. Bob felt the sweat running down the side of his forehead as he started to cut down through the fibrous layer.

Then he was through into the abdominal cavity, and the dark blood started to well out from inside. There was no indication of where it might be coming from. Bob felt weak and for a moment thought that he was going to faint.

"Why don't you open the belly up completely so you can see what's going on?" suggested Marianne calmly. She'd been around for years, and what she hadn't seen didn't matter.

Bob did so, and the trickle became a flood. "Get the suction!" he said. "And some big sponges!"

Marianne glanced sharply at him. He sounded as if he might decompensate at any moment. It wasn't his fault; the poor guy just didn't know what to do.

At that moment a head poked into the room.

"Bob? Need any help?" It was Dr. Janus Frankel, the department chairman.

"Yes, sir, I sure could use some!" Bob had never felt so relieved to see anyone in his life.

"I'll be right in," said Frankel. "Don't do anything, just keep the transfusions going." His scrub was the briefest on record, and he appeared beside Bob within a minute.

"Why don't you go over to the other side," he murmured. "Marianne, give me a pair of heavy scissors." He opened the entire incision and put his hand in halfway up to his elbow, feeling around inside Elmo's abdomen.

"Got it!" he said. "Here, suction all this stuff out. There's about three units in here, Anne," he said, "I hope you're keeping up with his losses."

"Third unit going in now, Dr. Frankel," said Anne. She had a pump going, and the blood was pouring into Elmo's veins. "His pressure's down to 80," she announced.

Dr. Frankel grasped the spleen in his right hand and brought it out through the incision, accompanied by great black clots. The bullet had not only made a hole but split the organ. He let the pressure off for a second, for demonstration purposes to Bob and the medical student, and the blood gushed out through the hole. Bob suctioned away all the blood. Dr. Frankel made it all look so easy.

Within a few minutes the arteries and veins leading to the spleen were clamped and cut, and the spleen itself had been removed. "Sometimes we try to save it," Frankel explained, but this one was too badly damaged. Then the search was on to see if any further damage had been done. Miraculously the bullet had missed the intestine and other vital structures in the area and flattened itself against the inside of a rib. Frankel brought the bullet out and dropped it with a clang into a metal kidney dish. "You'd better keep it," he told Marianne. "The police'll probably want it."

Later, after Elmo had been taken to the intensive care unit and everything was under control, Dr. Frankel asked Bob why he hadn't called his attending to come and help him. "That was rather foolhardy, taking on a case like that on your own, don't you think?"

Bob explained that Dr. Stringer hadn't had time to get to the hospital, but Dr. Frankel wouldn't drop the subject, asking for details of the time Bob had first called him, and exactly what had been said. Bob tried to protect Willie but to no avail.

"Thanks, Bob," said Dr. Frankel finally. "It's just lucky I happened to be around. Let this be a lesson to you: Don't ever get into a surgical situation you can't get yourself out of, okay? And I'll be talking the matter over with Dr. Stringer."

CHAPTER
ELEVEN

"Was that a good idea, do you think, to let the children see Dave Gilligan when he was having his epileptic attack?" Liz had her back to him, stretching up to put the dishes away in the closet. The espresso machine started its earsplitting whistle, then switched itself off.

"Coffee?" he asked her.

"Yes, please." Liz stood on a stool to put the cups in their appointed place. "It's odd, black coffee after dinner used to keep me awake, but not anymore."

Greg worked the little chrome-plated handles, filled two small cups, and put hers on the counter. He took a sip. Medaglia d'Oro: that was good coffee. "There wasn't much I could do at the time, but to answer your question, yes, I think it was a good idea."

"I think Edward was more upset than Elspeth. He hardly ate any dinner."

"I don't know that that was because of Dave Gilligan. The thing is . . ." Greg put his coffee cup down. Liz knew from his voice that he was about to make one of his pronouncements. "The thing is, our kids, and all the kids like them, growing up in comfort—even luxury, a lot of people would say—they only get a sanitized view of what life really is about. That's why I let them stay when Dave had his attack. They need to know that a lot of people around them are sick or poor, or both, that most people have tougher times than they ever will."

"Well, I just hope Elspeth doesn't get nightmares about it. You remember when Frosty got run over outside . . . ?"

"That was different. What she saw in the hospital was just

something that can happen to people. She shouldn't grow up thinking that such things don't exist," said Greg. "Do you have any of those after-dinner mints?" Liz shook her head and stared at him for a moment. She turned to the closet and brought down a small box with paper-wrapped chocolate mint squares. Greg pulled one out.

"It's simply because she saw something that most kids never see," he said. "If we didn't lock away our weak-minded citizens and put our old people away in homes, our kids would grow up realizing that these folks are all part of the spectrum of a community. In Europe, the village idiots aren't locked away in an asylum; they can do little errands, stuff like that."

"Greg, you're starting to preach," she said. "I'm sorry I asked."

The telephone rang. Greg picked it up and listened for a few moments.

"Okay," he said in a resigned tone, "I'll be right in. The emergency room," he said. "Some guy got stabbed in the leg. The police are bringing him in from across town, say they'll be there in ten minutes. There's a lot of blood, and they need a doctor there when they arrive. No idea who did it, of course. Which usually means there'll be another one later."

"But you're not on call, Greg," she protested. "Why do *you* have to go? You were going to help Edward with his French; he has a test on Monday."

"Roger Anderson's on call, but his wife says he's feeling unwell. At his age I suppose he's lucky to be feeling anything. So they called me. I won't be too long, and I'll help Edward when I get back. *Bon soir!*"

"*Bon soir,* yourself. Honey, they *always* call you when they're stuck. Why don't you tell them—"

Greg was already on his way out.

Liz slammed down her cup so hard, the dregs flew out and the handle broke off.

Darn, thought Greg as he climbed into his car, he'd forgotten to tell Liz the big news of the day: his call to Willie Stringer. He remembered the last time he'd spoken to Willie, the same day he'd seen Liz, sitting on a stool in the Chock-Full-o'-Nuts. He'd recognized her even though her back was turned, from the way she moved her shoulders. Liz had been shocked to see him, and for a second Greg had thought she wished it was Willie. But then she was so happy, she even cried a bit. A lot had happened, she told him. She'd gotten fed up with Willie, the whole scene, and on the spur of the moment she'd decided to visit her aunt in Edinburgh. She'd lived in a big, drafty old Georgian house with high ceilings and no central heating and had started music courses at the university. Soon afterward she'd met this guy, a commercial pilot who did charter work out of Abbotsinch, fallen in love with him, had a lightning-quick romance, and married him.

"On the rebound?" Greg asked her gently.

"No, it was the real thing," replied Liz, looking into his eyes. "Truly, the real thing."

It had lasted a year, she told him. Then one day Jack was supposed to pick up some passengers at Scone airport near Perth. It was foggy, and she told him to stay home, but he knew best. The search party found the plane the next day, burned out, in the trees at the top of a hill near the airport. A few more feet of altitude and he'd have made it. Greg almost wept for her, it was so sad. If it hadn't been for their daughter, Patsy, she said, she'd have gone mad.

Greg got to the hospital about one minute ahead of the ambulance. He could hear the approaching siren as he walked from the parking area to the emergency room entrance.

"They said over the radio that it's Big Vern," said Beth, who was doing a double shift and covering the emergency room.

"Oh, yeah?" said Greg with interest. "So somebody finally got to him, huh?"

Big Vern was the ranking pimp in town, a flamboyant black of about thirty who liked to wear broad-brimmed hats with big feathers, expensive silk shirts, and very tight pants. Very tight. He wasn't called Big Vern for his height. Everybody knew him in the emergency room, and he was pretty well hated. His girls would come in with bizarre injuries, and he always came with them, grinning and debonair, then strutted around the waiting room, shouting at everybody to hurry up, " 'Cause that girl's got to get back to work. Time's a-wasting and time is money!"

So everybody was awaiting his arrival with more than ordinary interest.

"Pity they didn't kill the bugger," said Emil, the French-Canadian orderly. Emil's father and grandfather had been lumberjacks in the forests of northern Quebec, and Emil was built like a lumberjack himself. He was a good man to have in the emergency room; most boisterous drunks took one look at him and instantly became more docile.

The siren got suddenly louder, then died as the ambulance swung around the corner, and the beam from its red roof-light flicked through the windows and around the walls of the trauma room. Then came the familiar high-pitched beep-beep-beep as it reversed to the ramp, and a moment later they heard the voices of the police officers and the ambulance men getting out of the vehicle.

Emil was already at the door when they opened the back of the ambulance. Big Vern was cursing and shouting at the top of his voice. One of the policemen climbed in. There was a barely audible thud, and Vern suddenly became quieter. Out came the stretcher, with Vern's broad-brimmed hat on his chest. There was a four-inch slash across the left thigh of his jeans, and blood was all over the front of his pants, almost black, and had soaked into the blue of the material.

Greg looked up as they wheeled the stretcher past the desk and quickly eyed the damage.

"I think you'll need to cut his pants off," he said to Emil. "It probably took him an hour to get into them."

"My pleasure!" said Emil with a broad, craggy smile. He picked up a huge pair of scissors from the orthopedic tray and followed the stretcher behind the curtain into the trauma booth.

There followed a wild scene of shouting and kicking and yelling. Big Vern was like a demon; he bit and flailed around like a demented man, shouting that nobody was going to cut *his* clothes off. Emil emerged, red-faced with exertion for a moment, then went back to the fray, while Greg waited. With two policemen, one ambulance attendant, Beth, and Emil, his presence would have been superfluous. Emil stayed very professional until Big Vern got Beth in the face with a backhand, then Emil moved so fast, nobody was quite sure what he did, but suddenly he was at the head of the stretcher doing something to Big Vern's neck. Big Vern went limp. Emil

immediately got to work cutting off his pants with the big
scissors.

Suddenly there was a shout of laughter from behind the
curtain, and Greg looked up in surprise. There was another
astonished giggle, then all of them must have started to laugh,
because it became raucous and loud. Greg could hear Emil's
basso roar over the others. Curious, he got up, went over to
the booth, and pushed the curtain aside. The policemen, the
ambulance driver, even Beth, holding her bruised jaw, were
rolling around, convulsed with laughter. It took Greg a few
moments to see what all the fuss was about.

Emil had cut away the entire left leg of Big Vern's pants,
and strapped to his bloodstained upper inner thigh with tape
was a large cucumber. Big Vern indeed!

Big Vern was awake again, glowering, tight-lipped with fury,
but he didn't say anything, not even when Greg cleaned off
the dried blood with a piece of gauze soaked in saline. While
he was doing this the two policemen left, still grinning, and
tried to catch Big Vern's eye on their way out to show their
pleasure at his humiliation. Greg spent a couple of minutes
carefully poking into the knife wound with a pair of tweezers
to see if there was any dirt or cloth left in it. The wound was
fairly shallow and no major vessels or nerves appeared to have
been damaged. Big Vern was quiet during the procedure,
letting out an occasional brief curse when Greg touched a
sensitive area and when he flushed the wound out with saline.
After sewing up the skin, Greg put a small dressing on the leg;
the knife had missed the cucumber by half an inch. Emil
wanted to rip the vegetable off and display it on the counter,
but Greg stopped him. Vern looked as pale as a black man
could, and Greg couldn't help feeling a momentary twinge of
pity for the man. In the merciless world in which Vern lived
and had carved out a niche for himself, macho pride was an
essential component of his survival.

"Thanks, Doc, how much do I owe you?" said Vern, trying
to summon up some of the old cockiness. He looked at Greg
with a strange kind of gratitude; the doctor was the only one
who hadn't taken advantage of his embarrassment.

"It's on the house, Vern," replied Greg with a magnanimous
wave of the hand, beating Vern at his own game. He knew

he'd never get paid, anyway. They could both hear Beth back at the desk, giggling on the phone. The news would be all around town in minutes, between Beth and the policemen, and if Big Vern didn't get out on his own, he'd be laughed out by his own girls and the other pimps—if they didn't kill him first. It was rat eat rat in this town, and Vern's position as top pimp had always been precarious, he knew; that cut had not been aimed at his leg. Vern figured he had a lot of fast decisions to make, and he'd better make the right ones.

"Here," said Greg, giving Vern a pair of disposable scissors and a tweezer. "Cut the stitches out yourself in eight days. Unless you prefer to come back here."

"Thanks, Doc," said Vern, grinning impudently. "Hey, anytime you want a girl or anything—"

"Get out of here, Vern." Greg looked at him with a kind of unwilling respect. "And watch your step!"

Greg got home about fifteen minutes later. Liz was still in the kitchen and Edward was with her, dressed in his pajamas, with his school notebooks and a couple of textbooks in front of him.

"Well, I didn't expect you back yet," she said, leaning back for a kiss. "Why didn't you tell me you'd be back so soon?"

Greg opened his mouth, then saw they were both grinning at him, hoping he'd rise to the bait. "Okay," he said, smiling back at them. "You are an impertinent pair, the two of you. *As-tu fait tes devoirs de français?*" he asked Edward.

"We're finished with that," said Liz. "We're now into advanced mathematics, with fractions. Ask your father about the ones we couldn't do," she told Edward, and got up. "I'm going upstairs to put away the laundry."

When she came back, Greg was telling Edward about Big Vern, and Edward was giggling about the huge cucumber. Greg repeated the story quickly for Liz.

"I've heard of him," she said. "A nasty piece of work. He deserves all he gets, and more."

"Well, if you'd seen him after he'd been sewed up, totally humiliated, with all the machoism knocked out of him, you might have felt differently," replied Greg. "For somebody like him, in the circles he moves in, he's almost better off dead."

Liz gave her shoulders a little twist, a body movement Greg

recognized. "You know, Greg, you're so nice, you make me sick. Doesn't it bother you what this guy, Big whatever, does for a living? He goes around in a big white Cadillac with mink seat covers, all paid for by the girls he exploits and beats up. And you're sorry for him! I suppose you'd feel sorry for Attila the Hun if he fell off his horse and broke a leg."

"Yes, I probably would." Greg tried to find words that wouldn't sound preachy, because if they did, Liz would be all over him. "The way I see it, my job is to help people who're hurt, not to judge whether they're good or bad." He glanced at her; okay so far, her face showed that she was still listening and not gathering her forces for a pitched battle. "There are other people to make that kind of decision, and I'm just as happy staying right out of it." Greg smiled at Edward, who was listening quietly to the conversation. "So I make it easy for myself and take care of everybody." He got up and put his hands on Liz's shoulders, then slid them down her back and brought her toward him. She resisted; as far as she was concerned, the discussion wasn't over.

"It really gripes me sometimes," she said. "Everybody takes advantage of you—the tradesmen, your patients, the other doctors. 'Good old Greg,' that's what they say, 'he'll take care of it, he won't get mad, we can sock it to him.' " Greg pulled her toward him in spite of some unwillingness, until she was talking to him over his shoulder. "What would it take for you to really get mad at somebody?"

Greg's hands fell to his sides, and she stepped back. He was surprised to see that she seemed angry and upset. He looked at her calmly, thinking about her question, and it was a few moments before he answered.

"I suppose if anybody messed around with you, or with the kids, did any of you some harm . . . yes, then I'd go after them."

Liz was only partly mollified. Her character was quite different from his, with a much lower flashpoint. People tended to be careful around her because her opinions were strong and she was a tough, uncompromising woman who hated weakness or indecision. Sometimes she wasn't sure about Greg. Was he just a patsy for everybody around, or was it simply that he hadn't ever been tested?

"Edward, look at the time," she said. "Say good night and take your books upstairs. And no reading in bed; you have school tomorrow."

After the usual attempts to wheedle a few extra minutes, Edward finally went off. Suddenly Greg remembered that he hadn't told Liz about his call to New York earlier on.

"Hey, you'll never guess who I talked to this afternoon," he said, his eyes twinkling.

"The Internal Revenue Service?"

"Nope. You give up?" Although he was looking directly at Liz when he spoke, he didn't see the sudden stillness that came over her when he told her about his call to Willie Stringer. "I don't think we have anything else on that day, do we?" he asked. Usually Liz was the one who did the inviting and the accepting.

She looked at the big calendar beside the refrigerator. "No," she said slowly, "we're not doing anything else next Friday."

When Greg and Liz went upstairs, everything was quiet; Edward's and Elspeth's lights were out, and even Douglas's room was dark and quiet. Often he left his music on when he fell asleep, and Liz would turn it off. She worried about Douglas more than about the others; nothing ever seemed to go right for him, although all the children had had the same upbringing. Where did he get that mean streak from? Why wasn't he interested in anything except that awful noise he called music? She got undressed, brushed her teeth, and got into bed. Greg hugged her quietly for a little while, then turned over and went straight to sleep.

Liz lay awake for a very long time, thinking.

CHAPTER
TWELVE

Head coach Wally Lenahan was not happy, for a number of reasons. At the top of the list was the strong suspicion that his wife was having an affair; he didn't know with whom, and it was driving him crazy. Another was that he wasn't getting along with the ground staff, particularly old man Kruger, and the track was not in good shape. One of his boys had sprained an ankle last week tripping on a rough patch, and the state athletic finals in Hartford were coming up only too soon. And now Edward Hopkins, his great hope for the two-hundred-meter, was letting him down at a time when he should be making his very best effort. Lenahan had even arranged to have the track open early twice a week before the school day started, but who the hell cared about the extra time and effort he put in? The kid had just come in a bad fifth out of five in a routine heat he should have won easily. Lenahan looked at his stopwatch: almost three seconds behind the winner, who'd come in at 29:45, and that was no great shakes. He jabbed viciously at the reset button. What a fucking job this was, working his ass off trying to get results from kids who didn't really give a shit about anything, while that whore Della . . . he looked at his wristwatch. If he called home now, she would have gone out already, or else she wouldn't answer the phone. Well, he'd try anyhow.

He started to walk back toward the coach's office when something caught his attention. The boys who'd just finished the race were in a tight little group around Dick Cargill, the assistant coach. Lenahan saw one of the boys buckle at the knees and slide to the ground. The others bent over him, and

Dick raised his head, looking around for Lenahan, and shouted something at him. But Lenahan was already on his way across the field toward them, on the double.

"I'm okay, really," the boy was saying as Lenahan came up. It was Edward Hopkins, and he was sitting on the grass, looking pale and a little dazed. Lenahan knelt down beside him and took his pulse. It was fast, faster than he could count, but then the kid had just finished running. Edward seemed to be getting better by the second and tried to struggle to his feet, but Lenahan made him sit where he was. "If you keel over again, you won't have so far to fall if you're sitting down," he said. "Did you eat breakfast this morning?"

"Sure, Coach," replied Edward.

"What did you have?"

"The usual, I guess, toast . . ." Edward was about to go on reciting his usual menu of a boiled egg and milk and Cocoa Puffs when he remembered that on this particular morning he'd only had half a glass of milk because he hadn't been feeling hungry. "Actually I only had some milk," he said apologetically, his soft voice even quieter than usual. Coach Lenahan's fists tightened. He always had had a short fuse, and needed to watch out for that. The headmaster had said something to him about it only a couple of weeks ago—nicely enough, of course—but Lenahan knew it was a warning.

"But you knew you were going to be running, didn't you?" Lenahan's voice was acid, sarcastic.

"Yes, Coach, but I really didn't—"

"And you know the rules, don't you?" Edward was starting to look green again, and Lenahan told him brusquely to get his head down between his knees.

"Ease off on him a bit, Coach, he's only a kid," muttered Dick Cargill, his hand on Edward's shoulder, but Lenahan turned on him with such fury in his eyes that Dick flinched. Lenahan opened his mouth to say something blistering but thought better of it and marched back across the field toward the sports building. He felt a surge of almost homicidal tension; any little thing now would make him explode. If he ever found out who Della was fucking around with . . . He decided not to call her—not now, anyway. On the way back he tripped on a small molehill, right next to the track. By the time he reached the steps of the sports building, his blood pressure was at a dangerous level and he'd forgotten all about Edward Hopkins, who was finally getting up, still pretty wobbly. Dick took one arm, and Edward's friend, Timmy, who was really a sprinter but had joined this race as a fill-in, took the other.

"I'm going to send you home, Edward," said Dick. He felt really concerned about him, and although Coach Lenahan seemed to think Edward was just slacking off, he was sure that the boy was not well. He didn't want to take responsibility for him at this point; he was only an assistant coach, not a doctor.

"Can your mother come and pick you up?"

"I think so. She should be home, I think."

"My mother could come over if Mrs. Hopkins isn't home," said Timmy quickly. Edward stopped and coughed as if something were at the back of his throat, then spat onto the grass. It looked red, and Dick and Timmy exchanged a concerned glance.

While the boys changed, Dick Cargill dialed the number Edward had given him. Liz picked up on the second ring. Dick explained that Edward had fainted after a heat and still wasn't feeling great. Would she be able to come and pick him up?

Ten minutes later Liz came fast around the corner and stopped opposite the main entrance of the sports building with enough brake and tire noise to make both Edward and Timmy grin. The boys were ready waiting for her, their running shoes, socks, shirts, and shorts already packed in their duffel bags.

She jumped out, breathless with concern, and seemed reassured when she saw them grinning at her.

"What happened?" she asked, her eyes going from Timmy to Edward and back.

"He sort of fainted. Did the coach talk to you?" asked Timmy. He didn't want to get the story wrong, and felt uncomfortable and out of his depth. He also felt responsible for Edward's illness although he knew that didn't make sense.

Liz took another look at Edward, trying to decide whether to take him down to see Dr. Davis or take him straight home. But Edward, in the manner of twelve-year-olds, looked just fine now.

"Coach Lenahan thought it was because I didn't eat much breakfast," said Edward, smiling although he still felt a little shaky. "Boy, was he pissed at me!"

"You don't have to talk like that, Edward," said Liz almost
automatically. "*Annoyed* would have done just as well."

Timmy and Edward exchanged grins as they got into the
back of the station wagon with their bags, but it wasn't their
usual look of adolescent complicity. This time they were just
trying to reassure each other. Timmy realized he'd never been
so scared in his life; when Edward fainted like that after the
race, he suddenly thought his friend, his very best friend, was
going to die, right there in front of him.

Liz made up her mind. "We're going down to see Dr. Davis,"
she said. "Although Coach Lenahan was probably right—you
should have eaten your breakfast."

Victor Davis was a colleague of Greg's; his office was on the
same street, about a hundred yards farther down, and only a
couple of blocks away from the hospital.

Liz swung into the parking lot at the back of his office and
noticed that the lot had been recently repaved. The office itself
was fairly new, a modern one-story building with big windows
and an elegant entrance faced in natural wood. The shrubs
around it were meticulously tidy, and the well-pruned rose-
bushes on each side as they came in were already sprouting
reddish leaves. It was quite a bit nicer-looking than Greg's
office.

Liz didn't know the receptionist, but the girl knew Liz's
name. Everybody knew Dr. Hopkins. "I'm sure Dr. Davis will
be able to see Edward; if you can wait there just a minute."
She disappeared into the back.

Edward looked around curiously. It was different from his
father's office, which had been a big old family home before
Greg had restored and modernized it.

This place was very clean and clinical-looking, but not as
friendly. It would be scarier for a patient to come here, he
thought, then remembered that now *he* was a patient. Sort of,
because he wasn't really sick, not like Dave Gilligan. Timmy
was looking at him with a strange expression on his face, as if
he didn't know him, as if Edward were some kind of stranger,
so he punched him on the arm to let him know everything was
all right. But Timmy just smiled in a funny kind of way and
didn't hit him back, which made Edward feel strange and more
uncomfortable than anything else that had happened that
morning.

Dr. Davis appeared at the door of his inner office and came toward them.

"Hi, Liz, hi, kids," he said to the boys. "Nice to see you here. Can I get you a cup of coffee?" he asked Liz.

"It's a nice office," said Timmy. "Is that a real palm tree?"

"Sure it's real. Real plastic," said Dr. Davis, smiling at Liz.

"Victor, I hate to bother you, but I wonder if you'd take a quick look at Edward. They called me from the school because he, well, I guess he fainted." Liz looked at Timmy for confirmation. "He's never done that before."

"Sure, of course. Why don't you have a seat over there?" He indicated a row of comfortable-looking chairs near the palm tree, and spoke to the receptionist. "Gwen, would you put Edward in Room three? Tell Mandy to get him undressed and get a urine sample." He smiled again at Liz and went back to his inner office.

Ten minutes later he came over to where Liz and Timmy were sitting. Edward walked behind him, tucking his shirt into his pants. The laces of his sneakers trailed, untied, behind him.

"I can't find very much the matter with him, Liz," said Victor. "He's in good shape, strong, healthy. He probably *did* faint because he ran without having had much breakfast."

Liz got up. "I'm sorry to have bothered you, Victor, but I thought it was best to bring him down. Thanks." She smiled at Edward, feeling relieved. "Tie your shoelaces," she told him.

"There's only one thing that bothers me, Liz," Victor went on. "There was a trace of blood in his stool, and he told me he either coughed up or vomited up a little blood this morning."

Liz looked at Timmy and Edward in surprise. They hadn't mentioned anything about it to her. "I think he should have an upper GI series." Edward looked at him questioningly. "It's a test, Edward. You drink some stuff that shows up on X rays, and it'll tell us if you have a stomach ulcer or something like that."

"A stomach ulcer!" said Liz in surprise. "Isn't he a bit young for that kind of thing?"

"Yes, he is," he replied, "but they do occur. When I was a resident, there was a boy of eight who had one, and he needed surgery. Not that we're talking about anything like that for Edward. I just want to be sure we're not missing anything."

He held out his hand to Liz. "I've made an appointment for him to have it at the hospital on Monday at 3:30, so he won't miss any school. Meanwhile I think Edward should take it easy for a few days—avoid spicy foods, things like that." He aimed a friendly punch at Edward, who turned to avoid it. He still wasn't feeling too great.

Liz took Timmy back to school and explained why he was late, then drove home with Edward, who was very quiet. He spent the rest of the day playing with his Lego blocks and dozing. He wasn't hungry, and Liz didn't force him; he probably had eaten something that had upset him, and there was no point in making him vomit again.

When Edward woke up the next morning, he heard his door open and his mother poked her head in.

"Oh, Edward, after all that excitement yesterday, I was going to let you sleep today."

"I'm okay. Really, Mom."

Liz came into the room and looked down at him. "You're going to stay right where you are," she said firmly. "I'll get some breakfast up to you in a few minutes."

Edward did not argue because when he sat up there was just a faint echo of yesterday after the race, not a pain, just a feeling . . . a greyness about the sensation in his legs, a kind of sluggishness in his system that he couldn't have described. Liz had noticed something, too, and it gave her a strange sense—not apprehension exactly—but as she walked down the stairs she knew that she'd done the right thing by keeping him home.

A few minutes later Douglas appeared at the door of Edward's bedroom, holding a tray. He put it down carefully on the floor over by the window, as far away from Edward as possible.

"Your breakfast, lord asshole," he said. Edward didn't feel hungry, but he got out of bed, picked the tray up, and got back in, balancing it carefully. He spilled a few drops of orange juice on the tray, then moved the tray to roll the drops around on it. Usually Edward could devour a huge breakfast, then look around for something else to eat. Today, although everything looked the same and the Cocoa Puffs were just as puffy as ever, none of it looked like anything he would want to eat.

Edward picked up a single Cocoa Puff, soaked it in milk, then traced out his full name, Edward Paul Hopkins, on the bottom of the brown plastic tray and watched the milk dry on the outsides of the letters. Then below it in smaller letters he wrote *asshole*, then smeared it out with his finger. Douglas used to hit Edward from time to time, but not recently. Once Edward had left his running shoes at home and Douglas had had to bring them to him at the track. Edward was sitting on the grass with his friend Timmy when Douglas came up behind him with one shoe in each hand and slammed them together with Edward's head in between, then threw the shoes at him. Edward had scrambled up; run after Douglas, who was much bigger but not as fast; tackled him; and started to pummel the daylights out of him. Timmy came up, watched for a minute because he hated Douglas, too, then pulled Edward off. Both boys were considerably bruised, Douglas's nose bled for almost an hour, and Edward had a black eye that changed from blue to green to brown over the next few days. After that Douglas had never laid hands on his brother again.

Dozing off into memory-dreams, Edward's eyes flickered for a few moments, then closed. A couple of hours later he woke slowly, not sure what had awakened him; then he heard the sound of his mother's cello in the sewing room. There was something disturbing about the way she was playing today; it seemed to exude a kind of sadness that crept through the walls and swirled around him. Her music always did something to him; he couldn't have explained what, but sometimes it took him to a place he knew but had never seen, and he had a shivery feeling, as if a part of his mind could look back a hundred years.

Liz finished the chaconne and sat, looking through the white-painted windows into the sunlit garden. She, too, felt her mind going back, but not a hundred years. Only about eighteen.

The sun was streaming through the window onto Edward's pillow; it hurt when he opened his eyes, so he closed them again, feeling the sun on his face and eyelids. What would it be like to be blind? he wondered. Would he be able to see that red glow in his eyelids when the sun shone on them, or would it just feel warm? He touched the sheet and felt its texture, then the blanket. Keeping his eyes firmly closed, he pulled the bedclothes away and swung his feet down. The carpet was soft and fluffy, but there was no way his toes could tell that it was blue. Did different colors feel different? He explored with his left foot until he felt the coverlet where it touched the floor. It had a different texture, and Edward thought it maybe felt cooler than the blue. How could you explain color to a blind person? He opened his eyes and went across to the table and turned his radio on; it was set at the only station he ever listened to, and the New York disc jockey was telling some scurrilous story about what Puerto Ricans do to their chickens before they cook them, which was so outrageous and funny, it made Edward laugh out loud. He loved this crazy man who said things that were so blatantly offensive, it made Edward's scalp actually tingle to hear him.

His legs felt stiff and strange when he walked to the top of the stairs. His mother had stopped playing, so she was probably in the kitchen with Daniela, the Spanish cleaning lady. He padded down the stairs, the wool carpeting soft on his bare feet. At the kitchen door Edward could smell the warm, toasty smell of ironing; Daniela was hard at work, her left index finger smoothing the material just ahead of the iron.

His mother looked up at him from the counter.

"Edward! Where's your robe? And no slippers!" Edward looked down as if he hadn't realized he was barefoot. Liz pointed at the laundry hamper. "Here, take these underpants back up with you and put them in your drawer. And don't come down again without a robe on and something on your feet."

"Hi, Daniela," Edward said, standing awkwardly by the refrigerator, his hand supporting the sagging cord of his pajamas.

Daniela smiled at him without pausing in her work. "You not feeling so good today, Eduardo?"

Daniela was a nice lady, always smiling, even though the big brown mole on the side of her chin made her look a bit funny.

"No, I'm okay," replied Edward.

"Then get upstairs before I beat you!" said his mother.

Daniela laughed, a happy, musical sound. She liked Edward, who had a habit of teasing her.

"Is it true what Puerto Ricans do to their chickens before they eat them?" he asked her, trying not to giggle.

"Don't ask me," said Daniela, taking a quick look at his face.

That boy sometimes had the devil in him. She held up the shirt and examined the collar critically. "Puerto Ricans?" she asked disdainfully. "How would I know what these people do with their chickens!" She started to laugh, a warm, involuntary, good-hearted laugh. She didn't know what Edward was going to tell her, but she knew it would be funny.

"Edward, will you get upstairs!" his mother cried, grabbing a wooden spoon and advancing on him.

Edward fled. "I'll tell you when I come back down, Daniela!" he called over his shoulder.

"He sounds pretty good now, your Eduardo," said Daniela, putting another shirt on the ironing board. She rolled her tongue around the r in his name. "He's a beautiful boy, Mrs. Liz. He will be a heartbreaker for all the girls." Daniela shook her head sadly. Spanish women like her knew all about heart-breakers, better than most women, certainly better than Americans. Daniela, herself, better than anybody. She could pick one out a mile away.

Edward squatted on the floor beside his bed and ate the cereal and drank the orange juice but soon felt very full and bloated. A long, stretchy, tired feeling spread all the way through his body and he got back into bed and pulled the bedclothes up around him, feeling cold and shivery. The radio was playing a song about a truck driver in Arizona, headin' for Albuquerque with a full load of memories.

Timmy would be wondering why he hadn't come to school.

When Edward woke again, it was mid-afternoon. He lay there for a moment, trying to remember why he was in bed at this strange hour. There was a clattering from downstairs; Douglas and Elspeth were home from school. Elspeth came straight up to his room and gave him a folded piece of paper with his name written in green crayon on the outside. She stood watching him while he opened it. It showed a colored crayon drawing of somebody in bed, with a big balloon tied to the bedpost. On the balloon was written in mauve letters "Get beter soon."

"Thanks," he said, not too graciously. "But I'm not sick."

"Miss Foster didn't come in today, so we got a free period. Ginger said she's pregnant, but I don't believe it."

"Just because she's not married?" asked Edward in a superior tone. "That doesn't mean she can't have one."

"I know *that,* stupid. Yesterday she said she had a toothache, so today she was probably at the dentist."

"Get lost, Elspeth," he said, swinging his legs out of bed. "I'm going to get dressed."

Suddenly the noise of Douglas's music blasted into the room. Elspeth went down the corridor, shutting the door to his room so the volume diminished to a muted roar. In the bathroom, while he was washing up, Edward noticed a red spot on the palm of his left hand the size of a pinhead, with what looked like slender red veins running into it, thinner than a thread. He wiped the soap off to see it better. It looked like a tiny red spider. It didn't hurt, so he forgot about it.

CHAPTER
THIRTEEN

"Well, what do you think of that, hearing from Greg Hopkins?" Willie was sitting on the edge of Ellen's four-poster bed, the one they used to sleep in until Willie moved into one of the other bedrooms. He looked at her obliquely; they hadn't talked about Greg or Liz for many years, but the topic was still loaded with all kinds of repressed emotion.

"Surprise, huh?" Ellen smiled with a touch of the old malice.

"Yeah . . ." Willie was being very careful. If anything real was going to be said on that topic, it wouldn't be by him, at least not at first. Ellen had always had a sixth sense about Liz.

"Do you want to go?"

"Sure." Willie had that ready, even the inflection, which said he'd love to see his old friend Greg again, school chums and all that sort of thing, but that's all. "If *you* do. And if you feel well enough."

"Why don't you go by yourself? Don't you think it would be better? You could get to know Liz all over again." Ellen was pouring the acid, getting ready to throw it.

"No way," said Willie decisively. He was ready for that too. "If you don't go, I don't, either."

Ellen heaved herself up on the pillows. She was wearing a Chinese silk robe with an intricate floral pattern. The cleavage showed her breasts, but all the life was out of them now. Willie remembered the luscious, swelling curves that used to be there, that she used to flash so brazenly and excitingly when Liz wasn't looking. He had been hypnotized by the sensuousness of her figure and how she used it: suggestive, maddening, like an Oriental dancer. It had all been an illusion.

It had taken years for him to get over that, the disparity between the promise and the performance, the fantasy and the reality. Ellen, it seemed, had been accidentally born into the wrong body. But that was before he heard about what had caused her frigidity.

They had been married for over a year, and Willie could not accept the fact that Ellen didn't enjoy sex. She tried her best, but nothing ever worked, in spite of Willie's acknowledged talent and extraordinary efforts. It drove him crazy, not being able to make her feel the ecstasies that he so wanted to share with her. Very often she cried afterward, the tears of a child forever on the wrong side of the window.

One disastrous night, after Willie had come on his own, then shouted and pounded the pillow next to her head in a fury of frustration, she finally told him what had happened to her when she was sixteen.

From the sound of it, Ellen must have been a hot ticket at the time. She used to go around with a lot of boys, she told him, and it drove her father crazy. If he'd had his way, he'd have kept her in a convent until he'd decided who she was to marry. Ellen sounded as though she had been pretty headstrong, pretty hard to control. She came in late most nights, and her father would shout and her mother weep, but to no avail. With her Mediterranean temperament Ellen really liked to have boys around, and she became pretty well known in her school and neighborhood.

Then, when she was almost sixteen, she fell in love. The way Ellen told it, the boy sounded like a nice kid. He was a student at U. Conn., very good-looking, and about six years older than her. At that age, six years was a big difference. He was studying physics and astronomy, and she listened wide-eyed to his stories of huge galaxies hurtling toward the edge of space at the speed of light, and how what he was learning was going to make space travel possible. He told her quite a few other stories too.

She spent all her spare time with him, and her father was really upset, worse than when she'd been playing the field because he figured that now she was a lot more likely to get herself into trouble. And Benny was really stupid around her father; he should have known better, because he, too, had a partly Sicilian background. He treated him like a boring old mustache Pete, and her father didn't appreciate that at all. Ellen should have known something was up when her father suddenly stopped saying anything derogatory about her young man.

One evening they'd gone down to New Haven to a rock concert, smoked some pot there, come back to town, and parked in the place they usually went to, a quiet spot near the campus. They still had one joint, and they smoked it, keeping the car windows closed. They talked a bit, and he started to take her clothes off, first unbuttoning her blouse—slowly, like in a dream—then her bra. They sat there for a while, both getting excited. He stroked her nipples so lightly, like a feather, she thought she was going to come right then.

Willie had interrupted to ask if she'd ever come before that time, but Ellen's mind was back in the car and she didn't answer.

Then Benny eased her out of everything else she was wearing. The car seat was cold and strange on her naked behind, but she felt a kind of wild, dangerous freedom surge through her body. Benny stayed fully dressed all this time and played with her and got her so worked up, she couldn't stand it. Then Benny stripped, too, and he was really something to look at, that boy, sinews and muscles and smooth sun-brown skin. He pushed her over on the seat and put her legs up, roughly, one on the wheel and the other on the back of the seat.

"Do you really have to go into all this?" asked Willie, getting angry. Then he looked at her drawn, white face and bit his tongue.

"Then somebody switched on their headlights right behind us. We'd never heard them coming. They yanked the door open on his side. I thought it was the police, because they used to come around from time to time."

Ellen's hands were gripping the sheets and the knuckles were white.

"The guy pulled Benny out, stark naked. There was another man there and they pulled something over his head and I could hear Benny shouting through it, but all muffled . . ."

Willie put his hand gently on hers.

"They took him back to the other car and pushed him in. I locked all the doors and grabbed my clothes. I'd never been so scared in my life, and my hands were shaking, so I couldn't get them on. I heard a scream, and then nothing. I didn't know what to do. The key was in the ignition, but I couldn't just leave him. I couldn't see the car because the high beams were on, but something was happening inside because the lights were moving, sort of shaking.

"Then I heard a door slam and they appeared at my window, dragging Benny as if he were dead drunk. The first guy banged on the window and I thought he was going to break it." Ellen looked up at Willie, embarrassed. "I had wet myself . . ." She hesitated. "Do you want me to go on, tell you the rest of it?"

"Yes. Please." Willie's mouth was dry.

"They let him go and he just fell, like a sack, right outside the car door. They went back to their car, reversed out of the lane, and were gone. It was dark, and I couldn't find the lights. Then I opened the door, and Benny was trying to sit up and he was shouting and grunting with pain, clutching himself. There was blood on the ground and dripping down his leg. I helped him get in the back; he could hardly move for the pain, and he was weeping now, still bleeding. I wanted to take him to the hospital but he wouldn't let me, so I drove him to his home and his brothers came out and took him in. Then I saw what they'd done. There was a piece of thick, hairy string, like twine, tied underneath his penis, which was okay, but they'd cut his testicles off. The string was like a tourniquet, so he wouldn't bleed to death."

"Oh, my God," breathed Willie. "My God!"

"I think that's why I'm the way I am," said Ellen. "My father had us both castrated that night. It was my sixteenth birthday."

Ellen was looking at him now.

"I think we should go. It's been a long time since we've seen them, and life's too short." Willie had heard Ellen use that expression several times recently. He kissed her gently, got up, and went into his own room. After all those years, they understood each other pretty well.

CHAPTER

FOURTEEN

It was always an adventure, going to New York City, and Elspeth and even Douglas wanted to come, but they would miss school, so Greg said no. Dr. Davis had made the original appointment for Edward's stomach X rays, or upper GI series as he called it, at their local hospital, but the radiologist only visited there twice a week and Greg wasn't too sure how competent he was, so they decided to have it done in New York, in the Pediatric Radiology Department at Children's Hospital, which was part of the Manhattan University Hospital complex.

Liz, of course, drove him down, and she decided to make a day of it. Edward had seemed tired and listless since the time he'd fainted at school, and he hadn't shown any real interest in anything, let alone running competitively. Coach Lenahan had called several times, but although he sounded sympathetic enough, Liz could tell that he was only interested in whether his two-hundred-meter star would be competing for him in the state championships. Liz thought him an unpleasant person, although Edward said he was a pretty good coach. Liz felt that Edward deserved a little vacation, and that she did, too, so after they'd finished at Children's Hospital they planned to go to Rockefeller Center for lunch and shopping, then the afternoon show at Radio City Music Hall before heading home. They should be back in plenty of time for dinner, but just in case, she put a couple of frozen lasagna cartons out on the kitchen counter with written instructions. Elspeth knew how to use the microwave and would be thrilled to make dinner for her daddy.

The appointment was for nine A.M., and the ride was easy enough until they got into the bad traffic on the Merritt Parkway. Edward watched the other cars as they crept along and told his mother each time he saw a Porsche or a Jaguar or other fancy vehicle. Liz wasn't listening; she was worried about being late and didn't like driving into New York, where the density of the traffic and the aggressiveness of the drivers scared her, and she wasn't too sure how to get to the hospital. By the time they finally turned into the hospital parking lot, her palms were sweating and her whole body was aching with tension.

Children's Hospital was quite different from the relaxed atmosphere of their little hospital at home, where everybody knew everybody else, where the nurses asked Liz how the children were, and the administrator would try to wangle another jar of that delicious plum jam she'd made last fall.

Not here. The place was so busy, it took her breath away; everybody bustling around, women in white coats marching with important strides down the corridors with students following like ducklings, bemused-looking visitors, technicians, nurses hurrying along the corridors, filling the elevators in chattering clumps.

The Radiology Department was on the ground floor. Edward was less bashful than Liz about asking for directions, and they finally got there.

"Did you notice they all said, 'And you can't miss it'?" asked Edward in his soft voice. His voice was never loud, but he responded to stress or excitement by speaking even more quietly. Liz had to make him repeat it, and by the time he'd said it again, they were under the sign: PEDIATRIC RADIOLOGY and STEINBERG RADIATION CENTER.

That sounded rather scary, Liz thought. It must be for kids with cancer. She grabbed Edward's hand and held on to it until they came to the desk. There were only a few people here, a contrast to the milling masses in the rest of the hospital, and the girl behind the desk was small and pretty and as nice as could be.

Yes, they had an appointment, and this must be Edward. "Hi, Edward, I'm Ginny. If you'll sit down over here . . . Mrs. Hopkins, we need you to fill in the forms; sorry about that, but we really use all that information. Now, Edward, I hope you didn't have any breakfast this morning." Ginny looked first at him and then at Liz.

"Nothing apart from the usual bacon and eggs, cereal, toast with butter and jelly," said Edward, looking as if the butter he'd just mentioned wouldn't melt in his mouth. "And two cups of coffee." Ginny gasped, then laughed when Liz shook her head.

"He didn't eat a thing, Ginny. Edward thinks he's being very funny."

They looked around the waiting area; most of the dozen or so dark red plastic chairs were occupied by mothers with one or two children, some in cribs. A girl of about fifteen with straggly hair was reading a book, sitting cramped between a large, still, untidy-looking woman with a three-year-old, and a young Hispanic girl with a very lively baby. The only two vacant places were next to a boy who looked about Edward's age, sitting with his mother. The boy's head was completely shaved, and an angry red scar outlined a large U-shaped flap on the left side of his head. Purple ink marks showed on several parts of his head. Edward hesitated, but Liz walked resolutely toward the empty seats, and Edward followed her. Liz smiled at the boy's mother, whose mouth moved briefly in acknowledgment. Liz sat in the far chair, and Edward sat down next to the boy, who took no notice and kept on staring in front of him.

Edward looked around the room; in spite of the presence of several small children, there was very little noise, as if something about the place kept everyone quiet. Like in church. Edward took a long look at his neighbor out of the corner of his eye, then his eyes moved around the waiting area.

"Did you notice there are no fathers here?" he asked his mother in a whisper.

"Yes, I did." Liz smiled. "They're probably all working." She was talking in her normal tone of voice, overcoming an impulse to whisper also.

The boy moved his eyes toward Edward for a brief moment. Edward said to him, "What are you here for? I'm getting a stomach X ray." Edward's voice cracked involuntarily between a whisper and his normal speaking voice. The boy kept looking straight ahead and said nothing.

"Answer the boy, Jacob," said his mother quietly.

"My head hurts if I speak," he said. His voice was high-pitched, with a metallic tonality. Edward thought, This kid's from outer space, an alien.

"He's here for radiation treatment," his mother said. She sounded as if she were used to doing Jacob's speaking for him.

"Where are you from?" Edward asked the boy, and the mother answered, "New Canaan, how about you?"

Edward immediately understood; he would have a conversation with Jacob, but his mother would do the talking; she knew him well enough to translate his unspoken words into speech.

Jacob's mother had some difficulty hearing Edward's quiet voice, but when he raised it, Jacob winced. She was determined that the conversation should go on; Edward got the impression that Jacob didn't get much opportunity to talk to other kids, and his mother wasn't going to let this chance go by, so she leaned across her son to hear what Edward was saying. They talked about baseball, which Jacob had played, then Edward mentioned that he did some running, and they talked about that for a little while. She had quite a pretty face, Edward thought, but it seemed to have become accustomed to the perpetually anxious expression she wore; Jacob must have been sick for quite a while.

"Jacob Milstein?" Ginny smiled over at him from the desk. "Room twenty-nine, Jacob, your usual." Jacob got up stiffly, still looking straight ahead of him. He turned and put out his hand to Edward with an awkward gesture. Edward took it, feeling embarrassed. Jacob just barely touched him, then he turned and went toward the door. His mother went with him, but as she rose from her chair she gave Edward a swift, grateful smile. Edward blushed, sure that everybody in the room was looking at him. After a few moments he turned to ask his mother what the purple marks on Jacob's head were for. She was looking at him with an expression he'd never seen before, and her eyes looked sort of blurry.

A few minutes later it was his turn, and Ginny took him to a changing room where he took off everything except his underpants and socks. She gave him a hospital gown to put on, a kind of long shirt that tied at the back. He managed the top tie, and when he emerged, Ginny did the one at his waist.

He followed her down a long, shiny, spotlessly clean corridor to a darkened room on the left at the far end. There was a kind of flat table in the middle of the room, with a black rubber pillow at one end. A big shiny box hung over the table; it had a series of small lights on it and a handle to move it up and down. A girl in a white uniform was pushing something into a container under the table. She looked up and smiled.

"I'll be right with you, as soon as I get this darned cassette unstuck."

They watched her for a minute, struggling with the equipment.

"This is Edward Hopkins," said Ginny. "He's come for an upper GI." She turned to Edward. "Carol will take care of you from now on. See you later!" Ginny went back along the corridor, and Edward was sorry to see her disappear back to the front desk. She was a really nice person, and he would have liked to get to know her.

Carol finally got her cassette in position and came over. She was prettier than Ginny, but she looked at Edward with a rather distant expression, as if she wished he were older. She explained that he would be lying on the table for quite a while, but first he was going to drink some white stuff that had a cherry flavor. To tease her a little, he asked if they didn't have strawberry, and she looked surprised and said no, most people like the cherry all right.

The doctor came in, a roly-poly man with a heavy gray apron that was a bit tight for him. "Edward Hopkins?" he asked, but he was talking to Carol. He didn't even look at Edward.

"Yes, right," she said. "Upper GI."

"Up onto the table," she said to Edward. "And watch your head. Lie down with your head on the pillow." She put on one of the heavy aprons; hers had colored flowers all over it.

The stuff he had to drink was okay for the first couple of swallows; as advertised, it had a strong cherry taste. But by the time he finished it, Edward thought he was going to throw up. The lights went out, and the doctor switched on what looked like a big television screen. Then they turned him, the doctor poked at his tummy, pushed up under his ribs, and every so often he said, "Keep very still now, don't breathe!" and Edward could see his leg move as he stepped on a foot pedal, then there was a whirring noise and a clatter from under the table, then they'd both go away for a while, then it would start all over again.

After a long time the big lights suddenly went on, and Carol said, "Okay, Edward, that's it. You were very good. Can you get back to the desk by yourself?"

Walking back down the corridor, Edward could feel the draft around his shirt and wondered if his bottom was showing. He twisted around but couldn't tell for sure. He held the tail of the gown around his legs when he got to the desk. He'd have been mortified if Ginny saw his backside.

"Well, how was it?" asked Liz as they came out of the main entrance. It was beginning to drizzle, and Liz put up her umbrella. She hesitated and looked around. "Which way is the parking lot, do you think?" she asked. Edward led her around the building to the parking area at the back. Liz gasped at the amount they had to pay at the kiosk: for that sum back home she could have parked outside City Hall for a week.

They drove downtown slowly, the traffic moving at half-speed because of the rain.

"How was it?" she repeated as they waited at the lights halfway down Park Avenue.

"It was okay, Mom," Edward replied. He was timing the traffic lights with his watch. "It takes exactly one minute and twenty-two seconds," he informed her, but she didn't know what he was talking about and ignored it.

"Did they tell you anything?" she asked as the traffic surged forward again. A cab sounded its horn right behind her. Edward turned around to look, and Liz, looking in the rearview mirror, caught the tail end of what looked like a crude gesture from her son, aimed at the cabbie.

"Don't *do* that, Edward! This is New York! That cabbie could easily just smash into us." Edward grinned at the cabbie as he passed on their left, but the cabbie wasn't even looking.

Edward didn't feel hungry, he told his mother, but she did, so they found a Chock-Full-o'-Nuts and stopped for a cup of coffee and a cream cheese and raisin bread sandwich, which was unceremoniously slapped down in front of them. "It's sad," said Liz as they left. "These places used to be so nice, and clean too. New York isn't what it used to be." Liz was shocked when she thought about it. It had been over four years since she was last in the city.

By the time they'd stopped at Brooks Brothers for a couple of shirts for Greg, and spent an hour wandering around Bloomingdale's, both Liz and Edward were exhausted, and they decided to miss the Radio City Music Hall show and head back home.

About the time they swung down the ramp to the Major Deegan Expressway, the roly-poly radiologist at Children's Hospital, Arthur Montefiore, sat facing an illuminated wall with a couple of dozen X rays on it. He had a microphone in his hand and was dictating into it.

"Edward Paul Hopkins, age twelve, upper GI series. The contrast material flows smoothly through the esophagus. Some rugosity is noted at the lower end, but the barium enters the stomach normally. There is no reflux or hiatus herniation. The stomach is of normal size and configuration, and irritability is noted in the antrum. There appears to be a small ulcer in the distal part of the stomach. Duodenum and small intestine are normal."

He looked again at the films, hesitating for a moment over the ones showing the lower end of the esophagus. Then he shrugged, put the mike down, collected the X rays, and put them into a brown folder with Edward's name on it. Not the very best upper GI series, but Carol, the technician, was new. She was bright enough, though, and she'd soon get the hang of things.

Arthur reached for the next envelope, pulled the top two films, and flipped them up on the screen. He picked up the mike and went on with his dictation in the same droning voice. "Joan Hendricks, age seventy-two, PA and lateral chest films . . ."

By the time Liz and Edward got home, Dr. Montefiore had called Dr. Davis, and Dr. Davis had called Greg with the news that Edward had a stomach ulcer. Greg knew that it was unusual at that age, but not unknown. Treatment would be with antacids, diet, and if that didn't work, with something called H2 inhibitors, which prevented acid from being formed in the stomach. Dr. Davis reminded Greg of the old aphorism from medical school: "No acid, no ulcer," and suggested that Edward should have an endoscopy at some point. Looking into the stomach through a flexible tube would give them all a better idea of what was going on.

So Edward got no lasagna, which he loved, but was given some rice and boiled fish, which he didn't like at all. The only one who thought it was funny was Douglas.

CHAPTER
FIFTEEN

"Greg, for heaven's sake, calm down. It's only a dinner." Greg was pacing up and down the length of the kitchen, wearing the look of a kid who's about to have his birthday party that evening.

"Are we all set? I mean, do I need to get any wine or anything?"

Liz gave him a long look, and he sat down at the counter and laughed, a bit embarrassed. "I know, I know . . . but it really is quite an occasion. God, can you imagine, eighteen years! I wonder if he's aged a lot."

Liz had been wondering the same thing and had tried to visualize Willie old and pompous, but she couldn't do it. And Ellen? A steel shutter had always come down in her mind if she ever went anywhere near that topic. Now, surprisingly, she found herself able to visualize and think about her without anger, as if Ellen were somebody she didn't know, somebody whose doings she'd only heard about.

"Willie has to go to some board meeting, so they won't be able to get here before eight."

Liz looked at him and laughed, shaking her head. Greg rarely came home for lunch, but here he was, at the kitchen counter eating a tomato. It upset her routine, but she was glad to see him because Willie and Ellen's impending visit was really beginning to disturb her.

Greg usually worked through lunchtime or had a quick sandwich or a cup of soup in the hospital cafeteria. His eating habits were precisely the opposite of what he recommended to his patients: he had a cup of strong coffee with sugar for breakfast, another later on in the morning, missed lunch as often as not, ate a big dinner in the evening, and nibbled on chocolate or cookies in bed. After worrying about it for a year or two when they were first married, now Liz just went along with it. It didn't seem to be doing him any harm; he still had more energy than anybody she knew.

Greg had mentioned Willie Stringer a couple of times since inviting them to dinner. Each time Liz had managed to turn her back to him so he wouldn't see her face; she had felt the sudden flushes coming straight from her heart up into her cheeks. Liz had never been a blusher, but she felt she was blushing now.

"I'm cooking a rack of lamb for them." Liz busied herself at the sink. There was no point in telling Greg that lamb was Willie's favorite dish, or that she'd angrily been unable to prevent herself from going all the way into Stamford to get it.

"Great. You never kept in touch with Ellen, did you?"

"No." A saucepan fell from the rack and onto the floor with a loud crash. Greg got off his stool to retrieve it for her, but Liz scooped it up in a second. Ellen, that bitch . . . It was strange, she'd felt almost benign about her until Greg actually spoke her name. For a second Liz remembered the last time she'd seen her. That whole scene had been permanently hacked into her soul, as if with a blunt penknife.

Willie . . . They'd certainly had some great times together, but now it took an effort to remember them because long ago she'd made a determined and mostly successful effort to forget about him altogether. It had been such a shock last week, when Greg first spoke his name, Willie Stringer, the words coming out of his mouth lit up in neon, with sparks flying from each letter.

Greg drained his cup of coffee and stood up. He was already late, although he'd only been home about fifteen minutes. Liz put his plate and cup in the sink and heard the scrunch of gravel almost immediately as his car backed down the driveway.

She felt more nervous about tonight now that Greg had gone. Taking the rack of lamb from the refrigerator, she examined it; the butcher had done a nice job for her, with those little paper crowns on the tip of each rib. Which piece would Willie eat? He'd surely know how much trouble she'd gone to, making his favorite dish. Would he read something into it? Something that wasn't there? Well, to hell with it, he could think what he damn well liked, him and his Ellen. It was all ancient history now. She had a new life, and a happy one—Willie would see that, and if he didn't, she'd damn well point it out to him.

Liz spent a good part of the afternoon preparing dinner. When Edward came home from school, he helped her put extra leaves in the big dining-room table, and Elspeth set out the silver. She would show them. Greg might not be a Park Avenue surgeon, but he'd done all right. Actually, the silver had belonged to her mother, but Willie wouldn't know. As the hour approached, Liz felt more and more confident that she would pass this self-imposed test of her own internal fidelity, and with flying colors.

She was even able to smile at herself for all the nervousness she'd suffered over the last several days when the thought of Willie crossed her mind. By now he'd be bald and paunchy, and she'd have a hard time not laughing when she shook his pudgy hand. He'd look at her hard, to see if there was still anything there, and she'd stare back, shouting a silent, contemptuous *No!* right in his face. Romance was great, but there was a time and a place for everything. She was past all that, and she'd been through too much. She could get all the romance she needed from listening to her daughter Patsy talk about her love life. Liz looked at the clock on the kitchen wall; Patsy was coming home today for the weekend, and if the traffic wasn't too bad, she should be home about five. Liz felt a kind of grim pleasure that her eldest daughter would be with her to meet the Stringers.

Ten minutes later Liz heard a car pull up outside, then Patsy's voice. A door slammed and a moment later Patsy came in, all breathless with excitement. She was a striking girl, full of life and energy, quite like her mother had been at her age, with the same big gray-green eyes. She wore her dark hair shorter than Liz had, with little curls around the nape of her neck.

"Derek wouldn't come in," she said, kissing her mother. "He has to get to Pittsburgh tonight."

"Derek?"

Patsy looked at her in astonishment. "Didn't I tell you about him? Well, later . . . Here, why don't I dry the glasses." In a moment Patsy had her sleeves rolled up and was hard at work.

"Who's coming to dinner?"

"Oh, some people you don't know, the Stringers. He was at med school with your father."

"Are you all right, Mom?" Patsy was staring at her. "You look sort of tense."

"I'm fine. Here, let me do that glass again, there's a smudge. How did your trip to Coney Island go?"

"With Ferdie? God, Mom, that was *two weeks* ago! Anyway, you're not going to believe what happened. Ferdie's real cute, a bodybuilder, spends all his time in the gym or talking about steroids." She paused, not sure about the last word. "Anyway, Ferdie's beautiful, but he looks at himself in all the shop windows. He didn't let me hold his hand. I had to hold his arm so I could feel the muscles rippling."

"Here, put the glasses on the towel."

Liz watched Patsy out of the corner of her eyes as they worked together. She was so young and alive, with such a mischievous, funny mind. She was so special.

"Well," Patsy went on, lining the glasses up in front of her like toy soldiers, "he lives in Manhattan, so he met me at Grand Central and we took the train to Coney Island." She grinned. "It's sort of nice to be seen out with him because he's big and blond, and like I said, he has these terrific muscles."

Liz smiled; she could see Patsy skipping brightly alongside this huge, lumbering fellow, chattering at him nonstop.

"Anyway, we were doing all the usual stuff and he took off his jacket and hit something hard enough to ring the bell, so I got a teddy bear, and then we did the roller coaster and stuff. There was this Chinese-food stand and we got some egg rolls, although Ferdie said they didn't have the right kind of calories or something."

"Empty calories?" asked Liz, just to show she was listening.

"Right. Anyway, ten minutes later we're getting on the train to go home when he starts making a funny noise, like wheezing, and his face is getting all puffy and sort of blotchy. 'I'm fine, okay,' he says, sounding really annoyed, but I think maybe he's having a heart attack or something, and I'm thinking about pulling the alarm, although that's not really going to do much good. Soon the poor guy can barely talk, and he says something about being allergic to MSG, that's the stuff they put in Chinese food to give it taste."

"Your grandfather has that too," murmured Liz, "but not that bad. He just gets a headache."

"By the time we get into the station, he's still all puffed up and wheezing, you know, like these really fat people when it's very hot? He can only get his words out one at a time, and I have to support him until I get a taxi to take him home. Can you imagine, *me* just about carrying this huge hunk? I finally get him home to his mother, but all he can say is he's never been so humiliated in all his life, that's all the thanks I got."

The glasses were dry, and Patsy put them in the cupboard, her indignant expression fading. She smiled, a quick flashing smile that showed her white teeth. Liz thought how much better she looked without braces, but they'd certainly done the job.

"He never called again, which didn't matter because I met this *hot* man named Derek."

By seven-thirty, Liz was bathed, dressed, and everything was ready. She took a long, guilty swig straight out of the sherry decanter to steady her nerves. She checked everything out in her mind: the potatoes were ready; the vegetables were prepared; the meat was cooking; Greg had opened the wine, two bottles, so they would have time to breathe, whatever that meant; and Douglas and Elspeth had been fed.

For Liz, the tension took a quantum leap about five minutes to eight, and then fifteen minutes later they all heard a car pull into the driveway. Edward and Elspeth, who'd eaten dinner in the kitchen with Douglas earlier, knew that something unusual was going on and ran to the window in Edward's room.

Moments later the front doorbell rang; they heard their father open the door and then a murmur of voices and laughter.

"Let me take your coat," said Greg to Ellen, after the hugs and handshakes. He wouldn't have recognized her; the sexy siren with the flashing eyes was gone, replaced by a rather bony-looking middle-aged woman with slightly sunken eyes and a look of ineffable tiredness. He made an immediate comparison with Liz's maturing beauty. There was no question about it; Ellen's fire was out. *She's ill,* thought Greg with compassion. *I hope she's being taken care of.* But Ellen still had great style. She slid out of her ankle-length blue mink coat, under which she wore a black silk dress with a Victorian pearl choker.

"My, it's a real beauty!" said Greg, stroking the soft fur coat before hanging it in the hall closet. Willie, now talking to Patsy, looked exactly as he remembered him, except for his gray hair. He looked perhaps a little sleeker, better cared for. Liz appeared from the direction of the kitchen, and there were hugs and more laughter all around.

"Now, what would you all like to drink?" asked Greg, leading the way into the living room. Almost as a reflex, Liz said to herself a vodka martini for Willie, and she knew the exact proportions he liked. Their eyes caught just for a second, just long enough for her heart to leap into orbit, and she thought, *My God, it's as bad as ever it was, what am I going to do?* She escaped into the kitchen to compose herself. Bloody Willie! He hadn't had the decency to change one bit, except for maybe the slightest jowliness, but somehow even that . . . And Ellen! Liz got a jolt of vicious satisfaction at her appearance.

"Mom? Do you need any help?" Patsy came bouncing in, full of energy as always.

"Yes," she said, improvising. "Put the plates in the oven, on low."

"Are you all right?" asked Patsy. "You look as if a ghost just bit you!"

"I'm just busy, that's all." Liz had to drag her eyes away from Patsy's face. She looked so like her father.

When Liz brought in the rack of lamb, she couldn't help looking at Willie, but he was deep in conversation with Patsy on his left. Greg got up to help Liz, but a thought struck him as he rose from his chair. "Willie, you're the surgeon, so do you want to carve?"

Willie looked up. "Greg," he said after a pause, "I never carve on anything that doesn't twitch."

Patsy laughed out loud. "Willie, you're just as disgusting as ever," Liz said, and Ellen smiled distantly. She had heard his joke many times before, and it didn't improve with repetition.

Willie was going great guns with Patsy. He smiled at her with those gray eyes that women didn't notice until they became his target, after which they had trouble forgetting them. Patsy felt cocooned, flattered by this handsome and successful surgeon who was concentrating all his attention on her.

"What musical instrument do you play?" He picked up her hand and looked at the long, slender fingers that were just like Liz's when she was her age. Then he looked at her lips. "They were made for better things than blowing across the mouthpiece of a flute." He grinned at her and she blushed. How on earth did he know?

"My mother must have told you," she said accusingly, but her eyes were soft.

"She didn't, I swear!" As usual, it had been a lucky guess. "Does your mother still play the cello?"

Greg was doing his best with Ellen, but she was uncomfortable and aware of the tension in the air, a tension only the two older women seemed to feel. Willie, who should have been more uncomfortable than any of them, seemed blissfully unaware of the electricity, but more likely Liz figured he knew exactly what was going on and was enjoying it. She looked over at him, laughing with Patsy, and felt a strange annoyance, which she refused to believe might be jealousy.

After coffee they went into the living room, where Greg served liqueurs and brandy. Liz gently sat Patsy down on the big sofa, with Ellen between them. "The men'll want to talk," she said, smiling. "It's been so long, they have a lot of catching up to do."

Greg and Willie settled into two big easy chairs next to each other, Willie waving away Greg's offer of a cigar. "Gave them up years ago," he said. "Ellen hates 'em, like most of the things I like to do."

Liz, making benign small talk about children and schools with Ellen and trying to get Patsy involved, kept one ear stretched to hear what the men were saying. She sat on the edge of the sofa to be closer. Willie had that infuriating patronizing look on his face, but Greg, good old Greg, was totally unaware of it. He was simply glad to be with his old friend and happy for him that he'd done so well. Willie regaled him with stories of the important people he'd operated on and how much money he had to make to keep up with Ellen's expenditures.

"Now tell me how things are going here," he asked, settling back with his brandy. "You certainly have a lovely home!" And a lovely wife, too, he thought, glancing momentarily across the coffee table. Greg told him about his practice, then the story about Big Vern and his cucumber, and they both had a good laugh.

When Greg told Willie about Edward and the stomach ulcer that had shown up on the X rays, Willie was suddenly all attention. When Greg asked him who he should get to do the endoscopy, Willie said he would do it himself, in the office, no problem. A pleasure. Greg was surprised, because he hadn't realized Willie did much pediatric work, and Edward was still just in that age group.

"I really appreciate it, Willie. Really." Greg almost had tears in his eyes. Having kids must do bad things to one's emotional stability, thought Willie. Luckily he didn't have that problem.

At eleven o'clock, as if the old grandfather clock in the corner had given a signal, Ellen got up and straightened her skirt. Five minutes later, after a flurry of warm thanks, hugs, kisses, and good-byes, the Stringers were in their car and backing slowly down the driveway.

Greg gave them a final wave, then came in and closed and bolted the door for the night. He found Liz and Patsy in the dining room, gathering up the glasses.

"Well, that was a great evening. Thanks for making such a splendid dinner!" He put an affectionate arm around Liz. "I hope you weren't too bored with all our reminiscences," he added, turning to Patsy. "We were all friends together, before you were even thought of."

Not so, thought Liz, looking down and starting to gather the dishes, not quite so.

She knew, as surely as she knew her own name, that Willie Stringer would call her and would want to see her. Right now she was sitting outside the honey trap, looking in, knowing that she couldn't help herself, that she would eventually step into it with full knowledge of the consequences.

CHAPTER
SIXTEEN

Greg met Victor Davis the next morning in the hospital. "We should get that endoscopy done on Edward," said Victor. "Who would you like to do it?"

"As a matter of fact, I've already asked an old friend of mine," said Greg. "Willie Stringer; he's a surgeon in the city."

"Good," replied Victor, "that's fine with me. I'd just as soon he didn't have it done here." The gastroenterologist, Dr. Mariani, only came twice a week, and he didn't normally do endoscopies on children. "Anyway, getting that scope down isn't easy with kids. I agree, better do it in the big city."

"Right. And this guy's pretty hot stuff. We were at medical school together."

"I don't know if that's much of a recommendation," Victor said with a grin, "but if he's okay with you, he's okay with me."

They walked together toward the records room; they both had charts to dictate.

"I saw Edward this morning." Victor hesitated. "He's not doing quite as well as I'd have expected. He wasn't feeling too good today, and Liz kept him home from school." Greg felt momentarily embarrassed that he hadn't known, but Liz would have called him if it had been anything serious.

He finished dictating his discharge summaries and headed for his office. The afternoon was balmy and mild, so he decided to leave the car in the hospital parking lot and walk over. It was only a couple of blocks away, and he enjoyed the fresh air, swinging his arms as he walked. The magnolias looked ready to burst into flower any moment now. Greg let his mind take a quick and rare vacation as he passed between his two places of work; he'd almost forgotten that a part of his brain knew how to enjoy the sights and sounds and scents of spring.

By the time he stepped inside his office, he felt clear-eyed, healthy, full of vitality and energy.

Louella was holding the phone out to him, saying, "Here he comes, Miz Hopkins, right now, in through the door."

Greg took it, mildly surprised. Liz rarely called him at the office; maybe she wanted him to pick up something on the way home.

"Greg?" Liz's voice was shaking, and a sudden cold fear grabbed Greg. "Greg, you need to come home now!"

"Liz, what's the matter? What—"

"Just come."

Greg was left holding the phone. He hesitated for a second, then turned and ran out of the office, down the street past the magnolias, which looked different now, menacing. He was out of breath by the time he got into his car, and his hand was shaking when he put the key in the ignition. He wheeled out of the parking lot, caught a rear tire on the curb. It bumped and squealed, then he was around the corner and heading fas toward the main street. He had to slow down going through the center of town, and the lights were against him at the corner of Main and Cypress. What on earth could be the matter? His hands gripped the steering wheel like a vise, and he could feel the tightness of the skin on his face. Liz? Greg felt sure she hadn't called about herself. Oh, my God, he thought, something's happened to Edward. He zoomed through the crossing, passed a small truck, and just avoided a car coming in the other direction. He could hear the angry sound of horns fading behind him. *Settle down, don't panic*, he told himself. *It won't help anybody if you get killed on the way home.*

He was out of the car almost before it skidded to a stop outside his house. Liz was waiting for him. His heart pounding, he ran toward her, searching her face for clues. She didn't give him time to say anything.

"Come upstairs, Greg!" and she strode ahead of him. Christ, it *must* be Edward. He followed her up, breathless with fear, but she went right past Edward's room to Douglas's door. Liz opened it, and he followed her in. There was nobody there, and he looked at her first with surprise then with a growing annoyance. What was this, some kind of joke? Liz got down on her hands and knees in front of Douglas's chest of drawers. She opened the bottom drawer and pulled it so far out, it almost dropped on the floor.

"Look at this," she said, turning her head toward him. At the back of the drawer was an open cardboard box half full of small transparent plastic envelopes. Also in the box was what looked like a bankbook and a notebook tied together with a rubber band. For a moment he stared, not comprehending, then he almost gagged.

"Oh, Christ," he breathed. "Is that what I think it is?"

For answer she pulled the box out, almost spilling the contents, and put it on the bed where he could reach it. Greg gingerly pulled out one of the small envelopes and held it up. Inside was a white powder, just enough to bulge the envelope slightly. He glanced at Liz, then opened it, took a little of the powder and tasted it, and made a face.

"It's cocaine, I'm pretty sure," he said.

"I figured it was something like that," replied Liz. She sat down rather suddenly on the bed. He sat down beside her, numb with shock, the cardboard box on his knee. He put his foot in the center of the open drawer and pushed, but it stuck, and he had to reopen it and ease it back into the closed position. Just doing that simple job helped, but only for as long as he was doing it. The two of them looked at the box as if it contained a time bomb.

"Where do you think he got this stuff?" Greg jumped up off the bed. "Who the fuck sold it to him? Was it at school? Who would sell dope to a fourteen-year-old kid? I'd like to—"

"Greg, I don't think that's the whole problem." Liz was white-faced but calm. This was the first time she'd really needed Greg to help her deal with a problem involving any of the children, and so far he wasn't doing too well. How would he cope when he learned the rest of it?

She picked up the bankbook and the little notebook, took off the rubber band, and handed them to him. Greg opened the bankbook, noting that it was in Douglas's name and was with the Hudson Savings Bank, not the one the Hopkinses normally used. It had a lot of entries, the first dated about nine months before. The sums varied in size, from $50 to

$250. Greg turned the pages. The balance as of two days before was $3,284.

"Not bad for a kid that . . ." At the same moment that Liz thought, God, he still hasn't understood, Greg's eyes opened wide with realization. He reached for the notebook, and his hands shook as he flipped the pages. It contained a list of names, written in Douglas's round, childish handwriting. Opposite each name was a dollar amount. There were several pages of this: a lot of names, most of them appearing several times.

He threw the notebook into the box and put his head down between his hands.

"He's been selling that stuff, Greg, not just using it."

There was a long silence, eventually broken by Greg. "What are we going to do?"

"Greg, that's why I called you to come back here. I don't know."

"Where is he?"

"At school, as far as I know. He went on the bus with Elspeth this morning."

Greg looked at his watch. Every fiber of him wanted to get out of this, out of this dreadful, unfamiliar nightmare of questions without answers; problems without the clear and clinical solutions he had been trained to deal with. "I have patients to see," he said without looking at Liz. "A dozen of them were already there when I left the office."

Liz said nothing but looked at him steadily with her clear eyes. There seemed to be a message there, but he couldn't, or wouldn't, read it.

"Well, there's nothing I can do here," he said, his voice raised defensively. "Let me think about it. Why don't you put all that stuff back in the drawer and we can talk it over when I get home."

"Okay, Greg," said Liz resignedly. "Go back to your office. I'll take care of all this."

Greg got up quickly. At the door he hesitated and looked back at her. Liz was putting the rubber band back around the bankbook and notebook. "I'll put it all in my own closet and lock it up," she said.

"Yes, right," he replied.

Liz waited until she heard the sound of the car reversing out of the driveway, then she took the box back into their bedroom and locked it in the top of the old armoire that had originally belonged to her great-grandfather. She looked at the old, faded sepia photo of him on the dresser, standing stiff and proud in his frock coat and square-cut beard with her grandparents and her mother, then only a swaddled bundle of lace and baby blankets. *They would be really proud of me,* she thought bitterly, *bringing up a son to be a drug dealer.*

Liz felt an ache throughout her entire body. Greg had let her down completely. If ever there had been a time for him to pick up the reins, figure out a plan of action and deal with the problem, this was it. And he'd just left her holding the bag as usual and gone back to the safe haven of his office to solve other people's problems instead.

Almost without realizing she was doing so, Liz went downstairs and made herself a cup of coffee and began to feel better. Greg would probably come up with a solution; he just needed a little time. At this point, as the director, manager, and mother of the family, she had absolutely no idea what to do next about her son, Douglas the drug dealer, probable user, possible addict.

Liz was startled by the sound of somebody coming down the stairs. Then she remembered that Edward hadn't gone to school; he must have been asleep during the time Greg was home. Liz felt embarrassed; even in that big house, she could usually tell when there was somebody else there. For a moment she wondered if Edward knew anything about Douglas's activities but thought it unlikely. Douglas was naturally secretive, and anyway, the two of them barely spoke to each other.

Edward just wanted something to drink; he felt okay, he said, just tired. He was going back upstairs to bed. Liz watched him go; he'd changed a lot in the last few weeks. All his energy seemed to have gone. Maybe he was just growing too fast; that was what Mrs. Mackintosh, his homeroom teacher, had suggested. Anyway, she was very glad that Willie was going to take a look at him. If there was anything really the matter, he'd find out.

Half an hour later Elspeth and Douglas came home from school, both hungry. After she'd given them each a big peanut butter and jelly sandwich they went upstairs. Liz hadn't been able to look Douglas in the eye, but he hadn't seemed to notice. She still hadn't the faintest idea what to do about him. She hoped Greg would have figured out something by the time he came home.

Suddenly there was a terrible noise from upstairs; she could hear Elspeth screaming and Douglas shouting in his hoarse, pubescent voice. She ran to the foot of the stairs and shouted up, "What's going on up there?" The noise went on. She heard Douglas use what the children called a swear, but it was the tone of his voice that struck fear into her. He sounded totally insane. Elspeth screamed again, and Liz ran upstairs, her heart in her mouth.

The noise was coming from Edward's room, and when she ran in, she couldn't believe her eyes. First she saw Elspeth, pounding on Douglas's back, and then she saw that Douglas had Edward by the throat and looked as if he were trying to choke him to death. She ran across the room and yanked him off, and he stood looking at her with an expression of such ferocity, her heart trembled. This was her son?

"What's going on?" she asked breathlessly. "What's all this about?"

"He's stolen stuff from my room!" said Douglas, pointing at Edward, who was rubbing his neck and looking as if he were going to be sick. "That asshole thief!" He started to go for Edward again, and Elspeth burst into tears.

"Don't you touch him," Liz shouted at him, "or God help me, I'll break your neck!"

Douglas paused and looked at her, his eyes glittering. Liz knew that if he'd had a gun, he'd have shot her dead right there and then.

"If it's the drugs you're talking about," Liz said, "I took them." Douglas gaped for a moment, then slouched toward the door.

"Fucking thief," he muttered as he passed her. She raised her hand menacingly, and he ran down the corridor. Nobody moved until they heard the door of his room slam behind him.

Liz sat down on the bed beside Edward, and Elspeth burst into tears again. All three hugged each other wordlessly. When she finally raised her head, Liz found her face was wet with tears too.

After she'd settled the children, Liz went downstairs and sat by the phone, her mind in a turmoil. Then she dialed New York City information. Even after they'd given her the number, she still hesitated, but finally she picked the phone up again, as if it were made of some contaminated substance. He was there, and the receptionist put her through immediately.

"Willie? I hate to bother you, but I need your help." After she'd told him everything that had happened, Willie was silent for a moment. She pictured him at the other end, tapping a pencil on his desk.

"Okay, Liz," he said finally, and a wave of relief spread over her even before he said anything more. His tone told her that he knew what to do. "I'll take care of it, and I'll get back to you. Don't worry, it'll all work out all right."

He put down the phone. He knew that Liz must be in desperate straits to call him like this. What was Greg doing? Why didn't *he* take care of it? Suddenly Willie felt profoundly sorry for her, and then for himself. They both deserved better than they'd got. As it happened, Ellen's parents were in New York, visiting their daughter. Willie reached for the phone: Angelo, his father-in-law, would know how to deal with this kind of stuff.

It was after nine before Greg got home, and he slunk in like a criminal. Sure, he'd been busy, but he could have made it back sooner. It was simply that he couldn't face up to it; he couldn't even think about Douglas at all. Throughout the afternoon he'd been doing things to take his mind off it; if he'd had Douglas's music system, he'd have had it on so loud it hurt, just so he wouldn't be able to think about the boy.

Liz took the heat off him at once. She seemed surprisingly calm.

"I had a talk with Chief Grunwald," she said gently, as if they'd previously agreed that she should do that. "He wants us to keep Douglas out of school tomorrow, and he'll come by the house about ten."

Greg's jaw dropped. "Grunwald? My God, he'll put him straight into jail! You know how he is about drugs, especially in the schools."

Liz smiled. "I've been on the phone a lot this afternoon. I think it's going to work out all right."

Greg looked at her silently for a few moments, in some awe.

He didn't want to know who she'd called, or who she'd spoken to. If she said it was going to be okay, he had perfect confidence in her ability and judgment.

"Do you think I should stay home? I mean, tomorrow, when Grunwald comes?"

"If you can, yes, I think it would show him that you care, that you're concerned."

"I'll be here," said Greg hurriedly. "Of course I'll be here."

They went to bed soon afterward, but for some reason they stayed apart and didn't touch each other at all. Liz lay awake a long time, feeling bruised and angry, both at herself and at Greg. She felt that calling on Willie Stringer for help had been a betrayal of her family, an admission of failure. And it had made her even more vulnerable to Willie. Liz could feel the warmth of Greg's body, sleeping quietly beside her. Why couldn't he take some responsibility for the family; why did he always leave it all to her? Because that's the way he is, she thought. As long as everything's going smoothly, Greg does just fine. He can't see why things *shouldn't* run smoothly, and he can't bear to be angry with people or have them angry at him. He always sees the good side in people, he is always anxious to help them. Maybe by helping them so well, he feels that it's an insurance policy that will protect him. Poor Greg; for him it's peace at any price.

She sat up suddenly, her fists clenched. This family could only afford one weak member. There was nothing she could do now about the present situation; she couldn't prevent Chief Grunwald from coming the next day, and she couldn't take back her call to Willie Stringer. But sure as hell she could prevent something like this from happening again.

CHAPTER
SEVENTEEN

"Douglas?"

Greg waited uncertainly outside his son's room. He'd gotten up early so he could be back when Kurt Grunwald, the police chief, came at ten, but then he realized he hadn't spoken to Douglas since Liz had uncovered his drug cache, so he padded down the corridor in his bare feet, meaning to . . . well, he wasn't quite sure what he meant to do, but he had a feeling of sadness and compassion for the boy, even if he didn't know quite how to express it.

He stood outside Douglas's door for a moment, listening, then cautiously turned the knob. It was locked, a major breach of family rules. Greg hesitated again. There wasn't really any point in waking the boy up, because he didn't know what to say to him, and it would just make him angry.

Greg went quietly back to shave and get dressed before going down to the kitchen to make himself a quick cup of coffee. He gulped it down, rinsed out the mug, put it on the empty drain board and took his car keys down from the hook.

He didn't hear the telephone; it started to ring as he was getting into his car. Backing down the drive, he felt like a burglar leaving the scene of the crime. He decided to stop off at the hospital before going to the office; there was an ambulance outside the emergency room, next to a couple of cars he didn't recognize. In the distance Greg could hear the sound of a police siren.

He went through the double doors. A small crowd of shouting people, mostly black women, stood around the nurses' station, and a smaller crowd of men, also black, stood around one of the cubicles.

"Here he is!" somebody yelled.

"Over here!"

"Keep that bitch away from me!" An agonized howl.

Greg could see poor old Mrs. Franklin behind the desk, overwhelmed by the women milling around her. *There must be somebody in the cubicle,* he thought. *I'll start there.* He pushed his way through the men, who didn't exactly block his way, but didn't get out of his way, either. A long, thin, scarecrow of a man was sitting on the examining table, trembling, holding a towel with both hands over his face.

"What's the matter with you?"

One of the men with him, also lanky, with big angry yellow eyes, hesitated and said, "She sucked on 'im, her back there. While he was asleep." He indicated a woman who was shouting the loudest, a big, bony creature wearing a tattered man's shirt.

"Let's take a look."

The man's arms became rigid and he wouldn't let Greg remove the towel. "Selly, tell this guy to get the fuck away from me." His voice was muffled from the towel.

"It's the doc, Elton. He's gotta see it, man!"

Behind him, the women started shouting again, and Greg bent down and spoke into his ear so Elton could hear him over the din.

"I can't help you if I can't see it."

Suddenly Elton pulled the towel partly away from his face, and Greg took a shocked step back. The man's right eyeball was hanging wetly down his cheek, held only by a whitish string, a bloody white glob stuck to the towel. The socket was a hole full of dark blood and shreds of tissue.

The tall black took one look, made a strangling noise, pushed back toward the nurses' station, and within seconds the fight was breaking out anew, the women screaming and pummeling him while the other men joined in the fray.

"Stay right where you are!" said Greg, pushing Elton back as he tried to join in again. He looked around for some help, but he could only see Mrs. Franklin. He shouted at the tall black. "Hey, Selly! Come over here! I need some help with Elton!"

Selly pushed his way back, out of breath, grinning, a long scratch mark now bleeding down his cheek.

"Here, hold this." Greg gave him a basin to hold while he poured it almost full of saline. Selly had to pay attention not to let it spill.

"Put your hands down," Greg told Elton. He turned to another of the men, a huge fellow with a gold ring in his ear. "I have to clear this up or it's going to get infected. You hold his arms. I don't want to lose an eye too."

The man hesitated, then rumbled with a bass laugh. "You're funny, for a honkie."

Somehow the situation seemed now to be defused, and when the police came crashing in a few minutes later, the group had quieted down and were either sitting in the waiting area or were looking on while Greg irrigated the socket.

"Any problems, Doc?" asked the sergeant suspiciously.

"This guy needs to go to Stamford," said Greg, putting on some Vaselined gauze and then an eye patch. "We can't take care of him here."

Greg washed his hands, went upstairs to do his rounds, then walked over to his office. The incident with Elton's eye had put him back half an hour, and when he looked at his watch, it was a few minutes to ten.

Kurt Grunwald was already there when he got home. He'd come in his own car rather than a police department vehicle; a thoughtful gesture. He was sitting in the kitchen; Liz had given him a cup of coffee, but the atmosphere seemed strained. Grunwald was not in uniform but in a dark business suit and tie. Greg looked at his stocky, muscular figure, pale blue eyes under surprisingly bushy blond eyebrows, and his military-style haircut. Greg didn't remember seeing him before. He must be in his early forties, Greg thought, and in good shape. His skin was Nordic, smooth, like soft, evenly tanned leather, with a few deep creases.

He looked relieved when Greg appeared. They shook hands.

"I'm glad your boy Douglas is going to help us with our controlled-substances problem," he said, sounding as if he were reading from a script. "As you know, the situation is getting steadily worse here in our public schools, and we're determined to stamp it out."

Greg stole a fast glance at Liz. She was looking steadily at Grunwald, concentrating on his face to keep her misery from climbing up into her conscious mind.

"I was just asking Mrs. Hopkins for some details," he said. His voice was wary, flat. "I'd like to see the box containing the alleged controlled substances, please." He sounds like a born law enforcer, thought Greg. Next he'll be calling Douglas a perpetrator.

"Sure, I'll fetch it," said Liz, putting down her mug. There was a brief, uncomfortable silence while Liz was out of the kitchen.

"Can I get you some more coffee?" asked Greg.

"Thanks, no, I'm fine," he said. Greg filled his own mug from the coffee machine.

Liz returned with the cardboard box and put it on the counter in front of the policeman. He opened it, pulled out one of the plastic envelopes, and did just as Greg had done. He put a tiny fragment of the powder on his finger and licked it.

"Yeah, right," he said. They watched him flick through the bankbook. He took rather more time with the notebook full of names, turning the pages slowly.

"I'll take this with me, if you don't mind," he said finally, putting the notebook in his coat pocket. "Of course, I'll be taking the substances with me too." He didn't crack a smile. "How long has this been going on, do you know?" His eyes swept from Greg to Liz and stopped there.

"We had no idea until yesterday when I was cleaning up his room," replied Liz. "But the dates in the book would suggest it's been going on for about nine months or so."

"Yes, well, I think it's time for us to have a chat with Douglas. I'm assuming he's here?"

"I'll go and get him," said Greg, putting down his coffee mug. He looked at Liz. Yes, she said with her eyes, he's up in his room.

"Why don't I come up with you," murmured Grunwald, and he followed Greg through to the hall and then up the stairs.

Douglas was behind the door; he'd heard the voices in the kitchen, and now the carpeted footsteps coming toward him down the corridor. It sounded like two people. *Shit*, he thought, *they're coming to take me to jail.* His bowels tightened painfully and he started to shake. He looked around the room. He couldn't get out either of the windows because he'd fall on the ledge around the basement. The footsteps stopped outside the door and Douglas held his breath.

"Douglas? Open the door, please. Chief Grunwald from the police department is here, and he wants to talk to you." It was only his father. Well, he knew how to handle him. If he just kept quiet long enough, his father would eventually just sigh and go away, back to his fucking patients.

Douglas sat down on the bed.

His father started to say something, but then a hard, scary voice Douglas had never heard before spoke up. The guy sounded as if his mouth were right up against the door.

"Douglas, this is Police Chief Grunwald. I'm giving you twenty seconds to get out of your room. Then I'm going to kick this door down and take you down to the department in handcuffs. I'm warning you now, you may get roughed up in the process."

Without knowing exactly why, Douglas leapt off the bed and quickly unlocked the door. He was unable to disobey that man's voice. It wasn't really that the guy terrified him, it wasn't so much that. That wasn't why he opened the door; the fucker sort of hypnotized him into doing it.

"What do you want?" Douglas was angry even at his own voice; it was halfway between a real voice and a whisper.

"Put on a shirt and come down to the kitchen," ordered Grunwald, turning on his heel and marching back along the corridor. Douglas emerged from his room like a badger leaving his lair, and followed him. Greg brought up the rear. Douglas didn't even look at the weak-kneed asshole.

In the kitchen, Douglas sat away from the counter, at bay, head down, bristling with silent resentment. Liz watched, agonized, biting the knuckles of her left hand.

From Grunwald's point of view the interview went surprisingly well. First he wanted to know whether Douglas was using the drugs himself. Douglas shook his head. Grunwald took a step closer to Douglas.

"When I ask you a question, you answer—you hear?" His voice was quiet but menacing.

"I don't use the stuff." Douglas's voice was a bare whisper, and it tore at Liz's heart to hear him like this.

"Have you ever used any controlled substances?"

"I sniffed some coke about six months ago. One time, maybe twice. I don't remember."

Then Grunwald wanted to know who Douglas's suppliers were but didn't sound surprised when Douglas said he only knew their first names.

"What type of vehicles do they use? Make and model? Connecticut registrations?" Then he wanted to know the routine for picking up what he kept on calling the "substances," how often they came, which day of the week.

Douglas answered sullenly, but as accurately as he could.

Once he looked up and said, "If they find out I told you all this, I'm going to get hurt bad." Liz caught her breath. This could become even worse than she'd expected.

"This information will be kept strictly confidential," replied Grunwald stiffly. Looking at him, Greg knew he wouldn't lift a finger to help Douglas if they came after him.

He pulled out the little notebook with the names of Douglas's customers and went over each name with him before putting it back in his pocket.

Finally he got up. "Stand up, you!" he said to Douglas in his crisp, flat voice. Surprised, Douglas stood up. "You have admitted to a major felony, and if I had my way, I'd have thrown the book at you. But because your parents have powerful and influential friends, I've been ordered to handle this differently." The contempt in his voice was so biting that both Liz and Greg cringed. Douglas showed no sign of even noticing. "But let me tell you"—he pointed a finger in Douglas's face—"if I ever hear your name connected again with any kind of drug problem, I will personally see you get sent down for the maximum number of years. Do you understand?"

Douglas nodded, looking like a whipped dog.

"One more thing." They all braced themselves. "I want you to give the money in this account to a charity. Any one you like. Send me the receipt as soon as you get it, okay?" Without waiting for a reply, Grunwald dropped the bankbook on the counter and picked up the cardboard box. "Thank you, Dr. Hopkins, and you, Mrs. Hopkins, for the coffee," he said. He didn't offer to shake hands when Greg let him out through the front door.

Nobody moved until Grunwald's car was clear of the driveway. Then Greg looked at Liz.

"Go up to your room, Douglas," he said. "I need to talk to your mother. Then I need to talk to you."

Douglas suddenly felt his courage coming back. "How come you need to talk to me now? Why didn't you ever talk to me before? Don't tell me, I know—you're too busy taking care of your fucking patients!" He pushed past his mother, who had taken a step toward him, and ran upstairs to his room.

Greg put his head between his hands, and Liz put a comforting hand on his shoulder.

"It could have been worse," she said, trying to smile. "I think Chief Grunwald put the fear of God into him, don't you?"

Greg nodded. Liz looked thoughtfully at him. "Did you notice how much Grunwald hated us? Not just Douglas, but you and me too?"

Greg raised his head, surprised. "Gee, I didn't get that impression at all. What was that he was saying about influential friends, by the way?"

"He must have meant Willie Stringer," she said, and then could have bitten her tongue. "I called him yesterday," she explained, "and Grunwald called me an hour or so later." Liz paused. "I think Willie must have talked to Ellen's father." And his father-in-law would have done the rest. Typical Willie Stringer. In spite of her annoyance, Liz had to laugh. He always used others to do his dirty work. This time, anyway, the end seemed to have justified the means.

Douglas slammed the door of his room behind him and locked it. The fuckers! His fucking parents, smirking and toadying to that fucking cop. Another cup of coffee, sir? Yes, sir, of course he's guilty, why don't you take him away and string him up by his balls? We don't want him, he's just a nuisance around here. He doesn't do his homework; no use around the house; please, we'll pay you to take him away. . . .

Looking in the mirror above the sink, Douglas made a face, the face he should have made to that cop. He dropped his pajama pants and took out his penis. Good and hard all of a sudden. It was the only thing in his life that seemed to work well. He watched himself in the mirror; his face got hot and red with the exertion. He thrust out his pelvis and worked on it like a maniac. The edge of the sink was cold against his thighs, but soon he didn't notice. It didn't take long; he squirted almost up to the mirror and left it dripping a thick yellow-white down to the top of the sink.

"Fuck you *all!*" he screamed at the top of his voice. He went over to his sound system and turned it up to full volume, until the windowpanes rattled in the frames. The noise was so loud it hurt, and that was the way he wanted it. He fell on the bed. The tears came from some hollow place in his chest and wouldn't stop.

CHAPTER
EIGHTEEN

"So how did it go?" Willie was calling Liz from the hospital between cases. Liz wasn't too pleased to hear his voice.

"Well, it could have been worse. He's a tough character, your friend the police chief." It was eleven in the morning and Liz was about to leave for the supermarket.

"Yes, so I've heard." Liz could hear the paging system in the background.

"Willie, you got to him through Ellen's father, didn't you?"

There was a brief silence. "Well, sure. He was the obvious person. There wasn't anything I could do myself."

"I understand that, but Grunwald was very resentful about having that kind of pressure put on him, and he as much as said so."

"Don't worry about it," said Willie airily. "As long as the problem's taken care of and Douglas isn't in jail . . ."

"Sure, but I don't like to have our local chief of police feeling that we've pulled a fast one on him, either."

"Hey, listen, that kind of thing's all in the day's work for those guys. It happens all the time. If he didn't know how to handle it, he wouldn't be the chief. Anyway, how did Douglas take it?"

"Pretty well, I think. He seemed pretty subdued, but he was almost friendly at breakfast this morning."

"Hold on a second . . ." There was a muffled conversation at the other end, then Willie said, "Liz, I have to go, they're waiting for me in the OR." He paused for a second. From his voice Liz could tell he was holding the phone close to his mouth. "You know how I felt when I saw you at your house, and I think you felt the same way."

"Now, Willie, we're going to have to talk about that . . ." Liz felt her resolve leaking away. She couldn't keep her voice steady, and Willie heard the resonance.

"I thought so," he said. "Which day is Edward coming for his endoscopy? You'll be bringing him, of course?"

"Tuesday. That's what you told Greg, anyway. Tuesday, eight A.M., nothing to eat after midnight, no breakfast, right?"

"Can you get away for lunch?"

"Sure. With Edward, of course." Liz smiled to herself. She knew Willie Stringer better than anybody in the world, and all the tricks he could get up to. She wasn't going to give in without a fight, not this time.

"Sure, bring him along, by all means." That was a surprise. The old Willie would have told her to dump Edward on one of her friends living in Manhattan. "He seems a real nice kid."

"You didn't see enough of him to tell," replied Liz sharply. "But thanks anyway." There was another pause, this time longer. Finally Liz said in a strained voice, "You haven't said anything about Patsy."

"Patsy? God, she's beautiful. It was really a shock. She looks so much like you, I almost asked her if she'd like to slip upstairs for a roll in the hay!"

"Willie, that's not funny." Liz knew he was joking, but she still didn't like it. "Listen, you'd better go and do your case or they'll finish it without you."

"See you Tuesday. Wear something green . . . you know I always liked you in that color."

Liz hung up and slowly returned to her present world. She felt the smile that had grown while she was talking to Willie fade from her face. She picked her shopping list up off the kitchen counter and absently read it through. Willie the Great. He still wore Camelot like an aura around him, just as he had when they were all students. Maybe it was because the only two men she'd ever loved were Willie and Greg, so she didn't have much to compare him with.

And for so long he'd been Willie the Bastard; Liz could not understand that she could possibly love him again, after what he'd done to her. Love him! She must be insane even to think of using that word in relation to him, but it kept coming back into her mind like the marching song of an approaching army, getting louder by the minute.

"I'll cure myself of this," she said grimly, not even aware that she'd spoken out loud. She took the keys to the station wagon and picked up the small stack of grocery coupons from the top of the refrigerator. "I'll remember every detail of what that bastard did to me. That should do it." Even as she said the words, she knew it was at least in part an excuse to think about Willie without feeling guilty.

She headed toward the shopping plaza a couple of miles out of town. The gas gauge showed almost empty; she'd have to fill up on the way there. Willie Stringer . . . Her mind felt a kind of contentment when that topic was programmed into it; it belonged there, somehow, although it had been forcibly evicted eighteen years ago.

A whole year she'd gone with him, the most exciting year of her life. Now—although she wouldn't have changed anything, not at this point—her life seemed numb in comparison, and nothing since those times had even approached the heights of ecstasy and happiness she'd felt then. They had both been so busy, Willie in medical school and she learning the cello and composition. When Willie had called, she'd run; when he'd said jump, she'd asked how high? And it was so out of character for her. Liz shook her head. All the other men in her life had always jumped for *her*; maybe that was why she'd never felt the same way about anybody else.

Liz passed a yellow school bus going the other way, and it brought her mind back to her children. She was getting to be like Greg, thinking about them only when they had problems. Elspeth goes along her sturdy way so well that maybe she misses out on attention; but she's Greg's little girl, and she doesn't seem to be suffering. Patsy was the same, maybe a bit wilder, more like her mother when she was that age. Liz laughed. Patsy tells all, and she's so funny about it. The girl goes through boys like a chain-smoker through cigarettes. *By the time I learn their names, she's on to the next one, or the one after.*

All these thoughts about Elspeth and Patsy were part of an avoidance system Liz's mind had worked out without her permission; it was circling around her two main worries,

Edward and Douglas. Actually, although she was concerned about Edward, everything with him seemed pretty well under control, and the fact that Willie was overseeing the situation took the load off her mind. But Douglas . . . A weight settled in the pit of her stomach. What were they going to do about him? Although there had been a slight improvement in Douglas's attitude since they'd found his drug cache, he still had that sulking arrogance when he was around her, and he vanished into his room when his father was home. What was going to happen to him? Liz knew perfectly well that if Douglas wanted to go on with his drug dealing, he would do so, regardless of the consequences; there was no way they could really stop him. He would have to want to stop on his own. They'd talked to him, of course, but he refused even to discuss any kind of outside counseling.

Liz's train of thought was broken when she came within sight of the gas station. She hesitated; for some reason she never liked filling up—it was like going to the dentist or the beauty parlor, basically a waste of time. But the needle was well into the red zone. She slowed down and pulled in.

A boy about Douglas's age came out, wiped the windshield, and checked the oil while the tank was filling. Liz didn't know whether to worry more about Douglas or about Edward. There was something that nagged her about Edward, more intuition than anything, but he wasn't eating properly and she was sure he was losing weight. His color wasn't quite right, either; sometimes, especially in daylight, there was a yellowish tinge around his eyes. . . .

"Your oil's okay, Mrs. Hopkins!" said the kid. Liz smiled and passed her Visa card to him. Maybe he was one of Douglas's friends; except Douglas didn't have any.

Back in the traffic, Liz remembered that she was going to do a rerun on Willie, and it was going to hurt, which was why she'd been putting it off, thinking about her children instead.

Willie Stringer. Willie the Lover Boy, Willie the King. King of Assholes. One whole year. They'd even been talking about getting married, or at least he had. Her father, who'd happened to be out of jail at the time, wasn't too impressed with the idea. Not trustworthy, he said. He should know. He must have recognized one of his own kind. . . .

Willie and Ellen. She'd never even thought of them as a possibility. That showed how innocent and ignorant she must have been then. At least he'd married her. Liz wondered what he'd seen in her then, and whether he still saw it. And now . . . what was Willie up to with her? Was he really making moves toward her, or was he just putting it on, out of habit? What could he possibly want out of it? An affair? With him in New York and her up in Connecticut? Without meaning to, Liz started to calculate how long it would take for her to get into New York, spend two or three hours there, and come back.

She turned her mind back resolutely to the moment when she walked in on Willie and Ellen, hoping that it would harden her heart against him, but instead, and totally against her will, she started to laugh at the memory of their startled expressions.

And then Edinburgh. Her aunt had been as nice as she could be, but those first few months had been just heartbreaking. So many times she had gotten as far as the travel agency, ready to go back to Willie whatever the cost, whatever the humiliation.

Liz shuddered at the mere recollection. After that her memories were much more blurred. Having the baby, and then, when she couldn't get work because she didn't have a permit, she'd come back, and New York had been like a new world. Meeting Greg like that, when she'd only come into the city to collect her transcripts . . . it still hurt when she thought about it, talking to Greg and wondering why it wasn't Willie who'd bumped into her; but he'd been so kind when she told him that story about her husband dying in a plane crash. And it had been quite a story, my God, the new Cessna, the storm, cloud-enshrouded hills, defective instruments. And when Greg had told her that Willie was married, she was sure she was going to faint—although she'd already decided she'd never see Willie again.

Liz finished her shopping in a retrospective haze. The best thing about domestic drudgery was that you never really had to put your mind to it. You could have two separate lives, one doing the laundry, the housekeeping, and the cooking, while the other went on uninterrupted inside your head. There was no reason the two should ever have to meet.

When she got home, she left the shopping bags on the counter. The children had heard her arrive and came down, all talking at once as usual, and she packed them back upstairs to do their homework. Liz went into the living room, where she liked to play her cello; the room had a better resonance than her old sewing room, and she now had enough confidence again to play in a big room. The cello case leaned against one of the tall windows, looking like a small, portly drunk. Every time she opened the old-fashioned wooden case, there were the tiny, threadlike scars of Willie's meticulous repair, and she could see him as if it were yesterday, working on the floor of her apartment with his little tubes of resin, totally absorbed, getting each tiny fragment back into its proper place.

Liz had started to play seriously again, and she could feel the expertise coming back into her fingers. Her bowing had improved, and there was a new sureness to her strokes. She was able to make music again, almost like the old days, without being hobbled by deficiencies in her technique. And when she played pieces she knew well, she could feel her spirit soaring free with the topmost notes, like Nils Holgerson, the little boy in the Swedish fable, flying up and away on the back of a goose.

Greg came in through the kitchen, and she stopped playing. "Please, don't stop, I love to hear you," he said. "I'll just put the groceries away." He went back into the kitchen and she started again, playing the first movement of the Elgar cello concerto. She could hear him in the kitchen, humming the theme with her. Liz was surprised that he knew it.

He came back in. "You and I are going out to dinner," he said. "Just you and I." As she was about to interrupt, he said, "The kids can eat on their own, for once in their lives." He saw Liz's doubtful expression. "Okay," he said, "we can get Katie Macklin to baby-sit. I'll call her right now."

He came back a few moments later, triumphant. "Katie'll be over at seven," he said. "It's all taken care of."

Liz was surprised. It had been a long time since they'd gone out together, just the two of them. Her spirits lightened; that was just what she needed today: for Greg to reaffirm his loving presence.

They went to Le Coq d'Or, a small but excellent French

restaurant just outside Stamford, and settled down in the red velvet seats.

"Well," said Greg, holding up his martini, "here's to us!"

"Right," said Liz, smiling. Greg remained a mystery to her in so many ways. She'd met Mrs. Parkinson, the nurse, in the supermarket, and had been told, in the most glowing terms, how Greg had single-handedly quelled a near riot in the emergency room.

"I heard about your adventure yesterday," she said. "That must have been quite an event for our little town."

"I was thinking about Willie and Ellen," he said, and Liz tensed. "How did you find Ellen?"

"I thought if I've aged that much, no wonder you're never home!"

"She's sick, don't you think?"

"Well, if she is, Willie can surely take care of it," replied Liz a little curtly. She had no intention of spending the evening talking about Willie and Ellen. "Honestly, I'm more concerned about Edward."

"He'll be all right," said Greg. "Willie's going to look after him."

"I know, but still . . . You know me, with the children I always worry, even when there's not much to worry about."

The waiter came to take their order, and Greg ordered a bottle of Cheval Blanc to go with the lobsters.

"You're pulling all the stops out tonight." Liz smiled. "Are you feeling guilty about something?"

"As a matter of fact, I am," said Greg, looking her straight in the eye. "About Douglas and all that . . . I really didn't help you much, and I feel badly about it."

"Well, so far it seems to have turned out all right," answered Liz. "He's been easier to live with since then."

"I hope it lasts," said Greg. "It's funny how different our kids are, isn't it?"

Liz stared at Greg for a moment, puzzled. Did he really think it was all over, that Douglas's problems were now at an end, just because Grunwald had tried to put the fear of god into him? But she didn't want to touch that one, not right now, anyway; and luckily the lobsters arrived.

Greg was grateful that they didn't come with the standard

New England white plastic aprons. Instead, the waiter tied extra large linen napkins around their necks, with a murmured *"Bon appetit, monsieur et madame!"* in Boston French.

"What I don't understand, Greg," said Liz over coffee, "is how you can be such a hero in the hospital and to your patients, and such a wimp at home."

"Wimp! That's tough talk." He shrugged. "I don't know, I guess I'm trained to take care of certain kinds of problems. I never did a course on how to handle drug problems in the home."

"I think you just dislike real confrontations," said Liz seriously. "You simply don't have it in you to get really angry with anyone for more than a moment or two."

"Well, I suppose there wouldn't be as many wars if there were more people like me." Greg smiled, but Liz knew she was getting a bit close to the bone.

"Sure, that's okay," she went on doggedly. She had to get this off her chest. "But in our present society, what happens is that people trample right over you. Somebody does something bad, like Douglas, and you feel sorry for them, look for excuses, and, I hate to say so, but you can lose their respect."

Greg looked around for the waiter. All this was getting a little heavy, and it wasn't really fair of Liz to be coming up with stuff like this when they were supposed to be having a good time.

On the way home, Liz held his hand, and they listened to a cassette of Jacqueline du Pre playing Bach. Greg had given her the cassette at Christmas, and she treasured it. For the first time in a long time they felt really relaxed and at ease with each other; Greg enjoyed their closeness, and when they went to bed and made love, she found that she didn't think about Willie at all.

CHAPTER
NINETEEN

Liz had every intention of wearing her white-and-black-checked suit when she took Edward to New York for his endoscopy. It was quite elegant and had been expensive, although marked down for the January sales. However, at the last moment she changed her mind and wore her long olive-green suede dress with a dark green belt and matching boots. She hadn't worn this outfit for a while, and Edward thought she looked terrific.

Willie's office was beyond anything either Liz or Edward had ever seen. Once the gilded elevator had taken them smoothly to the second floor, they stepped out onto a dark maroon carpet with a gold stripe along each side. To their left, as the porter had courteously informed them, were the smoked glass double doors that led to his office. Willie's sign was at the side, discreet gold on black, WILBRAHIM M. STRINGER, M.D., F.A.C.S. Liz wondered how many people knew that the *M* stood for Malcolm, after his grandfather.

Liz was about to push the door open when it opened automatically, so smoothly that Liz almost fell into the waiting room. Edward laughed, and some of the patients waiting in the big leather armchairs looked up. Liz was embarrassed, but only for a moment. She straightened her belt and walked across the deep, ivory-colored carpet toward the desk, with Edward following her. Liz would have liked to take her shoes off and feel that carpet with her bare feet. It was soft and thick; it would have been great for rolling around on. Her train of thought stopped abruptly at the receptionist's desk. Only it wasn't a desk but a wide glass table with a telephone console, a notepad, and a computer terminal on it. An attractive young woman wearing a figure-hugging burgundy business suit over a white silk blouse sat in a chromed chair behind it, smiling as they approached. Liz gave her a quick once-over. No problem there, Willie didn't get turned on by blondes. Immediately she felt annoyed with herself; all this seesawing about Willie was getting on her nerves; from one day to the next she didn't know if she hated him or loved him. That was totally out of character for Liz, who normally had pretty good control over herself. And anyway, she was here strictly on business. Family business. Her family's business.

"Mrs. Hopkins?" asked the girl, looking at Liz and then at Edward. Liz nodded, put her handbag on the table, and pulled out her Blue Cross/Blue Shield card and all the other stuff they needed in doctors' offices. Edward looked around, trying to identify the source of the soft, relaxing music that flowed into the waiting room, but he couldn't locate the speakers. The walls were ivory white, the same color as the carpet, with really colorful pictures on the wall, red and black shapes, some with yellow dots on a white background. They didn't seem to represent anything in particular.

"Dr. Stringer asked to be told as soon as you came," said the receptionist, unobtrusively checking out the suede dress with a swift, all-encompassing glance. Liz hoped there weren't any spots on it. The girl picked up the telephone, still smiling at her, pressed one button, and spoke softly into it. Thirty seconds later Willie appeared and came toward them.

"Liz, Edward, nice to see you both!" He didn't take his eyes off Liz, and she felt eaten up by them. "What a nice outfit," he murmured while Edward watched him with his big, thoughtful eyes. Edward was thinking how he'd like some Cocoa Puffs right now; it was only when he wasn't allowed to have breakfast that he missed it.

The endoscopy room was a bit like the place where Edward had his stomach X rays, except not so big. The nurse showed him the long, shiny black flexible tube that Dr. Stringer would be passing down to look inside his stomach. It was about as thick as his thumb, and had little mirrors and a light at the tip. Just the sight of it made Edward want to throw up. He couldn't imagine how that whole tube could ever get down inside him, then he remembered Dr. Davis's drawing; but it didn't make him feel any less apprehensive. Then Vera, the nurse, who was very beautiful and nice, gave him a shot with a tiny needle that he didn't feel, but soon he was feeling sleepy and glad to lie down on the table under the X-ray machine.

Vera woke him up, and before he had time to realize what was happening, Dr. Stringer was pushing that horrible tube down his throat. Edward coughed and gagged and tears came into his eyes; it felt like a huge red-hot pole being pushed down inside him. Vera had to hold him.

"Didn't you premedicate him?" Willie sounded annoyed. He wasn't too familiar with the equipment, which was on loan from the William R. Sheely Surgical Corporation, and it suddenly occurred to him that this was an adult instrument and a bit big for a twelve-year-old boy. And he was in a hurry; he'd slipped this endoscopy into the schedule and he was already running late.

"Yes, I did!" Vera was a little more emphatic than usual. She felt Dr. Stringer was being unnecessarily rough with the boy.

"Suction! Come on, Vera, I can't see a damn thing down here."

Edward subconsciously heard the whirr of an electric motor, but the doctor was hurting him so much, and he couldn't say anything or make a noise. He was choking . . .

"Easy, Edward, it'll be over soon," she whispered, and stroked his face. What a nice-looking kid. She bit her lip. Edward was crying soundlessly, the tears running down his face. Vera could feel her indignation rising. There was no need for the doctor to be so rough.

"Oh, shit!" Stringer's voice was a whisper. "Turn that suction up!" Vera saw the sweat suddenly rise on his forehead, like a sprouting of humid mushrooms. The fluid coming back in the tubing suddenly became red.

"We're in trouble here," said Stringer, his voice unsteady. "He's bleeding; it must have stirred up that ulcer."

Vera's eyes widened; she didn't think the scope was that far in. She looked at the white distance markers etched on the tube. The tube was forty centimeters in from the incisor teeth . . . but she didn't have time to think any more about it, because Stringer was shouting at her for medications and iced saline irrigating solutions. After a few minutes the emergency seemed to be over, the bleeding had stopped, and Stringer very gingerly withdrew the scope.

He said nothing to Vera or to Edward; he just washed his hands and left the room. Vera held on to Edward. Poor kid. Now Stringer would probably have to send him into the hospital.

Liz, sitting reading the most recent *Vogue,* saw him coming but didn't realize for a few moments that anything was wrong.

"Liz, we just had a minor emergency in there."

Liz could see that his hands were trembling ever so slightly. She rose from her chair and put a hand up to her mouth. "Oh, my God, Willie, is he all right?" A sudden feeling of doom came over her and she sat down quickly.

"Yes, of course, don't you get upset now." Willie's smile was gentle, reassuring. "He started to bleed from the ulcer and it took a while before it would stop. These things do happen from time to time. It shows how serious the ulcer is, though . . . so I've decided to admit him to the hospital."

"You mean, now? I'll have to call Greg."

"Of course." Willie Stringer had completely recovered his composure. "I was going to call him, anyway." His face became serious. "Liz, I'm warning you that this may require surgery. It was a big ulcer, and as you know, it hasn't responded to the medication. It sounds drastic, I'm aware of that, but it may be the best and the most definitive way of dealing with the problem." Willie listened to the speech he'd given so many times before; now, to him, it sounded almost like a recording.

"Can I go and see him now? Is he awake?" Liz was beginning to feel the dimensions of her fear for Edward; she'd known, she'd *known* there was something really wrong with him.

"Of course." Willie took her arm and squeezed it gently. "He's probably sitting up by now, drinking Coke!"

When Willie called, Greg was in his office. Stunned, he told Willie to go ahead and do whatever was necessary; he'd come down as soon as possible, and Liz should take a hotel room and stay in New York. The girl who'd checked them in took care of it all very efficiently. A room at the Algonquin, a short taxi ride away, would be ready for them.

After that Willie went back to his exam rooms, an ambulance

team came in wheeling a lightweight stretcher, and Edward went off, still too sleepy to feel embarrassed by the curious people who stopped to watch him being hoisted into the ambulance. Numb, Liz went with him, feeling she was participating as an actress in some kind of ghastly dream play.

The jolting when they pushed his stretcher into the back woke Edward up enough to wish that Timmy could have been there too. He would have really enjoyed the ride; they even used the siren most of the way.

At the hospital, Liz had to go to the business office while Edward was taken upstairs to the surgical floor. All he saw for the next ten minutes was a succession of ceiling tiles going by, some with long fluorescent fixtures, others with dark water stains in the corners and, in the elevator, ridged ones with ventilator grilles. To Edward it seemed that traveling on his back, he seemed to go much faster than just walking down a corridor.

There was a brief pause at a desk, while the orderly passed Edward's papers to the nurse. She stood up to see Edward and gave him a big smile, which made him suddenly feel better and less scared. She was just as happy to see him; up here it was geriatric city, with most of her patients incontinent and out of their minds.

"Hi, Edward. My name's Barbara. You'll be going to Room 2104, down at the end of the corridor." She flicked a look at the orderly to be sure he heard. "I'll come down to talk to you in a few minutes."

Edward just got a glimpse of her, and from his position he couldn't see exactly what she looked like, only a bunch of blonde hair and a round pink smile under a cap with a blue rim, but from her voice he knew that he liked Barbara. A few minutes later he was installed between the stiff white sheets of his strange new bed. Now that he had time to think about it, his throat was hurting a lot where the doctor had pushed that tube against it, and he was feeling tired and weak, like the time he'd fainted after running. He looked around his new quarters. On the wall opposite was a picture of a New England lane in the fall, with lots of brown and green and red leaves on the ground. Attached to the bed rail was a little control box with different knobs. He hesitated for a moment, then pushed one of them. The top of the bed started to move up. He spent the next five minutes finding out which button did what, until one of them made a little red light go on over his head. Almost immediately a drawly voice came out of the console. "Can I help you?"

Edward was startled.

"Oh, sorry," he said in his quiet voice. "I was just trying out the buttons."

For answer there was only a click. He wished his mother would come. Maybe she'd gone back home by herself. Suddenly he felt more alone than he ever had in his life, an awful, gnawing, scared feeling rising from somewhere deep inside him. Then the door opened, and a pretty, neat-looking nurse with blonde hair and lovely blue eyes came in. She wasn't very tall, but there was a sort of cheerful compactness about her.

"I'm Barbara," she said. "Do you remember me? I was at the desk." Instantly Edward fell in love. First she fluffed up his pillows, and she had this really nice smell, like flowers or something. She leaned over him and he wished she would stay there forever. Now it didn't matter too much if his mother came or not.

Barbara had a bunch of papers on a clipboard and asked a whole lot of questions about his illness. At first Edward wasn't sure what she was talking about, because he didn't think he'd been ill. But he told her about his X ray, and the medication and the diet, and then about the tube Dr. Stringer had put down inside his stomach. As he told her about it, she sympathetically took his hand in hers. It was soft and strong, and Edward was in heaven. Poor kid, she thought. How come nobody had told his parents about Willie Stringer?

The door opened again, and Edward thought it would be his mother, but it was a doctor in a white coat.

"Is this Edward Hopkins?" he asked Barbara, winking at Edward.

"Sure is. Now you take good care of him, Dr. Wesley," she said. "He's my new boyfriend." Edward blushed and felt embarrassed and delighted.

Barbara got up and went toward the door. "If you need anything, Edward, you just press that button and I'll come running!" She turned to the doctor. "He's Dr. Stringer's patient, Dr. Wesley." Edward didn't see the look that passed between them; he was just hoping she'd be back soon.

Bob flopped down on the chair and grinned at Edward. He was tall, strong-looking, with long legs and dark hair that kept falling over one eye. He asked a lot of questions, even more than Barbara had, then looked in his mouth, his ears, shone a light in his eyes, listened to his chest, and poked around his tummy. He took a lot longer with that, and kept on coming back to a place under his right ribs.

"Take a deep breath again," he said. "This'll be the last time," and pushed his hand up under his ribs. It felt funny, not a pain, but a kind of tightness.

"Liver enlarged two finger-breadths below the right costal margin," Bob wrote in his notebook. He hadn't examined too many twelve-year-olds; maybe that was normal.

Just as Bob finished and had gotten up to go, Liz came in. Bob introduced himself as the resident on Dr. Stringer's service.

"I've just been making friends with Edward," he said. "By the way, has he ever had any kind of illness, like hepatitis or anything?" *Might as well be sure,* he thought. *If it's in Stringer's notes and not in mine, he won't let me forget it.*

Liz thought for a moment. She was in such a whirl that she had to stop and separate the different medical problems her children had had. It was Douglas who'd had the flu so badly. "No," she said finally, "nothing, really, just colds and things like that."

"Good." Dr. Wesley looked relieved. "I don't know exactly what Dr. Stringer's plans are, but—"

"I've just been talking to him," interrupted Liz. "He's going to operate on him tomorrow morning."

CHAPTER
TWENTY

"Jesus!" Willie surveyed the papers strewn around his huge desk and bit his lip. He was not prepared for this; after the flurry of activity with Edward Hopkins, things had gone back to normal and he finished his office hours more or less on schedule. Only then did he have time to look at the day's mail.

The only good thing in it was a credit memo from the laundry service.

The first blow was a package from Myron Lipshultz, of Winkel, Stanley and Lipshultz, his accountants. Willie had the papers spread across his desk; his year-end figures, a decision from the Internal Revenue Service concerning a real-estate limited partnership he'd invested in, and a revised personal income tax return, which required a check, together with his and Ellen's signatures.

A lot of bills seemed to have come in today, and he'd put the usual ones—rent, utilities, telephone, office supplies, and so on—in a pile for the bookkeeper to take care of. Two, however, he put faceup separately on the desk. The first was from his insurance agent for $62,500, which represented the second installment of his annual malpractice premium. The second was from the famous interior decorator who had done the office. Willie had put down $50,000 and the bill was for the balance, $229,321.40. The word *please!* had been written in red at the bottom. The reason it had cost more than twice the estimate was mostly because the contractors had run into structural problems with the walls and ceilings. And with the price of furnishings, it was absolutely going through the roof,

and Tony had been just *livid* about it, but what could he do?
Of course Willie could get the stuff from Macy's, or somewhere,
if it was going to be *too* much of a financial burden.

Willie glanced at his watch. It was five-thirty, but Myron
would probably still be in the office. He looked in his directory
and dialed Myron's direct line. Willie had been in Myron's
office several times; it was even more luxurious than his own.

"Myron? Yeah, fine. . . . Listen, I got your package today.
. . . Yes. . . . A couple of things I didn't understand. What
about that limited partnership? You told me . . . Yes, I know
about that, but how can they make a new law retroactive? If
it's within a year? But surely . . . You invested in it too? I
suppose that should make me feel better. . . . Listen, that tax
bill is just out of sight. I just can't pay it. You should see the
other bills on my desk right now."

Willie's hands were sweating while Myron calmly told him
that he *must* pay the IRS because otherwise they'd come and
put a lock on his office door, impound and sell his furniture,
his car, until they'd made up the money he owed them. Those
guys don't fool around, he said, they're brutal. The decorator
could wait, though, no problem, but the malpractice insurance
should be paid too. Immediately. "Listen," said Myron, beginning to sound rushed, "I have to run. Have I covered everything? Okay, I'm going to be away for three weeks, yeah,
Bangkok, Hong Kong, a couple places. . . . Yeah, deductible,
it's a seminar . . . on the *QE2*, join it in Singapore. . . . Okay,
listen, if you have any problems, Marty Orenstein'll be here, a
fine young accountant we have complete confidence in."

And that wasn't all. There was a letter from some law firm
down on the Lower East Side asking for copies of office notes,
lab reports, X rays, and any other information pertaining to
one Elmo Harris, whose illiterate signature was on a release
form attached to the letter.

For a while Willie couldn't think who Elmo Harris was, then
he remembered the kid who'd been shot in the spleen. Shit,
he hadn't even seen the kid until the next day. Willie suddenly
went cold. Maybe that was why he was suing. Anyway, Willie
had to notify the insurance company immediately, he knew
that. Angrily Willie pounded on his desk. It really wasn't any
fun anymore, being a surgeon.

The thing that concerned Willie as much as anything was his income statement. Both his billings and his receipts were down for the third month running, and there seemed to be an increasing number of billings to Medicaid. This was a disturbing trend; he had a "high-class" practice, and more than just a few Medicaid patients could quickly change its entire character. God help him if people ever thought of him as a Medicaid surgeon!

It must be the house staff, he thought. *They're referring the garbage to me, and the good stuff, the patients with private insurance, are going elsewhere.* Well, maybe it was time for another party for the house staff. That usually helped. They could have it catered, do a bang-up one they would remember for a while. Obviously Ellen wasn't well enough to do it herself.

That thought brought his eye back to the note written in Vera's neat script: "Call Dr. Philip Carrera about Mrs. Stringer." The phone number was there, too, of course; good, efficient Vera. Willie reached for the phone, then hesitated. He'd call tomorrow; he'd already had enough bad news for one day.

As he was about to leave, the phone rang. The girl at the other end sounded surprised when he answered. It was Dr. Janus Frankel's office; would Dr. Stringer be kind enough to stop by tomorrow at eleven?

When Willie got in his car, he patted the steering wheel with both hands and thought about the IRS coming to take it away from him. Ridiculous! But as he started up the ramp all the other problems came down on him and he felt oppressed and tired, and his head started to throb. But it wasn't until he went through a red light and narrowly avoided a bad accident that he realized, for the very first time, that the careful weave of his life was unraveling and his affairs were getting precariously close to being out of control.

On top of everything, just when he needed to have some time off to straighten things out, he had Greg Hopkins's boy to operate on in the morning, and already he was feeling a bit anxious about that.

Edward Hopkins was first on the next day's operating schedule, the young and the old usually getting preference because of the greater risk of dehydration. It also meant that Bob Wesley had to get up half an hour earlier than he'd expected. Liz had called home from the hospital, and Greg had gotten Katie Macklin to spend the night at their house with Elspeth and Douglas. Liz also reached Patsy, who arrived at Grand Central Station around five in the afternoon, and went directly to the hospital. Before leaving for New York, Greg finished at the office, checked that everything was all right at home, and made it to the Algonquin by eight.

Early in the morning Edward was awakened by a nurse he hadn't seen before. She was large and motherly-looking but didn't say much except, "Turn on your side, hon." The injection hurt, but not for long.

Liz and Greg came in with Patsy, but they barely had time to give Edward a quick hug before the stretcher came wheeling up to the door.

"Okay, young fella." The orderly smiled. He was a friendly-looking man with graying hair and a very straight back. "If your name's Edward Hopkins, I'm taking you for a free ride!" He checked the name tag on Edward's wrist, transferred him to the stretcher, and off they went toward the elevator. Patsy walked alongside, keeping a hand on her young brother, who was looking flushed and sleepy. Greg and Liz followed disconsolately behind.

Bob Wesley was at the desk, writing something in a chart, heard the stretcher coming, and looked around as they passed.

"See you downstairs, Edward!" he said, glancing quickly at Patsy. They had to wait several minutes for the elevator, and by the time it arrived, Bob had finished his chart work and joined the little group. Liz was holding Edward's hand and talking to him softly about Timmy and his chances of winning the hundred-meter at the upcoming state championships. Edward's eyes were closed and he was almost asleep, but Liz kept talking to him, her voice low but sounding full of confidence. Her eyes never left his face. Greg wasn't doing so well. His face was ashen, and he didn't say anything because he knew his voice would break. Willie had told him over the phone that the best way of dealing with Edward's bleeding ulcer would be to cut the nerves that controlled the acidity of the stomach (no acid, no ulcer—that seemed to be the ultimate surgical credo, he was hearing it so often these days) and open up the outlet of the stomach.

Patsy couldn't believe that all this was happening to her little brother; surely hospitals and operations and that kind of stuff were for old people. She looked at her father, then at her mother; they were both silently panic-stricken, and it made Patsy's stomach curl up and twist with transmitted fear.

Bob came and joined them. The elevator indicator showed that Number 5 was making its laborious way up toward them.

"Must be tough in an emergency," said Greg, attempting a smile, "waiting by the elevator when somebody's in cardiac arrest ten floors away."

"It's not usually this slow," said Bob, looking at Patsy out of the corner of his eye.

"This operation on Edward, is it really necessary?" Patsy asked him bluntly. He didn't look like the sort of person who would lie to her.

Bob smiled. "If Dr. Stringer says it is, it is," he said, wishing he could feel more confident. He glanced at Edward; his eyes were still closed, but the breathing pattern showed he was awake. "It's the best way of dealing with an ulcer that hasn't improved with medical treatment." The truth depends on which service you're on, he thought. On the medical service he'd have said that Edward should go on a diet and medication for several months before even being considered for surgery, and then only after a very thorough workup to find out why he had an ulcer in the first place.

"If that's what Dr. Stringer thinks, it's okay with us," replied Patsy, looking at her mother, then at Greg. "We all have complete confidence in him."

Her parents nodded, beginning to feel a bit more cheerful. That's right, they thought, Willie knows what he's doing. Everything's going to be okay.

Willie hadn't slept too well, and the traffic made him a few minutes late, none of which improved his disposition. But when he stopped in the OR waiting area on his way to the operating suite, he was his usual able and confident self. Greg, Liz, and Patsy gathered around Willie in a tight, intimate little knot, and Willie put on his usual good preoperative show; he told them the operation would allow Edward to live a normal life without medication or fear of sudden hemorrhages and told them he expected it would take between an hour and an hour and a half.

Patsy put her hand on Willie's arm and saw a sudden strange look appear on her mother's face. "Thank you for taking care of Edward, Willie," said Patsy. "You know how we all appreciate you . . ." Liz immediately put her arms around him and gave Willie a quick hug. Then Greg shook his hand, too choked up to say anything. It was a very emotional moment.

Willie, walking back to the operating room, was surprised at his warmth of feeling for Patsy but immediately put his mind in gear for the operation ahead. Like many surgeons, Willie was able to divorce his personal knowledge of a patient as a breathing, thinking individual during the time he was operating on him. Under the brilliant lights of the operating room, inside the green surgical drapes, Edward, the boy with the soft, hesitant voice and quiet humor, was reduced to a problem, a set of expert technical decisions to be made. Willie seemed to be able to make that separation better than most; the residents said he'd still be cracking jokes if he was operating on his dying mother.

"Are we ready to go?" The tone of his voice told everyone around that he was in a dangerous mood. He glared over the screen at the anesthesiology resident, who obviously wasn't ready; he was still adjusting the ventilator and hadn't given all his medications. But today, everything was going to go at Willie's speed, whether they liked it or not. Without waiting for an answer, Willie picked up the scalpel and made a quick incision from the base of the breastbone, curving it out a lit-tle toward the umbilicus. The drapes heaved as the half-anesthetized Edward moved, unable to scream because of the endotracheal tube in his throat. Bob caught the suction tip before it fell on the floor.

"He's light!" shouted Willie over the screen. Bob and the scrub nurse exchanged a quick, scared glance. Willie grinned at Bob's set expression. "Don't worry, he won't remember a thing about it afterward."

The anesthetist, nervous to be working for Willie Stringer, quickly injected a dose of anectine; that would paralyze the kid so he couldn't move, even if he did feel the pain.

Bob was using electrocautery to stop the bleeding. Willie

sniffed at the spirals of smoke coming from the tiny blobs of charred tissue. Now that the operation had started, he seemed to be relaxing. "Love that smell—reminds me of those summer cookouts on the lawn."

Bob kept his eyes down. Sometimes Willie made him want to throw up. After he'd entered the abdominal cavity and put in an instrument to keep the incision wide open, Willie did his usual cursory laparotomy, checking the internal organs to see if they were normal. Of course, on a twelve-year-old boy, everything was bound to be normal.

"Take a feel, Bob. Tell me what you find." Willie turned away and washed his gloved hands in a bowl of warm saline. Liz, Patsy, the thought of his crippling bills, Ellen, his accountant, the IRS, all came to him in an unwelcome potpourri of disturbing thoughts and feelings, and he felt a faint sense of alarm; operating had always been sacrosanct, an island free of the outside world, and it now seemed in danger of invasion.

Bob put his hand inside and felt around. He remembered the routine: start with the liver, then the gallbladder, the pancreas, the stomach, and the spleen, close to it way out on the right . . . then the large intestine. . . .

"Okay, you've had long enough," said Willie, anxious to put away the demons. "Find anything you didn't expect?"

Bob hesitated for a moment. "I thought the liver was maybe a bit big . . . and the spleen . . ." Bob didn't sound too assured, and anyway, Willie didn't pay any attention. In fact, he probably didn't even hear him, because he was busy under the diaphragm, his fingers dissecting the tissues around the top of the stomach, seeking the two vagus nerves.

"You're going to have to retract hard, Bob," he said. "It's hard to visualize . . . in fact, the best way is to do it by feel. Here, feel the vagus nerves, down at the lower end of the esophagus, one on each side. You can always recognize it, it feels like a piece of string or cord."

Bob put his hand in, but try as he might, he couldn't feel what Willie was trying to teach him.

"Okay. Just retract while I put a right-angle around the nerve." He held out his hand to the technician. "Long scissors . . . silver clips . . . make sure they're in right . . . got it." Willie pulled out a thin piece of floppy, reddish tissue about half an

inch long and put it on a piece of moist gauze. He went back
to get the second nerve, cut it, and retrieved a fragment within
a few minutes. You have to hand it to him, thought Bob,
technically he's damn good.

"Now let's do the pyloroplasty," said Willie, looking at the
clock. His personal best for this type of case was fifty-four
minutes, and if he kept up the pace and Bob didn't get in his
way too much, he might just beat it.

The liver kept getting in the way, slipping out from behind
the retractors, and Bob became more and more convinced that
something was the matter with it. It felt stiff and was yellowish,
the same color as the liver of an old drunk they'd operated on
the week before.

"Wow, look at that vein!" said Bob. Indeed, there was a
whole nest of veins—big, bluish, bulging, and thin—located in
the tissues around the stomach and the spleen.

"Curious," said Willie, looking at the clock again. "Must be
an AV malformation." Bob had never seen one of those, but
he'd read about them. They were knots of swollen blood
vessels, both arteries and veins, hence the name. It was not a
very common finding.

Willie, his fingers flying, exposed the stomach where it
narrowed down to become the duodenum. He cut through the
circular muscle and was able to look into the inside of the
stomach. "See the ulcer?" Bob looked at the red mess and
nodded vaguely. He didn't see any ulcer. In fact, neither did
Willie, but there was no point in going on about it. Anyway,
the operation was almost over. Within ten minutes Willie had
completed the pyloroplasty, and he was ready to close up.

"Finish closing for me, would you, Bob?" he asked after
putting in a few sutures. "I'll go and tell the family that
everything's okay." Willie didn't like closing, anyway; it was too
boring and mechanical. He pulled his gown and gloves off,
dropped them in a bucket by the door, and left. The clock told
him the case had taken only forty-five minutes. Must be damn
near a record.

Willie specialized in dramatic entrances to the waiting room.
Dressed in his greens, he liked to keep his mask on until he
had almost reached the relatives of the patient he'd just
operated on, then rip it off with a flamboyant gesture. Greg,

Liz, and Patsy all got up when he appeared at the door. He stood in front of them, then pulled off his mask, revealing a tired but triumphant expression.

"Everything went just perfectly," he said, and Liz and Patsy hugged him wordlessly. Greg beamed from behind them.

"Didn't take you very long, did it?" he asked admiringly.

"Well, it wasn't the first one I've ever done of those." Willie tried to sound diffident.

"Was it a big ulcer?" asked Patsy, still holding on to Willie's arm.

"Big enough," he said with a smile. "Anyway, it shouldn't give him any more trouble now. We'll have him home inside a week, assuming that all goes well."

Greg was barely able to restrain the tears of relief. Liz watched him fight back his tears and felt for him. Poor Greg, he reacted to the feelings of the moment, like a child, without emotional hindsight or foresight. There were a lot of things he would never understand. Liz smiled sadly but without bitterness. After all, he was only a man; what else could you expect? Then, as she watched Patsy still holding Willie's arm, and the peculiar expression on Willie's face, a cold chill came over her heart. Surely, surely Willie had realized by now that Patsy was his daughter?

Edward woke up in the recovery room and turned his head away from the bright light. Immediately a dreadful pain shot through his belly and he cried out.

"Okay, you can give him some Demerol, fifty milligrams," said a man's voice, far, far away. A nurse's face appeared over his head and floated there for a long time, then it disappeared. He felt a pain in his butt and knew he was getting a shot. Then he felt he was going to vomit, and he tried to tell the nurse, but she was laughing with somebody and only came when she heard him retching. The pain in his tummy while he vomited was beyond anything he could have imagined, and it left him breathless and so weak, he couldn't move.

Edward kept very still, then the Demerol started to work and he drifted off again. When he woke up, there was a mask on his face, and the oxygen was making a hissing noise as it came through the tubing.

A blurry face appeared in Edward's field of vision, distorted, with thick lips and protruding eyes. Then it vanished slowly, like the Cheshire cat in *Alice in Wonderland*.

"He can go back to the floor, his pressure's okay now."

He could feel the stretcher moving, then trundling along the corridor, the ceiling lights flashing past, then his mother's face above him for a second, more lights, and then back into his bed, and that awful pain when they moved him.

Edward couldn't see the clock above his head, but the time he arrived back in his room was 9:17. Edward had exactly twenty-four hours of life left to him.

PART THREE

CHAPTER
TWENTY-ONE

The autopsy was performed the day after Edward's death, and Dieter Romberg, the pathologist, had agreed not to start until eleven, the time Willie expected to be out of the operating room. The autopsy suite was next to the Pathology Department, on the eleventh floor, one floor below the operating rooms. The service elevator was used to transport the bodies, and as might be expected in a teaching hospital with almost twelve hundred beds, it stopped pretty often at the eleventh floor.

The need to move corpses from the wards to the mortuary had always posed a problem, ever since some administrator decided that the public should not see such proof of the hospital's fallibility being trundled through the hospital corridors.

Barbara and an aide had the job of getting Edward ready; when a patient died within seven days of having a general anesthetic, it became by definition a "coroner's case," and the standing orders were that all tubes, intravenous lines, catheters, and so on were to be left in place. Their locations would be checked as part of the autopsy procedure.

The mortuary stretcher was alongside the bed.

"Okay, up he goes!" said Barbara, and the two of them lifted the sheet bearing Edward onto the top of the stretcher.

"I thought he'd be heavier," said Molly, the round-faced aide. She was normally pink-cheeked but not today. It was her first day on the surgical floor.

"Do you know how to wind it down?" asked Barbara, indicating the stretcher.

"No, this is the first time."

"Okay, come around to this end," ordered Barbara. She was surprised at how matter-of-fact she sounded. "See this handle? Pull it out and start turning. No, the other way, counter-clockwise."

The top of the stretcher started to sink.

"Oh, my!" said Molly, beginning to understand how it worked.

"Hold it!" Barbara pushed the edges of the sheet around the body. They could get caught in the mechanism and jam the whole thing, like a piece of material caught in a zipper.

Molly turned the handle, and Edward slowly disappeared into the depths of the stretcher. When the handle wouldn't turn any more, she stood up, breathless and red in the face from the exertion.

"Don't they have electric ones?" she asked. Barbara ignored her question.

"Here, take that end of the mattress," she said, and in a minute the stretcher had a sheet and a pillow on top and looked for all the world ready to receive a passenger. It just seemed a bit heavier than normal going around corners when they wheeled it down the corridor toward the service elevator.

Barbara had done a good job of controlling her emotions and felt proud of herself until she came back to the floor and saw the sad little pile of Edward's clothes and possessions waiting to be picked up by the family. She took a big, choking breath, walked quickly into the staff toilet, sat down, and wept.

Dieter Romberg was already angry, even outraged, in his quiet way. He'd finished going through the boy's hospital chart and a batch of late lab reports pinned to the cover. Even on such a brief examination, the boy's treatment seemed to have been cavalier, to say the least, and he had a bad feeling that the autopsy would confirm his worst fears. He tapped the speech-activated mike suspended above the end of the stainless-steel table, and the red light flicked on for an instant. He'd already gone around the stiff body and turned it over, carefully examining front and back.

"The body is that of a young male who looks approximately

the stated age—" He stopped. Pat Gonio, the technician, was looking at him.

"Head?" he asked, and Dieter nodded. Pat took a heavy knife and made a cut from behind the ear across the top of the head to behind the other ear, then peeled back the forehead onto the face before cutting around the skull. The noise from the electric saw was high-pitched and deafening. Dieter had to stop dictating until Pat had finished taking off the top of the skull. It was like a lid; the upper part of the brain sagged like Jell-O without its support.

"External appearances: normal postmortem mottling is noted in the thighs and back." He looked again at the tiny, still-red marks he'd noted earlier on Edward's body. "Four small spider nevi are present on the chest and one on the left palm . . ." Dieter had checked to see if these had been noted in the clinical records. Nothing on Stringer's notes, but that was to be expected. Bob Wesley hadn't seen them, either.

"A recent midline abdominal incision is noted. Sutures are in position and the wound appears to be in normal condition."

He stepped back from the mike. Pat had finished up top and was waiting to open up the chest and abdominal cavities.

"Pat, why don't you go ahead," he said. "Don't go through the incision, go around it, so we can see it from the inside. Call me when you're done; I'll be in the coffee room." He walked off, leaving Pat to get to work with his knife and electric saw. At the desk he told the secretary to call Stringer. "He's probably still in the OR. And call Dr. Wesley, too, will you? Tell him I have something to show him."

Sometimes Dieter didn't know whether it was worth the hassle of working in a teaching hospital; so many mistakes were made by junior doctors in training, so much responsibility was given to overworked residents. It *should* work, in theory, of course, with supervision by trained doctors. In fact, it should be better. But he knew that the junior doctors were often left to their own devices, although the increasing rate of malpractice suits had done something to improve that situation. But when you had somebody like Willie Stringer in charge . . .

Stringer and Bob Wesley came into the autopsy room together, both in their scrub suits. Stringer had been helping Bob to do a hernia. Walter English, the senior resident, usually

helped the juniors with simple cases, so when Willie volunteered
to help Bob, everybody figured that it had something to do
with the row he was known to have had with Janus Frankel,
the department chairman.

Dieter came back in at the same time, prepared for a battle.
Willie Stringer always gave him a hard time, especially if
something unexpected turned up. They gathered around the
table, and Dieter put on his thick rubber gloves. Willie looked
quickly at the opened abdomen. Everything looked all right—
externally, anyway. The back of the incision was closed; nothing
had ruptured.

"The liver looks a little enlarged, and maybe a bit pale, don't
you think?" asked Dieter with his soft Austrian accent, reaching
for the organ.

"Looks pretty normal to me," replied Willie, trying to keep
the acid out of his voice. "Yours would look pale, too, if you'd
bled to death." Those damn pathologists always tried to make
it look as if he'd missed something.

Dieter sighed. "We'll weigh it." He put a hand in the abdomen
and eased it partially out of the cavity. When you could see it
all, it certainly did look abnormal; the usually sharp edges were
rounded and the entire organ was a mottled grayish color.

"Postmortem changes," said Willie, getting in ahead of Dieter.
"No history of any liver disease that we know of." He glanced
at Bob for confirmation, and Bob nodded.

Dieter pointed out the spider nevi and Willie snorted. "That's
just some kind of insect bite. Of course I noticed that, but it
wasn't worth recording."

Bob looked hard at the tiny marks and felt his hands go
cold. He knew that spider nevi meant that Edward had probably
had some kind of liver disease, and he'd completely missed
those warning signs.

Dieter painstakingly pointed out the big spleen and the
enlarged veins behind and around the stomach.

"We saw all that," said Willie impatiently, and looked up at
the clock. "It's a congenital malformation. Let's look inside the
stomach and find the ulcer where the bleeding was coming
from."

With a pair of big scissors Dieter slit the stomach open,
starting at the lower end. They all looked at the grayish tissue.

Dieter held it under the faucet to wash away the mucus and some clotted blood. There was no ulcer. Nothing. Now it was Willie's turn to feel his hands going cold. Then Dieter slit the rest of the stomach open, right up into the gullet, and laid it open for all to see. There was still no ulcer, and no obvious source of Edward's fatal hemorrhage.

Dieter spread the tissues on the cutting board and flattened the rugosities in the lower end of the esophagus.

"There you are, Dr. Stringer," he said finally, in a strained voice. "Ruptured esophageal varices." There was a slit in the lining of the gullet. "When he was alive," said Dieter, addressing Bob, but keeping an eye on Willie, "those veins were full, about the size of your thumb." Bob gasped and looked at his thumb. "Any injury," Dieter went on, "like with an endoscope, could be the cause of a major bleed."

"But how did the veins get to be so big?" asked Bob.

"I think we're going to find that the kid had severe liver disease, obstructing the flow of blood through the liver. The blood backs up and the veins can get huge."

"Portal hypertension," said Bob, recalling. "What the terminal drunks get. But how . . . ?"

"From hepatitis, I would imagine," said Dieter, forestalling the question. "Did you see this?" He pointed at the lab slips. Willie snatched up the chart. Dieter, continuing to address Bob in his calm, German-accented voice, went on. "The bilirubin was 3.2, and the normal value is less than 1.0. Did you notice that he was jaundiced?" Dieter lifted Edward's upper eyelid with his thumb. In this light, there was no question that the white of his eye had a yellow tinge.

Willie slapped the chart back on the shelf, white with rage. "Why didn't you tell me about his bilirubin?" he asked Bob. His voice was chilly, almost shaking with anger.

"It wasn't back, Dr. Stringer. The lab—"

"We'll talk about all that later," interrupted Willie. "Let's get on with this autopsy."

"We'll get sections of the esophagus . . ." started Dieter, but Willie wasn't listening.

"Did you get a history of hepatitis from the parents?" he asked Bob brusquely.

"No, and I asked specifically." Bob was feeling sick and

thoroughly scared by the turn of events. It looked now as if his carelessness could have contributed to the boy's death.

"Sometimes people get hepatitis and never know it, but it can become chronic and cause progressive liver disease"— Dieter, still addressing Bob, pointed to Edward's liver—"and finish up like that." Willie made an impatient movement, but Dieter was not to be put off. "We had a similar case a couple of years ago," he went on in the same quiet voice. "The only difference was that he'd been diagnosed and treated for several years before he died, and that was before liver transplants became available."

The silence was thick enough to cut with a knife.

"Good theory, Dieter, but we won't really know until we've seen the microscopy slides, will we?" Willie tried a smile, but it didn't work. "Let me know when you have something definite to tell me."

Willie's face was set and grim as he left the autopsy area. This was just what he didn't need right now, on top of all his other problems. The fucking house staff, you couldn't ever rely on them not to mess things up. They always fucked up, always. And he couldn't sit on their tails all day long, checking everything they did. They had to learn by doing at least some of it themselves, for chrissake. His anger focused on Bob. Careless young fool, missing a case of chronic active hepatitis— he'd get his ass for this. He'd never liked working with him, anyway; he wasn't the kind who'd ever make a good surgeon. And Willie had certainly given him plenty of help. There were always lots of applicants for the residency program—they turned down a dozen good people for every one who got in.

He went back up to the operating room area to change and calmed down on the way. He'd write a report, complain to Janus Frankel, and get Wesley fired immediately. Then he remembered that his own standing with Frankel wasn't exactly at its peak at present, and his mood became more somber. In fact, the way things looked right now, he stood to come in for a fair amount of criticism himself.

"Fuck!" he shouted in the empty changing room, beside himself with anger and frustration. He pulled off his scrub shirt and threw it angrily on the floor. "Double fuck!"

* * *

Lilies. Lots of them. Greg tried to remember if they appeared
at weddings, too, or if they were only for funerals. He concentrated on their thick, curled, opaque whiteness. It was a pallor
more than a whiteness, a corruption of color, a place where
some shade or tint had been, but now bleached ivory, like
bone.

Organ music, soft, inevitable, penetrating like rain into the
recesses of his soul. Eighteenth-century music, heavy with the
essence of sorrow and pain; Bach, maybe. They must have had
a lot more funerals in those times, what with bubonic plague,
smallpox, and distempers of all kinds. Especially kids . . . even
a hundred years ago a child born into a Victorian family didn't
have much better than a one in two chance of reaching the
age of twelve months. The old gravestones told the story, with
all those names of young children.

Greg force-fed thoughts, any thoughts, into his head, anything to keep him from thinking about Edward's white, dead
face on the hospital pillow, but his mind kept swinging back
to it.

There was Timmy with his mother. Liz signaled to them to
come up to the front, and they sat down in the pew directly behind the five Hopkinses. The five remaining Hopkinses. Timmy's mother made an inarticulate sound and put a hand on Liz's
arm. Timmy, barely recognizable in a tie and jacket, sat down
on the edge of the hard wooden pew. When his mother sat
down, Timmy sat down, too, then slid unobtrusively along the
varnished seat closer to her. He kept his head down; he didn't
want to look at Greg or any of them. Liz glanced at him,
anxious to know how Edward's best friend was taking his loss.
Timmy seemed more subdued than she had ever seen him.
After a while he looked up at Elspeth, but just for a second.
His face was dry but she could see that he had been crying.

Out of the corner of his eye Greg saw Willie Stringer and
Bob Wesley come in. He didn't immediately recognize Bob; at
the hospital, he'd only seen him in a white coat. Both men
were wearing dark suits. They stood uncertainly at the back
until an usher showed them where to sit. It was really nice of
them to come, busy as they were.

The church was small and quite old, stone-built with a squat,
heavy steeple and solid pillars supporting Gothic arches and

windows. Most of the original stained glass was gone. It hadn't been of the very best quality to start with; storms, disintegration of the leading, and occasional vandalism had left only two of the original nine. Behind the altar was a representation of Daniel in the temple, and to Greg's left, a rather lugubrious-looking Christ was distributing fish, or maybe they were loaves. The colors had faded, especially the reds, which now had a bluish tinge, and both windows bulged in slightly. The other windows were clear, with small diamond-shaped panes, giving the lighting of the whole church a distracting gap-toothed effect. The first thing Greg had seen when he came through the felt-covered doors was a hand-lettered appeal for money to restore the windows.

"The Lord giveth, and the Lord taketh away. We are here today to bid farewell to Edward . . ."

Greg tried to keep his eyes off the shiny box that contained his son. Every few moments an internal scream tore him apart, and his mind and obstinate soul butted headlong into each other. Edward couldn't be gone, he was at home, waiting in his room, and he'd be there with that little quiet grin when they got home, asking what was for lunch.

Liz was holding his hand tight. Elspeth was on his left, looking around to see who was in the chapel. Douglas was on the other side of Liz, pale, shocked. For a kid who had often said how he hated his brother . . .

After Willie Stringer had come slowly out of Edward's room and broken the dreadful news to him, Greg had gone in for a few minutes and stood there, looking at his boy, feeling his heart breaking. There was a phone in the room, but he couldn't bring himself to use it, so he went back to the nurses' station and called Liz from there. It had been all right until he heard Liz's voice, then he broke into harsh, dry sobs and couldn't speak, while Liz, at the other end, with no idea of what was going on, got more and more frantic. He gave the phone to the nurse to hold while he regained control of himself. She could hear Liz's voice calling, "Greg, what is it, what's the matter?"

"Hold on, Mrs. Hopkins," she said, "your husband will be with you in just a second."

After he'd managed to tell her what had happened, he called Patsy's school, got her out of class, and told her. She said she'd come right home; they'd both get there about the same time.

In shock, Liz put the phone down and sat heavily on her bed, feeling that the world was falling in on her, crushing the air out of her chest. A blackness came across her eyes.

Blindly she reached for the phone and called the children's school, then in a daze drove there to take them home; it was essential to have them with her, partly because she might just go mad alone in that big house, but mainly because the family had to be together. She told them that Edward had taken a turn for the worse. It wasn't to protect the kids or anything like that; she simply couldn't get the words out: *Edward is dead.* If she had said it, it would have somehow made it real and irrevocable. As long as she didn't say it, there was a chance that it was all a mistake, that they'd be able to revive him, bring him back.

So Greg had had to tell them when he got home. Douglas went gray, then in an almost inaudible voice said he knew it. His mother wouldn't have taken them out of school unless something really weird had happened. Elspeth started to wail, and all four of them held on to each other in a tight circle and cried until they heard Patsy's car come in the driveway. She erupted into the kitchen, starting to weep as she came in, and fell into her mother's arms. Elspeth joined the two women, and the three of them clung together in a huddled misery of female mourning.

Greg and Douglas stood apart and watched for a moment, heartsick but unable to join them.

"Let's go into the garden," said Greg, and the two of them had gone out. Douglas's mind seemed split in two. One side truly felt the sadness of his own and the family's loss, while the other did a fast, guilty inventory of Edward's possessions, wondering what he could take over.

"Ashes to ashes and dust to dust . . ."

At the end of the service the rest of the mourners waited with ritual courtesy for Greg and his family to go down the aisle first. There were a lot of cars in the church parking lot. Liz saw Coach Lenahan near the back with a big, blowsy, restless-looking blonde. The limousine for the family was waiting outside. They all got in, then had to wait for the procession to form and the hearse to come up to the front. Douglas noted that it was a Chrysler, not the usual Cadillac, and about two years old.

It was only a five-minute drive to the cemetery, where the air was crisp and a breeze scuffled a few of last year's dead leaves around the gravestones. One of the undertaker's men was waiting at the gate and pointed up the gentle slope to the graveside. They passed two recent graves, as yet unmarked, on the same side, next to the sharp-edged hole and the earth-covered tarpaulin. Liz looked at the faded flowers still strewn over the new graves and decided to come back in two days to take Edward's flowers away before they looked like that.

Willie and Bob came up after them. Greg shook them by the hand, unable to speak. Willie gave Liz a long hug, and for a second she let herself be buried in that well-remembered warmth. Bob and Patsy looked at each other, remembering their liking for each other in the hospital, and impulsively he opened his arms to her and she came and held on to him. Bob turned and stood beside her, just as Willie was about to step into that spot. Willie hesitated for a moment, then moved down and stood between Patsy and Liz. His feet were getting cold, and he stood on the outside edges of his expensive thin-soled shoes, but it didn't help.

The graveside service was brief. Elspeth cried with the terminal desolation of her age. As the pastor spoke, a book in his hands and his robes billowing about his legs, Bob's hand found Patsy's, and thus he comforted her as best he could. She found her other hand taken by Willie, and she looked at him for a second without changing her expression. His hand pressure was firm, reassuring, and somehow loving. Patsy stood there, aware of a stream of messages coming in through the psychic receivers of both hands. She tried to listen to what the pastor was saying, but her hands spoke louder and overwhelmed the sound of him.

They all went back to the house afterward; Timmy's mother and Edna Macklin next door had insisted on giving Liz a hand with the food, although she hadn't really wanted their help. But Liz was tired, tired of everything, and didn't put up any resistance.

Willie spent some time with Liz; there was no question that their lives had come together again, he said very quietly so that no one else could hear, and he would be in touch. Ellen would have come but she wasn't feeling well. Liz just looked at him, too numb to take his words in. She felt anesthetized but aware of the suppressed pain that crouched in her mind, waiting to surface.

Willie left her and went to look for Patsy.

He found her in the kitchen with Douglas and Elspeth and smiled quickly at the two younger ones.

"Willie, it was really nice of you to come." Patsy hugged him and cried for a moment. Douglas and Elspeth exchanged a glance. Sometimes Patsy was one of them, sometimes she was a grown-up.

Bob came into the kitchen carrying a tray of almond cookies.

"I'm glad you're making yourself useful, Bob," said Willie coldly. "I plan on leaving in"—he looked at his watch—"about five minutes."

"Fine. You want one of these?" He passed the tray. Willie hesitated, then took one. He ate daintily, with his fingertips.

Bob had been talking quietly with Patsy ever since they got back from the cemetery; he liked her spunkiness and courage, and she appreciated his thoughtful and caring attitude. He promised to call her in New London; maybe they could get together sometime when things were less distressing.

On the drive back, there was a quietness, a tension, between the two men. Bob thought Willie was quiet because of the sadness they had participated in, and maybe from guilt. He thought of Willie's expression at the autopsy and wondered if he had said anything about it to Edward's parents. He didn't think so.

Willie didn't notice the silence and wouldn't have cared if he had. He hadn't wanted to bring Bob in the first place, but apparently he'd called Liz, and she'd told Bob he could ride up with him. Now Willie was immersed in his own thoughts and impressions: Ellen, Liz, and now Patsy . . . With such strong feelings about the three women in his life, he had some inkling that he might be on the edge of an emotional quagmire and walking straight into it.

He adjusted his seat, put all those thoughts aside, and went

back to trying to solve some of his other outstanding problems.
He bit his lip angrily, and his head started to throb again. How
was it that he, a successful New York surgeon, could be in such
a financial mess? It was even worse than he'd thought earlier.
He'd taken a bath in the October stock market crash, and that
was bad enough, but he'd had to sell most of the stocks he had
just to cover others he'd bought on margin. And there were
tax repercussions to that which he'd never even suspected.

They drove in almost unrelieved silence to the hospital,
where Willie dropped Bob off before heading home.

CHAPTER
TWENTY-TWO

"**I** need to see the doc!"

Greg heard Louella's voice raised in protest, then Big Vern's face appeared around the door of his office. He was grinning from ear to ear.

"Okay, Vern, what's up?" said Greg, not happy to see him.

"I got this thing on my leg." Vern undid his belt and pushed down his jeans. There was an angry-looking inflamed area at the lower end of the scar. "I took a needle, Doc, and tried to lance it, but . . ."

"In the exam room, Vern." Greg pointed at the door.

While Greg was taking care of the small abscess, Vern watched with fascinated attention.

"Sorry about your boy, Doc."

Greg nodded. There was nothing to say. He put a dressing on. "I thought you'd left town, Vern."

"Who, me? Are you kidding? No, Doc, *they* left town." Vern gave a wolfish grin.

The only thing that had saved Big Vern on the night of the cucumber was the fact that he had two brothers, both as mean and quick as he was. At the time Vern had been running five girls, two white and three black, and when he'd left the hospital and done the rounds downtown in his white Cadillac, they were gone. All of them. News travels faster than a speeding bullet, he knew it, and he wasn't Superman. Especially now. Downtown had a scary feel that night, and he knew what had happened. Teddy Black, who'd knifed him, must have started rounding Vern's girls up while he was still on his way to the hospital. Then what? He would keep them off the street until

Vern was finally taken care of, in case some of the girls were loyal and went back to him. Keeping the girls off the streets cost money, so he wouldn't want to waste too much time. Big Vern suddenly visualized his own body in the river—but not with a single shot in the back of the head like the Mafia did it. He'd be cut to pieces, and Teddy would make Vern's own girls help cut him up real good, just to make the point.

Vern passed a police car parked near one of his corners, without lights. He slowed. For a split second the streetlight shone on the driver's face: Sergeant Farrow. His eyes flicked over to Vern, and in the mirror Vern saw him reach for his handset.

Vern knew what that meant. He turned the next corner fast, suddenly sweating like a pig. *I'm one hot nigger,* he thought. *I'll be lucky if I see my breakfast tomorrow. Better run, get my ass outa town.* Almost panicking, he swerved to avoid a pedestrian, a drunk, weaving across the street. Just what he needed, to get pulled in on a manslaughter charge. He knew what the radio would say in the morning: "Vern Wilkins, aged thirty-four, was found hanged in his cell at police headquarters this morning. A known drug dealer, he had been arrested last night . . ."

Getting out of town wasn't such a good idea. He would stick out like a sore prick anyplace else, and it would take too long to get things started up and going again. Here he had his own pad, his own life-style. He just had to regroup, get his brothers . . . Yeah, his brothers and him, they'd take care of it. Vern turned down a narrow street and got on to the highway that led to I-95. He drove for fifteen minutes, cruising at a few miles an hour above the limit, checking from time to time in his mirror to see if he was being followed. When he came to the big 76 truck stop, he pulled in and parked between two eighteen-wheelers near the rear of the parking area.

The two phone booths outside the main entrance were too brightly lit. He went into the restaurant and found two more phone booths opposite the counter where they sold candies and cigarettes. He bought a pack of Marlboros and lit one. He had to wait for a minute as both phones were busy, and he spent the time leaning against the back wall, checking out the customers he could see at the counter. Nobody he knew, but that didn't necessarily mean anything.

Vern's leg started to ache; the local anesthetic was wearing off. He was lucky Hopkins had been there; not a bad guy for a honkie. If it had been that old shit Anderson, he'd have had the aides hold him down while he sewed up that cut—and no pain shots, either. Vern decided to call his brother Pete first, because the two of them worked together often, but the number was busy. He tried again, same thing. So he dialed the number of his younger brother, Vin.

"Vin? This Vern. Come get me at the 76 truck stop, can you? The one on I-95, between . . . Yeah, okay. Now. I mean now. And don't use your own car, okay?"

Vin came out in a black Chevrolet with sagging springs and a border of fluffy danglers around the rear window. Vern got in fast.

"Let's go get Pete," he said. "I'm gonna need some help tonight." On the way back to town Vern explained what had happened, and Vin laughed himself sick. In a fury Vern twisted his ear until it almost came off in his hand. But when they got to Pete's fourth-floor apartment on Thirty-fourth Street, they found him dead, his throat cut, blood all over the place. Vin stopped laughing. The phone was off the hook.

Vin was going to run out but Vern stopped him. "Take it easy. Before we go out of here, we gotta know where we're goin'."

So they sat there, ignoring the body on the bed. "It was Teddy Black, we gotta get him," insisted Vern. "Then nobody can do nothin' to us; we'll take over the whole area."

It took them only a short time to figure out where Teddy was; the giveaway had been the patrol car. Sergeant Farrow was guarding him until Vern had been taken care of. They found the car, still parked with its lights out in the same spot, half a block from Teddy Black's place. Vern parked the Chevrolet around the corner and they walked quickly back to Farrow's vehicle. Vin ran around to the passenger door, opened it in a flash, and was sitting beside the sergeant, his gun sticking in his ribs, before Farrow knew what had happened. Because of his leg, Vern was a bit slower getting in the back of the patrol car.

"Call your friend, Teddy," said Vin. "Tell him to come down here. You have something to tell him, but he has to come down to the car."

Farrow licked his dry lips.

"You guys are both dead," he said. "One way or the other."
He looked up and down the street. Not a soul, not even a cat.

"And we've always been so good to you," said Vin regretfully.

"Anything happens to us," said Vern, "and Chief Grunwald
gets the letter."

"What letter?" asked Farrow.

"The one that gives your bank-account number and the
deposits we made for you," answered Vern. "Now make that
call."

Farrow shrugged. All his life he'd taken the easy way. He
picked up a handset next to the regular police one.

Two minutes later Teddy Black came sashaying around the
corner. Vin got him in the face when he bent down to talk to
Farrow through the car window.

Less than an hour later Vern had his girls back at work.
They kissed him, told him how happy they were to see him
back . . . They read about Teddy in the papers next day. "Our
Vern," they said proudly, "nobody fucks around with him,
huh?"

Vern didn't tell Greg this whole story, just enough to last
through the opening of the abscess. Greg held up the small
hemostat; in its jaws was a piece of black thread about half an
inch long.

"That's what caused your abscess, Vern." He looked wearily
at him. "You left a stitch in; you should have gotten one of
your girls to take them out."

"They don't have the *time* for that kinda stuff, Doc. They too
busy workin'." He grinned and pulled his pants up.

At the door Vern turned, a strange expression on his face.
"If I can ever do somethin' for you, Doc," he said, "you know
I'm your man!"

Louella was furious. "Why doesn't he go to the emergency
room? He's going to give us a bad name, just by coming here."

Greg looked at her, all his sadness coming back like a leaden
wave over him. He shrugged, and it was an effort.

"He's one of God's children, too, Louella," he said, "and it's
not up to you or me to decide who's good and who's bad."

Louella snorted but said nothing. She felt so sorry for him
in every way, she could have cried.

* * *

There were no other patients, and Greg went back into his office and closed the door. He'd thought things would get better after the funeral; from the time of Edward's death until then, he had kept on imagining, from moment to moment, what was happening to his son. He visualized the nurses and aides preparing the corpse, the somber trip to the mortuary, Edward's stiffened body consigned to the bitter cold of the storage vault. The thought of Edward spending the silent, dark night there sent shivers through his marrow. He traced the desolate path he knew was followed by any patient who died after surgery in the hospital—the autopsy, being handled by the sleazy, mint-sucking undertakers with their carelessness and crude jokes. Now that Edward's journey was done and he was at rest in his tree-shaded grave, Greg hoped that he, too, would have some peace, but it didn't happen. He couldn't sleep; he dozed off fitfully, then awakened to the gnawing pain again. He tried reading in bed, and the same thing happened. His life became an oscillation between near unconsciousness and misery.

"Let's get away," said Liz, who was just as unhappy but had the blessing of being able to feel the support of her family. "Let's take a vacation, get a change of scenery."

"Why don't you go, and take the children?" he replied. "I can't . . . I have my patients to take care of." That was true, but he wasn't really taking care of them. At every possible opportunity he put on his boots and walked half a mile down the road away from the town, then across the field where the Kingstons kept their horses, till he came to the dry-stone wall that formed the far boundary of the cemetery. The first time he went that way, he found a thick growth of thorny bushes growing over the wall and tore his jacket scrambling through it, so the next time he took a pair of Liz's pruning shears and cleared a way for himself. It would have been much easier to get in the car and drive for five minutes around to the main entrance, but he did it the hard way as part of his penance. Had Greg been alive when it was considered normal to wear hair shirts, self-flagellate, and make pilgrimages on bare and bloodied knees, that is what he would have done. As it was, at least once a day he scrambled over the crumbling wall into the unused part of the cemetery, the end farthest from the main gates. There the ground was cleared of shrubs, but the grass grew in an undisturbed, thick profusion, absorbing noise like a fall of snow. Greg waded through the wet grass, around the dark, trickling boles of the silent yew trees, vaguely aware of the tiny bugs that he disturbed; they soared up and out of the grass to land again close by, like a moving cloud that kept pace with him. Sometimes the wind would bring the smell of fresh funeral flowers, or the scent of lilac. A few yards beyond the gravedigger's hut brought the limit of the long grass, marked by a curved margin where, every week or so, Old Rogo would sweep around on his aged mowing machine. Greg saw him several times; and his greeting was a peculiar half wave, half touch of the cap, a salute that acknowledged Greg, who was his family doctor, but also his own Polish serf ancestry and his present status as an American citizen. Coming through the cemetery the back way over the top of the hill like this, the first graves Greg encountered were the most recent, and for six days the most recent was Edward's. Then suddenly there was another beyond it, smelling of freshly turned earth and more flowers. Greg briefly resented the intrusion, mostly because he hadn't expected Edward to be superseded quite so soon.

Greg stood on the gravel path in front of Edward, seeing him through the thick brown earth, through the coffin lid and the shiny silky lining. There was never anybody else around, or at least he never saw anyone, except once, when he was on his knees and some old man came puffing noisily up the path. Greg got up, dusted off his trousers, and walked off in the opposite direction, embarrassed and annoyed at being disturbed. He was getting to know the place; its dark, humid stillness had slowly and gently wrapped its aura around him. It was his place—his and Edward's.

When Elspeth came home from school, she'd call the office, and if Greg wasn't there, she would come up to the cemetery to fetch him. She'd put her hand in his, wait for a bit, then gently lead him home. It made things difficult for Elspeth, who had understood that her brother was dead. But when she saw her father like that, she started to wonder, and began to have dreams that frightened her, although she couldn't remember what they were.

As long as Greg was doing something, keeping his mind occupied . . . When it was raining hard and he had to be careful not to slip in the treacherous wet parts of the hill, he was forced to concentrate on what he was doing and it was a relief. He positively welcomed getting his shoes full of muddy water and his clothes soaked. Sometimes he would hum the Twenty-third Psalm to the tune of "Brother James's Air," and that helped, too; walking through the valley of the shadow of death—he knew about that. Being there, talking to Edward, telling him what was happening to the people he knew, the people he was fondest of . . . that helped, too, but the pain was stayed only temporarily. The guilt blended with the pain until he couldn't separate them. All the whys came in serried ranks, marching against him. Why had he not seen that Edward was really ill? Why had he not listened? Why had he not spent more time with his son? Why, why, *why*? The voices shrieked at him, as anguished as he.

Timmy never came. Once, a few weeks after the funeral, when Greg was at his worst, he saw Timmy in the grocery store and smilingly told him that Edward missed him and would like to see him. Timmy mumbled some reply, then ran out, scared out of his wits. That night his father came around to Greg's house and visited with him for almost an hour. He'd come to ask him not to say things like that to Timmy, but after listening to Greg for a while he decided not to mention it. He left feeling sad and desperately sorry for Greg.

Greg's practice was also suffering. There was a lot of paper-work Louella couldn't do, and it started to pile up. She'd leave a stack of papers in a conspicuous place, hoping he'd notice and take care of it. Of course Greg knew about the bills, the overdue accounts, the office notes, the unanswered letters from the insurance companies, but he simply could not apply himself to the task. So the pile grew and became even more daunting. He would forget to return telephone calls; he came in late to the office with his wet, muddy boots and left early, always for the same destination. For a long time everybody was helpful and understanding; even Mrs. Jackson, the Gorgon in charge of Medical Records at the hospital, didn't report his failure to complete his charts. She put them away in a corner and finally got old Dr. Anderson to take care of some of the more urgent ones, the Medicare charts that had to be returned before the hospital got paid. Dr. Anderson grumbled, which annoyed Mrs. Jackson, because she knew how often Greg had covered for him when he wasn't feeling well or just didn't feel like going out.

In desperation, Louella called Liz, so Liz started to come down to the office once or twice a week and make the bank deposits and do some of the more urgent tasks.

In some ways things actually seemed to be better; now that he wasn't in the office or at the hospital all the time, Greg spent more time with Elspeth and Douglas. Elspeth went for walks with him, but always his steps would unconsciously start to take them toward the cemetery. Elspeth didn't mind; she was constantly there, like an anxious mouse, watching out for her daddy.

But one torment never let up. Greg had never really understood what had happened to Edward. Willie Stringer's explanations had been heard in numb belief; Willie's compassionate voice talking about unusual postoperative complications, bringing up the old saying about doctors' families always having rare complaints. But Willie had also said he'd send the autopsy report as soon as it came through.

It didn't come. Greg hadn't consciously waited for it at first, but he noticed, and as the days went by, he found himself looking for the mail and feeling disappointed when it wasn't there. Of course, he knew that those things took a while, and the last thing he wanted to do was bother Willie Stringer with something as trivial as that. And Willie never called; Greg didn't really expect him to, but it would have been nice, and it would have comforted Liz to hear from him, he felt sure.

Finally it got to be like an aching tooth and he knew he had to do something about it. He called Willie.

"Greg! Nice to hear you. How's the family? How's Liz?"

"Fine, Willie, we're doing all right. Liz is fine. Listen, Willie, do you remember telling me you'd be sending the autopsy report? Well, it must have gotten lost or mislaid, because I never got it. Could you have them send me another copy? I hate to bother you with something dumb like that, but I have to have it . . . I'm sure you understand."

There was a long silence, so long that Greg thought they'd been cut off. Finally Willie's voice came through, sounding tight and clipped. "Gee, Greg, I thought we'd gone over all of that. Is there anything I didn't cover?"

"No, Willie, of course you did. It's just that I'd like to see the actual, full report." Suddenly Greg felt a blast of anger go right through him, and it left him shaking. "Willie, I *want* that report. If you can't get it to me, I can call the Pathology Department and have them—"

"Greg!" Willie's voice was jocular, conciliatory. "Of course I'll get it to you. I'll put it in the mail myself. Is there anything else you'd like?"

"No thanks, Willie, I hate to put you to that trouble. . . ." Greg felt guilty about feeling such anger toward his old friend.

Tight-lipped, Willie put the phone down. Of all the people in the world he didn't want to talk to, it was Greg Hopkins. Like most surgeons, whose memories retain the flavor and texture of every clinical triumph, every victory over death or disease, Willie hated the discordant echoes of failure.

He had to see Greg's point of view; after all, it was his kid. But even that thought didn't have too much impact, maybe because he had never had any children of his own, or maybe because he assumed that his own not too profound relationships were basically the same as anybody else's. In his heart of hearts, Willie felt that a child could be replaced simply by having another one, and lots of people still had kids at Liz and Greg's age. A sudden thought passed through his mind. If *he* had died in childhood, he was sure, his mother would have wept, but they would have been tears of relief. And *she* would have made damn sure not to have any more.

Willie forced his mind back to Greg, and his head started to throb again. He had to do something about the autopsy report, but with all the things that were going on in his life he simply could not face up to telling Greg the truth about Edward. Willie made a decision that caused him to feel shaky for a moment. Then he got up, took the autopsy report out of his files, went into the main office, and made a photocopy, blanking out everything except the printed heading of the Department of Pathology and the date.

After the secretaries had gone, he took the cover off one of the electric typewriters, slid the headed paper in, and started to type.

Greg got the autopsy report in the mail three days later. It was a poor copy but quite legible. The report of the entire autopsy was there, and Greg gritted his teeth and read it all the way through. The summary put it all together. Cause of death: upper gastrointestinal hemorrhage secondary to a large peptic ulcer in the stomach.

It didn't tell Greg anything he didn't already know, but it made him feel easier, and that night he had his best sleep since the funeral.

CHAPTER
TWENTY-THREE

"Bob, I'll present the first case, the appendix, and you can present the Hopkins kid, okay?"

Bob Wesley was having trouble keeping his mind off Patsy Hopkins, and the thought of presenting the botched case of her brother really bothered him.

"Yeah . . . okay. I guess we can get ready for a shellacking on Edward."

Walter English shrugged. "If anybody gets shellacked, it should be Stringer." They knew it would never happen; the blame for anything that went wrong was inevitably passed down to the house staff.

Walter English looked at the clock. "Come on, we're already late," he said, and led the way to the door.

Complicated cases were discussed once a week by the full staff, and all deaths on the surgical service were also presented by the house staff at this time, which gave the meeting its rather gruesome name of Death Rounds.

There were unspoken rules; if a surgeon didn't want to discuss a case for whatever reason, he didn't appear. That meant that the resident would present the case briefly, and discussion, if any, would be minimal. This ploy might be used when the patient was important and the surgeon didn't want details of his illness to be known outside the hospital. In the old days, when only the surgical staff had come, the discussion tended to be open and direct, and comments and criticism flew around the auditorium like summer lightning. Now, when the meetings included people from social service, physiotherapy, the nursing staff, and even the patients' ombudsman, they tended to be much less frank. The specter of malpractice suits was never very far away, and it inhibited talk. Willie was fond of saying that being a surgeon in the late eighties was like being a Jew in Germany in 1939.

Willie was absent from the next meeting after Edward's death. It was held in the old surgical classroom, a sloping auditorium in which some of the greatest American surgeons had lectured and operated in the early days. It was part of the university building, separated by a corridor from the hospital. Janus Frankel sat at a desk on the dais, puffing on his pipe. The sweet odor of Balkan Sobranie tobacco wafted upward in the air-conditioned eddies and swirled around the NO SMOKING sign behind him. Walter English and his team came in, all in scrubs, and sat down on the front bench.

"Right, Walter," said Frankel with a hint of sarcasm, looking at his watch, "I'm glad you could make it. What do you have for us?"

So Frankel was in one of his bad moods; it was just as well to find out early in the proceedings.

"Just a couple of cases, Dr. Frankel. We'd like to present a rather unusual case of appendicitis and a postoperative death. The attending on call last week was Dr. Stringer. I'll present the first case, and Dr. Wesley will discuss the second."

Frankel nodded. "Your attending is here?" He looked around, puffing on his pipe. "Is Dr. Stringer aware that one of his cases is to be discussed?"

Walter and Bob exchanged a surprised look. "Yes, sir," said Bob. He'd happened to mention it to him yesterday, and Stringer must have received the notice they sent around each week.

"Well, Dr. English," said Dr. Frankel, "are you waiting for divine inspiration, or do you think you can start now?"

The case he presented was that of a previously healthy male, aged thirty-four, who had gradually developed a vague pain around his umbilicus on the evening of his admission to the hospital. He had drunk a can of beer, thinking it would help, but it only made it worse. About an hour later he started to feel nauseated and vomited soon after. The pain got worse and moved down to his right side. He developed chills and his wife took his temperature. It was high. As he was now in quite severe pain and it was getting worse, she took him down to the emergency room, where the surgical resident on call examined him.

"Who was the resident?" asked Dr. Frankel.

Walter checked the chart. "Bob, sir. Bob Wesley."

Frankel turned his attention to Bob.

"Well, what did you find?"

"Marked tenderness in the right lower quadrant of the abdomen, with rebound tenderness in the same area."

Frankel looked around. "Where are the medical students?"

There was a diffuse murmur from near the back of the auditorium. "Do any of you know what rebound tenderness is?"

One of the students, a tall girl with glasses and wearing a yellow shirt and jeans, stood up. "Rebound tenderness is when you push into somebody's belly and then let go suddenly and it hurts."

"What's your name?" asked Frankel sharply.

"Irene Stark," said the girl. She had the confident look of a Smith or a Barnard graduate.

Frankel paused for a moment, smoke drifting lazily from the bowl of his pipe. "Well, *Miss* Stark, if you ever want that title to change to *Dr.* Stark, I suggest you start by dressing in a more appropriate fashion. This is a surgical conference, not a discotheque." Miss Stark sat down, and a faint ripple of laughter went around. Students were always fair game at these meetings, especially the females.

Frankel turned back to Bob. "Then what?"

"We ran a lab on him . . . white-cell count was 12,500 with a shift to the left, electrolytes were normal."

"So you had some evidence of infection, which would support your diagnosis, right?"

Walter gave Bob a quick glance out of the corner of his eye: *Don't fall into that trap*, it said. But he didn't need to worry; Bob had been there before.

"At that point I didn't have a diagnosis, Dr. Frankel. I was just collecting data."

Frankel nodded.

"Urinalysis was normal, no red cells, no pus . . . abdominal X ray was normal. I got Walter to see him, and we decided to take him to the operating room."

"With the diagnosis of . . . ?"

"Acute appendicitis," said Bob confidently.

There was quiet for a moment while Frankel relit his pipe. A couple of the students started to talk very quietly, but he heard them and glowered over the bowl at them.

"Neither of you mentioned whether he'd had any previous episodes of similar pain," he said, turning back to the front bench.

"Yes, he did," replied Bob. "Several times in the last year, but they never amounted to very much. He did mention that he'd had some diarrhea with it."

"Is he a big man, fat?"

"No, sir—rather thin, actually." Bob looked at the first page of the hospital chart. "One hundred thirty-two pounds, five foot eleven."

A thought seemed to strike Dr. Frankel.

"Had he ever suffered from abscesses around his anus?"

Bob stared at him. Was Frankel trying to catch him out? Had he missed something? Some kind of venereal disease? AIDS? "Yes, sir, he did. He's had several abscesses opened over the last two years."

Frankel sighed and shook his head. Bob looked at Walter, who shrugged imperceptibly. He didn't know what the boss was getting at. He looked up into the auditorium to see if Willie Stringer had arrived.

"So, with a confident diagnosis of acute appendicitis, you took him to the operating room." Frankel's voice was quieter. It was an ominous sign. "What did you find?"

"An acutely inflamed appendix," said Bob. There was a faint titter from the gallery, instantly subdued.

"What else?" persisted Frankel. "What did the small intestine look like?"

Bob looked surprised at the question.

"There were quite a lot of adhesions around," he said. "The small bowel next to the appendix was a bit thickened, but nothing special . . ."

"And the appendix itself?"

"That was the unusual part, Dr. Frankel, because the swelling and inflammation reached beyond the root of the appendix to the cecum."

Frankel pointed to the blackboard. "Draw it," he said, "for the benefit of our apprentices up there."

Bob took the chalk and drew something that looked like a limp sock, foot down, with a narrow blind-ended extrusion like a long spur on the heel. "That's the appendix," he said, looking at Frankel.

"I'll take your word for it," he replied with disdain in his voice. There was a dutiful giggle from the gallery.

Bob took a piece of red chalk and filled in the spur and a little of the heel where the two joined.

Suddenly Frankel seemed to lose patience.

"So you took out the appendix, right? Just the way you always do?"

"Yes, sir." Bob was beginning to feel alarmed.

"Right. Let's see what the pathologist has to say." Frankel pointed behind Bob at a pale, obese young man with a round face and round horn-rimmed glasses. He got up and put a load of slides into the small carousel projector. While he was doing that, Frankel went up to the blackboard and wrote two words in large capitals: CROHN'S DISEASE. Bob turned to Walter and slapped his forehead. "Oh, Jesus!" he whispered, "I never thought of it."

Walter shrugged resignedly. Bob had a way of getting himself into trouble every time. He hadn't thought of Crohn's disease, either; it wasn't a common diagnosis.

The lights dimmed, and the first magenta-and-blue stained and magnified slides of the appendix showed up on the screen, accompanied by the pathologist's commentary. Yes, he said finally, it was a case of Crohn's disease. The next ten minutes were very uncomfortable for both Bob and Walter, as they suffered the sarcastic tongue-lashing in which Willie Stringer was obliquely included. At these meetings the attendings were only rarely attacked, and their sins were usually visited on the resident staff.

"All right, we've heard enough about that fiasco," Frankel said finally, but it was obvious that he was still angry. "What's next?"

"This is the case of a twelve-year-old boy . . ." Bob began.

Frankel was scanning the auditorium. "I still don't see Dr. Stringer," he said. "He *was* the attending, wasn't he?"

"Yes. He—"

"We'll postpone this discussion until next week," Frankel interrupted brusquely. "And I'll make sure Dr. Stringer's here."

There was a buzz of surprise. This was an unusual step. They all made a mental note to come next week; from the sound of it, there should be some sparks flying.

"What amazes me is that the transplanters never got to him," said Walter later, in the coffee shop, still talking about Edward Hopkins and mourning all the surgery that could have been done on him. He shook his head. "They have people from their team prowling around the floors, checking charts, and they'll take anything that's still breathing and has a blood pressure, any kind of live meat. It's the only way they'll ever get their program off the ground." Walter was holding his coffee cup in both hands, staring into the distance. For a moment he reminded Bob of a guy he'd met once in a hotel bar in Atlanta who'd explained to him in detail how he would deal with the nigger menace if it were up to him.

"They should go to the VA hospitals," he went on reflectively, "like they did for the first wave of kidney transplants. You can always find somebody there who'll sign a consent form, even if they're out of their minds."

Walter's beeper went off. The place was crowded and noisy, and he had to hold it up to his ear. "It's the emergency room," he said, getting up. "Some old broad from a nursing home with a cold leg. Maybe we can get an embolectomy out of it. Have you done one of those yet?"

Bob shook his head and followed him out. The coffee shop was crowded with nurses, especially near the door, where the cash register was. Walter bulldozed his way through, and Bob merely had to follow in his wake.

During a pause, while the Radiology Department was getting ready to do an arteriogram on the "old broad," Bob managed to get to a phone with an outside line, and he called the number Patsy had given him. It rang and rang, and he was about to give up when she answered. The phone was at the end of the corridor, Patsy explained, and they took turns answering it. Trudy had gone off somewhere, although it was her turn.

Bob had a sudden vision of Patsy's tearstained face at the funeral, and he wanted to hug her, to hold her tight in his arms.

"Hi, Patsy." He gulped, finding it unexpectedly hard to think of something to say to her. "How are you? Are you doing all right? I've been worrying about you since . . . since . . ."

There was a brief silence. "I'm fine, Bob," she said. "Life has to go on."

Patsy had gone home every weekend since Edward's death, although it was usually an ordeal. Luckily she had an inexhaustible store of energy and good humor, and her visits were awaited by all of them. In a way she was the bridge between the family before and the family after.

"Listen, Patsy . . ." He loved the sound of that name—he'd said it, rolled it around his tongue so many times—"listen, there's a big concert by Heavy Metal down on Strawberry Fields next Sunday afternoon. Would they let you out of your convent to go to something like that?"

"Sure. I just happen to be going to New York that weekend, anyway. That would be great, as long as I'm back here by ten. I have an eight-o'clock geology lab on Monday."

After deciding on time and place of rendezvous, Bob hung up and went back to the emergency room with a jaunty step. Setting up the first date with a new girl was always an exciting adventure, but Patsy was something special. And he'd chosen the right thing; she was into rock music, he could tell by the way she spoke. As for him, he supposed he was old-fashioned; he liked rock music like everybody else, but he was really a closet Mozart freak.

Patsy went back to her room with a thousand conflicting feelings. Hearing Bob's voice had brought back awful memories of the hospital and the funeral, but it also brought back the feel of his hand holding hers as they looked straight ahead of them, the wind reddening their faces. Heavy Metal—she didn't know too much about them, but she was sure it would be fun; she could just see it, everybody lying down all over Strawberry Fields, a pall of pot smoke hanging over everything.

Gently, she let down the arm of her record player on to the disc. Dennis Brain's stupendous recording of the horn concerto started up again, and she returned contentedly to reading the score, tapping out the rhythm with the fingers of her right hand.

CHAPTER
TWENTY-FOUR

Willie Stringer had missed Death Rounds that Monday because of a surprise visit to his office by his old friend Martin Penrose.

The day had started well; on the spur of the moment, while in the grip of the New York traffic, he'd called Patsy on his car phone to invite her to spend a day in New York. He'd put her up at the Plaza, they'd go to the 21 Club, the opera, the whole bit.

Patsy was surprised and flattered; she'd had the nicest impression of Willie when he'd come to their house for dinner and also when he'd come to the funeral with Bob. He seemed such an interesting and thoughtful man, as well as being wonderfully good-looking. Patsy wondered how many other surgeons would have taken the time to come to a patient's funeral.

When Willie got to the office, though, things started to go badly. Usually the porter parked his car for him, but today he was nowhere to be found, so Willie had to go around the block and wait in line. It took almost fifteen minutes, and by the time he'd parked and run up the stairs, he was already in a poor frame of mind.

There was a note on his desk from Dr. Frankel's office, reminding him that two of his patients were to be discussed at Death Rounds and would he please attend? Willie looked at his watch. Plenty of time.

Margaret, his secretary, came in with the printout of his day's engagements. At ten A.M., he had a meeting with a Mr. Martin Penrose. Martin! What was he doing in town? It was nice of him to come by, but he should know better than to come in the middle of a working day.

"See if you can reschedule Mr. Penrose," he said irritably. "Really, Margaret, you know better than to have people just dropping in like that, when I have to be at the hospital at ten."

"He's not dropping in, Dr. Stringer," said Margaret defensively. She looked at him through her huge round glasses. "He's with the Olympic Insurance Company, and he said it's important."

Willie took a deep breath and was about to get really sarcastic when the penny dropped. The Olympic Insurance Company was his malpractice insurance carrier, so Martin *was* coming on business. He glowered at Margaret, then shrugged.

"Okay. But I can't spend too long with him. I have to get to the hospital, so call me when he's been in here ten minutes."

"Yes, sir," she said in a cocky kind of way, as if she'd won some kind of contest. Margaret had been quite slim and attractive when he'd hired her a couple of years ago, but she had recently put on quite a bit of weight, and she now had a round face and the beginnings of a double chin. She did her job quite well, but her physical appearance had begun to irritate Willie. He resolved to fire her as soon as he could find a replacement.

For the next forty-five minutes he worked at his desk. The business side of his office ran like clockwork. When he was in the office, everybody knew it; he was more familiar with the books than his accountant, knew how many patients he'd seen each month for the last three years, and generally kept a very close eye on everything that was going on.

Feeling restless and irritated, he got up and strode around his office. There were no patients. He went into the lab; it was very modern and up-to-date, with sparkling white furniture and the newest equipment. Jackie Devlin, his senior lab tech, was working at the bench and looked up when he came in. She was a brunette with a rather long, subtly attractive face. Willie always thought she looked like a Modigliani.

"Do you need anything, Dr. Stringer?" asked Frankie. Dr. Stringer didn't usually come visiting unless there was a problem.

He stood there, thinking about other things, then looked at her. "Next weekend's a long holiday, Jackie. We'll be closed on Monday, so you won't need to come in."

"Right you are, Dr. Springer." Jackie smiled, but Willie had already turned and was on his way out. She raised her eyebrows, then turned back to the microscope. Last week the girls had said that he was acting funny, as if he had something on his mind.

"Yeah," Jackie had replied. "She's probably about 130 pounds, 36-24-36!" She wasn't very far off in her measurements, but it had not occurred to Willie to think of Patsy in those terms.

A light was flashing on the telephone console when he got back to his office. He picked it up and pressed the clear plastic button.

"Dr. Stringer? Dr. Dieter Romberg is on the line."

What could *he* be calling about? Maybe he was sick and wanted to see him professionally? But he knew that the pathologist didn't care for him too much, so that was unlikely.

"Dr. Stringer? This is Dieter Romberg, from the Pathology Department." Romberg's slow, Teutonic-accented speech occasionally made the unwary think that he thought slowly too. "I am now looking at the liver slides on your patient, Hopkins." Willie knew that when Romberg discussed a case on the telephone, he always did it from behind his microscope, so that any questions or details of tumors or organ structure could be discussed and answered there and then. "I see much fibrous replacement of the liver tissue, with thrombosis of some larger venous radicals, distortion of the portal triads—"

Damn him, thought Willie, he sounds as if he's gazing into a crystal ball, telling somebody's fortune. "Are you saying he had cirrhosis of the liver?" Willie interrupted. He felt suddenly weak and his face flushed uncomfortably. This was what he had dreaded, but expected to hear sooner or later.

"Yes, but if you would kindly allow me to finish, you will see that there is more." There was a brief silence, and Willie could imagine him changing the glass slides on the microscope and slowly turning the knurled control to bring the new one into bright focus. "Here we are . . . the lower end of the esophagus shows a network of large, collapsed veins with some bruising of the overlying mucosa. Dr. Stringer, did the patient have an endoscopy carried out previous to his surgery?"

"That could have been done by the tube we left in his

stomach, couldn't it?" Willie could feel the sweat coming out on his forehead and his head was beginning to throb.

"There were some other marks caused by the stomach tube, yes, but these were very minor and more recent. I apologize for repeating my question."

"Yes, we did an endoscopy the day he was admitted to the hospital. There was some bleeding, which I quickly controlled."

"Were you able to identify the source of the bleeding at that time, Dr. Stringer?"

The bastard's playing with me, thought Willie angrily, listening to Romberg's crafty, soft voice. *He knows damn well* . . . "At the time I thought it might be from an ulcer," he replied carefully. "But, of course, in the light of the pathological findings . . ."

There was a rustling of papers, barely audible to Willie.

"I'm looking at your notes, which your office kindly sent over . . . " Romberg began. *What notes?* "They describe an ulcer crater measuring three-by-three centimeters across, in the antrum of the stomach."

"That's incorrect," said Willie, grabbing on tight to the telephone and trying not to shout. "They must have sent an early draft of the notes, or mixed it up with some other patient's."

Romberg sounded relaxed and infuriatingly calm.

"Well, of course that's possible, but it has the date, the patient's name at the top, and, let me see, yes, it has your signature here at the bottom, Dr. Stringer."

Who the fuck had been sending out his endoscopy reports to Romberg without his permission? Somebody here was going to be looking for a job as of this afternoon!

There was a knock on the door and Vera came in. She hesitated when she saw that he was on the phone, then quickly wrote on the pink message pad on the desk before quietly going out.

Romberg's droning voice went on, with what Willie interpreted as a tone of superiority and reproof. "We examined the entire stomach and duodenum microscopically, without finding any trace of an ulcer."

"Well, those things can heal up really fast, you know, but of course down in your place you never see the good things that can happen to people, do you?"

"I'm sure you're right, Dr. Stringer. You know more about those things than I do."

You're damn right, you chair-borne slide-shuffler, thought Willie, you're damn right, *much* more. Then Willie's blood froze in his veins.

"I've discussed this case in detail with Dr. Gill, my department chairman," Romberg was saying, "and he feels we should refer it to the Surgical Quality Assurance Committee. Accordingly, I've sent all the appropriate materials to them."

"Sure, go ahead, do it!" Willie found himself saying, but the line was dead. He swore, softly and bitterly. That fucking self-righteous Kraut, Romberg! It was bad enough running a surgical practice these days, what with malpractice suits and insurance premiums going through the roof. But now the goddamn pathologists, the ass-bound bureaucrats of medicine, were getting into the act with a vengeance. Fifteen years ago, when he'd started off in practice, they never would have come after him like this. In the old days you could count on your colleagues to help you out if you were in trouble, not stick the knife into you and then turn it.

Willie picked up the pink message pad. There was a note in Vera's neat handwriting: "Mr. Tony Arbuthnot, Asst. Hosp. Administrator. Please return his call." This was followed by a telephone number.

The throbbing in Willie's head was getting worse, and it was beginning to make him feel physically sick. He dialed the number; he'd never heard of Tony Arbuthnot.

"Thank you for returning my call, Dr. Stringer. I hate to bother you with this, but I got a call this afternoon from a Dr. Hopkins in Wallingfield, Connecticut. Apparently he'd been talking to the Pathology Department, but they couldn't help him, and they put him through to me. What he wanted, apparently, was more details on an autopsy that had been performed on his son, who died here about . . . let's see, three weeks ago. Do you happen to remember the case?"

"Yes, I certainly do. My office already sent him the autopsy report. What . . ."

"It might be a good idea if you'd give him a call," suggested Arbuthnot smoothly. "He sounded concerned. I explained to him that this isn't something we get involved in, and in response to my inquiry he told me that you were the physician involved. I have his number here if you'd like it."

"No, we have it in the files," said Willie curtly. "I'll get in touch with him. Thanks."

Willie sat back heavily in his leather chair, aware of the throbbing in his head again. He'd been getting more of these episodes recently, especially when he was under some kind of stress; he should really see somebody about it.

Greg. What was his problem? What more information could he want? And why was he calling the Path Department? Willie reached for the phone, his hand shaking.

Greg was having a bad day, too; he hadn't slept and was too upset to shave. He was sitting in the kitchen in his robe, the copy of Edward's autopsy report on the counter, a magnifying glass in his hand. He'd been rereading it, and he had suddenly noticed that the date was in a different typeface from the rest of the report. Also, each of the pages had the same number at the bottom. With a feeling of physical nausea, Greg realized that it was a forgery. His immediate urge was to call Willie and confront him, but maybe there was some perfectly rational explanation.

He had called the Pathology Department at Willie's hospital, hoping to get some secretary to read off the original so he could compare it. He'd spent almost half an hour on the phone, finally talking to some administrator.

Dazed with fatigue, he went back upstairs to get dressed, but instead he lay down on the bed. He'd taken to spending the nights in Patsy's room; he couldn't sleep, and tossed and turned and put the light on to try to read, then dozed off. . . . That way at least Liz could get some rest. The worst time was always around five in the morning, when he was exhausted, and his mind took some strange turns, with all kinds of disturbing half thoughts, half dreams, all with almost frightening clarity— things that had happened long ago, his father, his childhood. . . . These thoughts appeared without warning, like long-forgotten hulks stirred up and surfacing from the deep after a cataclysmic storm. And the memories were not rusty or barnacle-encrusted; they had a febrile brightness about them that astonished Greg. More than once he thought he might be losing his mind.

When Greg was a child, his father hadn't been home very much; first he was traveling for a shoe company based in Salem, Massachusetts, and later for a pharmaceutical manufacturer. He was hardworking and diligent and eventually made a good enough living. Greg could remember the sound of his father shouting, relieving some of his tensions, which had scared Greg until he realized that he wasn't really shouting at his mother. He was always bursting with frustration and anger when he got home, and after he'd had a few gin and tonics (he'd always drunk rye until he joined the pharmaceutical company) and Greg had gone to bed, all the problems would bubble to the surface. Those ignorant quacks, he used to call them. . . . When his voice was raised, Greg would get up and stand behind the door in his bare feet, listening but not understanding much of what was being said.

"I've got this new drug, a beta blocker," he'd say from his comfortable armchair. His eyes were bright and his hand gripped his glass like a vise as he relived the highlights of the last six weeks. Greg's mother sat, placid now that he was home, in the opposite chair. She hardly opened her mouth when he was there.

"I start to tell them about it, and I can see their eyes start to glaze over, and I *know* they don't know what I'm talking about, but they never admit it. All they're waiting for is for me to finish and give them their reward for listening, a calendar, a couple of pens . . ."

What upset Greg's father the most, and made him shout the loudest, was the rudeness and arrogance he met with daily. How many times had he sat for hours in some waiting room, having given the secretary *her* gift (provided by the company), only to be told that the doctor had been called to an emergency, when in fact he'd just slipped out the back to avoid him! And how many times had he been humiliated by them, and smiled and taken it, when they'd then turn around and ask for a place on one of his company-sponsored cruises? Greg's father would have to thank them for whatever scrap of time they'd given him, shake their hands with a firm grip (at the orientation course, they'd even taught him the most profitable way of shaking hands), and smile, looking them frankly in the eye— "You *always* look them frankly in the eye," he'd been told solemnly, "and you also find out their birthday and their kids' names from the secretary, and you send cards."

But when he was talking to Greg, he never said a critical word about the individual doctors, only about his admiration for the profession. So when Greg had gone to medical school, he'd had an almost superstitious awe of the medical profession, and the feeling had persisted throughout his training. Even after he'd graduated and started up in practice, in his heart of hearts he'd never felt that he was a real doctor, not like the brilliant Willie Stringer. Greg always dressed the part, always went to the office in a dark business suit and well-polished black shoes, and his insecurities made him pay meticulous attention to every detail of his patients' illnesses. When he wasn't sure about a diagnosis, he'd get very uptight and order lots of tests, and then he'd try to make a diagnosis from the test results, and that rarely worked too well, and then he'd have to refer the patient to a specialist.

"I'm afraid I'm going to have to send you to a real doctor," he'd say to them, smiling, and they'd think what a lovely, modest man he was, not at all proud like most of them. But he knew that he was telling them the truth.

Greg turned his head on the pillow, suddenly wakeful. The phone . . . There wasn't an extension in Patsy's room, and he knew that by the time he got downstairs it would have stopped. Maybe it was the office. He lay back again, unable to summon enough energy to sit up. Louella would take care of it. Thank God for Louella—he'd never felt the same confidence with her predecessor, Mary Abbott, who'd been his nurse/secretary for about a year before Edward died. She'd really been a mistake. He'd given her the job on the strong recommendation of his patient, Mrs. Wellbourne, who was some kind of relative. She'd seemed a nice, capable enough person, with quite good references, but she wasn't as careful about records and filing as he would have liked. A couple of times he'd had calls from pharmacists about some prescriptions, and he couldn't find the appropriate records, and it had bothered him. But she certainly had had an affectionate disposition. Much too affectionate, in fact. Long after most people would have noticed, it suddenly struck him that Mary was making a play for him. He wasn't quite sure how to handle it, and decided to speak to Liz about it. When he told her everything that had been going on, the way she dressed and the way she would lean over him from behind when he was at his desk and press her breasts into his back, Liz's mouth hardened and she said he'd have to get rid of her; if that was too difficult for him, she'd be happy to come down to the office and do it herself.

Finally he'd gotten up enough nerve to the point of firing Mary. He gave her six weeks' notice and promised to give her a good reference, but she made the most awful scene. Greg shuddered at the recollection. It had been just dreadful, all that screaming and shouting.

Thank God for Louella. She had really kept the ship afloat during the time he couldn't cope, but now that he was better, he'd make it up to her. He'd give her a raise, or maybe a big end-of-year bonus. He'd ask the accountant, because whatever he did on his own would be sure to be wrong.

The fog of sharp glass shards was starting to roll around in his head again . . . the autopsy report . . . Greg closed his eyes. Since Edward's death, the overwhelming sensation in his head had been pain, but now it was making a transition to fear. Through his anguish Greg was beginning to realize that, even aside from the autopsy report, there were some very big unanswered questions about his son's death, and they hung around in his mind like wolves in the dusk, visible only when their eyes occasionally reflected the light.

When the phone rang again, he went downstairs to answer it. Although in a way he'd expected him to call, he was shocked to hear Willie's voice, and hung up quickly without answering, his heart pounding. He simply couldn't bear to talk to him.

CHAPTER
TWENTY-FIVE

"Well, Martin, good to see you!"

"It's been, let's see, almost eighteen years. My God! I must say you're looking good, though." And Willie was. His dark suit had been made for him by one of the best tailors in London, and he had lost a little weight over the last several weeks.

Martin, though, had become thicker around the waist, and although his bright blue eyes seemed as kindly as ever, most of the hair on the top of his head was gone, and the rest was a gray-beige color. In spite of that, to Willie he didn't seem much changed. He was well enough dressed, but the suit was off the rack and his shoes had thick rubber soles.

Martin put his heavy briefcase on Willie's big desk and sat down. His eyes flickered over the elegant, expensive furnishings, and the Utrillo on the wall behind the desk.

"If I had that," he said, indicating the painting, "I'd put it on the other wall where I could see it."

"That was always the difference between you and me," retorted Willie with a grin. "I always put my customers first. What I look at is the clock." He pressed a button on the console. "Don't put any calls through for the next fifteen minutes," he said, then turned back to Martin. "Now, what can I do for you?"

Martin's face fell fractionally. He had hoped for a nice chat about the old days before getting down to business. Willie hadn't changed.

"It's about a case I'm sure you remember, a guy by the name of Elmo Harris—"

Willie interrupted. "Martin, I thought you were in the drug business. How—"

"Oh, that was only for a couple of years. Soured me on the medical profession forever." He smiled. It was a thinner smile than his old wholehearted grin. "Medical insurance is more interesting, and I get my clients' undivided attention. Anyway, back to Elmo Harris. This is a really tricky one, and my directors are concerned about it."

Willie's eyebrows went up. "How come? He was almost dead when he came to the hospital, he was operated on, had his miserable life saved, and went home rejoicing. What the hell more could he want?" He looked at the clock. They would have started Death Rounds by now, and he was having trouble taking Martin and the Elmo Harris case seriously.

Martin sighed. "Well, for one thing, he's got himself a lawyer who's starting to talk discrimination, and he's trying to get the city administration into the act. And the newspapers too, of course, but so far nobody's taking him on."

"Big deal," said Willie, beginning to feel exasperated. "But the fact remains that he was properly treated and was healthy and had no complaints at the time he left the hospital."

Martin sighed again, and what was left of Willie's pleasure in seeing his old comrade evaporated. Martin opened his briefcase and pulled out a thick folder. Willie was surprised.

"If all that's on Harris, it's thicker than his hospital chart!"

"That's only part of it." Martin pulled a legal-size sheaf out of the file. "Okay, here's a partial list of the charges that refer just to you. I'm sure you know that Dr. Frankel and Dr. Wesley are also being sued. Right, here we are. Negligence, abandonment—"

"What's that?"

"Undertaking to care for a patient, then not providing the service."

"But I never undertook to do anything. I didn't even see him until the next day!"

"Weren't you on call for the surgical service that week?"

"Yes, but—"

"Then contractually you had an implicit obligation to see him, examine him, make a diagnosis, and personally perform or supervise any surgical procedure. Surely you were aware of that?"

Willie looked at Martin with growing irritation. His tone had been sharp, almost hectoring.

"He was properly taken care of under the supervision of the department chairman. Isn't that good enough for them?"

"No, it isn't. Your chairman's in deep trouble over that himself, and I understand he's far from delighted. He took on the care of a patient without making a preoperative evaluation, without an operative permit signed by the patient and himself, without previous explanation of the nature of the operation, the risks and possible complications . . ." Martin paused, then looked at Willie with a strange expression, and Willie suddenly realized that Martin was enjoying himself.

"Look, Martin, I don't think I should say anything more without an attorney."

"Right, of course. We've got one for you, one of the best. This is just a brief exploration of the facts so I can tell my boss how deep we're in—"

"This is ridiculous!" Willie's voice was rising; he deeply resented such interference and criticism from a nonprofessional. What the hell did Martin know about the job of a surgeon when he couldn't even get through his first medical school exams? "As soon as Harris's lawyer sees the case is going to be defended, he'll fold. He's just trying for some easy pickings, hoping you'll settle."

"Yeah. Not this one. We know him. He'll try every dirty trick in the book. Let me tell you right now, we're going to try to settle, but he'll make his demands so astronomical, we may just have to let it go to court."

Willie stood up, his eyes cold. "Thanks for stopping by, Martin. Your optimistic outlook has made my day. Now, if you'll excuse me, I have a meeting to go to at the hospital."

Martin put his papers away, in no hurry. "Couple of things, Willie. Don't discuss the case with anyone, not your colleagues, attorneys except your own, not the press."

"The press?"

"Sooner or later they'll hear about it. It'll make a good story, too: 'Discrimination in city hospital—wealthy Park Avenue surgeon refuses to treat dying black.' Well, it was nice to see you again, Willie. Do you ever hear from Greg?"

"Occasionally, yes, he's fine. In practice up in Connecticut."

"Say hi if you see him. I don't suppose I'll be visiting him

professionally. You'll be hearing from your attorney within a
day or two. . . . No, don't bother, I know the way out."

"Greg, come on, that doesn't make any sense." Liz sat up in
bed, annoyed at having to defend Willie Stringer, particularly
after the phone call from Patsy that evening. "Why on earth
would he want to give you a faked autopsy report? I'm sure
there must be some rational explanation."

Greg sat up, too, and put on the light. They both blinked,
and Liz said, "Did you have to do that?"

Greg was looking at her, and he had that drawn, haunted
expression again; the one he'd had for weeks after Edward's
death.

"He's hiding something, Liz. I know it. Remember, I've
known Willie for years."

Liz almost said something but caught herself in time. She
put out her arms to hug him, but he shook his shoulders in a
brusque movement that she knew well.

"I've been thinking about it ever since it happened," he said.
"There are too many things I don't understand, and I think
something major went wrong during the operation and he's
not telling us."

Liz sighed, beginning to feel exasperated. She was tired, and
at this time of night she really didn't think it was fair of him
to keep on ripping off the scabs of their tragedy.

"Don't you remember when he came out of the operating
room? His face? He was so pleased. If anything had gone
wrong, I'd have seen it on his face, I promise you."

"Liz, I'm telling you, something went wrong somewhere.
This afternoon I made a few phone calls. I spoke to Frank
Rosen in New Haven . . . I don't think you ever knew him.
Anyway, he's a staff surgeon and he teaches. He's an expert
on stomach surgery, and I told him the whole story. He was
shocked, really shocked. He said he'd never heard of such a
complication, not from that kind of surgery."

Liz lay very still; her heart was beating so fast, she hoped
Greg wouldn't notice.

Greg lay back and looked at the ceiling. Liz could still see
the stiffness of his jaw muscles. "He said I should get the
autopsy report, and I told him there had been a problem with

that, so he said I should call the Pathology Department directly. 'You're a doctor,' he said, 'they'll do it for you.' "

"Do you mind putting the light out?" asked Liz. "It's almost three." Greg turned on his side and clicked it off. In the darkness Liz's voice didn't sound so tense. "So what did you do?"

"I'd already called them this morning and got the runaround, of course. Those big places, they don't give a damn who you are. Finally some administrator told me to contact the physician who performed the surgery, so there I was, full circle, after a thirty-minute long-distance call."

"But you didn't call Willie, did you? Look, Greg, he's your friend, he's the one who did the surgery, and so he knows more about it than anybody. Why didn't you call him?"

"Liz, I talked to him last week, and I can't talk to him anymore. I'm going to call the head of his department in the morning, see if somebody can make sense out of all of this."

Liz could sense that Greg was feeling trapped and desperate. He hated the idea that his old friend might have done something unethical, and it hurt him to the bone to think that Willie had lied to him. At the back of his mind lurked the horrible thought that Willie might have neglected Edward and in some way caused his death.

"This is what I'd do, Greg. I'd call Willie up, tell him I was really concerned and wanted to go over the whole thing in detail. You can take an afternoon off and go into town, go out for dinner with him, whatever . . ."

Liz could feel Greg tense as she spoke.

"No, Liz. It's too late for that. I don't feel I can trust what he says anymore." Heavily he climbed out of bed. "I think I'll sleep in Patsy's room, sweetheart. I'm sorry I woke you."

Liz heard his footsteps padding along the corridor, and the creak as he opened the door to Patsy's room. Her heart was still beating fast, and she was beginning to feel a kind of fear she had never experienced. Willie, the man she'd loved more than anyone in her whole life, was beginning to turn into a monster before her eyes. He'd invited Patsy to New York, with God knows what in mind. Patsy had been indignant when she advised her not to go, to stick with men her own age. And all this stuff surfacing now about Edward . . . Supposing, just supposing, that Willie *had* done something dreadful, how would Greg react? Would he be able to sustain his anger long enough to *do* anything about it? Greg so hated being angry; he could always see the other person's point of view, often better than his own.

Liz sat up in the darkness, filled with a sudden sense of determination. If worse came to worst, and Willie had been responsible for Edward's death, she wouldn't wait for Greg to take care of it. She would have to. And she knew how she'd do it.

Patsy was late, and just a little flustered, although she would never have admitted it. This had the makings of the biggest weekend in her life. The Plaza, no less, and then a show of some sort. Willie was really the nicest man she'd ever met, barring her father, of course, but he didn't really count.

And then she was going to a concert with Bob the next day. She was really hitting the big time. How many girls did she know who'd gone out with two doctors in one weekend?

Of course, Bob was a kid, comparatively. Patsy had already decided that she liked older men, mostly because they could put her up at the Plaza. But Willie was really different—he was genuinely interested in her, and he was clever, he knew so many things. He made a welcome change from those heavy-breathing octopus types at the New London Academy, horny guys with short hair and a long reach. And Willie had been so nice, so supportive, not just to her but to all of the family. Patsy remembered gratefully how he'd hugged her mother at the funeral. But she hadn't been prepared for her mother's response when she told her about going to see Willie. She had been furious. Patsy grinned to herself. She was jealous! Maybe she had had something going with Willie before she'd married . . . There seemed to be a kind of understanding between the two of them in which her father didn't participate.

Patsy had promised herself that she'd finish the geology paper before leaving, because she'd never have time to do it when she got back. And it was really interesting. They were doing seismology; you could set off an explosion in the earth, quite a small one, and analyze the wave patterns that it set up. It made the whole earth ring like a bell. Patsy imagined hearing the massive earth chimes from the moon, or somewhere. But then, as she'd also recently found out, sound waves don't travel in a vacuum. So if you weren't actually on the earth, how could you tell what was happening? Did the moon and the planets ring too? Was the music of the spheres a reality, or just some old romantic crap? Did atoms and molecules also make a kind of music you could only hear if you were inside the orbiting electrons?

Patsy had always been a happy person, but now, absorbing all these new thoughts and information, she was experiencing a fresh kind of pleasure, an awareness of the complexity of the world around her. Everything she was learning made her look at the world differently, have new and unexpected thoughts about it, and there were plenty of people around with whom to discuss it all. Intellectually Patsy was in heaven.

The only big jolt in her young life had been Edward's death, and she still didn't know how much or how permanently it had affected her. Her friends told her she'd grown up a lot since it happened, but they usually hastened to add that she still had a long way to go.

Patsy swung her little white Subaru down the hill toward Route 32 and waited at the light where the drive joined the road. From there she could see the Thames River, the Coast Guard Academy high over its banks. The training ship *Eagle* poked its three tall masts up above the trees. A few minutes later she was heading down I-95; she sat back, put a cassette in the player, and settled down for the trip.

It took about two and a half hours to get into town, and then another hour to get through the Friday afternoon traffic around the park. But finally there she was, her tiny car jammed between two black limos, each about a block long, outside the Plaza Hotel. A uniformed man came out and helped her unload the car. Willie had said just to give him the keys, he'd take care of it. Inside, the hotel was huge, like a very fancy railroad station with chandeliers and carpets, and people milling around. She checked in, admired the flowers in her room, but didn't know if that was part of the service or if they had been sent by Willie. She went to the window and pulled the drapes back. The view was nice, she thought, looking down at the few horse-drawn cabs waiting outside Central Park, then over the trees. It was foggy, and she wasn't sure if she could see the edge of the lake or not.

She bounced on the bed. It was firm, and bounced her right back, like a trampoline. The furniture was solid and modern, in light-colored wood—oak, maybe. She didn't really know. Her friends would want to hear about every detail of the room, down to the color of the bedspread.

The telephone rang. It was Willie; he'd come and pick her up at seven. His voice was vibrant, even excited.

"Put on your nicest dress," he said. "Tonight we're going to the opera, then we're going to show you off at the 21 Club."

Willie really knows how to make a girl feel good, thought Patsy, putting the phone down and falling back on the bed. *When he talks to you, it's as if you're the only girl in the world.*

CHAPTER
TWENTY-SIX

Bob lay facedown on his bed, feeling as if he'd been kicked in the head. They'd really done a job on him at the Death Rounds. It seemed as if they'd all ganged up on him, the pathologists, Dr. Frankel too. Walter hadn't helped, just sat there looking at him with that funny expression, as if to say, Sorry, fella, but this time you're on your own. Willie had taken some of the heat off him, but not enough to make it look as if *he* were at fault. The auditorium had been packed, because everybody had come hoping to see Willie Stringer get it in the neck, but the attendings joined ranks and Willie had gotten out of it okay; not exactly smelling like a rose but okay. But they needed somebody to dump on, and Bob was the obvious one.

Dr. Frankel had taken the unusual step of telling Walter which cases to discuss, and the first one was the black man, Elmo Harris, the guy who'd come in a few weeks before with a bullet in his spleen. They hadn't discussed it at rounds at the time because they'd had too many other good cases, but for some reason Frankel wanted it on the schedule. Even now Bob went into a cold sweat at the recollection of the case. If Dr. Frankel hadn't come when he did, Bob was sure the man would have died. Anyway, Elmo had made it, and left the hospital a week later to go looking for the guy who'd shot him.

And Frankel had certainly hauled Bob over the coals on that one. "Our residency program is set up to avoid precisely this kind of situation," he said. "To take a patient into the OR without the experience to deal with what was obviously a serious situation was foolhardy in the extreme." He looked sternly at Bob. "Next time make sure your attending is in the operating room before you undertake this kind of procedure."

Bob noticed that he didn't look at Willie, who was sitting on the bench behind Bob and the rest of the team.

But all that was nothing, a mere hors d'oeuvre compared to what was to follow.

"The next case was deferred from last week," said Walter, facing the audience. "Case number 89-48521. Dr. Wesley will present it."

Bob stood up. "This is the case of a twelve-year-old boy who was admitted to the hospital about three weeks ago with a diagnosis of bleeding gastric ulcer."

Willie stirred in his seat. He was leaning forward, intent on every word. "Actually, if you look at my notes, the admitting diagnosis was upper GI hemorrhage," he said quietly. Bob looked at him. There was something in his tone—was he trying to tell him something, to warn him?

"Right, sorry. He had been feeling unwell for several weeks—"

"What do you mean by unwell?" interrupted Dr. Frankel. He was looking grim and annoyed. "In this context that's an unacceptable term that doesn't mean anything."

Bob felt that the atmosphere of the conference had changed suddenly; he'd been at enough meetings where someone was singled out for execution. The audience smelled blood; Bob hoped it wasn't going to be his.

"I'm sorry, Dr. Frankel. He fainted at the end of a two-hundred-yard race, and since then had felt very tired, often going to bed straight after dinner. His appetite was poor, and his mother thought he'd lost some weight, although she wasn't sure." Bob looked at Dr. Frankel, but his face gave him no comfort. For no reason, Bob suddenly felt he was on trial for his life.

He gulped. "Past medical history revealed childhood illnesses only. I spoke to the mother after the patient had died, and she remembered that he'd had a two-week period of tiredness and lassitude about a year before. At that time she noted that his urine was dark but put it down to dehydration and didn't think to mention it to anybody."

Bob went on to the clinical exam, which luckily he had done

quite thoroughly. He mentioned the fact that the liver had felt somewhat enlarged to him, although he wasn't sure if it meant anything in a boy this age. "He had an upper GI series a month ago, which showed an ulcer in the antral area of the stomach."

Frankel pointed to the radiologist, who flipped the X rays up on the fluorescent screens. Ted Markham was a third-year radiology resident, which you could guess because it usually took over two years to learn that particular elegant way of flipping the films up with the right thumb. He stood back, and somebody dimmed the room lights. "This is not a very good study," said Ted, "but of course it wasn't done here." There was faint laughter from the gallery, instantly hushed when Frankel told him to get on with it. "There is some distortion at the lower end of the esophagus," he said, using a slender metal pointer, "possibly due to varices." *Bullshit artist,* thought Bob. *He knows damn well they were varices, but I wonder how sure he would have been before the autopsy?* Frankel glanced over at the attending radiologist, who nodded his agreement.

"Show me the ulcer we've been hearing about," said Frankel.

Ted made a show of searching for it, then said, "Sorry, Dr. Frankel, I'm afraid I can't see it."

Willie came down from his seat and pointed at a shadow on one of the films. "That's what the Children's Hospital radiologist reported was an ulcer."

Ted looked at his attending, who also came down the steps at the side of the auditorium to get a closer look at the films. "No," he said, "I don't think so. I agree, it does look like an ulcer there, but only on that film. If you look on the later films—here . . . and here—that shadow's gone. It simply wasn't a very good study. Sorry."

Willie started to say something, then thought better of it and returned to his seat. He didn't seem particularly concerned, although Bob felt glad he wasn't in his shoes.

A few minutes later Willie interrupted the proceedings to describe the actual operation; he didn't mention the huge veins, the abnormal-looking liver, or the big spleen, and to Bob's astonishment Dr. Frankel didn't try to pin him down on any of these matters. But Frankel came back to life with a vengeance when Bob started to go into the details of the resuscitation attempts.

"Is Dr. Leibowitz here?" he asked. Bob and Walter exchanged glances. Sol Leibowitz was the medical resident who'd been first on the scene when they called the code on Edward Hopkins. He was up near the back of the auditorium and raised his hand. "Thank you for joining us, Dr. Leibowitz," said Frankel courteously. He always treats people on other services so nicely, thought Bob. Why doesn't he ever try it with his own people? "Would you like to tell us the sequence of events during the resuscitation?"

Sol hesitated. He'd been told to be at this surgical conference, but the last thing he wanted was to be the outside axman for Frankel. At first it had looked as if Willie Stringer was to be the target, but now it looked more as if they were going for Bob Wesley.

He told them about the resuscitation.

"Why didn't the anesthesiologist put in the endotracheal tube? Wasn't he there?" asked Frankel.

"He did come," said Sol carefully, "but he left soon afterward—"

"I told him he could go," interrupted Willie. "Everything seemed stable, and it didn't look as if he'd need to put in a tube."

"They looked stable? Minutes after a serious hemorrhage?" said Frankel, raising his eyebrows. "Well, I suppose it was a matter of judgment."

"His blood pressure was coming up, and he was conscious at that time," said Bob.

"What *was* his pressure at that time?"

Bob looked at the flow sheet. "Eighty over forty," he said, almost inaudibly. There was a long silence.

"Did you think of putting in a Blakemore tube?" asked Frankel finally. He looked up at the back of the gallery, where the students were. "Do any of you know what a Blakemore tube is?" After his comments last week to poor Irene Stark, they all lowered their eyes and hoped that Frankel didn't remember their names.

"Well, for your information, a Blakemore tube has a balloon on the end of it. It gets passed into the stomach and the balloon is inflated and pulled up against the lower end of the esophagus. It was designed to stop bleeding from esophageal varices."

Another silence while Frankel looked at Bob, waiting for an answer. "No, sir, I didn't. It never occurred to me, or to anyone else that I know of, that he could have varices."

He looked up at Willie, but there was no information to be gained from his expressionless face. Bob couldn't tell if he was waiting for the ax to fall on his own neck, or whether he'd been able to convince Frankel that Bob was the one who'd really messed everything up.

Frankel looked up at the clock. "We've run out of time, I'm afraid," he said. "The medical people have the auditorium next, and I can see them waiting outside." He looked at Bob and Walter. "There are a couple of things I'd like to discuss with the two of you in my office, if you have a moment."

Willie's face was devoid of expression as he slid between the seats, heading for the door, but his mind was seething in such a turmoil of anxiety and frustrated anger that he was as close to losing control as he had ever been in his life.

Bob Wesley and Walter English followed Dr. Frankel along the corridor to his office. Walter was confident that he had little to be concerned about except for the annoying fact that the problems had occurred on his service, but Bob was sweating slightly and walked behind the other two with a feeling of impending doom.

They went through the outer office where Maxine, the department secretary, handed Dr. Frankel a small pile of pink message slips, into the sanctum sanctorum, a rather plain room with a high, flaking ceiling and a tall, glass-fronted bookcase full of bound medical journals and reference volumes. Dr. Frankel went behind his large plate-glass-covered wooden desk and pointed to two high, straight-backed red leather-covered chairs, which looked as if they had been purloined from a bishop's waiting room.

Dr. Frankel sat down and spent a few moments getting steam up on his pipe.

"Walter," he said finally, taking his pipe out of his mouth and looking hard at it, "I'm concerned about some of the things that have been going on in the department recently." He paused; nobody moved a muscle. "In my experience, when one thing turns up like that at Death Rounds, it means that ten other problems have gone unnoticed."

Walter stared impassively back at Dr. Frankel. Three months and twelve days, that's what he still had to put in before getting out of here, back to the sunshine and clear air of Albuquerque.

Bob couldn't sit there and let Walter take the blame for something he had had nothing to do with. "The problems you're referring to were my responsibility, Dr. Frankel," he blurted out. "Walter . . ."

Frankel looked over at Bob as if surprised to see him there at all. "I'll be getting to your part in this shortly," he said, as if Bob had made a really impolite intrusion into an adult conversation. "What I want to emphasize to you," he said, pointing the stem of his pipe at Walter, "is that you are responsible for everything that happens on your service, whether you were directly involved or not."

There was another silence. Bob couldn't help moving uncomfortably in his chair, but Walter gazed stolidly back at Dr. Frankel. Three months and twelve days . . .

Dr. Frankel looked at the clock on the wall opposite him. "Two incidents," he said more briskly. "First, the black man who was shot in the spleen. Your junior resident took the patient to the operating room with insufficient preparation and without the expertise to handle the case properly. Luckily I happened to be around, but in spite of that, we may finish up with a four-million-dollar lawsuit on our hands."

Walter opened his mouth to speak, but Frankel put his hand up. "I don't want any discussion. We've had all we need at Death Rounds. What I'm saying is that you should know exactly what's going on on your service and prevent this kind of situation from arising."

The phone rang on his desk but he ignored it. After two rings they heard Maxine pick it up in the outer office.

"Secondly, the boy with the chronic active hepatitis. This case was woefully mishandled. He wasn't properly worked up, he had an operation he didn't need and which ultimately killed him. The resuscitation attempt was, in my opinion, also very badly handled." Frankel got up and walked around to the side of the desk, standing over Walter and addressing him. "As leader of the team, you have to have adequate support from your junior staff. If you feel that is not forthcoming, you are free to turn in an adverse report. As you know, there are lots of applicants for junior resident posts on this service."

Frankel went to the door and opened it. "That's all," he said curtly. "Now, if you'll excuse me . . ."

"Walter, I'm really sorry," mumbled Bob as they walked along the corridor.

"Don't give it another thought," said Walter airily, but he looked grim and didn't say anything more until they got to the surgical floor.

CHAPTER
TWENTY-SEVEN

Janus Frankel sat at his desk for a few moments after they'd gone, thoughtfully tapping the stem of his pipe and looking at the two envelopes on the desk.

"Maxine, get me the folder on Dr. Stringer." His voice was calm, but Maxine knew the inflections of it. The boss had been in a truly foul mood for days now; yesterday he'd been closeted with the university lawyers for over two hours, then that fellow Penrose coming from the insurance company . . . Boy, was he mad after that one! Maxine didn't like Janus Frankel, but she told the other secretaries how divine he was, mostly to maintain the desirability of her job in their eyes. To her he seemed hard, humorless, and he treated people like dirt, unless they were important or he wanted something out of them. But he was tough—she recognized that—and got things done.

Frankel opened the left-hand drawer of his desk and pulled out a round black-and-white tin of Balkan Sobranie tobacco. He filled his still warm pipe, wishing that Maxine would learn where all the files were. She was a great time waster.

Maxine brought the manila folder with WILBRAHIM STRINGER, M.D. typed on the tab and laid it on the desk.

Frankel pulled the letters out of their envelopes and reread them. The first was from Dr. Hopkins, the father of the boy who had died. He was apparently now a general practitioner in Connecticut—Frankel remembered him vaguely as a student; about the same time as Stringer himself, he recalled. Dr. Hopkins felt he had been misled about the diagnosis and the cause of his son's death and wished to talk to Dr. Frankel in person to clarify the situation. Frankel turned to the next letter. It was from the head of the Department of Pathology, stating that the case of Edward Hopkins, age twelve, was being referred to the Surgical Quality Assurance Committee, which was scheduled to meet in ten days.

He put the letters aside, then emptied the folder out on his desk. There was Stringer's résumé, a record of his professional qualifications and achievements, together with a small list of papers he had written or was coauthor of. In addition, there were three typed pages stapled together: the records of two complaints that had been made against him. The top sheet was a single-spaced account, written by the head nurse of the ICU, dated two years earlier. Stringer apparently had refused to come in to see a seriously ill patient in the ICU, although the head nurse and then the junior resident had both phoned to explain the need for his presence. A brief notation was scrawled at the bottom of the page in Frankel's predecessor's almost illegible handwriting. "Discussed with S," it read, "patient OK, will not happen again."

The second complaint seemed to have been more serious. Only a week or two after the first incident, Stringer had scheduled a routine operation, nothing special, just a gallbladder in an otherwise healthy middle-aged woman. She was admitted, seen by the anesthetist, and examined by the resident on call. At 6:30 the next morning, she had been given her premedication, 100 milligrams of Demerol and .01 of a grain of atropine. She was taken down to the operating room forty-five minutes later and put to sleep by one of the anesthesiology residents, who must have been barely awake himself. By 7:30, the traditional time when the first knife of the day is applied to flesh, Dr. Stringer hadn't appeared. They figured he must have been caught in the traffic, although nobody remembered his ever being late before. The head nurse called his office at 7:45, but of course there was no answer. Because of the pressure of cases, she decided to move Stringer's patient to wait in the holding area, still anesthetized, so she could open up the operating room for another case.

She tried to reach Willie at home. No reply. By eight, the anesthetist was having a fit and had terminated the anesthesia, but the patient vomited as he was taking out the tube, and inhaled some stomach contents into her lungs—a disastrous complication. She was transferred to the ICU where she had to be placed on a ventilator. By this time the head nurse had reached Willie's office manager, who informed them that Dr. Stringer was on vacation and was not expected back for four days.

Of course, Willie Stringer had come out of that one unscathed; he quoted the OR regulations, which stated unequivocally that patients should not be anesthetized until the surgeon was present in the operating room. Obviously he could take no responsibility for the subsequent complications. The one thing they almost caught him with was that the OR secretary remembered that Willie had scheduled the case himself. If they had been able to make that stick, they might have gotten him, but he came up with a signed statement from his appointments secretary stating that she had made the booking, not realizing that her boss was going to be away.

Not much, really. Frankel closed the file. He was well aware of the general feeling among the nurses and residents that Willie Stringer, though a clever and occasionally brilliant surgeon, had been involved in too many documented instances of carelessness, which even occasionally amounted to recklessness. As a result, both nurses and resident doctors were wary of him and on the lookout for trouble when dealing with one of his patients.

Frankel sat back. A wide puff of blue smoke rose and then hung in the air, as if he had started himself up and his motor was now on idle.

He free-associated for a moment, perhaps under the influence of the aromatic Sobranie blend. From the time he had been an assistant professor and Stringer a student, Frankel had harbored a strong personal dislike of Willie Stringer. He had tried unsuccessfully to block his appointment to the hospital staff, but he had only had a small voice back then. Now Frankel had been chairman of the Department of Surgery for just over a year of his two-year term. The senior men rotated that unsought-after post between them every two years, but Frankel liked the job and was good at it. He had a bigger goal in his sights, however; he wanted to be president of the American College of Surgeons, and to get there he needed a substantial power base, such as the post he was now in. Only it had to be permanent. Frankel had to do such an outstanding job that his senior colleagues would ask him to stay on.

Willie Stringer, as one of the "town surgeons," was an outspoken critic of the system and called the academics the "nonsurgical surgeons." "Who the hell are they to tell me what I can do and what I can't do?" he liked to ask his colleagues. "Those guys, who're lucky if they do a case a week, what do they know about surgery? They should stick to their teaching and research and let us take care of our own problems."

Stringer had deepened the divide, but not all the "town surgeons" agreed with him. The academics were doing a job they would hate to have, and disciplining themselves would become almost impossibly divisive if they were the ones who had to do it. At one of the department meetings somebody had even suggested that Willie Stringer be the next chairman, and although it was not meant seriously, the idea had been taken up enthusiastically, partly because it would teach Stringer a lesson but also because it would break what some considered the stranglehold of the academics over the town surgeons.

Janus Frankel was well aware of this; in a few quiet moments of evaluation he figured that Stringer's recent problems had isolated him, and he knew instinctively that this was the time to strike. A new mushroom cloud erupted from the pipe, and Janus Frankel pressed the button on his intercom.

"Get Dr. Furness for me, please."

A moment later he could hear the faint sounds of the paging system: "Dr. Furness, Dr. Andrew Furness, call 4104. . . ." The telephone rang, and a couple of minutes later Andrew Furness came into the room, closing the door behind him. Andrew was a tall, thin Scotsman with a long blue jaw and a watchful expression. Always impeccably dressed, he wore a long, old-fashioned, but spotless white coat over his pinstripes, with his initials neatly embroidered on the breast pocket, which contained a small slide rule clipped to it. Disdaining pocket calculators, he used it to figure out drug doses and electrolyte balances, just as he had when he was a surgical research fellow twenty years previously. Furness had abandoned academic surgery to go into private practice some years before; he had been in charge of the Pathology Committee, the Care Evaluation Committee, and a member of the Quality Assurance

Committee, and his Calvinist attitude had led to a near revolt among the surgeons, who suddenly found themselves hauled onto the carpet and reprimanded for all kinds of minor offenses. After a bitter struggle he had thrown in the academic towel and started up in private practice. He remained a capable, silent person whose stature increased as his responsibilities diminished.

"Andrew, thanks for coming over. I hope I didn't take you away from the operating table?" The mild jest passed by Andrew without response. The only time anybody remembered hearing his sardonic laugh was the day Jimmy Carter was elected president.

"Have a seat. I've got a real problem here, and I'd like your advice. It's about Willie Stringer . . ."

Frankel pushed the two letters across the desk toward him and put the other papers back in Willie's file. There was no need for Andrew to peruse those.

Andrew Furness read the papers in silence, then pushed them back at Frankel.

"So?"

"It looks as if Stringer's gone a bit too far this time," said Frankel, implying that this was not just an isolated problem. He pushed his chair back. "Did you know that the hospital's accreditation was in trouble last year?"

Anybody else's eyebrows would have gone up, but Andrew sat there impassively.

"Yes, the Joint Commission people were here to evaluate the hospital four months ago, and their final report arrived last week. For the first time in the history of this institution we only got a temporary accreditation, for one year, because of a number of problems they found. I went over the report with the administrator last Thursday, and believe me, it wasn't good reading."

"We've never had trouble in the past, that I know of," murmured Andrew. His thin lips barely moved, and he spoke as if a great effort were required.

"They really focused on two major problems. One had nothing to do with us, something about fire escapes from the patient areas, but the other has to do with peer review."

"Is that within their bailiwick?" asked Andrew. He had left Scotland twenty-five years before, but his accent was still strong.

"It certainly is. They said we don't police ourselves adequately, that the review mechanisms are inadequate, and that instead of doing proper critiques of our work, we go around patting each other on the back."

"That certainly rings a bell," said Andrew wryly. "Just don't fall into the trap I fell into."

"You were ahead of your time, Andrew," replied Frankel. "The thing is that with the malpractice situation the way it is now, we're being *forced* to do something about it. If we don't have satisfactory proof that we're doing a good job, they're quite capable of taking away our accreditation, and you know what that would do. We'd lose Medicare, Medicaid, and our patients would go to other hospitals. I needn't tell you that the administration won't tolerate even the possibility of that happening. If we don't do it ourselves, they're quite capable of setting up a review board from outside the department, even from outside the hospital."

"I see," said Andrew slowly. "Yes, I do see. How do you propose to handle this?"

"I wanted to hear your thoughts on the matter. You've had to handle that kind of difficulty in the past, I know."

"You could appoint a special committee to review Stringer's alleged misdeeds," suggested Andrew. "That way it would be done quickly and we could lay the whole thing to rest before it had a chance to get inflated."

"Good thought," said Frankel. "And from the point of view of this particular problem, a good solution." He put his hands flat on the desk in front of him. "There's only one difficulty I have with it. The JCAH would say that it proved their point: If we have to convene a special committee, it means that our existing system isn't adequate to handle this kind of thing."

"Yes, I see your point," said Andrew. "Let me think about it for a while. Do you mind?"

"No, of course not. Why don't we meet again, let's see . . ." Frankel looked at his desk calendar. "How about Friday, noon? I'll get some sandwiches in. There'll probably be a couple of other people joining us. I needn't tell you this is all very confidential."

Andrew gave him a thin, slightly lopsided smile. The two men understood each other quite well.

After Andrew Furness left, Frankel made several more phone

calls and had two or three more visitors. By the time he was ready to go to his next conference, a plan was taking shape in his mind. If he played his cards correctly, he could use this whole Stringer business very much to his own advantage. He would be seen as the strong leader who'd gotten rid of a dangerously incompetent colleague, and it would strengthen his claim to permanence as department chairman, increase his visibility with the College of Surgeons, and hugely increase his local power base. But he'd have to move very cautiously; he didn't want to do what Andrew Furness had done and fall into a trap of his own making.

Puffing away on his pipe, feeling rather complacent, he tried to look at himself and his work in a historical context. Where would it all lead? What would it be like, being a surgeon in ten or twenty years time? Would they still be able to find good people to take on the kind of responsibility he was shouldering? Or by then would lawyers have totally destroyed the practice of medicine? Already many of his colleagues were advising their children to choose other professions, even when there had been doctors in the family for generations, and the best young brains in the country were ignoring medicine and going to law school, headed for the top jobs in politics, business, and industry. God help us, he thought.

CHAPTER
TWENTY-EIGHT

Willie met Patsy in the foyer of the Plaza. When she got out of the elevator, he came toward her, looking marvelously handsome, she thought, wearing evening dress under a dark coat and a white silk scarf.

"My, you look wonderful!" he said, hugging her. Patsy wore a long dress of green silk with a plain string of pearls, and she did look stunning. His eyes twinkled at her. "It's a little chilly out." He slipped his coat off and put it around her shoulders. It was warm from his body, and Patsy gave a little shiver at the feel of it wrapped around her. He led the way to the door and ushered her to his BMW, waiting at the curb. To her faint surprise he opened the rear door; she'd thought she'd be sitting in the front with him. He leaned into the dark interior of the car.

"Ellen, this is Patsy."

For a second Patsy was thunderstruck. Ellen! It had never occurred to her that she might be coming too. Then she laughed, a big sudden laugh of relief, a laugh at herself. She gave Willie a huge kiss on the cheek and climbed in.

The opera was *La Bohème*, and it was the most stupendous performance. Patsy knew the music and had a tape of the opera with Maria Callas singing Mimi, but had never seen it, and from the moment the lights dimmed and the chandeliers rose up into the ceiling, she was in heaven. She sat between Willie and Ellen, who'd brought opera glasses, and they smiled to see her total absorption and enthusiasm. During intermission they went for a drink and shouted at each other joyfully over the noise of conversations around them. Patsy had that effect on people; she made them feel more alive, and happy to be with her.

"I wouldn't have minded having a daughter, if she'd been like that," Ellen whispered to Willie as they went back to their seats. Willie had worried that his wife might get tired, but she seemed amazingly happy and excited.

After the opera they went to the 21 Club. They didn't get one of the very best tables, but it wasn't in Siberia, either.

"Well, how did you like *La Bohème*?" asked Ellen after they'd been seated, but Patsy didn't hear her; she was gazing curiously around at the other tables.

"Is there anybody famous here?" she whispered, and Willie smiled. Her enthusiasm and wonder were totally endearing.

"Probably," he said, careful not to look around, "but actually I think they're mostly business people here tonight, Wall Street types, you know."

"*La Bohème* always makes me feel sad," Patsy said to Ellen. "It must have been tough being a student in those times, huh? No student health service, stuff like that . . ."

"I suppose so," replied Ellen. "But they probably figured they were better off than the generation before *them*."

"And at least they weren't dragged out of the classrooms and put into uniform to die on some battlefield, so they probably felt privileged," added Willie rather absently. He could see that Patsy was attracting more than a few admiring glances.

"To starve in a garret? Come on, Willie!"

The waiter approached with the menus. Patsy was intrigued to see that hers didn't have the prices on it. "How did he know that *I* wasn't taking the two of *you* to dinner?" she asked, her eyes mischievous after Willie had explained. "I read the other day that most of the wealth in the U.S. is now in the hands of women, so I could have been!"

"Quite true. Luckily for me, Ellen gives me a little pocket money every Friday," murmured Willie with a quick, amused glance at Ellen, "and the waiter is aware of that." He immersed himself in the wine list while Ellen discreetly pointed out to Patsy some of the minor celebrities at other tables. "Let's see, if you're both having the Dover sole and I'm having the poached salmon, I think a little Meursault would wash all of that down nicely, don't you?"

There was a slight commotion as a group of half a dozen people came in, heralded by loud laughter as they entered from the lobby. Patsy put her hand up to her mouth. "Was that . . . ? Is that . . . ?" she whispered, awestruck after they'd gone past.

"Klaus Von Bulow? Yes, I think it was."

She couldn't help staring, then a wicked look came over her face. At that moment Patsy looked so like Liz, he could have hugged her. "Willie," she whispered, "why don't you go over and borrow a little insulin. Tell him we're fresh out." She giggled delightedly behind her hand. "Go on, I dare you!"

"You're bad!" Ellen smiled at her with more amusement than she'd felt for a long time. "If your father could hear you, I'm sure he'd take you across his knee and give you a good spanking!"

"Poor Daddy," said Patsy, suddenly sobered. "I don't think he raised his hand to me once in his life. Maybe he should have."

"How is he coping now? Last time I spoke with him . . ."

"Better, I think, but it was a terrible blow. It was dreadful for my mother and the rest of us, too, of course, but somehow it was worse for him. He's sort of isolated himself."

"It sometimes takes a while." Willie reached over and touched her arm with genuine sympathy. He really wished he could do something to ease the hurt of that whole family.

The wine waiter appeared, cradling a bottle wrapped in a white cloth.

"Patsy, I'm sorry I brought that subject up, let's talk about something else."

The wine waiter poured a mouthful of wine into Willie's glass, expertly turning the bottle as he finished pouring, lest a stray drop fall onto the snowy white tablecloth. Willie swirled the wine around in the glass, sniffed it, took a sip, thought about it, then nodded.

"Have you ever sent wine back?" asked Patsy while the waiter filled the glasses. "I bet they'd have a fit!"

"I have, but not here. The wine's usually pretty good," replied Willie. He was enjoying Patsy's innocence and enthusiasm, but it gave him the strangest feeling of déjà vu: Patsy was so like Liz, it twisted his heart. It was as if Liz had stayed the same age and only he had gotten older. He glanced at Ellen almost guiltily, but she was chattering happily with Patsy. He put his hand on Ellen's knee and squeezed it gently, and she glanced at him, surprised.

"Did your parents ever talk about when we were all students together?" he asked carefully. "We hung out a lot, the four of us."

"Not too much. So how come you never visited until about three months ago?"

"It's a long story, and I'll tell you some time. How's the sole? Here, let me fill up your glass. Do you drink like your father or like your mother?"

"Like my father, of course. My mother gets dizzy after one drink, and silly after two. My father—God, I've seen him put it away when he's on vacation, but you'd never know it to look at him."

"When we were students, he could drink any of us under the table and never show it." Willie smiled, remembering. "You'll have to get him to tell you about some of our exploits."

For dessert, Patsy decided to have a *bombe flambée*, but Ellen, who was beginning to look tired, didn't want anything. Willie was quite satisfied with coffee and a cigar.

"I really like the smell of that," said Patsy, sniffing the smoke. "There's something rich and elegant about it. Is it a Havana?"

"You know they're not allowed in this country," he replied with mock reproof. "But luckily I have a friend in Switzerland who takes the labels off and mails them."

"Are you two going to the concert tomorrow afternoon?" asked Patsy innocently.

"Concert? Not that I'm aware of."

"The one in Strawberry Fields," said Patsy. "Bob Wesley invited me. I thought maybe you might be going too."

"No." Willie couldn't help speaking a little abruptly. The ash fell off his cigar and onto the tablecloth, and Patsy scolded him. "You think *I'm* a bully!" she said after he complained about her strictness. "It's just as well for you that you didn't marry my mother!"

Ellen arranged to take Patsy shopping the next morning; she picked her up in the hotel lobby and they had breakfast together in the coffee shop. Then they walked along the south side of Central Park, basking in the warm sunshine. It was one of those gorgeous blue-sky green-tree days that New Yorkers like to point at when the critics complain about the climate; there was enough of a breeze coming off the ocean to keep everything cool, swirl skirts up, and make boys stare and girls giggle.

Ellen asked if Patsy would like to ride in one of the horse-drawn buggies that went clopping lazily past. Somewhat to her relief, Patsy said no, but she would like to go to Tiffany's and get something small for Elspeth and Douglas.

"Mom says it's always better to get something inexpensive in an expensive shop than the other way around," she said with a smile.

By the time they came out of Tiffany's with four little blue cardboard boxes tied in ribbon, Ellen was walking slowly and seemed out of breath. Patsy looked at her with concern.

"Are you all right?"

"I think maybe I should get home now," she replied, annoyed at her weakness. "I'll just get a taxi, and I'll drop you off at the hotel."

Patsy thanked her and got out of the cab outside the Plaza; at that moment, looking into her eyes, she realized that Ellen wasn't just feeling tired; she was dying.

Bob Wesley picked her up at the hotel.

"Boy, you really travel in style, don't you!" he said, awed, looking around her room. "Do you always stay here when you come to town?"

"Only when I have a sugar daddy to pay the bill," she said, trying to sound coy. "Actually, this is the first time I've ever come to New York by myself, so there!"

After last night, when everything had cleared in her mind about Willie and she could understand the nature of the affection she felt for him, she'd had a marvelous sense of emotional freedom, as if her feelings could now roam anywhere again; she hadn't realized what a serious conflict had been in her heart.

Now, though she felt free, she was still a bit uncomfortable with this big, serious young man who seemed to take up so much space in the room. He brought back memories she didn't want to have. He was now wearing sneakers and jeans and a yellow shirt, but she still saw him in his white coat.

The concert was terrific, sort of. Actually, they finished up a long way from the podium, and what with the wind and the traffic noise, the music would have sounded better through a third-rate hi-fi, but the feel of it—the atmosphere and the excitement—was all there. They held hands and somehow got the hang of each other, although they barely spoke until afterward; but they knew each other immeasurably better by the time they walked back, hand in hand, through the warm evening to the Plaza.

Up in her room, they talked and laughed, and he told her about his uncertainties concerning his career, how he didn't really feel or think like a surgeon; and she told him a bit about what she was doing, about the alpha and beta seismic waves; and gradually they got closer, and they moved over to the bed because it was easier for him to put his arm around her there, and he felt light-headed from her perfume and the warm fragrance of her and she trembled a bit at the feel of him so close and hard, although his touch was light and gentle.

And slowly their clothes came off. They could never explain just how, or who started it, but at the end it wasn't slowly anymore but with a quick scrabbling and the sudden freedom of air on their bare skin, swelling and softness and heart-stopping wetness and wildness and pleasure.

Later Patsy sat up suddenly. Bob opened his eyes and feasted on the sight of her body, incredulous. He couldn't believe he had made love with this exquisite, cool creature sitting there, looking so calmly and unselfconsciously at him with her big green eyes.

"By the way," she said in a perfectly normal voice, as if they were having coffee together in a restaurant, "Dad asked particularly if you would call him. He said it would be too difficult to reach you at the hospital."

Bob pulled a brown arm from under the sheet and squinted at his wristwatch. He sat up, rubbing his eyes. "God, I haven't slept so hard for years." Patsy put her hands on the back of his neck and stroked his shoulders. It felt wonderful, relaxing and intimate. He reached for her, and Patsy slid out of the bed and stood looking at him.

"You make that call first."

Bob clambered stiffly out of the bed. He hadn't realized how tired he was from his impossibly long hours.

"Okay, but you promise to come back to bed afterward?"

"No promises."

Patsy gave him the number, and he dialed direct. Greg answered after one ring, as if he'd been waiting by the phone.

"Hi, this is Bob Wesley. Patsy told me . . ." Patsy, sitting on the bed, saw his face tense. "Yes, I did." He glanced quickly at Patsy, then turned away from her. "Didn't Dr. Stringer . . . No, okay. . . . Hepatitis, chronic active was the final . . . No, actually the bleeding was from esophageal varices. There was no ulcer, no. I'm sure Dr. Stringer would have . . . Yes, sure, they sent me a copy. I'll get it to you in the mail tomorrow. . . . Right, yes, we went to a concert. . . ." He turned to Patsy, his face white. "Here. He wants to talk to you."

Bob went and sat down heavily in one of the cane-backed chairs. That fool Stringer had told Dr. Hopkins that Edward had died of complications of a stomach ulcer, and Bob felt the shock and fury his news had caused. This was just the first gust of the hurricane to come. He looked at Patsy; he could see her eager youth, and a flood of warm feeling enveloped him. She was a marvelous girl and would need somebody to hold her hand in the approaching storm. Somebody like him. Or would she turn against him when she knew the facts?

CHAPTER
TWENTY-NINE

Liz stopped playing her cello when Greg picked up the phone, although she could just as easily have played more softly. She'd only recently felt confident enough to play when there were other people around, and it still didn't take much to inhibit her. But this time, watching Greg's face, she quietly put the instrument back in its case, snapped it shut, and waited, with a sense of doom that increased by the moment. She could guess, more or less, the tenor of the conversation from Greg's responses. First she thought it was Willie, then she realized it must be Bob. And it was bad news, there was no doubt about that. She went and sat straight-backed on the sofa opposite him, like a defendant waiting for the jury's decision.

"Yes, hi . . . nice of you to call. How are things in New York?" Already Greg was gripping the phone tightly. "Did you enjoy the concert?" His face was tightening with the strain, waiting for the pregame anthem to finish.

"What was the final diagnosis?" Greg couldn't restrain himself. "Oh, Christ . . ." Liz already knew enough to brace herself for the end of the call. Douglas had stopped writing at the desk and was listening, his eyes fixed on the paper in front of him, and Elspeth, always the first to sense atmosphere, came and sat on the big sofa very close to her mother, whose near presence partly canceled the poisonous vibrations coming from the phone.

"Do you have a copy of the autopsy report?" Liz expected Greg to glance at her, include her, but he stared into the phone as into the eye of a skull. "Hepatitis . . . hemorrhage from esophageal varices. . . . I see. . . . Thanks, Bob. . . . Yes, if you would. . . . It should get here by Wednesday. . . . Yes, let me speak to Patsy."

Douglas raised his eyes when Greg put the phone down, and watched him. Greg stood there, looking at all of them.

They all held their breath. Almost before he said anything, the tone of his voice chilled Liz's heart.

"Willie Stringer killed Edward," he ground out almost inaudibly, staring past her at the wall. Liz looked up at him and saw the veins of fury suddenly standing out on his face. She had never dreamed he could look like this; there was the look, the pain of a tortured animal there, and his lips were pulled back like a wolf in a trap. But Liz was already on her feet and shouting, "How could he? How could he have *killed* him? Greg, for God's sake, what are you talking about?"

"That fucker!" he screamed at the top of his voice, not even talking to her. His hands jerked up the table next to the wall, and the big vase of pink phlox, a heavy crystal ashtray, and a bottle of white wine and two glasses from before dinner flew up in the air and smashed on the floor as he stood there, raging, his fists clenched.

Liz was petrified, unable to speak, but she signaled the children to go upstairs this instant, not to say anything, just go.

Greg banged both fists on the table. "He killed Edward! Our child!" he shouted at Liz, to make her realize the full import of what he was saying. "Our child!" he repeated more quietly. Liz wanted to hold him, but at that moment she was too frightened of him. His eyes were staring, red-rimmed. She had never seen him like this. Absently he bent down and started to pick the broken glass and pottery off the floor, putting the wet pieces and the flowers back on the table.

"I'd thought about killing him, if it was his fault," he said, quiet now. "But I'm not going to. I'm going to ruin that bastard." He came toward her, and Liz's hands tightened on the back of the chair behind her. He put his hands on her shoulders and stared at her with that terrifying, insane look. "Did you hear what I said, Liz?" He shook her shoulders with a sudden uncontrolled rage. *"I am going to destroy Willie Stringer!"*

Douglas and Elspeth sat listening together on the top step

of the stairs. Elspeth started to cry silently, but Douglas ignored her. He didn't understand anything about the liver or hepatitis or any of that stuff. But he did understand that the man who used to be his father's friend, Dr. Stringer—the man with thick gray hair who'd come to dinner and talked a lot to Patsy—had somehow killed Edward. Douglas, firmly in the grip of powerful adolescent male hormones, felt a sudden primitive violence rise in his blood, and had Willie been there, he would have leapt on him. Instead he swallowed his bile and went up to his room. He had friends who would help him decide what to do.

Elspeth sat at the top of the stairs for a while. Her tears were only for her father, who seemed so different; Edward no longer existed except as a memory, and she couldn't understand what had happened to cause all this retrospective alarm. Edward was dead, and nothing could be done about that.

For an hour Greg raved and wept and screamed obscenities, while Liz tried to calm him. He was going to destroy the bastard, he kept on saying, pounding on the cushions. Liz, still frightened by the force of his passion, wondered how he was going to turn his rage into action. Greg was certainly slow to rouse, and made every effort to avoid confrontations, but the barrier had been breached now. In the midst of the storm, Liz felt that finally she had a bulwark to protect her, even if that bulwark was on a heaving, pitching ship.

What would he do? Quick visions of Greg and Willie locked in hand-to-hand combat flashed before her, but somehow the fantasies wanted depth; each man lacking the necessary commitment to the other's annihilation.

But she could feel that commitment taking shape and growing in her own mind and spirit. If all else failed, she knew that she could do it.

The next morning, Greg called Janus Frankel in Manhattan; he remembered him without affection from his days in medical school. Frankel was surprisingly affable, and gently interrupted Greg's diatribe.

"Look, why don't you come into the city and we can discuss the whole problem more fully? How about tomorrow? We can go out and have a quiet lunch rather than talk here, okay? I'll meet you in the main lobby at about twelve."

Greg took a taxi from Grand Central to the hospital and got there a few minutes after twelve. He was feeling strained and tired, worn-out now that his anger had exhausted itself. He'd barely slept the night before, and he was feeling and looking his age. There was a moment when he felt his whole body shake, going through the main door of the well-remembered lobby, but it only lasted a second. Dr. Frankel was at the main desk, unmistakable in his elegant gray suit, gray-striped shirt, and a dark red tie the color of— Greg was learning how to cut off the chain of thoughts inside his head.

"Dr. Hopkins?" Frankel recognized him and came forward, hand outstretched.

"Yes, sorry I'm late, the train . . ."

"Perfectly all right. The place we're going to is just a couple of blocks down. It's within walking distance."

They walked into the hot concrete street. The sun shone like an oven lamp through the alien, yellow chemical haze. They threaded their way among the people crowding the sidewalk, then turned the corner and were able to walk side by side. Dr. Frankel kept up an intermittent flow of small talk, which Greg answered politely but briefly; he had never been good at this urbane kind of time-filling chitchat. Although he seemed benign enough now, Greg remembered how he'd felt as a student about the arrogant and sarcastic Dr. Frankel.

The restaurant they went to was small and not yet crowded. A waiter in a well-worn dinner jacket came briskly up to the table, gave them each a menu and asked if they would like drinks. Frankel looked at Greg, who shook his head.

"Ice water will do fine for me, thanks."

"It was good of you to come all this distance," said Frankel, putting down the menu a few moments later. "Did you drive?" Greg shook his head. Frankel leaned over and said rather confidentially, "The médaillon de veau is particularly good here, by the way."

I wish he'd cut out this pseudo-sophisticated bullshit, thought Greg, tense again, and irritated. *We're not here to evaluate the food.*

"I came to discuss two things. First, the crime I believe was committed against my son, and second, this autopsy report"— Greg took the folded sheets from his inside pocket—"which I believe is a forgery." As he spoke, he felt that his language was too strong and that it would put Frankel on his guard against him.

But Frankel did not seem at all taken aback. He took the papers and glanced at them.

"May I have these?" His eyes were glistening. This was exactly what he needed; he was well aware that much of the case against Stringer depended on clinical judgment and could go either way, but with this he could nail Stringer to the wall, without any doubt.

"No, I'm afraid not." Greg reached out and put them back in his pocket. "I'm getting a little cynical these days."

Frankel blushed. "Yes, of course, I understand that," he said. "However, this document may be necessary to establish proof."

"I'll be happy to submit it when a properly constituted inquiry is made," said Greg stiffly. "Until then I prefer to hang on to it myself."

"Sure," said Frankel. "I appreciate how you must feel."

Like hell you do, thought Greg, trying to keep the bitterness out of his eyes.

The waiter came back to get their order. He had long, greasy black hair and dirty fingernails.

"You know Willie Stringer pretty well, don't you?" asked Frankel, cutting his bread roll in two with surgical precision.

"I think we were best friends," replied Greg.

"Oh, I see. That must certainly make it more complicated for you."

"Honestly, I don't care about that anymore. I just want to get this . . . matter cleared up, so that I know exactly what happened. And if there was any negligence, I want to be sure it is properly punished."

The veal arrived. It was sliced thin and covered with some kind of brown sauce with tiny mushrooms. Greg sat back while two other waiters came around with four different kinds of over-cooked vegetables, followed by the inevitable ritual with a two-foot-long pepper mill. After Greg, irritated, waved the waiter away, Frankel—who had been watching his guest with benign but clinical interest—picked up his knife and fork and asked, in a casual way, "Are you willing to take a personal, active part in the process, if your participation seems necessary at some point?"

"What do you mean? Isn't my being here actively participating?"

"Yes, of course, but what I meant was maybe coming to a hearing, presenting that document in your pocket, things like that."

"If it's necessary, yes, of course. I'll be glad to." Greg attacked his veal as if it were Willie Stringer's throat, and Frankel watched him thoughtfully. He would have to be careful; if Greg Hopkins had become a fanatic or a zealot, his presence at an inquiry could do more harm than good.

"I'm more angry than I've ever been in my life," said Greg, pausing; he saw what was passing through Frankel's mind. "I've never thought of revenge as anything I would ever want. But I'm not crazy, if that's what you were wondering. If I have to testify about Edward, I guarantee I won't hurt your case."

"Now wait a minute," said Frankel, feeling that things were moving along too fast in Greg's mind. "Nobody's talking about testifying just yet. I was talking about an in-hospital inquiry. What we need to do is find out the facts, and then, if it looks as if—"

"You already know the facts. Tell me, has Stringer ever had problems like this before? How many other people has he killed or maimed?" Greg's voice was raised, and Frankel put both hands up, palms facing Greg, and smiled.

"Hey, Greg, take it easy. Yes, there have been problems before, but obviously we can't bring them up. We'll have to judge this case on the basis of the evidence presented."

"What exactly are you planning to do? What do you hope to achieve from all this?"

"We have a strong interest in maintaining the highest standards on our surgical service," said Frankel, trying not to sound too pompous, "and my colleagues and I are determined to discipline anyone who doesn't come up to those standards."

"Discipline?" asked Greg. "You mean rap them over the knuckles and tell them to behave in the future?"

"No, I don't mean that at all. I'm talking about withdrawing his hospital privileges."

"Couldn't he just move to another hospital?"

Frankel smiled. "Not anymore. With the malpractice situation nowadays, any surgeon who loses his privileges at one hospital is functionally dead. None of the other hospitals would ever take him on. Their legal people wouldn't let them take the risk."

"That means he's going to have to fight for his life." Greg paused, a piece of veal impaled on his fork. "In case you don't know it, I want to warn you that Willie Stringer's a tough cookie, and he has a fair amount of political pull. He'll get some hotshot lawyer and keep you all tied up for years."

Frankel sighed. "That's certainly a possibility. But I hope we can handle it in a way that will avoid that."

"Well, that's up to you. I'm sure you know the politics of all that kind of stuff better than I do." Greg put down his knife and fork and wiped his mouth with the napkin. "I just want you to know that I'm approaching this matter on all fronts. I'm writing to the New York State Medical Association, the American College of Surgeons, his local medical society . . ."

Frankel had started to shake his head even before Greg finished speaking. "Gee, Greg, I hope you haven't done that."

"No, I haven't yet. Why?" Greg's face instantly became closed, suspicious.

"I most strongly suggest that you do nothing further at this point. If you do, it will force him to get legal help, and as you said, that could tie us up for years. If you let me handle it my way, I think we'll have a better chance of success. The College of Surgeons and all that can come later."

Greg wiped his palms and looked at Frankel, trying to make up his mind whose side he was on. Was he genuine about going after Willie Stringer, or was he just looking for a way to get his colleague off the hook? Greg paused and took a long, hard look at the man on the opposite side of the table, then mentally shook his head. This guy Frankel, he could practically smell the ambition on him. If Frankel were protecting Willie, he would just stonewall, maybe have a quick whitewashing inquiry, go through the motions at a nice slow pace. And he certainly wouldn't be here having lunch with Greg. He wouldn't even have talked to him on the telephone.

At this point Greg was willing to go along with his instincts. "Okay. How long do you think all this is going to take?"

"A few weeks, minimum. But I don't want you to say anything more to Stringer. Nothing at all—no phone calls, letters, nothing. And don't talk to him if he calls you, okay?"

"I wasn't going to, anyway," replied Greg. "I just want to be sure that this whole thing is going ahead, not just getting sidelined and forgotten."

"You have my word on that, Greg. I'm going to go ahead as fast as I can, but you understand I have to step very carefully, for all kinds of reasons."

Frankel paid and they left the restaurant, bowed out by the waiter who had served them. Greg looked at him with distaste.

On the way home in the train, Greg felt grimly content about his meeting. Frankel, in retrospect, seemed genuine, and anxious to see that the Stringer business was fairly and promptly resolved.

He pulled out the *New England Journal of Medicine* from his pocket and stared unseeingly at the cover, reflecting on the way things got done in this complicated world. *There are usually several reasons why people like Frankel take a certain course of action,* he thought, *and I'm only being allowed to see one of them. If that.*

Janus Frankel also was well pleased with the way things had turned out. He felt confident that he could control Greg's anger; he'd have to talk to him often and convince him that progress was being made; otherwise, he could easily make some hasty move that would blow his whole plan sky-high.

Back in his office, he called home. When could we have the Stringers to dinner? he asked his wife. No, just the two of them. Yes, this Friday would be fine. She would take care of it; she had to call Ellen, anyway—about the hospital flower show.

CHAPTER
THIRTY

In the several months of his career as a drug dealer, Douglas had made more than just money. He now had a good working knowledge of how the system functioned, and he had a fair number of contacts in parts of the town his parents didn't even know existed.

One afternoon, a few days after he learned that Dr. Stringer was responsible for his brother's death, Douglas put his books in his school locker, slammed it shut, and padlocked it. This week all the kids were smashing their lockers shut with as much noise as possible, and the noise was deafening as he walked down the corridor toward the back exit. He found his bicycle in the rack, unlocked it, and rode off, sitting up straight, his hands clasped behind his head as soon as he got into high gear. Coming around a corner, he leaned to one side and swerved close to a bunch of girls who'd just come out of the school library. They shouted after him, and he grinned, looked around, and almost lost his balance. The laughs and catcalls followed him to the next corner.

The weather was fine, with a few high, wispy clouds and a strong breeze that pushed him along from behind as he sped through the gates. He turned left, swinging around a yellow school bus, but now the breeze was coming from the side and quite gusty, so his hands went back on to the handlebars. It didn't bother him; the gesture had already been made in the place where it mattered.

Another school bus and a couple of cars were stopped at the intersection of Orchard and Church; Douglas sneaked expertly between them with millimeters to spare, looked quickly each way, then sped across, against the light. The driver of the school bus honked angrily, and Douglas waved a monodigital signal back to him without looking around. A few minutes later he was downtown, weaving and swerving through the traffic, causing heart spasms wherever he went. To Douglas, his bicycle was what the cello was to his mother, and he played it with a virtuosity approaching hers. At the intersection of Main and Marvin, he slammed on the front brake, leaned forward to lift the back wheel off the ground, swung it around, pivoting on the front wheel, and rode off down Marvin, where it was suddenly quiet, with warehouses on both sides. Then he turned right into Plum Lane, which was just wide enough for two people to squeeze past each other or for one bicycle to ride down. Plum Lane was a notorious place, especially at night, and smelled of vomit, beer, and urine at any time of day. Plum Lane led into Commerce Street, as a drain empties into a sewer.

Commerce Street, as far as the local authorities were concerned, didn't exist. Potholes from the previous winter abounded there, deepening and crumbling a little more each time a cruising john's car lurched into one. And it couldn't have been on the Sanitation Department's map at all; piles of ancient garbage littered the corners, some in misshapen black plastic bags. There were five bars on Commerce Street, four on one side and Flanagan's on the other, marked by a large shamrock leaf proudly painted in nausea green on the window. All the other store fronts on both sides of the street were boarded up. Halfway down on the left, two doors from Flanagan's, a derelict house had burned out two months before, leaving blackened walls and blinded windows, maybe because the fire department hadn't known where Commerce Street was.

The main business carried out on Commerce Street was not mentioned in the town's multicolored brochure, nor was it reported to the IRS or represented in the Chamber of Commerce; it was carried out in the grubby little rooms with drawn blinds on the second and third floors above the bars. This was Big Vern's home territory, and here he was king.

Douglas caught sight of Vern, leaning against the corner, his big hat and high-heeled cowboy boots making him look like something out of an old Western, and squeaked to a stop in front of him, doing a specially impressive pivot before dismounting.

"Yo', muthafucka," said Vern amiably, "where yo' bin?"

"Out of business," replied Douglas. He told Vern briefly about the demise of his operation.

"My name in yo' 'dress book, asshole?" Not that Vern really cared.

" 'Course not. You never supplied me. I always used the best."

"Then whaddaya want? Yo' daddy would shit if he knew you was down here."

Douglas explained, and Vern watched him with his yellow eyes, amused at first. Every few moments his glance flickered over Douglas's shoulder and along Commerce Street, where shadowy figures in short leather skirts and fishnet stockings lounged briefly in the doorways.

"No way," he said when Douglas finished. "Get back to your own fuckin' end of town."

"Okay, I'll do it myself, then," said Douglas.

"You'll get caught, you dumb shit, you don't know nothin' how to do it, where to put it, nothin'." But Big Vern could see the stubbornness in the boy. It would all end badly for him; the kid didn't have half the street smarts he thought he had.

"I have a frien' who'll do it," said Vern after a moment. "But it'll cost ya big."

"How big?"

"Five, six C's . . ." He saw Douglas flinch. "For me he'll do it for less, maybe. Say four total, if it's in New York."

Douglas grinned. He could find that amount without too much trouble. His confidence returned.

"You take MasterCard?"

"Ha, fuckin' ha. Cash with the order, man."

"No problem. I'll be back in a week. Who's in charge if you're in jail?" Douglas swung one leg over the bar of his bicycle, grinning.

"Fuck off, honkie kid. And say hiya to your dad!" he shouted after him as Douglas disappeared in the direction of Plum Lane.

It would take a bigger deal than he'd ever handled to make

that amount in one go, thought Douglas as he pedaled fast toward his own part of town. A vision of Chief Grunwald rose up in front of him, and he flinched for a second. He knew what he was risking, but there was never any question in his mind. No one else in the family had the guts to do it.

There were four people in the small surgical conference room that Friday at noon. The place was normally used for small seminars, research group conferences, and so on. At one end was a projector screen, now rolled up to the ceiling, and at the other were four large gray filing cabinets full of old departmental minutes, copies of ancient grant applications, and other dusty rubbish nobody would ever look at again. Between the files and the screen was a long, square table with four high-backed chairs down each side and one at each end.

The group occupied the end of the table nearest the door, with Dr. Frankel sitting in the chairman's place. At the other end were several plates of sandwiches and a red-eyed coffee machine that intermittently made deep intestinal-sounding rumblings.

The door opened and Andrew Furness slipped in unobtrusively. "Sorry I'm late," he said. "I got caught in the traffic."

Dr. Frankel smiled. "I didn't realize you'd have to come in specially. You know Dean Sampson on your left, and of course Dr. Gill from Pathology, and Dr. Latimer, our chief of staff."

Andrew nodded to the other men and sat down. Dr. Frankel glanced around the table as if he were counting heads.

"I've talked to each one of you briefly about this matter. Did everybody receive copies of the letters, the operation notes, and the autopsy report?"

There was a general nodding of heads. He knows his stuff, thought Andrew rather grimly. Get them nodding agreement about something, anything, right at the beginning of a meeting. It sets the tone.

"The facts, I believe, speak for themselves. We have here a case that had an inadequate work-up, an incorrect diagnosis, an unnecessary operation, an ineffective resuscitation, and a fraudulent autopsy report to the next of kin." Frankel looked over his glasses at the men around the table. They all stared at their papers; nobody spoke.

"What we need to decide here is what to do about this problem in our midst."

All this seemed a little hasty to Andrew. Brought up in Scotland, where he had been taught from an early age that the underdog is to be automatically and fiercely defended, he felt uneasy at this instant assumption of Willie Stringer's guilt. To his knowledge Willie had never been invited to answer those accusations. He checked through the papers in front of him again.

"Are you saying that this autopsy report here is fraudulent?" he asked, holding the stapled sheets up.

"Dr. Hopkins was sent an autopsy report on Pathology Department notepaper from Dr. Stringer's office. That report differed materially from the original you have in your hand," replied Frankel.

Andrew made a show of looking for it in his papers.

"It's not there, but I've seen it. At present it's in Dr. Hopkins's possession."

Andrew nodded. "Can you get copies for us? I'm sure—"

"Dr. Hopkins has expressed his willingness to bring it in person. Until then, you have to take my word for it."

Andrew nodded again but felt uncomfortable that such a key exhibit was not available. He looked at the faces of the men around him. Had Frankel selected them because he felt they would go along with whatever he suggested? He smiled to himself at the thought. Frankel must have had another motive for choosing *him*. Were the others known to be enemies of Willie Stringer? Certainly he was no particular friend of his, but not an enemy, either. . . .

Suddenly it struck him. This was a power group, and each individual had been chosen on those grounds alone. They were almost certainly as yet uncommitted; he felt sure that Frankel was too clever to have tried to influence them before the meeting. But if Frankel could make them see things his way, this group could cut a swath a mile wide. And Willie Stringer would be in that swath. . . .

"Have there been any previous problems with Dr. Stringer that you know of, Dr. Frankel, or is this an isolated case?" Dr. Latimer was asking. Although he was chief of staff and had been around for a long time, he was an internist, mostly interested in research, and barely knew that Willie Stringer existed.

Frankel put both hands on the manila folder and took his time answering. "There are a number of complaints about him here in his personal file," he said, tapping the folder. "But I don't think it's appropriate to discuss them here. We're concerned only with this case at the present time."

"Sure, of course. I have no desire to compromise him in any way, I assure you." Latimer had both hands up, palms out in a disclaimer, backpedaling so fast that he almost fell over. But the message was clear: Stringer's record was far from satisfactory. Latimer felt rather proud to have extracted this piece of important information—for free, so to speak. It always helped when one could find out little extra things about somebody; it made them more three-dimensional, and one felt more confident if one had to make a decision about them.

Andrew stared impassively at his papers. What Frankel was doing was becoming clearer by the minute. The somber insinuations about past misdeeds . . . those complaints, if they existed, could be about anything. Maybe one time he'd left the water running in the scrub sink.

"How well is Stringer regarded by his peers?" asked Dean Sampson. He was a large man, paunchy and good-looking in an arrogant way, with big, fleshy lips. As dean of the Medical Faculty, he had more experience of power struggles than most of them. There was no point going on about the facts; those had been settled. He would show these clinical types how to cut through the bullshit and get down to business; otherwise, this meeting could go on all day. He pushed his seat back, every button on his white coat doing its duty. "What I mean, to be quite frank, is how broad is his power base? We don't want to get into—"

"A good point, Dean," interposed Frankel smoothly. He had hoped to keep the politics out of it for a little while longer. "His position used to be quite strong, but he has rather a divisive attitude and I think some of his friends are now taking a distance. What do you think, Andrew?"

"He does tend to be independent, yes, I agree," replied Andrew rather noncommittally. For some reason, the Scots accent was heavy on him today.

Frankel suppressed a frown. Maybe Andrew Furness had not been the best choice for this advisory group; he tended to be legalistic and hard to point in any one direction.

"Let me put this problem in the perspective of what's happening in medicine today," he said. His voice was incisive and clear. "As a professional group, we've never been under as much attack and criticism from the public, from the media, from the legal profession, as we are now."

He looked around at his audience. They were all listening intently.

"There are pressure groups in existence now," he went on, "that want to take the disciplining of doctors, our colleagues, out of our hands entirely and hand it to outside bodies made up of housewives, trade-union officials, and clergymen." A faint collective rumbling of agreement and a feeling of circle-the-wagons solidarity ran through the group. They were already aware of rumors of something of the kind, but hearing it enunciated so clearly sent a shiver up their collective spines. Andrew alone remained unmoved. "The reason for this, of course," Frankel said, his voice rising with feeling, "is that they recognize that up to now we've done a bad job of it. A *lousy* job, if I may say so; and what's more, we know it!"

There was a pause, during which Frankel could feel the tide of opinion strongly with him. He knew he was accurately expressing the feelings of most of them.

"I've talked to a number of department chairmen around the country about this problem," he said, indicating the seriousness with which he was taking it, "but only in the most general terms, of course. All of them, without exception, told me that they were under great pressure to root out their own bad eggs." Undismayed by his own mixed metaphors, Frankel paused. This was a smart group, and there was no need to underline the point he was making. So far they seemed to be in total agreement.

"I read the JCAH report on this hospital," said Dr. Gill, the chief of Pathology, a morose-looking individual with a shock of very black hair over a long, lined face. "I must say it made sad reading. They also said we're not doing enough policing of our own people."

"And as a result we only have a one-year accreditation instead of the usual four," added Frankel quickly. "And for an institution of this importance, it's a real smack in the face." Frankel sounded thoroughly indignant. He knew that so far things were going well. He was ringing all the right bells.

"Are those sandwiches for us?" asked Dean Sampson, his eyes sweeping greedily over to the far end of the table. "Because if they are, may I suggest a recess for just long enough to grab them?"

Much of the remainder of the meeting was given over to evaluating the strength of Willie Stringer's response to any disciplinary moves.

"What we don't want is for him to get some high-powered lawyer representing him in all this," said Frankel. "Then we'd need to get the hospital and university lawyers, and before we knew it, they'd be making the decisions which it is our moral duty to make ourselves."

"Quite agree," mumbled Dean Sampson through the last pastrami sandwich, "but I think I'll pass it by our legal boys— quite unofficially, of course. They might come up with some good ideas on how best to handle this."

"How about letting the Quality Assurance Committee deal with the problem?" asked Andrew quietly. "It's already on their agenda, and that's their job, after all."

"Good thought," said Dr. Frankel. "The only problem is that the next meeting is scheduled for almost a month from now, and you can see we're under quite a bit of pressure to move fast on this one."

"Couldn't you bring the meeting forward and hold it next week sometime?" persisted Andrew. He would feel much more comfortable if a duly appointed body took responsibility for the matter.

Frankel rubbed his chin thoughtfully. "Yes, I see no reason why we shouldn't." He took out his pocket calendar and flipped the pages. "We could have it on Tuesday. What do the other members think?"

"Sounds good to me," said Dr. Gill, also checking his diary. "I'm on that committee, too, of course. But I think this group here should continue to meet in a kind of overseeing capacity, just to make sure the ball isn't dropped."

"Dr. Latimer?"

"Yes, indeed . . . proper channels . . . always best in the long run." He seemed to be deep in contemplation, probably thinking about his damned liver enzymes, thought Frankel.

Dean Sampson had already gotten up. The meeting had lasted long enough. "Fine with me," he said, heading for the door. "When do we meet again?"

"Just a second," said Frankel. He was writing in his little book. "Emergency meeting, QAC, Tuesday the twelfth," he muttered as he wrote. "Same time, same place next week, if that's okay with everybody?"

Andrew Furness stood by the table, gripping the back of his chair, a slow flush spreading over his face as he realized how profoundly Janus Frankel had outsmarted him. To call an "emergency meeting" of the Quality Assurance Committee would instantly inform all the members that an unusually serious matter was to be dealt with, and it would put Willie Stringer at an immediate and serious disadvantage. And it had been his own suggestion.

Janus Frankel went back to his office, well pleased. In retrospect, asking Andrew Furness to join the group had been a masterstroke. Everybody knew him to be a fair and just man, and his presence would reassure anyone who might think it was some kind of kangaroo court set up to destroy Stringer. The others seemed happy, too; sometime in the future he would suggest that the group become an official and permanent body charged with the broad task of monitoring professional competence in the medical and surgical staff. He knew that Willie Stringer certainly wasn't the only one at fault. Without even trying, he could think of half a dozen staff members who could do with a thorough review of their professional activities.

Andrew Furness left the meeting with a feeling of profound uneasiness. This business of peer review was great in theory, he thought, but it could so easily be subverted; at worst it would allow a powerful individual to wreak vengeance on any physician unfortunate enough to cross his path, all in the name of improving the standards of medical care.

CHAPTER
THIRTY-ONE

It could have come from the beautiful Vera, Willie's nurse and confidante, who had lunch with Maxine, Frankel's chatty secretary, or possibly somebody had seen Frankel and Greg going out of the hospital together. But Willie Stringer quickly discovered that Greg was coming after him, both barrels blazing. He kicked himself for making that stupid forgery; it would have been so much better just to tell Greg frankly what had happened, but it was too late to worry about that now. What he had to do was stop Greg before he did too much damage. Willie felt sure that a long heart-to-heart talk between the two of them could have taken care of it, but Greg wouldn't answer the phone, or else he'd hang up. And Willie, for the first time in his life, was running scared. In the last few days he had made a few hurried, ill-thought-out decisions under pressure. And he'd gone to see Chris Gorham, his internist, because of the headaches.

"I know you guys are under a lot of stress all the time, Willie," Chris said, "but you're wound up tight as a piano wire. Is there anything special going on in your life?"

"Well, Ellen hasn't been well, and . . . it's just been one thing after another the last few weeks."

Willie looked around without making it seem too obvious. This was a really luxurious office; different from his own, but Chris must have spent a fortune here. The oak paneling in his private office had come from an old English manor house in Surrey, he'd told Willie on a previous visit, explaining the origin of the elegant linenfold pattern to him. In fact, the

whole place had an English look; there were hunting prints on
the walls of the examining rooms and a red-faced nobleman
in hunting pink by Gainsborough in his office. Like Willie, he
had his best piece on the wall behind his desk, facing the door.

"Willie, your blood pressure's up again. Just about off the
scale. You're really going to have to take this seriously. Are
you taking your medication?"

"Yes," replied Willie, then a little defensively, "Most of the
time. It makes me drowsy sometimes, and I don't want to doze
off at the operating table."

Chris grinned complacently. "Why don't you take some time
off? Take Ellen somewhere, sea, sun, all that kind of thing.
You really need to get away and relax."

If you could see my bills, thought Willie, you wouldn't even
suggest it.

"Right you are, Chris," he said, getting up. "I'll go back on
the pills. Thanks for your time, I appreciate it."

Out front, the girl behind the Hepplewhite desk told him
that there was no charge, of course, but if he had insurance
coverage, they would like to collect it.

Willie's office was only two buildings away, so he walked back
fast, because he had patients waiting. Off the scale . . . it wasn't
surprising with what he'd had to put up with recently. But
he'd really have to watch it. He took a small pink pill out of
his pocket and swallowed it, then took another. It tasted foul
without water to wash it down.

He saw two patients in quick succession, then there was a
pause in the action. Willie sat at his desk, his head in his hands.
What the hell could he do about Greg? If he kept on with this
vendetta, he could cause all kinds of trouble. Willie raised his
head. Angelo! Why hadn't he thought of him before? Angelo,
obviously. He knew about this kind of stuff. He reached for
the phone, checked the area code, 203, right, then dialed
Angelo's number.

"Angelo? Hi, this is Willie. . . . Everything's fine, yes, Elena's
doing okay, considering." Elena was her baptismal name, but
she'd dropped it in high school. Too Italian, she'd said. "Angelo,
I need to see you. There's been a real problem come up here
and I'd like your advice." Willie paused for a moment. "I know
you can't get away, sure. I was thinking of coming up to

Hartford. . . . Yeah, tomorrow will be okay; I don't have any surgery and I can cancel office hours. I think there's a flight from La Guardia around eleven, gets into Hartford at noon. Can you meet me? Okay, it's a Pilgrim flight. . . . Thanks, Angelo, I appreciate it. See you then."

Angelo Petrini put down the phone. There was something strange going on with his son-in-law in New York, and it made him feel uncomfortable. This was the second time he had asked for some kind of help in the last few weeks, after years of nothing at all. They came for Christmas most years, him and Elena, and even then, during the family celebrations, he had always made it pretty obvious that he couldn't wait to get back to New York.

It wasn't any trouble with his daughter, he was pretty sure. Her mother had spoken to her the night before and there weren't any new problems, just the usual stuff about how dull her life was and how the medicine was making her sick.

Maybe he needed money? He certainly made a lot, but with his malpractice insurance costing what it did, and all the money he'd spent on that fancy office, it was possible. Or he could have gotten into some trouble with a woman. Angelo was a man of the world and had figured Willie out pretty quickly. But no way would Willie come to him with that kind of problem. He knew better than that.

Carmen, Angelo's wife, had gone to bed long ago, and he went prowling around his house, switching off the lights. Although his garbage business pretty well ran itself these days, he'd always been a hands-on kind of person. Two or three times a year he'd spend the day with his men on the trucks, just to remind them that he wasn't only a city councillor and a powerful politico.

Angelo stood under the big chandelier in the entrance hall and looked up the wide, blue-carpeted stairs. This house of his, it was more like a mansion, with its six bedrooms upstairs, each with its own bathroom, the study, the library. His father had bought it for him when he got married, and the first thing he'd done was to pull the bookshelves out of the library and put in a pool table with a big lamp over it. The yard was dark, and he switched the floodlights on, illuminating the front of the garage. His was the only house in that very exclusive area that didn't have a sophisticated burglar-alarm system. Angelo didn't need one.

Willie never enjoyed flying, particularly in small feeder-line aircraft such as the Pilgrim Airlines de Havilland. It was cramped and bumpy, and who could take seriously a pink-cheeked boy pilot who also took your luggage out to the plane? He was glad to get out at Windsor Locks, the airport serving Hartford; there was a new pleasure in feeling solid ground under his feet. It was cooler up there than in New York, and the wind blew his hair into spikes as he walked across the tarmac from the plane.

Angelo was waiting for him inside the terminal, bulging in a gray coat with dark blue velvet lapels. Angelo was a big man, about six feet tall, built along the lines of a sumo wrestler, with a huge belly and thick arms. When he was younger, he had complained that he could never find clothes to fit him, but now he had his silk suits and cashmere pullovers especially made for him in Florence. Angelo's face was astonishingly handsome; smooth-skinned, with dark, clever eyes that his associates hoped would never hood over when they were around.

Willie had brought only a briefcase with him, and they walked in silence through the terminal toward the main entrance. A pale green Cadillac of the largest and most recent model was parked exactly opposite the entrance, surrounded by NO PARKING signs. A uniformed policeman nearby touched his cap as Angelo climbed in.

"Good flight?" Angelo asked. Willie was always surprised by the deep, croaky voice. Somehow it didn't fit his appearance.

"Not bad," replied Willie, while an automatic voice from somewhere in the car courteously reminded him to fasten his seat belt. The car slid silently through the parking lot and headed along the road toward Hartford. Willie enjoyed the scenery, getting used to the ride of the big Cadillac. It felt different from his BMW; more like driving around in a drawing room.

"How long are you staying?" Angelo never wasted time with small talk.

"There's a flight back this afternoon, leaves at two," said

Willie, still feeling shaky from the flight out. "I've got a seat booked."

"Do you want to talk here in the car, or do you want to go to a restaurant or what?" asked Angelo. "The car isn't wired, I can tell you that for sure." Angelo grinned sideways at him, and once again Willie felt glad that Angelo was not his enemy. He always had that thought somewhere at the back of his mind, and it helped him to take good care of Ellen.

"Let me take you to lunch," said Willie, looking at his watch. "What's that place, the Italian restaurant we went to a few times?"

"You mean Barrolino's," said Angelo. "Sure, we can go there. It's not bugged, either, if you're interested. Victor Barrolino —he's a friend of mine—has his own equipment, checks every day before he opens." Angelo laughed. "Can't be too careful, right?"

He looked at Willie as though he expected an answer, so Willie said, "Yes, right."

Angelo picked up the car phone and called the restaurant. He'd once told Willie he remembered every phone number he'd ever used, right back to his childhood. He didn't do it on purpose, he said. He could look up a number as well as somebody with an expensive education; he just didn't need to.

"Yeah, we got a table," he said. Willie imagined some bewildered party being hastily relocated while a waiter quickly changed the tablecloth and cutlery and sent the boy running across the street for a bunch of fresh carnations.

Short of putting out a red carpet across the sidewalk to the car, their reception was royal. Victor, shorter than Angelo, but similar in build, opened the door himself, and the air was suddenly thick with *buon giornos,* hands on shoulders, broad gestures, and throaty, effusive Sicilian family laughter.

"First tell me about Elena," said Angelo once they were seated in the red velvet-covered chairs at a table slightly separated from the other diners. He'd put on his glasses to peruse the menu, and didn't raise his eyes when he spoke.

"She's doing reasonably well," replied Willie cautiously. "The cancer hasn't got any bigger since she started the chemotherapy, but it makes her sick, and she's lost some weight."

"How come you didn't find it sooner? You're a doctor, aren't you?" Angelo's eyes narrowed for a second, and Willie felt the frightening power of the man.

"First, it's not my field. Secondly, I've always insisted that she be checked out fully every year. There's nothing else that I or anybody else could have done." Willie spoke curtly; he didn't have to feel guilty about Ellen's illness too.

Angelo was still watching him. "What's *your* problem?" he asked.

Willie took a deep breath. Angelo was one of the few people who could always put him on the defensive.

"Remember that kid who was peddling drugs? Well, it's the same family, his younger brother . . ." Willie outlined what had happened, and how the boy had died the day after the operation.

"Wasn't that the girl you'd been going with before you and Ellen got married? Liz Phelan?"

Willie acknowledged the fact. Angelo gave him a long, knowing look and shook his head. "Aside from the kid dying, you still haven't told me what the problem is."

Willie had decided to forget his pride and tell Angelo everything. "I did something really stupid." He explained about the faked autopsy report. "I was just trying to save him some unnecessary worry. There was no way to bring his kid back." Willie could feel Angelo's contempt coming at him across the table.

"All this is probably nothing to some of the stuff you've done in your day," he added, forcing a grin and looking squarely at Angelo. He wasn't going to be intimidated by this mafioso, even if he was his father-in-law. A moment later he found out that it had been the wrong thing to say. Angelo seemed somehow to get larger, and his eyes really narrowed this time.

"Willie, what I do doesn't concern you, and I'm not here asking for your help. But I'll tell you this, as a businessman: *My customers always get what they pay for,* and if something goes wrong, *they get told.* Nobody's perfect, but I never cheat them— and that way they usually come back."

Willie was about to protest that it wasn't a fair comparison but thought better of it. There was no point in getting into an argument now. "Greg, the kid's father, is coming after me," he said to Angelo. "I don't know what to do about it. He thinks

I'm responsible for his son's death. He won't talk to me, and he's starting to make trouble at the hospital."

Angelo's eyes bored into him. "What really happened is you fucked up the surgery, then tried to cover it up, right?" he asked. Willie started to protest, but Angelo raised his hand. It was huge, like a shovel.

"It doesn't matter," said Angelo quietly, accentuating each word. "You want this guy off your back, right?"

"Yes, I suppose so." Willie hadn't really thought of it in quite these terms; he just wanted to be rid of the threat to his career.

"You told Elena about all this?"

Willie hesitated. "She knows part of it . . . yes, more or less."

"That's a mistake." Angelo spoke with heavy authority. "A man should never bother his womenfolk with his business problems." He was silent for a few moments. "I'll take care of it," he said after thinking it over. "I have some connections in that town, aside from the police. But in this kind of situation it would be better if he came over to your side, rather than just eliminating him, wouldn't it?"

Willie's mouth fell open. "Eliminating him . . . my God, Angelo! There was never any question of—"

"Shut up, Willie." Angelo leaned over toward him, and Willie felt physically afraid, although Angelo was twenty years his senior. "You got a fire, don't tell the fireman how to put it out. Now, when you go home, you be sure to tell Elena her daddy loves her and he's taking care of everything, okay?" He pointed a finger at Willie. "Don't forget!"

Angelo had brought a copy of the *Hartford Courant* with him into the restaurant. Now he partially unfolded the paper and read it through the rest of the meal, holding it in his left hand and eating with his right. He did not say another word to Willie. After coffee Willie tried to pay with his American Express Gold card, but Victor laughed, slapped him on the back, and waved the card away. "It's all taken care of!" he said. Angelo took him back to the airport without another word.

During the bumpy plane ride back to La Guardia, Willie tried to doze, but there was too much going on in his head. What on earth was Angelo going to do? Willie felt he might have unleashed the furies on Greg and his family; he had a sudden vision of a car pulling up outside Greg's house in the middle of the night and two gunmen coming out and killing everybody inside. Surely it would be just a warning, something like that? Surely that was all that was needed? But Angelo didn't fool around with warnings, or at least he didn't think so. All the gruesome gang murders he could remember passed through his mind; he saw newspaper photos of sheet-covered bodies with only the feet showing, and a trail of blood running into the gutter.

And Liz . . . his blood ran cold at the thought of her getting hurt. His last conversation with her had not been too friendly. She had called to warn him off Patsy, and he felt her fury when he laughed, and she'd asked, in that tight, angry voice of hers, if he'd realized that he was Patsy's father. How could he *not* have known? It was strange having a daughter, but he really felt wonderful about it. Willie had decided that he would make up for lost time. The only thing that bothered him was that Patsy didn't know, and under the circumstances, maybe it wasn't the moment to tell her. He wondered if all this business with Greg would damage his relationship with her. Greg was sure to tell her about the fake report . . . Willie winced at the thought. He had gotten so attached to her warm, funny, irreverent self. That weekend had been wonderful, and she'd looked so beautiful in that green dress, smiling at Ellen and him across the table at 21 with her shining, excited eyes. And Ellen had really liked her.

But now . . . how would she look at him the next time they met? Would she turn against him too? Willie's heart tightened miserably. He couldn't bear the thought.

Suddenly he felt very tired. The burdens were getting too much for him: Ellen's illness, the practice, Frankel, the decorator, the IRS. He wished he could do as Chris Gorham had suggested and take a few days off so he could catch up with himself, stop running, just long enough to get a grip on things again.

He must have been dozing because when the plane lurched, he woke up suddenly and shook himself. This was no way to think! He'd been brought up to face problems squarely— "Evaluate and overcome," his father used to say. His father. Everybody seemed to have known him better than Willie did. At the hospital, people still told him stories about the old man when he was head of the Pathology Department: he was a legend. Delightful, caring, talented, hawk-eyed, they said; old Dr. Stringer had been loved by one and all. It was a pity he'd never taken the trouble to get to know his son. Willie could remember him coming back from the hospital with his old leather briefcase with the curly straps. He'd pat Willie on the head and ask him if he'd been a good boy, and that was it. Except for the aphorisms. Every time Willie heard about stitches in time, or better safe than sorry, it put him back on his father's knee, looking earnestly into the already old and rheumy eyes, hearing about people who could be wise with a penny but foolish with a pound. "A pound of what?" he'd ask, but his father already would have gotten up and disappeared into his study. To Willie the sound of that heavy door closing behind him was the ultimate symbol of fatherhood.

Willie looked out of the plane window. They were flying at about three thousand feet, and he could see the misty gray of Long Island Sound far over on the right. That meant they would be landing soon. He checked his watch: three P.M. There would still be a lot of traffic coming into town.

One of his colleagues had a plane of his own, which he flew up to Maine where he had a summer house, and as he didn't use it much, he'd tried to interest Willie in buying a half share. Just as well that he hadn't had any ideas about taking him up on it, Willie thought. Another financial burden was something he didn't need.

Money, money, money—that seemed to be what concerned him the most these days. As a medical student, he hadn't cared about money and had said so to whoever would listen, but Greg, who was poor, had said it was easy to talk like that when you were rich. Wait till you get married, have a house and kids, Greg had told him; it's all you'll think about. They were playing around at the City Island beach at the time, escaping from the city heat, and Willie's answer had been to hold Greg's head under water for about a minute. After that time, whenever Greg said something Willie didn't agree with, Willie told him he was brain-damaged from that prolonged ducking.

But really, he didn't even like money, he just had to make a lot to keep from going broke. And he was pretty generous too. He and Ellen contributed to the ballet, the opera, and all kinds of special events and appeals to which friends were always asking them to give. *"Noblesse oblige,"* as his mother used to say, when unwillingly doing something for the lower classes.

What parents he'd been born with! He remembered visiting Greg's folks up in Port Washington and being surprised that they not only talked to each other but even seemed on quite good terms with each other and with Greg. Since he'd been pretty successful by the usual standards, Willie assumed that his parents couldn't have done anything too terrible. Was it because of them that he liked to have women around him? What kind of insecurity was it? Was it because he had felt unloved as a child? Willie shrugged to himself. It's too easy to blame your parents; that's why the shrinks are so rich. They relieve their patients of all responsibility—place it on the mother who told them ghost stories in the dark or the father who diddled with them in the bath—so it's never their own fault, whatever part of their lives they happen to be screwing up. Just like Catholic confession and absolution, only more expensive.

There was a grinding, whining noise as the flaps went down, then a few minutes later the rumble from the descending undercarriage. Then they were over the expressway, thick with traffic, flashing lights zipping past; there was a thud, a jolt in the back, and they were down, rolling toward the terminal.

The only nice thing about flying, he thought, hunting for his car along the avenues of the short-term parking area, is that you can leave your troubles behind and below and think about things you normally don't have time for. It's not a bad thing to be forced to sit for a while and ponder. On the way back to town he had a sudden strong feeling of his own mortality. He just hoped that when he died, it would be quick; he didn't want time to review his faults and deficiencies. That would take a while, he thought. And he wanted Patsy to care enough to miss him when he was gone. Someone had to love him enough.

CHAPTER
THIRTY-TWO

That weekend, after giving the matter a lot of thought, Liz decided to drive up to Bridgeport to see her parents. She didn't invite Greg or any of the children to come with her, and she announced her plans with a tight-lipped look that didn't encourage questions.

Once in the car, she buckled her seat belt automatically, then sat there for a minute, hunting for a cassette. She must seem like a typical, basically good, law-abiding housewife, she thought; nobody would ever guess what was going on in her mind by looking at her. And in fact, at this point she sometimes felt she didn't know herself, either. She thought of those stories about the ordinary guys with ordinary fears and weaknesses who were flung into battle situations and suddenly became heroes; maybe it took that kind of stimulus to bring out her own basic instincts. If Edward hadn't died, they might never have surfaced at all. And now, what was Willie doing with Patsy? Her hands tightened on the wheel until her knuckles cracked. That bastard, he was like a shotgun aimed exclusively at her family.

Liz backed out of the drive too fast; luckily there was nothing coming down the street. She collected herself and concentrated on her driving until she was out of town and clear of the heavy traffic.

Maybe it was a hereditary trait, her tendency to bouts of blinding fury, those waves of rage that came over her when she thought of what Willie had done to her, to Edward, to the rest of her family. She knew that her father tended to respond like that, and with less provocation. Like the time when she

was about ten and a guy who had come to the door with a
questionnaire had mocked her mother because she couldn't
talk normally. It was one of the rare occasions when her father
was home, and he erupted from the living room where he'd
been reading the paper, caught the man by the hair, and
banged his head against the door post until he fell on his
knees, right there at the door. Her father's knee had come up
fast and hard. . . . A couple of weeks later Liz found a tooth
between two stones on the path by the door, hunted around
and found two more. And her grandmother, an Oklahoma
pioneer—there was a whole slew of stories Liz had heard about
her. Nobody messed around with that lady, no sir, not if they
wanted to stay in good health. She'd mangled her hand in
some machinery, and her husband fainted when he saw it. So
she'd put a tourniquet around her wrist and cut off four of
her wrecked fingers with a paring knife.

But Liz really knew that the main cause of her rages was
frustration because Greg wasn't doing anything about Willie.
Nobody was protecting the family.

What Liz had in mind was really quite in keeping with her
own family tradition; but it still shocked her.

It seemed strange pulling up outside the house she'd spent
so many years in; it was like returning to a past life, though
she remembered the details well. The eaves and the brown,
wood-shingled walls seemed to smile at her, and the corner
under the door where the milkman used to leave the bottles
beckoned secretly. Liz sat in the car for a few moments, enjoying
the peace of this old, unassuming street. There were only a
few cars, mostly aging but well kept, and the gardens in front
of the narrow houses were immaculate, as if they were participating in a street-wide competition. The air was still and hot,
and Liz could hear the bees through the open window. She
could just see past the house into the backyard; the wooden
swing set her father had built for her was still standing, and
had done service for all her children since then. It was probably
the most permanent thing Mike Phelan had ever done, aside
from buying the house. That had been an investment before
he'd gotten married, using the proceeds from his current scam.
At the time he'd been an investment adviser in New York,
working from a public telephone in Rockefeller Center under

the name of Julius Mandelstam Investments. He didn't look at all Jewish, but as none of his clients ever met him, it didn't matter. When Liz was born, her father was in a federal prison. She was almost three before she saw him, but she liked him immediately and they had gotten on pretty well ever since. Her mother had somehow managed to handle it; she'd been able to instill in her daughter the standard values of honesty, self-respect, and straight dealing to which she personally adhered, while observing her husband's life of ring-around-the-collar crime with resignation. When he was in prison, she went to visit him every week, but she never took Liz. It was just an unavoidable but expected absence, as if he were an engineer working in Bahrain. Now Mike had retired, having carefully squirreled away most of his ill-gotten gains, and he spent much of his time lamenting the fact that he was too old to take part in the new scams of the computer age.

There was a movement behind the low hedge, and a khaki back appeared over the top, then disappeared again. Her father was gardening, keeping up with the neighbors. He heard the car door slam and straightened up, his square Irish face red with exertion. He pushed the white porkpie hat back off his brow with his wrist and looked her up and down as he always did.

"Didn't you bring the children?" he asked, looking aggrievedly at her with those still piercing china-blue eyes. "We never expected you'd be coming alone." Liz closed the gate and went over to kiss him. The smell of his sweat was nostalgic.

"Your mother's inside," he said. "She's going to be disappointed."

Mike stuck his spade in the earth again. There was a pile of tulip bulbs in the wheelbarrow next to him, and he was having trouble again with the roots that grew in from the tree in the street and choked the flower beds. He chopped at them angrily with the edge of his spade.

"Dad, please don't fuss with those roots. Greg sees people every day with bad backs from doing that."

Mike swung his spade stubbornly.

"My grandfather cut peat and carried it through the bog for sixty years, man and boy," he replied in the rich brogue time had only mellowed, "and he never had a bad back in his life."

Liz smiled affectionately and kissed him again, wondering vaguely who her grandfather had really been. According to the dictates of the situation, he had been variously an engineer on the Irish railroads, the owner of a lonely pub near Tipperary, a dock foreman in Dublin, and a small builder just outside Cork. As a child, Liz had known intimate details of at least six grandfathers but had never met any of them.

Her mother was in the kitchen, sleeves rolled up on her sturdy arms, a chicken on the cutting board, the scent of oregano and garlic in the air. The window air conditioner was on, vibrating in the sash in a slow, well-remembered rhythm. She smiled and turned her head so Liz could kiss her on the cheek; one hand was holding a large earthenware pot and the other was stirring. A strangled snorting noise escaped her and Liz hugged her tightly. She never had any trouble understanding her; in fact, some of the strange sounds conveyed feelings that would have been difficult to express in words.

Liz spent a quiet day and a half with them, her tension and worries sliding off her like scales, leaving her resolve intact. She told them all they needed to know about Greg's difficulties, and Mike was surprisingly sympathetic, because in the past he'd always said Greg would never amount to anything and didn't spend enough time with his family. "You're a fine one to talk," Liz would tell him, and he'd reply, "Well, you didn't turn out too badly in spite of it, did you?" A familiar domestic impasse from which each retired the winner.

Her room hadn't changed much. They'd put a folding bed over by the window for Elspeth, but the curtains, the wallpaper with little pink roses (once she'd tried to calculate how many there were on the entire wall, at three roses per square inch), were all the same. The old chintz-covered chair and the big pillows with machine lace around the edges were still there, fat and cozy-looking.

Her parents' bedroom was directly opposite, and on the day she left, after finishing her packing, she went quietly across to their room, pulled the petit-point-covered chair across to the old armoire, stood on it, and searched quickly on top of it. There was an aged leather briefcase with a torn strap and two big cardboard boxes. The gun was between the two boxes, covered in dust, still in its leather case. The last time she'd looked at it, it was loaded, but that had been years ago. She'd just have to take a chance. She took the gun, went back to her room, wrapped it in her robe, and put it in her overnight bag, tucked in with her other clothes.

As she drove off she had a momentary qualm: Suppose they had a burglar and Dad went for the gun and it wasn't there? Maybe she should call him when she got home and tell him? He would be mad as hell, and then he'd call Greg, she was sure of it. She wondered if the gun had been registered with the Bridgeport Police Department. Probably not—as a convicted felon, her dad would not be eligible to own one.

When she got home, there was a note on the kitchen counter. They had all gone off to McDonald's for supper. That lazy little Elspeth, Liz thought; she'd told her exactly what to make and where everything was. But she knew what had happened— as usual, Elspeth had gotten out of it.

Liz took her bag upstairs and put it on the bed. She unwrapped the robe from around the gun and took it carefully out of its case, handling it gingerly. It was a .38 Webley, a serious weapon. She broke it, the way her father had shown her to when she was about thirteen, and saw that it was still fully loaded. She squinted down the barrel. It had been well oiled, but that was years before, and it felt gummy. She spent the next hour taking it apart and cleaning it, surprised that she remembered how. As she put it back inside the case she heard the car turning into the driveway. Liz put the weapon in the bottom of her sewing box. Nobody ever looked in there.

Willie Stringer had been to Janus Frankel's apartment once before, at a departmental cocktail party for a visiting professor from Sweden, but he was surprised and a little suspicious when Ellen told him of the dinner invitation.

"Is that all she said?" he asked. "Is anybody else going?" Then, a little later: "Did she say what the occasion was?"

Ellen shrugged. "Maybe they're electing you Stud of the Year, who knows?"

Willie gave a swift, annoyed twist of his shoulders and went off to his study. She knew just how to irritate him, although a lot of her present brittle anger seemed to be a by-product of her illness. Ellen went back into her bedroom and sat down on the stool in front of her dressing table, her shoulders sagging with tiredness. She tried to rub the aching part over her shoulders. God, look at those bones! Her shoulders used to be soft, rounded, and quite alluring.

She forced herself to look in the mirror. Her hair, which had not too long ago been dark and silky, now had the crinkly, brittle texture of straw, with lots of white threads in it, and her eyes looked like great dark holes in her face. In a panic, she switched on the ring of lights around the mirror—surely she didn't really look quite that bad? The soft lighting helped, but not much. *Christ, I look like a burned-out building,* she thought. *It's that chemotherapy. I didn't look like that before.*

She took a comb, a fine tortoiseshell one with a silver back, and pulled it through, trying to make her hair look smooth. When she looked at the comb, there were great strands of hair in it. She hadn't felt anything, barely the pulling of the comb in her hair.

That was Ellen's moment of decision. No more chemotherapy, no more doctors. At the back of the bottom drawer of the dresser she had a small white cardboard box with one hundred 100-milligram capsules of Seconal, which she'd bought in Mexico City three years earlier. She knew what to do when the time came, when the pain became too bad. She would wash the Seconal down with gin, some night when Willie was away for a convention or a meeting.

Suddenly her whole spirit revolted against the idea of killing herself. She had too many things to do, too much to see. God damn it! Ellen stood up. She wasn't going to give in to this tumor! A few years ago she'd skimmed through a book by some guy who'd beaten cancer. She could call up Brentano's and they'd get it for her. If he, a mere man, could do it, then so could she.

The Frankels lived on East Eighty-fifth Street, in a good enough building but not in the same class as the Stringers'. As an academic, Janus Frankel couldn't equal Willie when it came to earnings, and the woman he'd married had no money at all, or so Ellen had heard.

Still, the apartment was very well arranged, with lots of flowers and some quite nice pieces of Early American furniture.

The meal was unpretentious and quite delicious, and the Frankels were excellent hosts. After dinner Janus gently guided Willie into his study, where he poured a measure of fine, amber-colored Armagnac into each of two crystal balloon glasses.

"Well, that was a really superb dinner, Janus," murmured Willie, comfortable but watchful in a huge leather armchair. "Your wife certainly is a great cook."

"Willie, we have some things to discuss," said Janus. "I thought this would be the best venue. I'm sure you're aware that your ex-friend, Dr. Hopkins, has started a ball rolling that may be difficult to stop."

Willie waited, his heart contracting. He could feel the blood rushing to his head and tried to remember if he'd taken his blood-pressure pill.

"Now, it's perfectly obvious to me that you were let down badly by your house staff, and in particular by the junior resident, Bob Wesley. But in view of the allegations made, and which are specifically directed at you, we have to do something."

Janus Frankel got up and brought over a box of cigars.

"They're from the Canary Islands."

Willie reached into his inner pocket and pulled out his own big cigar case. "Here, try one of these. They're Havanas."

Janus took one and put his own box up on the mantel, then sat down facing Willie. "I've given this matter a great deal of thought, and I think I have a possible solution that will satisfy all parties."

Willie raised one eyebrow but said nothing. His head was pounding as if he'd had two cups of strong coffee too many. He wasn't sure if he could trust this smooth son of a bitch, but he might as well listen.

"Obviously we're going to have to have some kind of hearing, to go over the facts and make recommendations." Frankel amputated the end of his cigar with the gold cutter Willie had passed him, and after carefully lighting the cigar he looked over the glowing end at Willie. Frankel couldn't tell much from his expression. He waved the cigar in a deprecating way, as if the whole thing could quickly be resolved among friends and colleagues. After all, where was the old-boy network more powerful than in the medical profession?

"This is how I think we can put it all together, Willie," he said, as if he were making up his mind then and there. "For a start, I've decided to fire Bob Wesley. It's not just because of the Hopkins business, but the implication will be that he was fired specifically for that reason. Then when the matter is discussed at the hearing, it will appear that blame has already been assigned, and not to you." Frankel's calm eyes surveyed Willie, and he wondered if Stringer was a chess player. If not, he wouldn't be familiar with the concept of sacrificing a minor piece in order to gain a stranglehold position.

Willie still hadn't said anything; he twirled the stem of his glass and listened.

"When is all this going to happen, Janus?"

Frankel, listening with meticulous care to the nuances of Willie's voice, relaxed one notch. He could tell that one of the evening's major hurdles had been jumped successfully; he had at least gained Stringer's partial confidence.

"As soon as I can get a review committee together. We're being pressured by Dr. Hopkins, as you know. I've been able to persuade him not to contact the State Medical Association or the College of Surgeons, but I'm sure we won't be able to hold him off indefinitely."

"Fine. I'll talk to my attorney in the morning and see what he has to suggest. He'll probably need all the documents that I don't already have."

Frankel's cigar glowed red in the dimly lit study, and he shook his head thoughtfully. "Willie, I don't think that's a good idea, and I'll tell you why. If we get your lawyer into the act, then the hospital lawyers and the university lawyers will have to come in too." He paused to give Willie time to think it out for himself. Then it wouldn't sound so much as if he were dictating the course of action. "That will put them into a de facto adversarial position with regard to you."

Willie could feel the muscles in his back tensing up again, and waited for the throbbing in his head to return. "What you're saying is, keep the lawyers out and let's settle this between ourselves, between physicians?"

Frankel nodded vigorously. "That's exactly right, Willie. This is the kind of thing we have to do ourselves. We all know the kind of stresses we have to work under, but lawyers . . . well, in my experience, all they do is complicate things. Don't you agree?"

Willie stood up. "Janus," he said, "Ellen and I have had a great evening. I thank you, and I think it's time for us to go home."

Frankel got up, too, obviously disappointed. "Think about it, Willie, and please try to see that I'm trying to deal with this as discreetly as possible."

So you can have me discreetly thrown out of the hospital on my ass, thought Willie as they walked back into the living room.

On the way out Janus put his hand on Willie's shoulder for a moment, in the friendliest of gestures. There was no doubt whose side he was on.

CHAPTER
THIRTY-THREE

Coming home from the hospital, Greg felt he was going to explode with anger. He turned into the driveway and stopped outside the back door with enough suddenness to send the gravel flying from under the wheels of his car. Liz looked out and just had time to see the set of his shoulders before the door banged open. She braced herself and for a second thought of packing the children off to Edna Macklin's, but there wasn't time. Douglas and Elspeth, who were sitting at the kitchen counter eating a post-school snack, froze as he came crashing in. Their father's moods had been unpredictable and sometimes frightening since Edward's death; everything he did somehow seemed to be related to it.

Greg looked at the expressions on their faces, stopped, and laughed, in spite of his fury. They looked as if he'd come in swinging a machete at them.

"Hi, gang," he said, putting an arm around each of the children as they sat on their high stools. He looked over at Liz; she could see the anger coming back into his face.

"God, Greg, what's happened?" she asked. She couldn't think of anything she'd done that might have caused such a reaction.

Greg straightened up.

"Liz, you're not going to believe this." He was still tight-lipped with annoyance, but Liz and the children immediately relaxed. Whatever it was, his voice told them it had nothing to do with them. "I was finishing rounds at the hospital when old Dr. Anderson came up, smiling that stupid, senile grin . . ."

Liz raised her eyebrows. Greg always used to speak nicely about the old man and had always covered for him when he was sick.

"Anyway, he asked about you and the kids, just as nice as could be. Then all of a sudden he puts his hand on my shoulder, as if he were some sort of father confessor, and says, 'Hey, Greg, I know you've been under a lot of strain lately, and we're all really concerned about you.' 'Right,' I said to him, 'you know, it was tough, sure, but things are settling down.' He's still got his hand on my shoulder, and he's looking at me with this funny expression. 'Don't rock the boat, Greg,' he says. 'We have a duty as professionals to stick together, you know.' I didn't know what he meant, so I asked him. He steps back and says, 'You know, Willie Stringer. Lay off. Get off his back.' And he just turned and went away down the corridor, leaving me standing there like a dumb—" He glanced at the children, who had stopped eating and were listening with rapt attention.

"Who the hell does he think he is, anyway, that brain-dead old buzzard?" He looked at Liz, his lips compressed in a way she had come to know well. Suddenly he seemed to calm down.

"Could I have a cup of coffee?" he asked. Douglas and Elspeth exchanged a quick glance and went back to their snack.

"Why do you think he said that?" asked Liz quietly, her mind working hard. She put a spoonful of instant coffee into his mug and poured some boiling water over it, then handed it to him. His hand was still shaking from the emotion.

"I don't know why he said it. None of his goddamn business, anyhow. I didn't even know he knew Willie Stringer; he's never mentioned him before, I'm sure of that."

"So what does that tell you?" asked Liz in a quiet voice that stopped him in his tracks. He looked at her, puzzled.

"It tells me he's an old atherosclerotic buffoon who's getting his big red nose stuck into other people's business."

Elspeth giggled from the other side of the counter. "His nose isn't that red," she said, and Greg smiled at her in a preoccupied way. She didn't miss a trick, that kid.

"Well, Greg, to me it suggests that maybe somebody put him up to it."

"What?" Greg looked at her in amazement. "Who on earth would want to do that?"

"Somebody acting on behalf of your dear friend Willie, I should think, don't you?"

"My God! I bet you're right. Have you ever heard of such a thing?" he asked, suddenly indignant again. "Sending a message like that, you'd think it was some kind of a mafia organization—"

He stopped suddenly and looked at Liz, his mouth opening slowly. They both had the same thought at the same time. The stubborn look came back into Greg's face. "If he thinks getting people like Anderson to apply pressure, if he thinks that's going to help him, he's got another think coming."

Liz said nothing but scooped up the children's plates and put them in the dishwasher. She had met Ellen's father when she and Ellen were roommates in New York, and he'd taken the two of them out for dinner. Ellen had wanted to go to Mama Leone's, and he'd grumbled that it was just a tourist trap. He suggested another place, a *real* Italian restaurant, but Ellen had started to sulk, and she'd gotten her way. Even though he'd lost out to Ellen on that occasion, Liz remembered the size of him, and the expression on his face when he wasn't getting what he wanted. She'd thought him pretty scary at the time. From what she had heard since, he hadn't gotten any less scary.

She looked at Greg. He was so vulnerable. For so many years he'd worked so hard, done his job, taken care of his patients, and somehow lost his way in the world because he was so immersed in his own little part of it. Liz suddenly had a grabbing fear for him. That business with Dr. Anderson was just a warning shot across the bows; if Ellen's father was involved, he would have no compunction about his methods. If Greg persisted against Willie Stringer, there would be real trouble, she was certain of it.

The turnaround in Greg's opinions and feelings about Willie had been sudden, triggered by the call from Bob Wesley, but Liz's own struggle to the same conclusion had been more gradual. She had tried to keep her image of Willie intact, but the cold realization had grown within her until she couldn't ignore it any longer. The breathtaking horror of it, that his carelessness had taken away her son forever, became a sickening part of her life. This must be what having cancer is like, she thought. Sometimes for a few seconds, as she woke up, her mind was clean and free, the way it had been before. Then it would all come back in a rush, like filth smearing over the windows, and it would be like that all day long, the sun never getting through. She did her day's work automatically without pain or pleasure, grateful that she had something to do to keep her mind from focusing. It was like the pain from a toothache she could control by herself; when her mind could be elsewhere, it was just a dull ache, but when she thought about it, it was like a drill directly on the nerve.

For quite a while, before she'd made up her mind and gone to get the gun from her parents' house, she had suffered the pain like an animal, thinking only about the pain itself. It had taken Liz a long time to change the focus from the pain to what had caused it. To *who* had caused it. And the first flickering of hatred had appeared as a tiny, malignant point in her mind, visible only from time to time out of the corner of her eye, disappearing as soon as she looked directly at it.

Willie had never called her. Possibly that might have done something to arrest the process. Last time Patsy was home, she'd told her about her weekend in New York and laughed at the sudden expression on her mother's face.

"Come on, Mother, he's like an uncle! Anyway, he's really nice, not like *that* at all." For a moment Liz had thought of sitting her daughter down and telling her the whole truth, but she'd decided not to. It really wasn't the right time, and anyway, the amused look on Patsy's face had reassured her that she hadn't fallen under Willie's spell. But she would have to tell her, when things were a little more stable in the family. Then Patsy had said how difficult Bob was finding things at the hospital. Patsy had always seen the funny side of her relationships with boys, and although she was occasionally angrily tight-lipped about them, she could usually come up with a good story about each one. But she was hesitant about Bob, and Liz could sense that she was a little afraid of the feelings that were surfacing. For a start, she had a purely commonsense worry about getting involved with somebody as unsure about his job and his future as Bob was. She wanted to help him, but she wasn't sure which direction was best for him. He'd invested a lot of time and energy into becoming a surgeon, but he himself had the feeling it wasn't for him. Maybe everybody in training had had that feeling at some time; maybe it was just a passing discouragement he would get over in due course.

"Did you come home just to tell me about Dr. Anderson?" Liz asked Greg.

"Not really. Things are very quiet at the office these days."
He smiled without bitterness. "That new fellow, Dr. Ahmet,
who works out of Anderson's office, I think quite a few of our
patients have gone over to him." He held his empty coffee mug
with both hands. "You know, we've never asked him here for
dinner or anything. I don't even know if he's married." Greg
shook his head. "I'm really going to have to shape up." He
looked up at Liz suddenly. "I think that guy Frankel may come
through—he sounded as if he was really genuine, wanted to
clean up his department. And I got the impression that this
isn't the first time Willie Stringer's done something terrible."

"I don't know, Greg, you know how those big-city guys stick
together. They have to, or the whole system would fall apart
around them. I don't know if I'd trust your new friend Frankel
any more than the rest of them."

"Well, I think he's okay." Greg put his head between his
hands. "All this is like some kind of horrible dream. Every
morning I wake up and think maybe it's over, and Edward will
come on rounds with me today, and we can have Willie and
Ellen over for dinner again."

Liz went and hugged him silently. "Just in case you ever
wondered," she said, "I'm on your side, one hundred percent."
She emphasized the last three words, and he looked at her
with surprise and gratitude.

"I don't know where all this is going to take us, Liz, but you
do understand I have to do it, don't you?"

Bob Wesley was on call in the emergency room, and business
was already getting brisk. Aster Hicks, his bête noire, was on,
and he knew he needn't expect much help from her. On the
other hand, the ER doctor was Don Aminoke, a tall, aristocratic-
looking Nigerian, a hard worker with a good sense of humor,
prime requisites for working full-time in the ER. What Don
called the Friday Night Knife and Gun Club had been unusually
active, but although they'd had superficial cuts and one spent
bullet embedded in an already well-scarred gluteus maximus,
nothing big had come in. On the radio scanner they had heard
about two DOAs, but they had gone straight to the morgue,
bypassing the emergency room.

"Hey, Bob!" The desk nurse, who couldn't see him, was

calling down the corridor just as he came out from examining an old man with urinary retention. "There's a gal in Booth eight, an abscess, she needs an I and D, she's been waiting a while."

Bob poked his head around the curtain of Booth eight.

"Hi . . ." Bob hesitated—the woman was unusually attractive, beautiful, really, and well dressed in an elegant sweater and designer pants. Not the usual level of ER clientele at all. She smiled up at him, very self-possessed.

"Hello. I'm Hazel Mordino. Are you going to be my surgeon?"

Bob grinned. "It depends on what's the matter. Let me take a look."

She rolled up her sleeve to show an angry-looking abscess the size of a half dollar just below the elbow. Bob was quite taken aback.

"How long have you had this?"

"Oh, a couple of days. I thought it would just go away."

Bob frowned; there was something here that didn't click, that he didn't quite understand. Otherwise, she looked perfectly healthy.

"I should really do a complete physical," he said.

Hazel bit her lip, obviously annoyed. "That won't be necessary, Doctor. I'd just like you to take care of my arm. Otherwise I'm fine."

"Are you diabetic, Hazel?" She shook her head. "On any kind of medication?"

"No." Hazel obviously didn't want to be examined, and Bob was tempted simply to open the abscess and pack it, give her an antibiotic, and let her go home. He hesitated, reached for the latex gloves folded on the sterile dressing tray, then stopped. He couldn't do it that way. It was sloppy medicine, and he knew that it was only too easy to pick up the habit of taking shortcuts. And he wasn't so terribly busy that he didn't have time. Hazel was getting really irritated by the delay, but Bob excused himself and went to find Aster. The rule was that patients should be undressed and put into a hospital gown, not only to save their own clothing from getting messed up but to allow the doctor to examine the patient more thoroughly.

Bob was puzzled; abscesses like that don't usually just happen to normal healthy people, and Hazel looked, well, upper-class.

He wondered whether she might have diabetes without knowing it; it causes a reduction in the body's ability to fight infection.
He checked the slip of paper with her routine blood and urine
tests; her blood sugar was within normal limits, and there was
no sugar in her urine.

He went looking for Aster and found her having a surrep-
titious cup of coffee in the tiny alcove where the medications
were stored.

"That girl with the abscess, she's fully dressed. I'd like her
in a hospital gown, please, just like everybody else."

"She didn't want to get undressed, Dr. Wesley," said Aster,
annoyed to have been found slacking off, especially by him.
"And in any case it's only a small abscess on her *arm*." She
emphasized the last word.

"Don't waste my time," he snapped. "Get her undressed. I
shouldn't have to tell you."

Aster tightened her lips and mentally prepared yet another
report on Dr. Robert Wesley, who had insisted on *completely
disrobing* a young female outpatient whose sole complaint was
a tiny abscess on her arm. But she went, after slamming down
her coffee mug on the medicine counter.

The young woman was duly undressed, not without some
resistance. When Bob came behind the screen, the first thing
he saw was Aster's annoyed expression, but when he lifted the
sheet covering Hazel, he couldn't suppress a quick, horrified
intake of breath. Both her legs were swollen and inflamed, a
ghastly mess of weeping sores and purulent ulcers. Bob stood
there for a moment, hardly believing the contrast between her
attractive, carefully made-up face and the dreadful lesions on
her legs. Gently he examined the rest of her, unable to look
her in the eye. There were a few similar but less gross sores
on the front of her abdomen. What on earth *were* those
appalling lesions? Did she have some kind of cancer that was
eating her up? Aster's face was gray, and she looked as if she
might be sick at any second.

He turned his head to look at Hazel's face. "How long have
you . . . how long has . . . have your legs been like this?"

Hazel's calm expression suddenly seemed to quiver and
disintegrate. Her eyes brimmed with tears and she started to
sob quietly, but she didn't say anything. Bob stared at her legs,
revolted and puzzled.

Then the light dawned. Of course. Hazel was a heroin addict, and the leg ulcers were the result of injecting the contaminated drugs under the skin in an attempt to get into a vein. That was also the cause of the abscess on her arm. Then Bob, looking at her more closely, noticed some irregular bluish marks on both legs. He recognized what they were immediately, although only a few years ago it would have been a diagnosis of such rarity that he never would have even heard of it. The lesions were Kaposi's sarcoma, he was sure of it. And the rest of the picture fit. This girl with such a beautiful face had AIDS, almost certainly transmitted by infected needles used to sustain her addiction. He looked at her with a kind of disbelief and sadness. She would probably be dead inside a year.

Suddenly a loud cry startled them all.

"Help! Help me!" A hoarse shout came from the direction of the entrance doors, and both Bob and Aster flew down the corridor, relieved to get away. A short, thickset, elderly black woman was trying to run toward them, half carrying, half dragging a boy who looked about five years old. His mouth was open and he was wheezing horribly with every breath; his eyes were rolling and he seemed barely conscious.

"It's an acute asthmatic attack," said Aster before they'd even reached them. "He'll need IV aminophylline."

Bob ignored her. "What happened?" he shouted.

"He was eatin' his dinner an' he sort of choked and coughed and went blue. We live just across the road, and . . ."

Bob already had two fingers inside the child's mouth. He could feel something at the back of the throat.

"Hold him by the arms!" he told the woman, who must have been the child's grandmother. "Quick!" He put his own arms around the boy's chest and compressed it suddenly. A piece of meat shot out of the child's mouth like a projectile, and he drew a huge, wheezing breath and promptly vomited all over Aster's uniform.

Aster instinctively drew her hand back, and Bob caught her eye. If he hadn't been there, she'd have knocked the child right across the corridor.

"Oh, dear me, nurse, I sure am sorry. Herbert! Herbert, look what you done!" The whites of Herbert's eyes were showing all around, and he stared at Bob, then at his grandmother, as if he had suddenly been wakened from a nightmare.

"That's all right, ma'am," said Bob brightly. "Don't give it another thought. It's all in the day's work, isn't it, Nurse Hicks?" He smiled his most dazzling smile at the furious Aster, then took out his stethoscope to listen to Herbert's chest. Sometimes a smaller piece of meat could stay lodged in one of the smaller bronchial tubes.

"Sounds pretty good," he said after checking both sides, front and back. He noticed a rounded bulge on the middle of Herbert's tummy, just below his belly button. "Did you know he has a hernia here?" he asked, pushing a finger into it.

"Is that what that is?" she said. "It's gettin' bigger."

"He should have it fixed," said Bob. "It's no big deal; he'll be able to go home the same day. Nurse Hicks here will make an appointment for him to come to the outpatient clinic on Tuesday."

"You couldn't just do it now for him, could you?" asked the grandmother uncertainly, poking at the soft bulge with a gnarled old finger. Herbert took a deep breath and howled, the tears beading up on his fat cheeks.

" 'Fraid not." Bob grinned. "Meanwhile try to get him to chew his food a bit more, or mash it up for him, huh?"

"From now on this boy ain't gettin nothin' but thin soup 'n' grits, not at my house, no, sir!" She put Herbert down, caught him not too gently by the ear, and started to head for the door. Bob heard her say, "Wait till your ma hears about this here, you're gonna catch it!"

Bob straightened his shoulders and prepared to go back to talk to Hazel. He would have to persuade her to come into the hospital, and she probably wouldn't want that, because she'd soon start going into withdrawal, even if they put her on methadone. And if there is one thing an addict fears beyond fire and torture, it is withdrawal.

Don Aminoke came out from one of the booths where he'd been treating a woman with a bee sting. "Talk about an allergy," he said, pointing back to the booth. "That one swelled up like a poison toad when she got stung, and unswelled right down again with some IV cortisone. Sort of disconcerting. Like a balloon deflating right in front of your eyes." He looked sharply at Bob. "What's the matter with you?"

Bob told him about Hazel.

"Hey, man, as long as you weren't a customer of hers, what do you care?" Don always tried to sound callous and tough, but Bob had seen him with his own eyes, at two o'clock one morning, paying for a taxi to take two scared teenage girls home to Queens. What they were doing in Manhattan at that time, he didn't know, and he didn't ask.

"It was the contrast that really got to me," replied Bob, a bit embarrassed to show any kind of emotional reaction around the emergency room. "Her face is so calm and beautiful, and her legs . . . Just looking at them, I almost puked."

"What are you going to do when you finish here?" asked Don curiously. "I don't mean this shift. I'm talking about when you finish your residency."

Bob looked over his head to the activity board. Everybody in the booths had been seen, and all was quiet for the moment, a brief lull in the war.

"Let's see if we can drum up some coffee somewhere," he said. "Maybe there's some in the X-ray Department." The on-call technician usually had a pot brewing.

"There is. I already checked it out," said Don. "It ain't great, but it's better than nothing."

The two of them walked along the darkened hallway toward the X-ray Department. There was a light on in the tech's room; the Mr. Coffee machine's red light was on and there was coffee in the pot, but the tech wasn't there.

Bob and Don each served themselves, using paper cups from a stack by the machine, and sat down in the two old, worn easy chairs.

"First time I've sat down all day," said Don. "It's not been that bad, just go, go, go."

"How do you like working here?" asked Bob. "Don't you miss getting to know your patients, that kind of stuff?"

"Are you kidding?" Don stretched his long legs luxuriously out in front of him. "That rabble? The kind of people we see here all day? No, sir. When I'm done, I'm done. Nobody calls me when I'm off-duty. I don't have to worry how some patient's doing, because it's not my responsibility. I'm a free man, Wesley, something you will never be!"

For a second Bob thought it was funny, but there certainly was some truth to it. At this point Bob was looking around at other ways of spending his life besides being a surgeon, on call to the world twenty-four hours a day for the rest of his working career. Maybe it was a matter of attitude, too, but there was no question that the doctors who were the most respected by their peers were the ones who devoted their entire lives to their work. Nobody seemed to think of reproaching them for their broken marriages; for their children, who grew up paternally deprived and hardly knowing who their father was. What did women doctors do? It must be even worse for them, the ones who also had a husband and children to take care of. But then, Bob tried to think of the names of famous women doctors, and he didn't come up with many . . . Marie Curie, Helen Taussig, the cardiologist. Certainly no really big names today, nothing to compare with Christiaan Barnard or Michael DeBakey or a dozen others. Maybe workaholism was more a disease of males.

So where did that leave him? How did he want to spend the rest of his life? That thought turned his mind to Patsy, and he smiled secretly to himself. He carried her around with him all the time in his head and in his heart; kept on seeing her for a second in the corridor or the cafeteria, when his breath would catch until the girl turned around, and of course it was someone quite different. Supposing, just supposing, that one day he asked her to marry him and she was dumb enough to agree; what sort of life would they have together? Patsy was planning to be a geologist, he knew, so she would be going all around the world digging holes and setting off seismic explosions and so on. Unless she got a home-based job. But what about him? Maybe he could become a general practitioner, like her father. Maybe he could even join him in his practice; there certainly seemed enough work there, the poor guy was hardly ever home. And he might really be happy to have somebody else to share the work with.

Don was getting up. "I have some paperwork to do," he said. "I'll tell the girls you're here." He dropped the paper cup in the trash can and left, looking carefree and relaxed. Maybe that *was* the life, Bob thought, following him with his eyes; being an emergency room doctor—

Hazel! Bob jumped up; he had completely forgotten about her and followed Don back into the emergency area.

Bob had noticed a disturbing trait about himself some time ago; he didn't know whether it applied to other people, too, but he found that he tended to forget, at least for a time, about things that were particularly disturbing to him, as if his brain was trying to rid itself of unpleasant or distressing material.

He heard one of the telephones ringing, and as he came around the corner, the secretary held out the phone to him. It was Patsy, calling from New London.

"God, Patsy, I was just thinking about you." He spun around, delighted, coiling the cord around himself. The desk nurse grinned and gave him the thumbs-up sign.

Then his face changed, and he turned abruptly from the nurse, who was still watching. After a couple of minutes he put the phone down slowly. Patsy, almost in tears, had finally told him her father had just been arrested. They said he'd been illegally prescribing dangerous drugs.

CHAPTER
THIRTY-FOUR

Louella had let them in, thinking it was a routine check, and both men sat quietly in the waiting room until Greg had finished seeing his patients.

The one who did most of the talking was Henry P. Gray, Jr., a burly young man with thinning blond hair who looked as if he'd played football at some stage in his career. He had a slow, deliberate way of speaking, as if his thoughts had some difficulty making their way to the surface, and was an inspector from the Federal Drug Administration. The other one, whose name Greg didn't remember, had been sent by the State Medical Board; he was a wiry little fellow in a tight gray suit whose eyes were continually moving around Greg's office as if he expected to find a stash of cocaine or heroin hidden in one of the filing cabinets.

"We'd like to look at your office records, please, Doctor," said Henry after showing a badge fixed to the inside of his wallet. "We're particularly interested in your narcotics file."

"Sure," said Greg, taken aback. "What's this all about?"

"We're here on the basis of a complaint filed yesterday against you in federal court in Hartford," he replied. "Does your secretary have the narcotics file in her office?"

"Yes, she does. I'll get them."

"Thanks, Doctor, don't bother. We'll do it. We just need to have your official permission to examine them, that's all. Oh, and by the way, do you use numbered prescription forms?"

"Yes, I do. May I ask who made the complaint?"

Henry and the other man looked at each other, and Henry shrugged.

"A Ms. Mary Abbott. She worked for you, so she knows, I guess," said the man from the SMB, looking directly at Greg.

"Knows what?" asked Greg sharply. "I haven't done anything illegal."

There was a brief silence.

"Right, Doctor. We'll go through and take a look at the records and the prescription forms now, if that's okay."

Greg ushered them back into the outer office.

"Louella, these gentlemen are here to look at the narcotics file. Give them whatever they need."

Louella glowered at them but reluctantly brought down the heavy file from the top of the drug cabinet.

"You always keep the book up there?" asked Henry casually. Louella's mouth tightened even more, but she said nothing. She put the blue, hardbacked file on the desk. Henry shrugged and took off his jacket. He had big muscular arms with hair that came over his wrists. "The prescription forms—you keep them in there?"

"Yes. There are a couple out, I think. One in my desk drawer . . . Louella, do you know where the other one is?"

Silently Louella picked up a pad of forms from off her desk and passed it to Henry. They both saw the glance that passed between the two visitors.

"I have to go to the hospital, Louella," said Greg, annoyed but not too concerned. Ever since he had fired Mary Abbott, he'd had a feeling that she'd find a way to cause some kind of trouble. "You can call me there if you need me."

Louella didn't call, but when Greg got back, she was sitting in tears at her desk. The two men stood up when he came in.

"Can we speak to you in the office?" asked Henry.

He closed Greg's office door behind them as if the place now belonged to him.

The reason he gave for taking away Greg's narcotics license was that more than seventy prescriptions for amphetamines, methadone, and Demerol had been signed by him and issued to individuals who were not on his list of patients and whose addresses didn't exist.

"That's nonsense," said Greg. "Let me see them."

Henry opened his briefcase and took out a wad of prescriptions in a thick rubber band. They looked as if they'd passed through a lot of hands. Greg looked at the top one. It certainly looked like his handwriting. It was dated over a year ago. He made a quick calculation; at that time Mary Abbott had still been working for him. He flipped quickly through the rest of the stack.

"I didn't write a single one of those," he said.

"Of course not, Doc," said the small man, grinning.

The reason he gave for immediately suspending Greg's license to practice medicine was that his FDA license to prescribe drugs had been suspended.

"There will be a hearing as soon as possible, probably within the next two weeks," said Henry. "You will be advised by registered mail."

"I hereby warn you that practicing medicine without a license in this state is punishable by a fine and a prison sentence," added the small man, trying to keep the satisfaction out of his voice.

When they left, the two men chatted for a moment in the street. Henry said, "Okay, you take the newspaper office and I'll handle the hospital."

Greg sat numb, looking at Louella.

"Somebody put her up to it," she said. "She never would have the guts to do it herself."

Greg sent Louella home, took the phone off the hook, and sat in the unnaturally quiet office, his head in his hands, feeling like a boxer who'd just survived a lethal bout only to get hit by a bus. He thought of calling Liz, but there was no point in adding to her problems. After a while he called Daniel Levine, the attorney who'd handled his will and the purchase of his house and office. Daniel didn't sound his usual affable self, and hesitated for a second when Greg said he wanted to see him urgently.

"I'm sort of booked up, Greg. But, okay, how about this afternoon around three?"

Willie Stringer would have marched right across the street and stormed into the attorney's office, but Greg acquiesced. He figured there was no point in antagonizing his own man. "Okay, then," he said. "Three o'clock."

Greg had never felt so tired, or so alone.

After a while he called the Medical Society office in Stamford.

They were sympathetic and cheered him up somewhat. "We have a lawyer who specializes in this kind of thing," they said; "let us know if you need him."

"Thanks," replied Greg, "but let me see what my own guy here can do."

There was a knock on the door but Greg ignored it. "A fine and a prison sentence," the man had said. The knock was repeated, and Greg went to look through the side window. It was Mrs. Gilligan, pushing a wheelchair with Dave in it. She saw him and smiled. Greg didn't have the heart to send her away. He opened the door.

"Come in. The office is sort of closed right now." Greg was embarrassed and couldn't bring himself to say he'd been shut down.

Dave's eyes were rolling, the muscles of his face occasionally twitching in what looked like pleasure.

"How's he been?" Greg helped her put him on the examining table.

"Better, much better, Doctor," she said with a smile. She had the same shy, slightly fearful look about her. Greg left her to find Dave's folder in the files. There was a recent lab slip attached to the envelope.

"The lab values are pretty good," he said after checking the column of figures. "His phenobarb level is about right. How often is he having the fits now?"

"They're way down, Doctor, thanks to you." She smiled, a gentle, grateful smile, and Greg felt suddenly like a charlatan. He wasn't allowed to practice medicine now.

"His last one was two days ago, and it was just a little one. He just shook for about a minute. Do you think they'll ever go away completely, Doctor?"

"I certainly hope so," he said, trying to sound encouraging. There was no way he could tell for sure, but he felt he had to keep her hopes up. "They're coming out with better drugs all the time now, so I think there's a good chance."

Greg gulped. "Mrs. Gilligan, there's something I have to tell you. Today some inspectors came and took away my license." His fingernails bit into his palms. "But it'll be all right. I don't need to tell you I've done nothing wrong."

Mrs. Gilligan looked at him in disbelief, then she started to cry quietly. "That's just terrible, Dr. Hopkins, just awful." She dried her tears with the back of her sleeve. Dave made a bubbling noise, and a trail of saliva ran down the side of his mouth. She wiped it away gently with a tissue.

"Doctor, there's just one thing I want to say to you." She hesitated, her large brown eyes uncomfortable, as if she were about to take some kind of liberty with him. "And John—that's my husband—I'm sure he'd agree with me."

Greg looked away at Dave, to make it easier for her, whatever she had to say, and waited. "We know what you've been through, Doctor—with your boy, I mean—and now with the problems you're having. I don't want to sound interfering or anything, but you've always taken such good care of us, and I want you to know we think the world of you, Dr. Hopkins."

Embarrassed at her long speech, she quickly opened the wheelchair and sat Dave up. In an uncomfortable silence, Greg helped to get him into the wheelchair, and they eased it out of the cramped examining room. At the door, Greg smiled and tried to say something to her, but to his mortification the tears welled up in his own eyes, and he had to turn abruptly away.

Daniel Levine was about forty-five, with a kind of studied sloppiness in his old wrinkled blue-and-white seersucker jacket and gray flannels. Some people thought he cultivated the I'm-just-a-country-lawyer look that had become popular near the end of the Nixon administration. He sat now in his equally sloppy-looking office, rocking gently in a high-backed chair, surveying Greg, who was sitting uncomfortably on the edge of the client's chair. The lawyer's stiff body language spoke volumes. His manner was formal, distant.

". . . no warning, no appointment, nothing," Greg was saying. "They just arrived, went through my stuff—files, prescription records—and shut me down. Just like that. I still can't believe it." He paused, looking at Daniel. "There's something going on here I don't understand, but I have my suspicions."

"I heard something about it at noon. Nothing to those charges, really, is there?"

"Of course not." Greg looked at Daniel in some surprise. "You had to ask me that?"

"Greg, I want you listen to me, and listen good, please. Look around this office. I don't have a teletype, a cellular phone, or any of that fancy stuff. I get most of my information flown in. A birdie, a large and powerful birdie, has told me you're trying to get even with some doctor in New York."

Daniel raised both hands to stop Greg from speaking. "Please, let me finish. This birdie doesn't like that at all, as he said the doctor is a friend of his. The birdie, by the way, could eat you and me both in one gulp."

"What is this shit about birdies?" Greg stood up, raising his voice. "Are you talking about Angelo Petrini? Or if not, who? Why do you have to talk like we're in the middle of some kind of nursery rhyme?"

"I didn't want to mention names. Just a word to the wise."

"Daniel, what the hell are you doing? As my attorney, aren't you supposed to be on my side?"

Daniel stopped rocking his chair. "As your attorney, I feel my job is to warn you when you are running into danger, and that, Greg, is exactly what you're doing. If certain people really start to pay serious attention to you, then God help you, because I won't be able to." He steepled his fingers under his chin and his blue eyes fixed on Greg. "Now, if you could tell me that your interest in the New York surgeon is at an end, I have no doubt that charges would be withdrawn, apologies made, corrective statements put in the papers, all that stuff. Possibly some other problems might evaporate too. Do you read me?"

Greg was staring at him in disgust.

"And if not?"

"If not . . ." Daniel considered him for a few moments, during which Greg decided that he had never trusted him, anyway. "If not, they'll do worse things to you than you can imagine."

Greg got up slowly and went to the door. He turned, his face red with anger. "Daniel, you can shove your advice right up your ass, up there with your birdie!"

The door slammed, and Daniel's chair started to rock again, forward and back, forward and back.

I was just telling him how the real world works, he thought.

Outside the offices of Levine, Strauss, and Levine, Greg paused, blinking in the strong sunlight. A white Cadillac drove by, and a black hand momentarily appeared at the driver's-side window. The driver kept his eyes straight ahead. It wasn't a wave but certainly a hello of sorts. It took Greg a moment to figure out who it was: Big Vern, of course, Big Vern of cucumber fame. An irrational wave of optimism swept over him; if Big Vern could survive *his* problems, then he himself could survive this. At least nobody was trying to cut his cucumber off. Not yet, anyway.

CHAPTER
THIRTY-FIVE

"I'm telling you one more time, and that's it!" said Big Vern with a gleam in his yellow eyes. He had a short fuse, and all this was taking time away from his business. "You listen to the man and shut up. Don't say nothin', 'cause you don't know nothin'." He sat back. If the kid hadn't been the doctor's son, he'd never have gotten into this business in the first place.

Douglas looked from him to the small man who'd been sitting with them for the last fifteen minutes. He had a white, rather pasty face, with mousy hair, a slightly receding chin, and a thin neck made even scrawnier-looking by his collar, which was a couple of sizes too big. He spoke very quietly, with an accent Douglas couldn't place.

"Take it from me," he said. "Shooting ain't no good, not these days, unless you have an organization behind you. Other people can get hurt, you get seen—recognized, maybe—you have to get away." He looked at Douglas like a teacher with a willing but stupid pupil. He didn't normally waste his time with this kind of deal, but things had been quiet and he had a temporary problem of liquidity.

"The way to do this job right is with a car bomb, detonated by a time switch. It doesn't take a big one, either—a small briefcase full is plenty, as long as it's in the passenger compartment."

Douglas still wasn't convinced. "With a car like that he's sure to have an alarm system. How . . . ?"

The little man grinned. "Vern here gonna be helpin' you?"

Vern hesitated, then nodded. There was no way the kid could do it by himself.

"Well, if Vern's working with you, you don't have to worry about no alarm system."

Vern made a decision.

"Take a hike," he said to the little man. "Come back in five minutes. And don't talk to any of them girls in the street, they'd suck ya in and pop ya out like a plumstone."

"Look, kid," said Big Vern to Douglas when the little man was out of earshot. "You want revenge for what this guy did to your bro, right?"

Douglas nodded. He felt he was getting out of his depth with car bombs and such like. What he wanted was to get the guy Stringer killed, without all these complications.

"Okay, let me tell you something. You kill people when they're a real danger to you, before they fuck *you* up. When you want *revenge,* you don't kill them, you hurt them, hurt them bad, so they think about what you done to them every day. See the difference?"

Douglas shrugged. Yes, he supposed Big Vern was right. He'd never thought about it like that.

Vern suggested a couple of ways to do it; he, Vern, would help him. A dumb-shit kid like Douglas needed an adult to keep him out of trouble.

When the little man came back, Vern asked him how much the bomb would cost.

"Two grand, including full instructions." He winked at Big Vern.

"This kid ain't got nothin' like that kinda money," said Big Vern. "He's gonna stick with something simple, like shoot the fucker's kneecaps off him."

They both looked at Douglas, who stared back at them.

"Yeah, right," he said.

In cases where physicians and drugs are involved, both the law and the medical associations move swiftly.

Greg's appearance before the disciplinary committee of the State Medical Association took place as scheduled. He was represented by the lawyer recommended by the association, a man with considerable experience in such cases. As the hearing progressed, Greg became more and more anxious; the man seemed tired and lackadaisical in the conduct of his defense and didn't bring any witnesses. In the meantime it was shown by the inspectors that Greg's handling of records and narcotics files was grossly negligent. To Greg and Liz's growing concern, it was beginning to look as if things might go badly for him.

Then his attorney called a surprise witness, who turned out to be no less than the distinguished New York surgeon, Wilbrahim Stringer. He described Greg in glowing terms, having known him since medical school, and said that there had been some major error and there was no way that Greg Hopkins would be culpably involved in illegal drug activity. As Greg's lawyer had already established that a prescription pad and a signature stamp had been reported stolen from Greg's office during a break-in almost two years before, and as there was no evidence that he had ever seen the persons named on the prescriptions, the committee finally gave Greg the benefit of the doubt. He was let off with a stern warning. Any more of this kind of carelessness and they would rescind his license.

"Well, I think you should thank your good friend for taking the time to come up here," said his lawyer, putting a friendly hand on Greg's shoulder. "He certainly saved your bacon today!"

He snapped his big legal briefcase shut and went on his way, jaunty with his success.

Greg went looking for Willie to thank him, but he had disappeared. It was getting late, and by the time Greg and Liz had gathered up all their papers and headed for home, it was already dark. Greg was shaken and silent, terribly upset by the whole episode, while Liz sat there quietly. She knew she didn't need to do more than be there to comfort him.

"Greg, could we stop at Safeway and get some milk? With all this I forgot to go this morning. Sorry!" She put her hand on his knee, and her touch was a relief to him. Greg turned right at the light, in a turmoil about the afternoon's proceedings. What on earth had possessed Willie Stringer to come all the way up here to defend him? Maybe he'd misjudged him. He certainly wouldn't have done it if he'd set up the whole thing, would he? And the nice things he'd said . . . he obviously didn't bear any kind of grudge against Greg for stirring up the hornet's nest in New York.

"Maybe I should call the whole thing off," he said, glancing at Liz. "As the man said, Willie really saved my bacon today."

"They weren't going to do anything, anyway," said Liz dryly. "It was obvious that the whole thing had been set up by that bitch, Mary Abbott." But her words lacked conviction. She knew as well as Greg how close it had come.

They pulled into the Safeway parking lot, and Greg waited in the car while Liz ran in for the milk. He still felt unsure about what he should do next; would he be betraying Edward if he abandoned his crusade against Willie Stringer? Or would it be better to call Janus Frankel in the morning and tell him he'd decided not to go ahead with it? After all, Willie was only human, and presumably the whole thing would make him deal with his patients more carefully in the future. Nothing was going to bring Edward back.

They passed the town hall, then the new Holiday Inn, which had opened a week or so before. Liz was just saying that it was supposed to be very nice inside and that they'd gotten a New York chef to get the restaurant started when Greg saw the back of a big white BMW in the parking lot on the other side of the sidewalk. With a shock he remembered that Willie Stringer had a car just like that, and he thought he'd recognized the white and blue of a New York license plate. But of course there were lots of other white BMWs.

He slowed, thinking hard, then decided to go around the block. Liz looked at him in surprise when he turned left instead of right, but she didn't say anything.

As they came around again Greg slowed in front of the hotel parking area and almost stopped when he came abreast of the big white BMW. Sure enough, it *was* Willie's, and the custom plate confirmed it—WMSMD.

Without even thinking about it Greg drove into the hotel lot and parked the car.

"I'll just be a minute," he said. "Willie's in there, and I want to speak with him . . . to thank him, I suppose."

He looked at Liz with slight embarrassment, but she said in a normal tone, "Go ahead, Greg. I hope you find him. It's going to be crowded in there." She sat very still while he walked quickly over to the back entrance of the hotel.

Greg hurried down the long corridor to the front lobby of the hotel, which was full of Japanese car dealers and their wives, laughing and calling to each other. He fought his way to the dark bar, which was crowded, and he pushed his way through slowly. Willie was nowhere to be seen.

He went back to the lobby and asked if Willie was staying there, but there was no one registered by that name. Greg started to feel disappointed; his old, warm feeling for Willie was begining to creep back into his consciousness in spite of himself. He was about to head back to the parking area when it suddenly occurred to him that Willie might be having a meal before going back to New York, and he felt unaccountably guilty that Willie should have to eat in a restaurant in Greg's town.

There was a big group waiting at the door, and a pretty girl with a deep décolleté was guiding people to their seats. Greg edged his way through and started to scan the heads of the diners. There were at least a hundred people there, and it took several minutes before Greg saw Willie, sitting at a window table. He had just started toward him when he saw who was sitting at the table with him. On one side was Greg's lawyer, the one who'd been recommended by the medical association, and on the other side was the fat, middle-aged doctor from Stamford who had presided over the proceedings that afternoon. Greg stopped dead, his mouth open with shock. A waitress bumped into him from behind, but he never even felt it. So the whole thing had been a setup, designed to embarrass him into getting off Willie Stringer's case. It was their laughter, their obscene, guffawing laughter, which Greg saw and felt more than heard; that offended him most. He restrained himself from striding over, tipping the table up and beating Willie into unconsciousness.

Slowly he turned and went back to his car. He got in, started the motor in silence, and drove down the street, turning right at the corner.

"That bastard!" he said a few minutes later. Then he told Liz what he'd seen, and Liz, afraid and concerned about him, held his arm tightly all the way home.

Bob Wesley was in the middle of rounds with his team when his pager went off. Call extension 4990. The chairman's office? What on earth could Dr. Frankel want with him? Walter English

gave him a strange look, one of embarrassed sympathy. Whatever it was, Walter knew about it.

Although he wasn't aware of any new problems that might
have attracted the attention of Dr. Frankel, Bob answered the
page with a sinking heart. "Come to the office," said the
secretary. Her voice, too, was strange; usually she was formal,
brisk, and quite unimpressed by the charm of the residents.
Now her voice was bright, too friendly. He was shown straight
into the inner office, and she wouldn't look him in the eye.

"Yes, Bob, come on in," said Janus Frankel.

Bob went into the room.

"Sit down. Now, Bob, I'm going to come straight to the point.
For a while we haven't been satisfied with your work here. I
know it's a very demanding, very tiring, and difficult job, but
we have standards of patient care to maintain, and, Bob, I'm
truly sorry to have to say this, but you're not meeting them."

A sudden lightness came over Bob. His mind seemed to soar
out of the office and look down on what was happening as if
it were somehow a third person, separate from him.

He smiled at Frankel. "Are you firing me?"

Frankel's eyebrows went up. The kid seemed to be almost
pleased.

"I'm really sorry, Bob. Of course we'll give you a good
reference. I know that Dr. Ostermann at the VA is looking for
a resident at your level, and you might find it not quite as
stressful."

"I decided a little while back that surgery wasn't for me,"
said Bob, choosing his words carefully. "It simply doesn't work
as far as I'm concerned. I like to be able to get to know my
patients on more of a long-term basis, and—"

Dr. Frankel stood up. He had no intention of listening to
Bob Wesley's thoughts on the problems of surgery as a discipline. He held out his hand. "Thanks for your help, Bob. Of
course we'll pay you through to the end of the month. As of
now, you are relieved of your duties except for any charts you
have to dictate, stuff like that. You'll get your final check when
I hear from the Records Department that all your paperwork
has been completed. Hey, Bob," he said with a spurious
bonhomie that made Bob want to puke, "stay in touch, okay?"
He put his hand briefly on Bob's shoulder.

Frankel felt no more compunction about this unjust move than a chess player at sacrificing a piece. In this case there was no doubt that the end justified the means. As long as Willie Stringer was convinced that Frankel was on his side and agreed to attend the hearing without bringing in a lawyer, it was worth doing.

Bob went back to finish rounds with Walter, feeling as if a huge load had been taken off his shoulders. He knew that surgery wasn't his vocation, but he was angry that he'd been fired so ignominiously.

Suddenly he stopped. Stringer! It must have been Stringer who'd put Frankel up to it. Everything started to fall into place: he'd been so angry about the Elmo Harris episode and blamed him for Frankel getting into the act; and then the awful Edward Hopkins fiasco; and then, of course, there was Patsy. He was jealous, the old goat!

In the old days Willie, in his perverse way, might have been flattered to learn how many people were making plans for his demise. But not now. Somebody from the Department of Immigration and Naturalization was coming to the office that afternoon; Vera, his nurse and good friend, apparently did not have a work permit or even a valid visa. He knew she was from Germany, but it had never occurred to him that she might be working for him illegally or that he was breaking the law by employing her.

Not only that, the IRS people were coming the next week, and his accountant was still in Hong Kong, or wherever the hell he'd gone, and wasn't expected back until two days later. Nothing was very amusing now.

CHAPTER
THIRTY-SIX

Bob had promised to go up to New London to see Patsy, and with his newfound freedom he was able to get there earlier than he'd expected. Patsy's last class finished at three, so they walked across the campus, through the gates into the arboretum, and strolled hand in hand through the quiet paths, enjoying the cool, protective shade of the oaks and yews and rare pine trees.

Bob wanted to tell her about Frankel firing him, but he knew it would upset her, so he concentrated on enjoying the peace and quiet of the place with her, although it wasn't easy. When they came to the edge of the little lake, two mallards took off like missiles and vanished over the tops of the trees, leaving little pockets of disturbed water on the surface.

Patsy was weaing a gray skirt and a plain white blouse, and her freshness and beauty made his hands tremble.

They stood looking out over the water. The sun was now below the treetops, shining through the tight network of black branches like the flames of a divine fire. He put his arm around her and drew her to his side. They both stared straight ahead, unbearably intent on each other's presence, aware of every movement, every breath each of them took. His hand moved gently up to her breast, and she didn't stir or draw away. The feel of her made him light-headed, as if he couldn't stand being separate from her another moment.

"No, Bob. Not here," she murmured, turning. She put her arms around him and held herself hard against him, just for a moment, and all the passion was there, all the young desire of her whole being. Then she pulled away and went back up the path toward the gate, almost running. Bob stood for a second, then ran after her, all kinds of wild, predatory passions surging during the short chase. They walked quickly back to her room, hand in hand, without saying another word.

Patsy looked at her watch.

"Judith won't be out of class for thirty minutes," she said as she locked the door.

Later they went down to the Pizza Hut. Judith Porter, her roommate, was expecting her friend Timothy, so Bob bought four large pizzas although Patsy said they'd never eat them all.

When they got back, Bob carrying the pizzas, Timothy had arrived, and the two of them were sitting on Judith's bed. Judith, who was looking bored, brightened up noticeably when she caught sight of Bob, and her eyes flickered appreciatively over his broad frame.

"Boy, that smells good. . . . This is Timothy Scales, by the way."

God, thought Bob, *if somebody introduced me in that tone of voice, I'd be out the door in one second.* He stuck out his free hand, balancing the pile of cardboard boxes in the other, and Timothy shook it silently.

Judith rolled her eyes at Patsy, while Timothy kept his eyes fixed on the pizzas. Patsy and Judith found plates and a knife.

"This one's got everything," said Bob, opening the top box. The enticing aroma was now mixed with the unmistakable odor of hot cardboard, but it didn't bother anybody. "Mushrooms, green pepper, onions, pepperoni, extra cheese . . ."

He sliced it up with a flourish and passed it around. With a grin he gave two pieces to Timothy, who made a sandwich out of them and started to wolf it down.

"I see there's another of those nuclear subs over at Electric Boat," said Bob indistinctly through a mouthful of pizza. It was still very hot, and he blew the air out of his mouth. "Doesn't all that radioactivity bother you guys, living between the naval base and that nuclear power station, whatever it's called?"

"Millstone," prompted Judith, smiling at him. "Millstone One, Two, and Three. It doesn't bother us at all, does it?" She turned to Patsy, flicking her smooth blonde hair out of her eyes. "It's easier to find each other now that we glow in the dark." They all laughed, except for Timothy, who was too busy with his pizza.

"It's a more classy kind of pollution, anyway," said Patsy, her eyes not moving from Bob. He looked so relaxed and somehow in charge of himself. "Better than the carbon monoxide you have to fight through in New York."

"We went to this concert in Strawberry Fields—" started Bob.

"Don't tell me, I've been hearing about nothing else since Sunday night," said Judith a little tartly. "By the way, she never got around to telling you that she really prefers Haydn and Mozart to heavy metal."

If Judith thought that was going to be a fatal dig, she was disappointed. Bob looked at Patsy, openmouthed.

"She's kidding, right?"

"No, as a matter of fact"—*It might as well come out now,* she thought, *even if it makes him think I'm a freak*—"I enjoyed the concert. I loved it. But I'm really into the classical stuff. Sorry."

"What do you mean, sorry? Finally I've found something to talk to you about!" He stood up and stuck out a declamatory hand. "No more long silences! No more embarrassing pauses in the conversation! Now we can talk about Köchel numbers and sonata form and all that stuff. Wow! Can you imagine a relationship that's more than just sex?"

Judith and Timothy exchanged a glance, and Judith moved a little closer to him on the bed. Maybe he wasn't such a tiresome guy, after all; at least he didn't go in for all that crazy long-hair stuff.

Bob wanted to hear the Dennis Brain horn concerto, so Patsy pulled it carefully out of its sleeve and placed it on the turntable.

Timothy yawned. "Let's go for a walk, huh?" he said to Judith. She got up immediately, looking relieved, and put on her shoes. They said good-bye and were gone almost at once.

Bob and Patsy sat close together on Patsy's bed. She could feel the strength of him, and she had a woman's more profound understanding of the bond that was growing between them. Up to now she had worn boys to the cinema or a dance like she would wear a new dress. They weren't more important than that, sort of exciting to be around but totally forgettable after a week or two. And they still kept on coming, as if there were a line of them waiting to go out with her. As soon as one was discarded, his best friend came calling with a bunch of flowers.

Maybe they all thought they'd be the first. Well, they could forget about that now. She had Bob.

There was a closeness and a distance, a comfort and an unease with Bob. She felt unsure, attractive, inadequate, in control. All her emotions and feelings were topsy-turvy, and it was thoroughly disconcerting. But this was the first time she'd been on the threshold of falling in love. The strange thing was that when she'd been driving back from New York, she'd thought almost as much about Willie Stringer, although in quite a different way, of course; a kind of bittersweet feeling of something outside her grasp.

That had been a strange weekend, and the impressions of the people who had populated it roamed around in her head. Ellen, trying to hold on to life but unable to respond to its physical demands; and Willie, the perfect sort of uncle until she heard from Bob's own mouth what he'd done to Edward. It had all come out in a torrent, and afterward Bob had felt guilty because he felt he'd been self-serving, passing the criticisms he'd gotten from Frankel on to Willie Stringer—although Willie was the one who really deserved it, certainly more than he did.

What Patsy had been concerned about was the effect this new information would have on her father. Emotionally he was still shaky, although he'd been a bit better the last time she'd seen him. It would have a terrible impact on him, she knew, but she had no way of telling where those revelations would lead.

Somehow Patsy had managed to insulate herself from most of the tension that had built up in her family. Edward was dead; she grieved but life had to go on. She thought about him often and sometimes cried softly in her bed at some particular memory of him. The one that came most often to her was the night of her high-school prom, when she'd first appeared in her long dress. Edward had been picking up his school books at the bottom of the stairs when she started to come down, and he'd watched her with what she thought was awestruck admiration. "Wow, Patsy, I don't care what anybody says, I think you're *beautiful!*"

Driving back from that New York weekend, Patsy had stopped at the Big 76 truck stop for a cup of coffee. She liked those places; there was a kind of mystery, a flavor of faraway cities, rolling plains of wheat, and endless deserts surrounding those lean, cigarette-smoking truckers with their worn cowboy

boots, in sole command of the giant trucks that sat in the
parking lots, their huge motors clicking occasionally as they
cooled off, wearing their mud-encrusted license plates like
medals from Arizona to Maine.

"Let me turn it," said Bob when the record came to an end.
"It's really fantastic. I've heard the horn concerto lots of times,
but never played like this."

"I'll get my dad to put it on tape for you if you like," she
said. "You know, he really likes you. He said you're an honest
doctor. I know that sounds funny, but he means—well, it means
he likes you, I guess."

"I feel bad about what I said to him on the phone," said Bob
soberly. "I was upset with Willie Stringer for a lot of reasons."
He looked hard at Patsy, who understood immediately what
he meant. "Willie's really not a bad guy, and I hope your father
isn't going to do anything on the basis of what I told him."

"Poor Dad. He's so upset about Edward, I don't know if he's
ever going to get over it. I went home the day before yesterday,
and he was looking so old all of a sudden."

"Patsy, I'm thinking of getting out of surgery."

"Why, Bob? I thought you loved it. What happened?"

"It's a lot of things. When I'm working, my stomach is in a
knot all the time. I feel responsible when anything goes wrong
on the service, and I just know that I'm not like them—I mean,
not *built* like the surgeons. I don't *think* like them." Bob took a
deep breath. "And Dr. Frankel fired me today."

Patsy put her arms around him in a spontaneous, protective
gesture and buried her head in his chest.

"How could he?" A thought struck her. "Has it got anything
to do with . . . well, you know, Edward?"

"Maybe, but it doesn't really matter. To tell you the honest
truth, I'm more relieved than anything."

"What are you going to do?"

Bob stroked her silky hair. "I don't know. I think I'd like to
go into general practice."

"That's what I thought. Get your coat, we're going home to
talk to Dad."

"Patsy! We can't just arrive like that! For one thing, he might
be out. And anyway, what do you have in mind?"

"Something he said. Okay, I'll call to make sure he's home.
It's only fifty minutes from here."

CHAPTER
THIRTY-SEVEN

Ellen Stringer had changed a lot in the last few weeks. For much of her married life she had been cantankerous and sarcastic with Willie, but now that she felt the shades of her life closing around her, she had suddenly become more thoughtful and appreciative of him than she had ever been.

Now she was more worried about Willie than about herself; not only was he not eating well but also his essentially spiky, irritable arrogance had been replaced by a kind of mental numbness, as if more things were happening to him than he could handle. What seemed like a profound emotional weariness had set in; at the office, where his presence used to have a galvanizing and occasionally frightening effect on all the staff, he now came and went almost unnoticed, and they all thought him much nicer, more agreeable.

Ellen mentioned the idea of a vacation again; Willie thought about it and considered Ellen's limited life expectancy. She would probably be in a wheelchair within six months, on continuous pain medication soon after that, and she'd be dead inside a year.

"Where would you like to go?" he asked, coming over to the bed to sit by her. "We'll go as soon as all this business with the hearing is over, and that shouldn't be too long." He reached out for her hand. Ellen had always had delicate hands with long fingers, but now they were almost skeletal. "God, your fingers are cold!" he said, and held her hand between his own, their healthy pink contrasting sadly with the pallor of her skin.

Ellen indicated the pile of travel folders in front of her.

"I've just been figuring," she said, and her eyes lit up with a kind of febrile excitement. "The only place we've been to in the Caribbean was Bermuda, and that was years ago."

"Bermuda . . ." He was going to remind her that Bermuda was in the middle of the Atlantic, not in the Caribbean, but thought better of it. He smiled a little sadly to himself; even a couple of months ago he would have snapped at her for saying such a stupid thing. But now, if she thought Bermuda was the same as Barbados, it was all right with him.

"Sounds good to me. Where would you like to go? Barbados? Antigua? You name it and I'll get reservations."

Ellen gently took her hand out of his and reached for the folders the travel agents had sent her. She had made a long list on a piece of her headed notepaper.

"First we should go to Jamaica. Here, look at this, look at the mountains. They're called the Blue Mountains, and they're not far from Kingston, and they grow the best coffee in the world up there, or that's what it says, anyway." Ellen stopped, a little out of breath, and he smiled at her.

"I'll get Vera to make the reservations for the end of next month, how about that?" That's if Vera hasn't been deported back to Germany by then, he thought. He smiled at her. Perhaps the sunshine and sea air would make her feel better, maybe even reverse the awful cancer growth.

"And next year," continued Ellen before she'd quite gotten her breath back, "it'll be St. Thomas in the Virgin Islands."

"I'm afraid you won't qualify," said Willie, holding her hand tight to prevent the tears from coming into his eyes, "but maybe we can get a special dispensation." He put his head lightly on her shoulder. Her bones felt as if too much pressure could break them.

"The year after that will be Barbados," she said, her voice fading. "You remember the Eisensteins went, and they said it was just—" Ellen coughed and pulled out her handkerchief. With a shock, Willie saw the blood.

"How long . . . ?" he asked, indicating the red spot.

"Oh, a week or two," she said with a smile. "It's always just a little, no big deal."

But Willie, with his painful fund of knowledge, knew that those little specks of blood meant that Ellen's tumor had spread to her lungs. She would never see Jamaica, let alone Barbados.

This time the tears came into his eyes, and he buried his head where her neck met her shoulder, holding her tight.

"Easy," she said, and he knew she was smiling at him the way she had when his passion used to get the better of him. "Take it easy or you'll break me in half."

Holding tightly to Ellen, Willie felt something slipping, slipping forever away from him. His sleek, well-polished, and obedient world, which had been so securely under control, was now losing its outlines, like the melting turrets of an ice palace in the sun.

Willie showed no such signs of weakness at the hearing.

The committee was composed of the same people Dr. Frankel had summoned for his conference some weeks before: Dr. Gill, the senior hospital pathologist, who only knew Willie Stringer by repute; Dr. Latimer, the chief of staff, who had been pulled away from his study of liver enzymes for this inquiry and felt annoyed at the waste of time; Dr. Sampson, the portly dean who couldn't pass a sandwich or a piece of pie without reaching for it; and Dr. Andrew Furness, the surgeon, affectionately dubbed the silent Scot by the house staff.

Dr. Frankel had made every effort to help the proceedings seem relaxed and informal; he appeared surprised when Willie came accompanied by his attorney, a noted lawyer well practiced in the field of medical disputes. He was short, balding, and inoffensive-looking, tightly fitted into a dark business suit and carrying a huge legal satchel that looked far too big for him. Willie introduced him, ignoring the reproachful look Janus Frankel gave him. The lawyer said that he was at this moment merely holding a watching brief and would only interrupt the proceedings if his client's rights were infringed upon or threatened. Janus got started as soon as everybody was seated. There was a lot of material to go over, he explained, which was why he'd chosen to hold it on a Friday afternoon and Saturday morning, in order to interfere as little as possible with everyone's schedules. Also, it would attract less attention from the rest of the hospital.

A photocopy of Edward Hopkins's chart was set on the table in front of each place, together with the autopsy report and copies of Willie's admission notes and endoscopy report. On top of each little stack of papers was a blue-bound copy of the hospital bylaws.

Janus Frankel put a small tape recorder in the middle of the table.

"Willie, we decided to record the sessions, in case there's ever any argument about what was said. Is that okay with you?" He glanced at Willie and then at the attorney.

"Sure," said Willie, "just let's get on with this. I'm playing golf on Saturday afternoon, and I don't want this to drag on until then." This provoked a ripple of comfortable mirth; Willie felt a little better and helped himself to some coffee from the machine in the corner, bringing a cup over to his attorney.

Janus Frankel called the meeting to order, then said that the committee had been convened to consider some allegations of mistreatment of a case, number 89-48521, brought to their attention by a report from the Surgical Quality Assurance Committee and also by a Dr. Gregory Hopkins, the father of the child, a general practitioner in Connecticut. He smiled encouragingly at Willie over his glasses, as if to say, "We're your friends, your colleagues, and we'll get through this as soon as we can."

"Before we actually start, I'd like to mention that I strongly suggested that Dr. Stringer voluntarily agree not to be represented here by an attorney, but he appears not to have accepted that suggestion." Dr. Sampson nodded knowingly and grinned, and the others looked inquiringly at the attorney. "Of course," murmured Frankel, as if it were an afterthought, "that is perfectly within his rights." He shuffled through his papers, although he knew exactly where everything was—every note, every report.

They started with Willie's admission note; this was a brief description of all the pertinent clinical history and findings on physical examination before admission. According to the hospital bylaws, admission notes had to be dictated into the hospital system within twenty-four hours of the patient's admission.

Frankel read the note; it was just the right length, to the point, and gave a good summary of the findings. Willie had noted that during the endoscopy there had been some brisk bleeding but had thought he could see an ulcer in the far end of the stomach.

The first sour note was struck when Dr. Gill asked mildly about the date of the transcription on the bottom of the typed sheet. The transcriber's initials were followed by the date, which, as he pointed out, was three days after the boy's admission.

"Then it was actually dictated after the boy had died?" asked Dr. Sampson, munching on a doughnut, the remainder of which sat in front of him on a paper napkin.

"Really, I don't remember," said Willie. "At the time I had twelve patients in the house, and anyway, sometimes the secretaries get backed up, and they don't get the stuff typed immediately."

"There are two dates here," said Dr. Gill, holding up the paper. "One says date of dictation, the other date of transcription, and they're the same."

"I checked that point," said Dr. Frankel. "Mrs. Kaminsky, the head transcriptionist, said that it was actually a quiet time for them, and they were right up-to-date." He smiled, happy for Mrs. Kaminsky. It wasn't always so easy for her, he knew.

There were no further comments on the admission note, but Willie felt that the atmosphere had chilled a little. The committee members could all draw their own conclusions.

The rest of the afternoon was spent going over the hospital chart and the autopsy findings. Bob Wesley came in for a fair amount of criticism, particularly for missing vital clinical signs in his history and physical examination. Frankel leaned over to switch the tape recorder off for a moment.

"I want you all to know that I was forced to fire Bob partly because of this," he said. "A substantial part of the blame for this tragic case rests with him."

Willie got up for another cup of coffee.

"Isn't the captain of the ship responsible?" asked Dr. Sampson, and as Willie was at that moment opening a packet of sugar, he missed the warning rise of Janus Frankel's eyebrows. Dr. Sampson's question died on the wind. The attorney saw the byplay but remained impassive.

Willie spent an uncomfortable hour trying to reconcile his recorded findings during the operation with those at the autopsy, and he could feel the attitude of the committee hardening against him.

At five o'clock Frankel looked at his watch. "I think we've done enough for today," he said. "Thank you all."

At the door he put his hand on Willie's shoulder for a moment. "Sorry to be putting you through all this," he said encouragingly. "Actually I think it's going pretty well, don't you? By the way," he went on, "Dr. Hopkins will be here tomorrow, and we'll try to dispose of his evidence as fast as possible."

Willie waited until everyone else had gone, then he turned to his attorney.

"How did it go?" he asked, his attempt at insouciance clearly forced.

"It went well," replied the attorney grimly. "For them. I expect you realize that they are well informed, well prepared, and out to get you. By that I mean they will press to have your hospital privileges suspended and probably take it to the State Medical Board to have your license revoked."

Willie tried to control his dismay and shock, and the attorney went on. "I've seen several cases like this; when a powerful group wants to get rid of a physician, it's very difficult to stop them. We'll fight it to the last, of course, but I want to be sure you know what we're up against."

Willie waited, speechless, while the attorney packed his papers in his voluminous case. Then, feeling dazed, he went up to see a new patient he had admitted through the emergency room. Just as he was getting out of the elevator he heard a voice behind him. It was Andrew Furness.

"Do you have a second, Willie?" Without another word, Furness led the way into the small room where the residents did their dictating and closed the door behind them.

"Willie," he said without preamble, his Scottish accent quite marked, "that committee is setting you up for the high jump, and they're only waiting to see that . . . questionable autopsy report sent from your office to Dr. Hopkins. I would strongly suggest you talk to Dr. Hopkins and persuade him not to appear tomorrow, and to have him destroy that report. If it ever appears, Willie, you're sunk."

Andrew looked at him with a kind of sympathy. "I thought he was a friend of yours."

* * *

Willie was shaken to the core of his being. There was no question in his mind that Andrew Furness was right, and with the proper kind of paranoid retrospection he could see how Frankel had put it all together, step by cautious step, like a Shoshone Indian planning a baited trap for a wily old bear.

But he could still get out of it; Andrew was right about that too. He'd thought that his appearance at Greg's hearing would defuse Greg's anger and might make him drop the whole vendetta.

The only recourse now was to talk to him, explain what his actions were going to lead to. He felt sure that Greg, despite his anger, wouldn't want to see him totally destroyed. And anyway, he thought, with a partial return of his old confidence, if he could only talk to Greg for a while, he could get him back on his side. He'd always been able to do that in the past.

Willie reached for the phone and got an outside line. He located Greg's number in his address book and dialed it. The phone rang in the kitchen, and Liz picked it up. A wave of sheer anger hit her when she recognized the voice, but she controlled it.

"Liz, I'm sorry, but I really need to speak to Greg."

It was strange, talking to the man she had planned to visit in Manhattan in order to shoot him dead in his office. She felt that any jury would let her off when they heard the facts. Now she had a wild idea, an alternative plan that appeared, fully formed, in her mind.

"He's not home yet, Willie," she said, her mouth suddenly dry. With a huge effort she made her voice sound calm and conciliatory. "I don't expect him for another hour or so."

There was silence for a second, and Liz could feel the uncertainty, the shakiness, the near panic in Willie. An artery started to throb in her temple, and the wave of hatred came over her again. Out of control, Willie was even more despicable than when he was his normal, arrogant, uncaring self.

"Willie, I think it's time we settled our problems. It's breaking up my home, my marriage. I know Greg's planning to come in to New York tomorrow, and I know why. There's a chance to defuse this situation in time to prevent another disaster. You'd better come out here now, and deal with him face-to-face."

She heard Willie's shocked intake of breath.

"I can't come out there," he said. "Greg doesn't want to see *me*."

"I'll take care of that," said Liz, forcing the confidence into her voice. "If you leave New York an hour from now, you can be here before nine. Do it, Willie."

Willie's hesitation was almost palpable, and the corners of Liz's mouth drew back with tension as her hand clenched like a vise around the phone.

Willie thought of Ellen, sitting at home waiting. There were not that many evenings left for them now.

"Okay," he said dully. "I have to go home first." He thought of telling Liz about Ellen, but his pride didn't allow him to do that. "I'll get up there about nine."

Immediately after Liz put the phone down, the extension in the upstairs bathroom was replaced softly, and Douglas went down the stairs two at a time, through the kitchen, and out onto his bicycle, heading downtown as fast as he could go.

Liz went into the living room, took the cello carefully out of the case, and tuned it by ear. The feel of the wood, the robust character and mellow age of the instrument, was a kind of comfort to her, and she started to play, slowly at first, then with a growing confidence and fire. She played Elgar and Debussy, Bach and Prokofiev, and her soul went into the music and it soared and swelled, her hands and fingers in the most perfect coordination. In all her life she had never played with such passion.

Elspeth, who usually didn't pay much attention to her mother's playing, sat on the floor by the door, enthralled, while Liz played on, gathering strength, immersed, swallowed up by the music, with a growing intensity and a wild feeling of desperation that sang out of the house and lost itself in the waving treetops in the garden, taking her youth, her love, and her joy up into the heavens, lost to her forever. And from far away, the sound gently returned, came back into the house, and slowly seemed to disappear into the instrument itself.

Liz held the cello against her silently, reluctant to put it away. She stroked the wood, feeling its ancient resonance, admired again the familiar, polished curves, the shiny ebony fingerboard, and the worn, carved pegs. After sitting very still for several minutes, she rose abruptly, and put it back in its case, then untwisted the mother-of-pearl cap to loosen the tension in the bow. She closed the case slowly, as if she were closing a coffin.

Willie drove home as fast as he safely could. Luckily, most of the Friday evening traffic was in the opposite direction, and it didn't take too long. He left his car in the parking garage below the apartment building and took the elevator to his penthouse apartment.

Ellen was in bed, surrounded by a new batch of travel brochures. Her hair, now so straight and thin, was tied up in a red bandanna. She was having difficulty breathing. She'd spat up a fair amount of blood today, she said, but now it was better; she felt she'd gotten rid of whatever it was that was making her cough. She just felt too tired to make dinner, but there was some nice stew. All he needed to do was put it in the microwave for a couple of minutes. Willie was shocked at the change in her since breakfast time, and suddenly he saw clearly what he'd been denying steadily for so long: Ellen was not only dying; she now had only a few days to live.

"Is there anything I can get you?" His heart filled with compassion as he looked at her.

"A new set of lungs, maybe?" She started to cough again, and this time there was some bright red blood at the corner of her mouth when she put down her handkerchief.

"Ellen, I have to go in a little while. I need to go up to see Greg," he said, his eyes not leaving her face. She looked up at him, and the muscles in one eye seemed to be trembling.

Ellen could feel his nervous energy, the tension of a man near the breaking point. She knew Willie wouldn't be going all the way up there without a very good reason, especially now; he had been so attentive to her recently, and only the most pressing cause would make him leave her when she was obviously so sick. Of course, she knew about the hearing—but with the look on his face she didn't want to be told anything about it. She was just too tired, too weary to shoulder any more burdens. In her own mind Ellen had already turned her face to the wall.

Willie didn't feel hungry, so he just made himself a cup of

strong coffee in the espresso machine before leaving. Not that he'd have problems staying awake.

There was still a fair amount of traffic leaving Manhattan, and Willie, enclosed in his luxurious BMW, became more and more tense as he swung on to the Wilbur Cross Parkway, heading east. Everything was swirling around in his mind; the thought of losing his license to practice medicine, which his attorney had so somberly informed him was a distinct possibility, ate at him. If that happened, then what would he do? All his life had been devoted to medicine, and he'd assumed that he would die in harness. He had neither the training nor the temperament for any other occupation. His mind switched with a nervous rapidity back to Ellen, and he imagined her flipping through the colorful guides to the Caribbean that she would never see, every so often looking at the clock, watching it tick away the remaining minutes of her life.

The worst thing that was happening to him, although he didn't know it and wouldn't have thought of it in these terms, was that the malignant genie of fallibility had started to grow and spread in his mind, and in a surgeon, as he would have readily acknowledged, this was a terminal condition. With the decisions that he had to make daily, involving life and limbs and vital organs, uncertainty was deadly and destructive. Now that he knew his colleagues were casting a cold and disapproving eye on his every move, he had lost the sureness, the feel, and the confidence that allowed him to do his job. He sensed it but didn't yet know it; as a surgeon, he was dying.

It was almost nine o'clock by the time he pulled up quietly behind Liz's station wagon, yanked on the emergency brake, and sat back for a moment to steady himself. This was going to be an ordeal, and he knew it.

CHAPTER
THIRTY-EIGHT

Patsy opened the door within seconds of his ringing the bell. He searched for a sign of their former friendship, but there was none. She wouldn't even look at him.

"In here," she said.

She led the way through the hall, walking fast, as if to get away from him. Willie heard someone switch off the television as they approached, then he followed her into the spacious living room, remembering the last time he'd been there. It looked different somehow, less bright, less friendly. Now the shades of color in the chintz curtains seemed to clash, and the people sitting there in the room were like white-faced statues. He saw Liz, in a straight-backed chair, her eyes cold; and Greg on the sofa, his lips tight together, staring at him; and Bob, sitting on the floor, his head bent. Patsy sat down beside Bob. There was one empty chair next to the sofa.

Nobody moved.

Willie stood, painfully aware of the bitter atmosphere surrounding him. He ignored the others and spoke directly to Greg.

"Greg, I came to talk with you, at Liz's request. I'd like to do that, but in private, if you don't mind."

When Greg replied, his voice was calm, controlled, and Liz glanced approvingly at him.

"If you have anything to say, you can say it in front of everyone here. This is my family, what you left of it."

Willie's eyes moved over to Bob and then to Patsy, sitting beside him. There was a bright flicker of diamond on her finger. He sat down in the chair, putting his hands flat on his knees. The material of his trousers absorbed the moisture from his palms.

"Let me start at the beginning," he said quietly. The muscles of his face were so tight, it was only with a big effort that his voice came out the way he wanted it to sound.

"I first saw Edward at your request because he had been vomiting blood, and an X ray done in New York had shown an ulcer in the lower part of his stomach." He looked at Greg and then at Liz, but their expressions did not change.

"As a special favor to you," he went on, and Patsy gave a contemptuous snort, which he ignored, although it hurt him, "I saw him in the office and did the endoscopy, although I usually just deal with adults, as I told you at the time." Willie was getting into his stride, and his confidence returned enough for him to glower back at them.

"We know all that," said Greg. His voice sounded rather hoarse. "Get on with what you came to tell us."

"At the time Edward came into the hospital," went on Willie, doggedly pursuing the story in chronological order, "I was extremely busy and had some very sick patients in the hospital. That night I got home about one A.M." He fixed his gaze on Bob. "In situations like this, attending surgeons have to depend on their house staff to do the detailed history taking and clinical exam." He paused. "That happened to be Bob's duty; he missed the diagnosis of chronic hepatitis and was fired as a result."

Patsy took Bob's arm and held on to it, but she didn't say anything.

Willie's tension suddenly tightened; he had to do something, so he used the only weapon he had. And, even in his desperation, he knew as he spoke that it wouldn't help him; it wouldn't bring Patsy's affection back.

"Did they"—he pointed at Liz, then at Greg—"did they ever tell you who your father is?" He stood up, shouting. "Patsy, did they ever tell you that *I'm* your father?"

Patsy got up, sat on the arm of Greg's chair, and put her arm around his hunched shoulders. She looked defiantly at Willie. He didn't intimidate her.

"Yes, they did. And this is my *real* father, right here." She hung on to Greg's arm, and he felt her sincerity, her commitment. "He's the person who's always been my father, who's always been here, who brought me up, who loves me."

Willie turned to Greg, realizing that he was the only one he had any possible hope of influencing.

"Look," said Willie, his tone suddenly changing but with the same look still in his eyes, "we were best friends in med school and you knew me pretty well. Can't you see how devastated I am by all this? I know what it's done to you, your family . . ." Willie took a step forward, to stand directly in front of Greg. "But don't you also see what it's done to me—when you entrusted Edward to me, and he died in my care? Don't you see what that's done?"

Greg looked at Willie with a glimmer of sympathy. He never would have thought that Willie the Great could be reduced to this. And it must have hurt terribly, the way Patsy had just rejected him.

"Every surgeon makes mistakes," Willie went on, stepping back and addressing them all. "We all do. We try to avoid them but they happen. They have to happen; medicine isn't an exact science, you all know that. All we can do is do our best and try to keep the errors to a minimum." He took a deep breath; he was really having difficulty controlling his voice now. "If every time a surgeon made a mistake you got rid of him, stopped him from operating, taking care of his patients, pretty soon you wouldn't have any surgeons left at all."

There was the sound of voices outside, and a car door slammed. Liz leaned over to Patsy. "Where's Douglas?" she whispered, suddenly anxious. Patsy pointed up to the ceiling; she thought he was with Elspeth upstairs, watching television.

"The only good thing about mistakes," Willie continued, sounding and feeling increasingly desperate, "is that we can benefit from them, use them to avoid future ones."

Liz sat back grimly, her eyes going from Willie to Greg. With a feeling of resigned anger she recognized the signs in Greg's expression. He was already vacillating, sympathetic in spite of himself, good old soft-hearted Greg, about to go over to Willie's side as he'd always done, always. . . . She got up quietly and left the room.

Willie's agitation and apparent sincerity was having its effect

on all his audience, and they listened, fascinated and apprehensive.

"Greg, for God's sake, what do you want me to do? I can't
bring Edward back, although heaven knows I wish I could. My
record is as good as any surgeon in the hospital, and better
than most. Who's going to win if you destroy my practice and
my reputation? Who's really going to benefit from that? Are
you? And what about Ellen—what about the effect of all this
on her?" Willie was shouting at them now, pouring his rage
and frustration out on them; his head was throbbing and they
all seemed to be staring at him with a kind of fear—except
Greg, who was looking over Willie's shoulder and whose whole
face was changing.

At the summit of his fury, Willie turned to see what Greg
was looking at and found himself staring into the barrel of a
gun, held steady in Liz's hand.

He stared at her for a few seconds without comprehending,
and at that moment his blood pressure peaked and a blood
vessel burst inside his head. The lights seemed to flicker and
move in the ceiling, and the gun wavered in a circle and went
out of focus. His right arm was tingling and suddenly he
couldn't feel his right leg, and he fell, twisting on his left one,
very slowly it seemed, and his face slackened as he went down,
and all the anger faded away because there was no longer any
anger or sorrow or happiness for him. It didn't hurt at all
when he fell, but his face was on the carpet, and it was scratchy
on his cheek. He looked up at the people around him, their
faces above him white, blurry ovals. He didn't know who they
were but it didn't seem to matter. He asked them to help him
up but they just kept looking down at him. It was very strange;
he was asking them to help him up, but the sound coming out
of his mouth was not what he expected, more like a blowing.

Liz stared down at him, disbelieving, her gun still unfired in
her hand. A sudden suspicion that he was faking grabbed her,
and she raised it again.

Greg was on his knees beside Willie. When Liz saw his
distraught expression, she finally understood something about
him, something she'd known but never fully comprehended.
Greg was a paragon, a model doctor, primarily the property
of his patients, any patient, anybody he thought he could help.

And that knowledge defined her position, too, of course, and a sudden, unexpected feeling of relief spread like a warm tide through her mind.

"He's had a stroke," said Greg, looking up at her. "A bad one. You'd better call an ambulance."

Greg made Willie as comfortable as possible; he was breathing well, but his face was slack and his cheek billowed out when he exhaled. The ambulance should be here in a few minutes, thought Greg, standing up. His knees cracked. He'd have to move Willie's car to let the ambulance into the drive.

"Here, Bob, take over. You need to keep his chin up. I'm going to move his car."

Bob kneeled down and gazed at the man who had been at the center of such an incredible vortex of anger and despair. Willie was looking at him, but there was no recognition in his eyes, and after a moment his gaze drifted away. He seemed ten years younger; his face was a healthy pink, with all the lines of tension and frustration smoothed out.

Greg found Willie's car keys and went outside; the sky was full of stars, and there was a chill in the air. He slipped past Liz's station wagon, opened the door, and got into Willie's car. He didn't even see the briefcase tucked behind the driver's seat, wouldn't have thought anything of it if he had. Greg started the car up and drove it carefully into the street, leaving the parking lights on. He could already hear the ambulance siren, probably less than half a mile away. They arrived at the same time as he reached the back door, and they ran in with their folding stretcher. Bob decided to accompany Willie to the hospital; he could see that there were other things going on with Greg and Liz, and he didn't want to be around. He grabbed Patsy, and she went with him.

Greg was in a kind of trance, numbed by all that had happened. He helped close the ambulance doors, getting a last glimpse of Willie's expressionless face, and after the taillights of the ambulance disappeared from the end of the driveway, he walked slowly back into the house. Only Liz was in the living room, and Greg saw with a start that she was still holding the gun. He wondered if the ambulance men had noticed, but they'd probably been too busy with Willie.

"Put that thing away, Liz," he said quietly. "I wish you hadn't pulled that trick with Willie. You know perfectly well you wouldn't have shot him."

But, first with disbelief and then with horror, he watched as she slowly raised the gun and he saw her finger start to squeeze the trigger.

"No! Don't do it!" he shouted, and moved toward her with his hands outstretched. But he was too late. The explosion was deafening in the confined space. There was a crash from behind him, and he turned to see the shattered cello case fall over, splinters and shards of wood on the floor, twisted strings hanging out, still moving.

Slowly Liz walked toward him, a long wisp of smoke still trailing from the barrel of the gun.

"It's all over, Greg," she said, and his heart died within him as he watched her. He knew it would be more than he could ever bear if she left him now.

CHAPTER
THIRTY-NINE

Elspeth's frightened face appeared at the door. She hesitated for a moment, then ran to her father. She stood protectively in front of him, facing her mother.

"Was she shooting at you?" she demanded.

"No, of course not! Your mother—"

He was saved from explanation by the sound of a police siren, which wailed, came around the corner, then died. Car doors slammed, and there was the sound of feet pounding up the drive.

The back door buzzer rang and Chief Grunwald appeared, rather disheveled, as if he'd dropped everything and run when the call came, as in fact he had. With him were a uniformed sergeant and another police officer, both of whom crowded in behind him.

"I'd like to know what's going on here," said Grunwald, standing by the door, his feet apart, eyes moving from Greg to Liz, and then over to Elspeth. "We got a call about a carload of drugs, then the ambulance got called out here. Somebody get hurt?" He sniffed the air.

"Nobody got hurt," said Greg steadily. "A friend of mine was visiting, and he had a stroke, right here. That's why we called the ambulance."

"That his BMW outside? The one with the lights on?"

"Yes," said Greg. "I moved it to let the ambulance in."

Grunwald nodded to the police officer, who went out again through the back door. They heard his footsteps on the gravel.

"Where's Douglas?" asked Grunwald.

"Upstairs," said Elspeth. "His music's on so loud, he probably didn't hear anything."

Grunwald nodded to the sergeant.

"You don't mind if we talk to him?" he asked Greg while the sergeant moved quickly toward the stairs. He returned after a few moments, with Douglas in front of him.

The sergeant shook his head. "Nothing," he said. "The noise up there . . ." He stuck a finger in his ear and rotated it, as if he were trying to revive a blown-out eardrum.

Grunwald obviously wasn't so sure. "Big Vern's a friend of yours, isn't he?" he drawled, his blue eyes scanning Douglas's face.

Douglas's expression was totally impassive, but his mother could feel the smoldering violence just below the surface. So could Grunwald, who had a strong feeling that sooner or later this boy was going to come to a sticky end. He just hoped he wouldn't be the one holding the gun when the time came.

"Mind if I use the phone?" he asked. Greg nodded, and Grunwald called for someone to come out and pick up the BMW.

The officer came back in holding a briefcase. "It wasn't even in the trunk," he said. "It was right behind the driver's seat."

He put it on the table and opened it. It was stuffed full of small glassine packages.

"Now, I wonder how that briefcase got there," said Grunwald quietly, looking at Douglas.

"Don't look at me," said Douglas. "He must have brought it here. I'm not in that business anymore, remember?"

Grunwald continued to stare at Douglas, then his eyes moved to Liz, then to Elspeth, before finally resting on Greg with a glimmer of unexpected sympathy. He knew what Greg had gone through already with Edward, and he had a good idea of the kind of problems they would be having with Douglas. They'd have been better off, he thought, if Douglas had been the one to die in the hospital.

Grunwald had been unwillingly pitted against Greg by out-side pressure from Hartford, and he deeply resented this interference. Especially as Greg Hopkins was the best doctor in town, was known to take good care of his patients, whoever they were. Judging from what the ambulance men said on the radio, the guy at the center of it all, the New York surgeon, wasn't going to be causing too much of a stir from now on.

"I don't know what's going on in this house," he said finally, after glancing at the fragments of the cello and the hand-sized hole in the wall where the bullet had gone through. "And I don't think I want to know." His eyes switched to Greg. "I'm not even going to ask to see your gun license."

Douglas moved, and Grunwald's eyes hardened. "On second thought, I'd better have the gun," he said. "No questions asked, as nobody got hurt, okay?"

Liz went to the sofa and pulled the gun out from under the cushion where she'd put it when she heard the police coming in. Silently she handed it to Grunwald, who sniffed the barrel, broke the weapon, extracted the five unused shells, and put them in his pocket. He hesitated, still uneasy, but he then made up his mind.

"You understand there may be some questions about all this later on?"

Grunwald stood silent for a moment and gazed at a spot somewhere between Greg and Liz. "I should tell you we're all sorry about what happened to Edward. I hope your family can get over it now and get back to normal."

He turned on his heel and left.

After the tow truck had clanked off with its load, Greg spoke with an unusual sternness in his voice.

"I think we'd better all sit down here. We have a few things to talk over."

"I'll go and make some coffee," said Liz, heading toward the door.

"Later," said Greg. "Right now I want everybody here. Douglas, tell me about that briefcase in Dr. Stringer's car."

Douglas explained, in a whiny, defensive tone that infuriated Greg. "For God's sake," he interrupted, "just tell us what happened. Skip the excuses."

Douglas stopped, took a deep breath, then continued his story simply and directly.

"He killed my little brother," he finished, "so I wanted to kill him. Simple. I was going to get a car bomb, but it would have cost too much."

Liz gasped and put her hand up to her mouth.

"Nobody else was going to do anything," went on Douglas accusingly. Greg avoided Liz's eye.

"Don't you see that you just committed a crime? Planting drugs like that! Douglas, I can't believe it!" Greg shook his head. Where on earth did the boy get his criminal impulses?

"Okay, Dad, this is how I see it. When you found out this guy killed Edward, you made a fuss, tried to get him punished?"

Liz started to say something, but Douglas talked right through her. "I know, because I heard you on the phone—and talking to Mom. Then what happened? The law came down here, and suddenly *you* were in trouble. You won't ever win because you don't do things yourself; you hope other people'll bail you out."

Greg felt the blood leaving his face. It was painful to have his own son see through him so clearly.

"Well, I'm not going to live like that." Douglas stood defiantly, his feet apart. "Nobody's ever going to bully me, because they'll find out they get hurt worse."

"Where did you get those ideas?" asked Liz quietly. "At school? From TV?"

"I got them right here at home," replied Douglas. "I saw what happens when you don't fight, when you let other people roll over you."

"But if everybody did that, Douglas, don't you see, we'd go back to being cavemen, with everyone for himself." Greg was appalled by his son's whole attitude.

"But your way doesn't work, Dad!" Douglas's voice was strong with conviction. "Look at Big Vern. If he'd gone to the police for help, he'd be in jail or dead now. And it's just the same for you, and you're a doctor, an important person." Douglas shook his head with frustration. It was quite obvious that his parents couldn't or wouldn't understand what he was saying.

"I agree with Douglas," Elspeth piped up suddenly. "God helps him who helps himself."

"All right now, that'll do," said Liz, taking command again. "Elspeth, have you finished your homework? Upstairs, please, we need to talk to Douglas without your comments. Up you go!"

Elspeth dragged herself reluctantly up the stairs.

Greg and Liz stared at Douglas, trying to make themselves

believe that he was still one of them, still part of the family.

"What did I do wrong?" asked Liz quietly. She didn't know whether her question should be addressed to Douglas or to Greg.

Neither of them paid any attention to her.

"I think I know what you're saying, Douglas," said Greg. "But in a civilized community you can't take the law into your own hands like that." Douglas started to say something, but Greg raised his hand. "I agree with you that sometimes the proper procedures don't work, but surely they're better than blowing each other up when you have a grievance."

Douglas shook his head, and Liz wept inside. She knew that it was his stubbornness, his inability to see things other people's way that would finally be his undoing, maybe even get him killed. She got up and put an arm around him, but he shook her off without looking at her. Liz sat down again. Nobody spoke for a few minutes, then Douglas got up and went to the stairs. Halfway up, he stopped and turned back.

"What I really wanted to do was shoot the fucker's kneecaps off," he said, then continued up to his room, feeling rather proud of himself. And he could do it too. With a little practice, and with Big Vern showing him how.

The words should have chilled both his parents, but it didn't have the expected effect; Douglas's voice, which had broken a few months before, occasionally reverted to its higher, childish pitch, and had done so now. Surprisingly it helped Greg and Liz put everything in perspective. Douglas was still just a kid, experimenting with different ways of doing things, still terribly unsure of himself, with the precarious cockiness and arrogance of adolescence. His present attitude was not necessarily the one he'd be stuck with as he grew older.

It was clear, however, that one of the things Douglas needed was a stronger role model, a father whose decisions he could respect and which demonstrably worked, at least most of the time.

"We have a lot of work to do," said Greg, his eyes on the top of the stairs. "Or, rather, *I* have a lot to do."

"It's not just your problem, Greg. It'll take our united efforts. Douglas isn't back in our camp yet, not by any means."

"Liz, just before Grunwald came in, you said it was all over."

Liz came and sat beside him on the sofa.

"Yes, Greg, I did." She pushed her hand through her hair, and Greg saw a single long white one among the brown. A feeling of such tenderness came over him, he wanted to hold her in his arms and never let her go.

"What I meant was that Willie is finally out of our lives, and now . . . well, now it's just you and me, Greg, for better or worse." There were tears in her eyes, and he wiped them gently away with his index finger before putting his arms around her.

The phone rang, and Greg sighed and went over to pick it up. It was Bob. Willie was still semiconscious, his blood pressure was very low, and the doctor there had decided to transfer him to the hospital at Stamford as soon as possible.

"Bob's a good doctor," said Greg, coming back to her. "And he'll do a lot for the practice, don't you think?"

They talked about that for a while, and then the phone rang again. With a kind of premonition, Liz went to answer it.

"Thank you, Bob" was all she said.

"Willie's dead," she said quietly. "He had a cardiac arrest while Bob was phoning last time. There was nothing they could do."

A long silence followed. Greg sat immobile, shocked.

"He wasn't a bad man, Liz, you know, he really wasn't." Tears sprang into his eyes at the thought of his friend, and Liz put her arms around him again and held him tight. Greg would never change, she realized, but maybe his weaknesses were ultimately his greatest strengths as a human being, as a doctor. It all depended on one's point of view.

Greg detached himself gently. "I'd better call Ellen," he said.